Praise for *Joe College*

"Tom Perrotta gets it right. . . . one of the few convincing portrayals of college life I've ever come across . . . a comic novel so enjoyable you'll find yourself turning the last page in no time."
—*Newsday*

"It takes a sharp eye and a light touch . . . to take on the back-to-school genre as knowingly as Mr. Perrotta has. . . . An overwhelmingly pleasing book."
—*The New York Times*

"Proves yet again that Perrotta's books are sheer pleasure."
—*San Francisco Chronicle*

"*Joe College* is funny, honest, and a fabulous read, especially for anyone who's tried to fit in and let go—and to figure out which parts of themselves to hold on to in the process."
—*Salon.com*

"Perrotta transforms eighties nostalgia into art."
—*Entertainment Weekly*

"If Salinger's Holden Caulfield had hit the books a bit more assiduouly, and gotten out more, he might have turned into this story's engaging. . . narrator and protagonist Danny."
—*Kirkus Reviews*

"I have a new favorite book, *Joe College,* and this is why: Tom Perrotta wrote it; an irresistible and accidentally heroic voice narrates it; angst has never been more delicious, food funnier, or Yale more accessible. What a great pleasure."
—Elinor Lipman, author of *The Inn at Lake Devine*

"Perrotta serves up a hilariously satirical eighties cocktail, with an Ivy League twist."
—*Glamour*

"Perrotta . . . is in full control of his quirky comic sensibility."
—*Publishers Weekly*

"With his new novel, he has delivered another sweetheart . . . Perrotta has established a slightly befogged comic landscape that's his alone."
—*Newsweek*

"With perfect pacing and dead-on detail, Perrotta never lets you forget that growing up is the most emotionally explosive and morally fraught story around. I loved this book."
—Antonya Nelson, author of *Talking in Bed*

"Perrotta . . . has drawn Danny so exquisitely . . . that you feel as if you know him pretty damn well . . . Danny is delightfully likeable—a Huck Finn of higher ed."
—*Washington Post Book World*

"Perrotta's eye for the minute, often skewerable, detail or reminiscence proves just as sharp and cunning as it was in *Election*. [A] quirky comic tale of young love and angst."
—*US Weekly*

"No one chronicles growing up in suburban New Jersey in the late 1970s and early 1980s better than Perrotta. . . . [he's] a master of the light comic touch and wry social observation."
—*Library Journal*

"*Joe College* succeeds as a fast-paced, fun read."
—*Los Angeles Times*

"A painfully funny, unsparingly accurate examination of the life of an eighties era 'Yalie.' Perrotta cuts quickly to the heart of the matter; the incremental betrayals, encroaching obligations, and conflicted motivations of a working class intellectual. Class warfare has rarely been so funny or so on target."
—Anthony Bourdain, bestselling author of *Kitchen Confidential*

Joe College

Also by Tom Perrotta

Election
The Wishbones
Bad Haircut: Stories of the Seventies

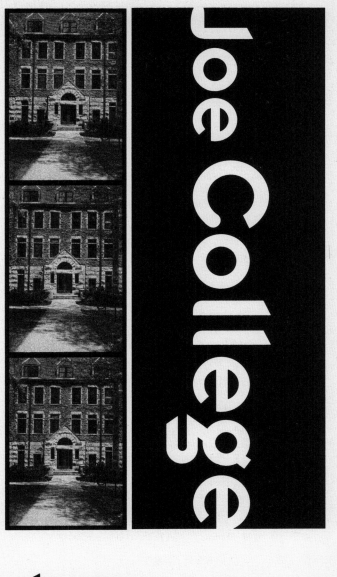

Joe College

tom perrotta

St. Martin's Griffin ☙ New York

www.stmartins.com

Book design by Victoria Kuskowski

Title page and part title image used curtesy of Photodisc

Library of Congress Cataloging-in-Publication Data

Perrotta, Tom
    Joe College / Tom Perrotta.
        p. cm.
    ISBN 0-312-26184-5 (hc)
    ISBN 0-312-28327-X (pbk)
    1. College students—Fiction. 2. Family-owned
    businesses enterprises—Fiction. 3. New Haven
    (Conn.)—Fiction. 4. New Jersey—Fiction.
    I. Title.
PS3566. E6948 J64 2000
813'.54—dc21   00-031722

First St. Martin's Griffin Edition: October 2001

10 9 8 7 6 5 4 3 2 1

In Memory of Chris Zenowich

acknowledgments

I'd like to thank Nick "Food Dude" Castagna for educating me in the ins and outs of the lunch-truck business, and Mike Colicchio for making it possible—*Joe College* wouldn't have been written without their help. I'm also grateful to Mark Dow, Tom Feigelson, Byron Kim, Kevin Pask, and Hajime Tada, among others, for their enduring friendship and for the memories they shared and inspired during the writing of this book. Thanks is also due—as always—to Mary Granfield for her good company and good advice, and to our kids, Nina and Luke, for being such wonderful distractions. My thanks, as well, go out to my agent, Maria Massie, and my editor, Elizabeth Beier, for their unswerving support and enthusiasm.

What is that feeling when you're driving away
from people and they recede on the plain until you see
their specks dispersing?

—Jack Kerouac, *On the Road*

part one

An Ordinary Evening in New Haven

pencil dicks

All through that winter and into the spring, when our Tuesday- and Thursday-night dinner shifts were done, Matt and I would sit at the long table near the salad bar and plan his end-of-the-year party, our voices echoing importantly in the cavernous wood-pan- elled dining hall.

"What do you think?" he asked. "We gonna need more than two kegs?"

"Depends, I guess. How many people are coming?"

"A lot." Matt fixed me with those weirdly translucent blue eyes of his, eyes that sometimes made me think I was looking straight into his head. "I'm just gonna plaster the campus with signs that say, 'Party at Matt's.' As far as I'm concerned, the whole school's invited, plus all of Jessica's friends from Columbia. I wouldn't be surprised if a couple hundred people show up."

"A couple hundred? Your landlord's gonna freak."

"I talked to him. He's cool about it."

"Cool about a couple hundred people?" I hadn't had much experience with landlords, having lived only at home and in dorms for the first twenty years of my life, but even I had enough sense to be skeptical of this claim.

"Lance is a party guy. Two glasses of grain alcohol and he'll be sliding naked down the banister to answer the door."

"Grain alcohol? Who said anything about grain alcohol?"

"You can't have a really good party without it. Not the kind of party I'm talking about."

"That stuff'll fuck you up," I said, trying to sound as though I were speaking from experience. It was a tone I'd pretty much mastered in my first two and a half years of college.

Matt looked away, a private, dreamy smile softening the intensity of his face. I followed his gaze down the long center aisle of the dining hall, taking quiet satisfaction in the order I'd imposed on what only an hour before had been total chaos. While Matt had been working the dish line, feverishly sorting the dirty plates, glasses, and silverware from trays that came streaming toward him on the conveyor belt, I'd been clearing tables, straightening chairs, emptying ashtrays, laying down fresh paper doilies and clean water glasses, propping up table tents, and wiping the floor with a big hairy dust mop. All the dead guys on the wall, the former masters and rich donors and esteemed scholars, looked down upon my handiwork with solemn approval. They appreciated a clean dining hall and were glad I had made myself useful.

"What I really want," Matt mused, "is a party where everyone gets laid who wants to."

"There's a name for that."

"I'm not talking about an orgy," he said, apparently disappointed in me for thinking that he was. "I'm talking about a situation where everyone gets lucky in their own way."

"Sounds like an orgy to me."

Nick, the Tuesday-night chef, emerged from the kitchen and trudged over to the table to join us for a final cigarette before heading home or out to a bar, wherever it was he went after work. I always did a double take when I saw him in street clothes. Out of uniform he struck me as a plausible human being, an average guy in a belted leather jacket, rather than the sweaty buffoon he impersonated during working hours, a malcontent in a puffy hat muttering an incessant profane monologue as he tossed sprigs of garnish onto trays of scrod in white sauce and meatless baked ziti.

"What's up, pencil dicks?" he inquired, pulling up a chair at the far end of the table as if to illustrate the gulf between us. There

didn't seem to be anything hostile in the gesture, just an acknowl-
edgment of fact. We were college boys; he had to work for a living.

"Matt's planning an orgy," I informed him.

Nick nodded calmly, as though he frequently received advance
notice of such gatherings.

"An orgy, huh? When's it gonna be?"

"End of the semester," said Matt. "You comin'?"

Nick adjusted the flame on his Zippo before lighting up. This
was in 1982, back when smoking was commonplace in the dining
halls and dorms, and many seminar tables were matter-of-factly
equipped with ashtrays.

"Kristin gonna be there?" he asked.

Kristin Willard was a prep school girl from Greenwich who
worked the serving line a couple nights a week, a long-limbed
beauty with an overactive social conscience who could break your
heart even in one of those hideous blue synthetic shirts they made
us wear on the job. Nick had a crush on her just like the rest of us,
only worse.

"Fuckin' A," said Matt. He said this a lot when Nick was around.
"You think I'd throw an orgy without inviting Kristin?"

Nick wiped at the moustache of sweat droplets that was as much
a part of his face as his eyes and nose and gave a shrug that indicated a certain lack of faith in our judgment.

"Knowing you asswipes," he grumbled, "it'd probably just be
the three of us."

5

Still wearing his paper dining-hall cap—this was a peculiar affec-
tation of his; sometimes he even wore it to class—Matt walked me
to my entryway and waited by the door with a strange air of
expectancy, as if he wanted me to invite him in. He was often like
this when we parted company on work nights, and I got the feeling
he wasn't too keen on returning to his off-campus apartment. He
had transferred from the University of Michigan a year earlier and

still seemed a bit adrift, unable to find his place in the social formations that had crystallized before his arrival.

"I got a shitload of reading to do," I explained. "Two books of *Paradise*-fucking-*Lost* and as much of *Middlemarch* as I can stomach without slitting my wrists."

As a defense against looking like a weenie—a term I'd never even heard of until I arrived at Yale, a hotbed of weenies if there ever was one—I had recently adopted the strategy of complaining bitterly about my reading, even to people like Matt, who understood that I didn't mean a word of it.

"More Whitman for me," he said.

"Whitman? Don't you have to finish that Shakespeare paper?"

"I'm so deep into Whitman, I can't even think about Shakespeare right now. As far as I'm concerned *Leaves of Grass* should be the frigging Bible."

"The Gospel According to Walt," I said, stepping aside to clear a path for two cute sophomore girls in humongous thrift-store overcoats.

"Gross, hankering, mystical, NUDE!" Matt recited, shouting the words like a crazy person in a bus station. The overcoat girls stopped in their tracks, whirling to regard him with startled, disdainful expressions. I directed my attention to Sterling Tower—it was lit up again, glowing like an ad for Higher Learning—attempting to create the impression that my proximity to the maniac in the paper hat was purely coincidental. " 'HOW IS IT I EXTRACT STRENGTH FROM THE BEEF I EAT?' " he continued, pleased beyond words by Whitman's inscrutable inquiry.

"Hey," he said, his voice returning to normal as the girls disappeared around the corner into the courtyard. "Wanna grab a slice later on?"

"I can't. I really have to make some headway on *Middlemarch*. I hate going to seminar unprepared."

He nodded; even in the dark, I could see the disappointment on his face.

"All right, man. I guess I'll see you on Thursday then."

On the way up to my suite, I had to stand aside to make way for the Whiffenpoofs who lived across the hall. They came barreling down the stairs in their tuxedos, belting out "The Lion Sleeps Tonight" in impeccable three-part harmony, off to yet another command performance. Trip winked at me; Thor greeted me with an upraised fist. Nelson Harriman, who was wearing a white silk scarf and looked, as usual, like he'd stepped out of *The Great Gatsby*, managed to toss out a quick, "Hey, guy," in between the nonsense syllables of the song.

When I arrived at Yale in 1979, I'd been totally unprepared for the centrality of singing groups to campus life, the excitement that surrounded the news that so-and-so had been tapped to be a Spizzwink or an Alley Cat, the presence of one group or another at every official university function you could think of, the number of people who'd tell you proudly on Sunday morning that they'd spent Saturday night at a "jamboree" featuring Red, Hot & Blue and the Duke's Men. I remembered wanting to laugh out loud the first time I saw the S.O.B.'s at our freshman dinner, their heads bobbing up and down like pistons as they mugged their way through that stupid song about putting the lime in the coconut, then slowly realizing that nobody else at my table seemed to find this spectacle even remotely idiotic.

My alienation from the singing-group subculture had only grown stronger in the months I'd spent living across the hall from Nelson, Thor, and Trip. It wasn't that they were bad guys—with the possible exception of Trip, who seemed suspiciously eager to put in a good word for the South African government whenever the subject of apartheid came up. What amazed me was the amount of time the Whiffenpoofs demanded from them, the way their membership in the group seemed to define their entire identity. Most of their time outside class was consumed by Whiffenpoof functions; even their vacations were given over to Whiffenpoof tours. It was true that they got to sleep with Whiffenpoof groupies and visit great Whiffenpoof places—you couldn't brush your teeth next to one of them without hearing about their latest junket to Monaco or Bermuda—but it still didn't seem like a worthwhile trade-off to me. The way I saw it, no amount of sex or travel would compensate for the humiliation of belonging to a group with such a stupid name. For my money, it would have been only marginally more embarrassing to claim membership in "The Shitheads" or "The Dingleberries."

When I got upstairs, Sang, Ted, and Nancy were sitting in the common room with their coats on and backpacks at their feet, listening to Steely Dan's *Gaucho,* the album of the moment in Entryway C. They could procrastinate like this for hours if no one had a paper or a problem set due the next day, playing the same side over and over again while desperately reassuring one another that they were off to the library any second. These reassurances would continue until someone bowed to the inevitable and shyly floated the alternative of pizza.

The sight of them made me doubly glad I hadn't invited Matt in. The few times he'd mingled with my suitemates, the results hadn't been encouraging. Matt had completely misread the ethos of our suite, deciding it was his duty to monopolize the conversation and impress my friends rather than sit back and let us regale him with anecdotes from our shared history, which was all we really demanded from a guest.

"Danny," Ted commanded, before I'd even had time to unzip my coat, "you've got to tell Nancy about that time Seth went off on the fire alarm."

Nancy was Ted's girlfriend, and had long ago attained the status of honorary suitemate. She had a room of her own in Pierson, but had abandoned it in October, soon after she had begun sleeping with Ted. Their cohabitation had continued even after Ted rotated out of his single into a bunk bed–double with Max.

(Privacy turned out to be less of an issue than might have been expected, since Max was purely nocturnal, and didn't even think about going to bed until long after Ted and Nancy had headed off to classes.) I once asked Ted why he and Nancy didn't spend more time in her room, and he explained that Nancy's roommate was living with her boyfriend there, so it would have caused a lot of confusion if Nancy'd tried to reclaim her bed. In any case, Max, Sang, and I didn't mind having her around. She was a lot cooler than Ted and seemed to think the rest of us were pretty great, too.

"I'm sure Nancy's heard that story a hundred times," I said.

"That's okay," Nancy assured me. "I don't mind hearing it again."

I glanced at Sang, who was paging through the phone directory with curious ease, despite the fact that he was wearing very large ski mittens. He came from Southern California and found winters in New Haven all but unbearable. He put on his down jacket in mid-October and didn't even think about taking it off until we'd reached the sunny side of spring break. His ex-girlfriend Eve claimed he used to sleep in it every once in a while.

"I have to take a shower," I said. "Why don't you tell it?"

Sang glanced up from the Yellow Pages. He didn't seem to be searching for anything in particular.

"Tell what?"

"The story about Seth and the fire alarm."

He pulled off one of his mittens and ran his hand over the top of his stiff new crew cut. As part of the grieving process for Eve, he'd decided to change his look from California surfer to Red Chinese nerd, and was clearly fascinated by the new topography of his head.

"I have to go to the library," he said, removing his thick black eyeglasses and polishing them with great deliberation on the tail of his corduroy shirt. He put his glasses back on, tossed aside the phone book, and stood up. "I'm gonna be up half the night as it is."

Ted turned back to Nancy, resigned to telling the story himself. He had that jerky grin on his face, the one that made you want to like him even when you knew that, deep down, you had grave reservations.

"He wailed on that thing with a baseball bat," Ted explained, reducing the story to its essentials. "It's the middle of the night, everyone else is leaving the building, shuffling downstairs in their nightgowns and bathrobes, and this guy is standing there in these tartan plaid boxer shorts, no shirt or anything, beating on the fire alarm with this aluminum baseball bat, screaming, 'Take that, you fucker! Take that, you fucker!'"

"Wait a minute," said Sang, who'd decided to sit back down. "Don't forget, this was like the fifth time in a row the alarm had gone off in the middle of the night. Lots of people were pissed."

"Yeah," I said. "Not to mention the fact that the alarm was right outside our door."

"He didn't stop," Ted continued, unperturbed by our interruptions. "The alarm stopped ringing, but he just kept beating on it for like a half hour. The cops came, but they were afraid to go near him."

"Come on," I said. "It wasn't a half hour."

"I'm exaggerating," Ted explained. "It's an effective storytelling technique."

"He was clinically depressed," Sang pointed out. "He'd been acting kind of weird for a couple of months at that point. Remember? He and Max actually had a fistfight over whether Texas was bigger than Australia."

"Australia's bigger," Nancy said uncertainly. "It's got to be, right? It's a continent."

"The funny thing is," Ted went on, "he didn't hurt the fire alarm at all. Those things are basically indestructible."

"Ruined my bat, though," I said. "Dented the shit out of it."

"Turned out to be the first time in his life he'd ever swung one," Sang added. "Can you imagine? An American guy, nineteen years old, never even swung a baseball bat."

"That was probably like half his problem," said Ted, who was taking a class in Abnormal Psych.

"Is he okay now?" Nancy asked.

"Max was in touch with him for a while last semester," I said. "He's taking a couple of classes at community college, trying to get it back together. He was supposed to come visit for the Harvard game, but his parents wouldn't loan him the car or something."

"Get this," said Ted. "Did you know it's like a federal crime to damage a fire alarm? There was talk of the university pressing charges, but they let him off with counseling."

Sang cast a plaintive look at the door.

"We should call him."

Ted kept shaking his head in delight, as if the story got better and better the more he thought about it. He hadn't been friends with Seth, and didn't seem to notice that the rest of us found the memory of his breakdown upsetting rather than hilarious. He raised an imaginary bat over his head and brought it down hard on an imaginary fire alarm.

"Take that, you fucker!" he said, dissolving into giggles.

The door to my single was closed. I opened it to find Max sprawled out on my bed, barefoot and shirtless, reading *Assassin's Diary*. Every bone in his rib cage was visible, clearly articulated against its taut sheath of skin. He was a dedicated vegetarian, the first I'd ever known, and his thinness was the source of both amazement and concern for the rest of us.

"Hey," he said, eyes straying from the page to issue only the briefest flicker of greeting. "Wanna know something cool? Arthur Bremer was all set to kill Nixon in Toronto, had a spot along the motorcade and everything, but missed his chance because he decided at the last minute to run back to his hotel room to change into a shirt and tie. He wanted to look respectable on the evening news after he was arrested for killing the president. Isn't that great?"

After John Hinckley's attempt on Reagan's life the previous year and the revelation that he'd done it to win the heart of our fellow Yalie, Jodie Foster, Max had become fascinated by the links between Hinckley, the movie *Taxi Driver,* and the story of George Wallace's would-be assassin, Arthur Bremer, who seemed to be at the root of it all. He had the feeling that the tangled knot of history, pop culture, celebrity, class resentment, insanity, and sex contained some essential nugget of truth about our society. He'd gotten an Am Stud grad student to agree to supervise an independent study on the subject, but the department had nixed the project, leaving Max to pursue it on his own, to the detriment of his actual classes.

"Uh, excuse me," I said. "I was under the impression that this was my room."

Max looked around, my autographed picture of Uncle Floyd and the crooked Mark Rothko print confirming the fact that this was indeed the case.

"Yeah, well, I got home from the library, and Ted and Nancy had barricaded the door to my room. You weren't around so I figured I'd borrow your bed for a while."

"Well, your room's free now," I said, sounding harsher than I meant to.

He sat up, looking more bewildered than hurt, and ran his fingers through the knotted mop of his curls. Sang and I had once pressed him on the issue of hair care, and he'd finally admitted, after much prodding, that he didn't actually own a comb or a brush and did all of his grooming by hand.

"Sorry, man. Didn't mean to violate your space."

"Don't worry about it," I said, suddenly feeling like a jerk. Only a few weeks earlier, this room had been his, so it was a little weird for me to be pulling rank like this. "I'm kinda stressed. I've got a lot of reading to do tonight."

"I'm outta here," he assured me.

He hopped off the bed, took a couple of steps toward the door, then stopped. He closed his eyes for a few seconds, grimacing with the effort of recollection.

"Oh, yeah," he said. "I forgot to tell you. Cindy called again last night."

highlighting

Somebody must have had a deadline, because the suite was empty when I got back from the shower. Naked except for the towel around my waist, I stood for a moment in the common room, savoring the silence and the rare sensation of privacy.

Unlike most of my friends, who claimed they couldn't get any work done in their rooms, I found it impossible to work anywhere else. The library was just too distracting—too many people, too many noises, too much searching eye contact with total strangers, not all of it friendly. I knew from bitter experience that it was possible to spend three hours in the main reading room and get about ten pages of reading done. The more remote corners of the library were no better. The carrels up in the musty stacks of Sterling, where Sang spent most of his time, were far too creepy and desolate for me. It was like a horror movie, the way you could hear footsteps echoing down the endless corridors as they approached, the sound growing louder and clearer by the second, until you expected a crazed fifth-year senior to yank back your head and slit your throat, leaving you to bleed to death all over your Tocqueville. The closetlike weenie bins in the Cross Campus Library were disconcerting for an entirely different reason. The partitions between the different bins didn't reach up to the ceiling, so noises traveled easily. I often thought—sometimes with more certainty than others—that people in nearby bins were having sex rather than studying, a suspicion aggravated by Ted and Nancy's frequent boasts of weenie-bin assignations. Whenever this happened, I found myself oscillating between intense self-pity and equally intense feelings of arousal, neither state of mind particularly conducive to the kind of concentration demanded by a book like *Middlemarch*.

I had another problem with *Middlemarch*, though, one that afflicted me even in the safety and solitude of my own room, and slowed my laborious crawl through the novel to a virtual standstill. The problem was highlighting.

I had seen highlighters before coming to college; I just hadn't understood what they were for. I thought of them, quite simply, as yellow Magic Markers, objects for which I had little use in the present, and for which I could imagine little use in the future. It certainly wouldn't have occurred to me to mark up my books with them, or with any other writing instruments. My high school textbooks were school property; we weren't supposed to deface them, period. This prohibition made sense to me. I was always annoyed when I received a book that someone else had underlined or commented on. My own reading experience was somehow diminished by the visible traces of a third party who was neither me nor the author. I spent more time than I should have wondering why the previous reader had marked one passage rather than another, or comparing my reactions to my predecessor's, though, to be honest, the comments generally didn't extend far beyond *Yes!* or *How True!!* or *Hester Sucks Dick!!!*

But then I got to college, where I suddenly found myself surrounded by an army of people wielding yellow highlighters, carefully illuminating the crucial passages in their reading, the main ideas, the provocative metaphors, the striking epigrams. Some highlighted judiciously, selecting only a key word here and there, while others did it wantonly, scribbling furiously over whole paragraphs. One of my freshman roommates used a ruler to keep his highlights straight; another guy I knew, who had taken an expensive class on improving his study habits, kept an array of highlighters at the ready to color code his texts for handy reference at exam time.

By the end of my first semester, I was already hooked. By the middle of my junior year, the period I'm referring to here, I could no more imagine reading without a yellow highlighter in my hand than I could have imagined going to bed without brushing my teeth.

What happened with *Middlemarch* had happened to me with other books, but it had never caused me so much difficulty. Too much of the book seemed to demand highlighting. George Eliot wrote with such sustained profundity that I found myself coloring over line after line after line, sometimes covering entire pages with a thick coat of yellow neon. Every now and then I'd forget myself and absent-mindedly highlight a completely banal sentence, something on the order of: *"I shall take a mere mouthful of ham and a glass of ale," he said reassuringly.*

After I had slipped up in this manner a number of times, I decided that I needed some other mark, some way of distinguishing truly important highlighted passages from the ones that were slightly less important or not important at all. Over the course of two hundred pages I had improvised a byzantine system involving highlighter, underlines, and marginal punctuation marks. What a truly major passage looked like is hard to re-create, though I can report that the people who sat next to me in seminar often felt the need to comment on my thoroughness.

In the end, my reading process had been warped into a strange kind of inventory taking, in which I was forced to divide the book into miniscule units, weighing the present sentence against all sentences that had come before, trying to find a place for it in my mysterious and ever-shifting hierarchy of classification. A more reasonable person might have simply declared a moratorium on highlighting, but that struck me as the coward's way out, hardly better than not reading at all.

My concentration was further disrupted by guilty thoughts of Cindy, whose calls I'd been dodging for the past several weeks. I knew we needed to talk, but I figured that if I avoided her long enough, she'd get tired of waiting and supply my half of the conversation on her own, thereby sparing me the unpleasantness of having to be the bad guy. She wasn't getting the message, though, and her persistence was starting to worry me.

Cindy was a girl from home. We hadn't moved in the same circles in high school, hadn't been well-enough acquainted even to sign each other's yearbooks. I had forgotten all about her until my first day of work the previous summer.

God knows I hadn't wanted to spend the summer riding shotgun in the Roach Coach, selling plastic-wrapped danishes to tired-looking factory workers. I would much rather have been in Manhattan or Washington, D.C., interning for a magazine or a congressman, but nothing had come through that paid enough to make either plan even remotely plausible. In the end, it had come down to the Roach Coach or the forklift for me, and the Roach Coach at least offered the promise of novelty, as well as a boss who wasn't going to address me as "Joe College" and reserve the shit jobs especially for me.

I met her outside a small manufacturing plant in Union Village that looked like a scale model of our high school. I'd already made change for her dollar before I paid enough attention to her face to realize that I knew her.

"Cindy, right?"

She gave me back the same squinty look. I raised the bill of my baseball cap to help her out.

"Danny? What are you doing here?"

"Helping my dad."

"Dante's your father?"

I hesitated a second before saying yes, not because I was embarrassed or anything, but simply because it was hard for me to get used to hearing my father referred to as "Dante." Like me, he normally went by "Danny" or "Dan," but for some reason had decided to use his given name on the truck.

"He's a trip." She shook her head in cheerful reminiscence, as if she and my father were the ones who'd gone to school together.

I took a moment to really look at her. At Harding, she'd always just faded into the background, but out there, in that sunstruck

Monday morning industrial nowhere land, she seemed mysteriously vivid, a person worth getting to know.

"Aren't you at Harvard or something?" she asked.

"Yale."

"Wow." She shook her head in sincere wonderment and glanced down at the coins in her hand. "I guess I don't have to count my change."

"You better," I told her. "I'm an English major."

Cindy was a religious coffee drinker and made it a point to stand on my line instead of my father's. From our brief exchanges, I learned that she worked full-time in the office of Re-Coil Industries, a company that manufactured a revolutionary kind of nylon hose for use in a highly specialized machine whose name she could never remember. During the school year, she took night classes in accounting and marketing at Kean College. She still hung out with her high school crowd, but said it was getting boring. She went to the gym whenever she could and was thinking about buying a new car.

At the beginning of the summer, my attraction to her was tainted by doubt and disapproval. I was dismayed by her hair, the outdated *Charlie's Angels* thing she was still doing with the curling iron and blow-dryer. She was big on pastels and had a weakness for matching culottes and blouses, an ensemble my mother referred to as a "short set." She chewed Juicyfruit, painted her nails, and didn't skimp on the eye shadow. The girls I liked in college favored baggy sweaters and objected to makeup on political grounds. On special occasions they wore thrift-store dresses and cowboy boots. They didn't devote a lot of time to their nails, and a surprising number of them had mixed feelings about shaving their legs. I had the feeling they wouldn't have approved of Cindy.

As the weeks went by, though, my reservations began to crumble. Who was I to be a snob about hairstyles and nail polish? Maybe I went to Yale nine months of the year, but right now I was back

19

home in New Jersey, spending my days speeding from one godfor-saken industrial park to another in a truck with a cockroach painted on the front doors, trading stale quips about Jodie Foster with guys who wore their names on their shirts, and cultivating an impressive tan on the lower two thirds of my left arm. What did I care what the girls I went to school with—girls I hardly knew, from places like Park Avenue and Scarsdale and Bethesda and Newton and Buck-head and Sausalito and Saratoga Springs and Basel frigging Switzerland—what did I care what they would think about some-one like Cindy, whom they were never going to lay eyes on or have a conversation with anyway?

I was lonely that summer, and her face lit up every time she saw me. She complimented me on my new glasses, asked what I did to stay in such good shape, made frequent comments about what a jerk her ex-boyfriend had been and how she hadn't had a date for the past eight months.

Sometimes she wore a tight denim dress that buttoned down the front, and she always smelled like she'd just stepped out of the shower. Even in that little candy-striped jumper I hated, you could see what a nice body she had, that she worked out but wasn't a fanatic about it, not like some of the girls I knew at school, girls who ran so much their bodies were just bones and angles. Cindy smiled a lot and had a distracting habit of touching me ever-so-lightly on the wrist as she talked, maintaining the contact for just so long, but not a fraction of a second longer. I'd spent my entire high school career pining for girls like her. Two years of college had changed me in a thousand ways, but not so much that I didn't get a little dizzy every time she uncapped her cherry Chapstick and ran it lovingly over her dry, puckered lips.

My mother had been telling me all year that my father needed a rest, but I hadn't realized how badly he needed one until I'd spent a few weeks on the job. He looked like he'd aged ten years in a matter of months. He had indigestion from too much coffee, hemorrhoids from driving all day, and the haunted, jittery look of a fugitive from justice. He talked to himself more or less incessantly, often in a hostile tone of voice: "You idiot!" he'd say, slapping himself in the head the way they did on those V-8 commercials, "you forgot to refill the cup holders!" A slow driver in our path could trigger a rage in him that was frightening to behold, a teeth-grinding, horn-pressing, dashboard-pounding fury that made me think he was just a couple of red lights away from a massive heart attack or a full-scale nervous breakdown.

It was painful to compare this frayed version of my father with the optimistic, rejuvenated man he'd been the summer before, the risk taker who'd chucked his job as assistant manager of a Pathmark and gone deep into debt to buy the lunch truck and route from a guy who was calling it quits after thirty years in the business. You could see how excited he was by the uncharacteristic boldness of his decision, how proud he was to finally be his own boss, to own a truck with his name on it. He spent entire weekend afternoons washing and polishing it in our driveway, making that black-and-silver lunch wagon shine. His high spirits manifested themselves in the very name of the truck, which had previously gone by the more prosaic moniker of Eddie's Breakmobile. If people were going to call you the Roach Coach anyway, he'd reasoned, why not beat them to the punch?

It wasn't hard to see what had defeated him. Running a lunch truck is grueling, thankless work, marked by long hours, low profit margins, and constant time pressures. If a company's coffee break is at 10:15, you'd better be out in the parking lot at 10:14, open for business. Nobody wants to hear about the traffic jam or the flat tire that held you up, though they're more than happy to give you an earful about the sludgy coffee or how you supposedly shorted them on the ham in yesterday's sandwich. It starts to grind you down after a while.

By late June I knew the ropes well enough for my father to start taking Fridays off, leaving my parents free to spend long weekends relaxing at their campground near the Delaware River. (They loved it there, though Camp Leisure-Tyme always struck me as a grim parody of the suburban life they were supposedly getting away from, trailers lined up one after the other like dominoes, all these middle-aged couples watching portable TVs inside their little screen houses.)

My first day in charge, hustling from one stop to the next, singlehandedly taking care of the customers we usually split between us, I carried in my mind a comforting image of my father crashed out on his hammock in the shade of a tall tree, empty beer cans littering the grass below. The following Monday, though, he confessed that he'd been a nervous wreck the whole day, unable to do anything but deal out one hand of solitaire after another, mechanically flipping the cards as he tormented himself with elaborate disaster scenarios involving me and his precious truck.

Cindy asked me out on a Friday morning in early August, the third day of what turned out to be the worst heat wave of the summer. It was only ten o'clock, but already the thermometer was well into the nineties. I felt wilted and cranky, having awakened at four in the morning in a puddle of my own sweat. She worked in an air-conditioned office, and I could almost feel the coolness radiating off her skin.

"Poor guy," she said. "Looks like you could use a cold one."

"A cold two or three sounds more like it."

"Why don't you come to the Stock Exchange tonight? A bunch of us hang out there after work on Fridays."

"I just might take you up on that."

"Great." She smiled as though she had a question for me, but then decided to keep it to herself. "I'll keep an eye out for you. Come anytime after six."

I drove through the day in a miserable heat daze, stopping every now and then to soak my head in the spray from someone's lawn sprinkler. When it was finally over, I took a shower and fell asleep on the living room couch for a couple of hours. It was close to eight by the time I finally made it to the restaurant, and Cindy was alone at the bar.

"I thought you stood me up," she said, not even bothering with hello.

"Where's everyone else?" I asked. "Wasn't there supposed to be a bunch of you?"

"They left about an hour ago. Jill's brother invited us to a party down the shore."

"You could have gone. It wasn't like we had a date or anything."

She nodded slowly, trying to look thoughtful instead of hurt.

"I see them all the time. I thought it might be nice to be with someone different for a change."

I climbed onto the stool next to hers and played a little drumroll on the bar, feeling unexpectedly calm and in control.

"It is nice. How come we didn't think of this a month ago?"

She reached down and squeezed my leg just above the knee. It was a ticklish spot, and I jumped in my seat.

"I've been waiting for this all summer," she said. "I can't believe you're really here."

I wouldn't have predicted it, but Cindy turned out to be a talker. She drank three glasses of rosé with dinner and held forth on whatever popped into her head—her indecision about buying a car, her crush on Bruce Springsteen, a bad experience she once had eating a lobster. She had so many opinions my head got tired from nodding in real or feigned agreement with them. She believed it was better to die in a hospice than a hospital and thought tollbooths should be abolished on the parkway. She disapproved of abortion, loved trashy novels, and was angered by the possibility that rich people might be able to freeze their bodies immediately after death, remaining in a state of suspended animation until a cure was found for whatever had killed them.

"It doesn't seem fair," she said. "When you're dead you should just be dead."

"That's right. It should be available to everyone or not at all."

"I want to travel," she blurted out. "I don't just want to rot around here for the rest of my life."

I looked up from my Mexi-burger, startled by the pleading in her voice. She smiled sheepishly.

"I don't know what's gotten into me. I'm not usually such a chatterbox. I hope I'm not boring you to death."

"Not at all. I'm happy to listen."

And I was, too, at least most of the time. Even when she recounted in minute detail a complex dispute her mother had had with the cable company, or tried to convince me that I needed to read *The Late, Great Planet Earth,* I still found myself diverted by the unexpectedness of Cindy and touched by her need for my approval. I wasn't used to thinking of myself as someone other people needed to impress. Until quite recently, in fact, I had generally felt the obligation moving in the opposite direction.

"Do I sound stupid to you?" she asked.

"What makes you think that?"

"I'm just going on and on. I'm not even sure if I'm making sense."

"It's nice," I said. "I'm having a good time."

She stuck one finger into her wineglass, stirring the pink liquid into a lazy whirlpool. Then she transferred her finger from the glass to her mouth, sucking contemplatively for a few seconds.

"You're sweet," she said finally, as if pronouncing a verdict. "You're sweet to even put up with me."

She decided she was too tipsy to drive and happily accepted my offer of a ride home. We maneuvered our way through the crowded parking lot, bodies brushing together accidentally on purpose as we walked. It was still muggy, but the night had cooled down just enough to be merciful. I reached into my pocket and fished around for the keys.

"Oh my God," she said, grabbing me roughly by the wrist. "You're driving me home in this?"

I had spent so much of my summer in and around the Roach Coach I didn't really notice it anymore. But her startled laughter made me look at it as if for the first time: the gleaming silver storage compartment with its odd, quilted texture, the old-fashioned cab, the grinning cockroach on the passenger door, emblem of my father's rapidly fading dream. The roach was a friendly-looking, spindly-legged fellow, as much person as bug, walking more or less upright, with white gloves on his hands and white high-top sneakers on his feet. He seemed to be in a big hurry to get wherever it was he was going. DANTE'S ROACH COACH, said the bold yellow letters arching over his head. Beneath his feet, a caption read, COMIN' ATCHA!

"It's all I have," I said. "My parents took the station wagon to the campground. We can take your car if you want."

"That's okay," she said cheerfully. "How often does a girl get to ride in a lunch truck?"

I opened the door and helped her up into the cab. Then I circled around to the driver's side, climbing in beside her. An open box of Snickers bars rested on the seat between us, along with a parking ticket and a stack of coffee cups decorated with a Greek-column motif. Cindy helped herself to a candy bar. I started the truck.

"Kinda melted," she informed me, struggling with the taffy-like strand of caramel produced by her first bite. "You should keep these things out of the sun."

Five minutes later we pulled up in front of her house. I shut off the ignition and headlights, turning to her with one of those dopey what-now shrugs that was the best I could muster in the way of a suave opening gambit. She nodded yes, sliding toward me on the seat. I moved the candy bars and coffee cups on top of the dashboard, out of harm's way.

I hadn't been kissed all summer, and the first touch of her tongue on mine released me from a prison I hadn't even known I was in. All at once, the boundary between myself and the rest of the world disappeared; a sudden weightlessness took hold of me, as though I were no longer a body, just a mouth filled with tastes and sensations. For some unidentifiable period of time, I lost track of who and where I was.

When I could think again, my first thought was, *This is amazing!* My second was, *She's a secretary!* The thought was so jarring, so ridiculous and uncalled-for, it made me pull away in confusion. We sat there in the humid cab, separated by a distance of maybe a foot, breathing so hard we might as well have just delivered a refrigerator. She ran one hand through her formerly neat hair and looked at me as if I'd said something peculiar.

"What do you want?" she asked, her voice low and urgent.

"Want?" I said.

"Why are you even with me?"

Instead of answering—or maybe by way of answering—I kissed her again. This time it felt more like real life, two bodies, two separate agendas. I put my hand on her breast. She removed it. I groaned with disappointment and tried again, with the same result. Instead of backing off, though, she kissed me even harder, as if to reward my persistence. I wrenched my mouth away from hers.

"My parents are away for the weekend," I whispered. "We'd have the whole house to ourselves."

She ignored the invitation. Her face tightened into a squint of pained concentration.

"Tell me what it's like," she said.

I didn't bother to pretend I didn't know what she was talking about. In some strange way, we'd been talking about it all night.

"It's just college," I told her, leaning back against the door, trying to calm my breathing.

"How'd you get in?"

"I applied."

"Yeah, but—"

"I don't know," I said. "I did really good on the SATs. Much better than I expected."

This was my standard answer whenever anyone at home asked me how I'd gotten into Yale. It was easier to write it off as a fluke than to go into all the other stuff, the AP classes I'd taken, the papers I'd written for extra credit, the stupid clubs I'd joined just so I could list them on my application, all the nights I'd stayed up late reading books like *Moby Dick* and *The Magic Mountain* with a dictionary beside me, the endless lists of vocabulary words I'd memorized, the feeling I'd had ever since I was a little kid that I was headed out of town, on to bigger and better things.

"But it's hard, right? They give you a lot of homework?"

The word "homework" seemed jarring to me; it had dropped out of my vocabulary the day I graduated from high school.

"I didn't know what homework was," I admitted. "High school's a joke in comparison."

"It must be fun, though. Living in a dorm and everything."

"It's okay. The food's a little scary."

"I did really bad in high school," she said. "My mother was sick a lot. Then I got involved with this older guy. Before I knew it, the four years were gone and I hadn't really learned anything. Now I feel so stupid all the time."

"An older guy?" Just the phrase made me a little queasy.

"I was a cashier at Medi-Mart. He was one of the supervisors."

I remembered seeing her a lot at Medi-Mart back when we were in high school, thinking she seemed more at home behind the register than she did walking the halls of Harding.

"How long'd you go out?"

"Two years." She looked away; all the life seemed to have drained out of her. "He was married and everything. You must think I'm horrible."

I reached for her face, gently steering it my direction. She was teary-eyed, but happy to be kissed again. This time I tried some new strategies, nibbling on her lips and licking up and down the salty length of her neck. Within minutes she was breathing in quick, trembly gasps, murmuring encouragement. When she seemed ready, I tried maneuvering her onto her back, but she went rigid, not resisting exactly, but certainly not cooperating.

"What's the matter?"

She gave me a glassy-eyed smile of incomprehension.

"Nothing."

"Are you sure?"

"I love this," she said, running her tongue around her chapped and swollen-looking lips. "I could kiss you forever."

Three weeks later, I was starting to believe her. All we ever did was kiss. Nearly a month of heavy making out, and I hadn't even succeeded in getting my hand up her shirt. I couldn't figure out what I was doing wrong.

Other than that, we had a pretty good time together. Sometimes we went to the movies or out to dinner, but mainly we just shopped for cars. It was the consuming quest of her life. We read the stickers, quizzed the salesmen, took demos out for drives— Civics and Corollas, Escorts and Omnis, K-cars and Firebirds, Mustangs and Rabbits. But despite all our work, she seemed no closer to making a decision. New or used? Automatic or stick? Foreign or American? Hatchback or sedan? Every night we started from scratch. There was always another dealership, new variables to ponder. I started to wonder if she saw car shopping and kissing as ends in themselves—wholly satisfying, self-contained events—rather than starting points on the road to bigger things.

I think I would have lost patience with her a lot sooner if the end of the summer hadn't been looming over us from the start. Every day, in some process of withdrawal that was as subtle as it was relentless, I looked upon her less and less as my actual girlfriend and more and more as a potential anecdote, a puzzling and amusing story I would share with my roommates in one of those hilarious late-night conversations that I missed so much when I was away from college.

Cindy saw it differently. As I retreated, her attachment to me intensified. She hated the idea that I was just going to pack my bags and disappear, leaving her right where she was at the beginning of the summer. The average night ended with her in tears, me awkwardly trying to comfort her. Shyly at first, then more insistently, she began to explore the possibility of continuing our relationship after I returned to school. We could write and talk on the phone, couldn't we? I could come home for occasional weekends and vacations. It was do-able, wasn't it? Then she brought up the idea of visiting me in New Haven.

"It's not far, right? And I'll probably have my new car by then." I saw how excited she was by this prospect, and how hard she was trying not to show it. "It'll be really cool, don't you think?"

I didn't think it would be cool at all, but it seemed even more uncool to say so.

"Where would you sleep?" I asked, in a tone that suggested simple curiosity.

"Where would you want me to?" she asked, her excitement tempered by caution.

"What I want doesn't seem to matter."

"What do you mean?" Her voice was quiet now, a little defensive.

"What do you think I mean?"

"Tell me." Even in the darkness of the Roach Coach, I could see that she was getting ready to cry again. I hated it when she cried, hated how guilty it made me feel, and how manipulative she seemed in her misery.

"My parents are away," I told her. "We can do anything we want to. So why are we sitting here arguing about nothing?"

Something suddenly seemed very interesting to her outside the passenger window. I let her stare at it for as long as she needed to.

She came over the following night. It happened to be the Saturday before I left for school, our last chance to take advantage of the empty house. She made the decision herself, after I made it clear that I wasn't much feeling like going anywhere.

I had everything ready when she arrived. Hall and Oates on the record player, Mateus in the refrigerator, candles in the bedroom. In my pocket I carried two Fourex lambskin condoms. (Fourex were my condoms of choice in those days. They came in little blue plastic capsules, which, though inconveniently bulky and difficult to open, seemed infinitely classier than the little foil pouches that housed less exotic rubbers. I used the brand for several years, right up to the day someone explained to me that "lambskin" was not, in fact, a euphemism.)

We drank a glass of wine and went upstairs. I lit the candles. We kissed for a while and started taking off our clothes. Her body was everything I'd hoped for, and I would have been ecstatic if Cindy hadn't seemed so subdued and defeated in her nakedness. She sat on the bed, knees drawn to her chest, and watched me fumble with my blue capsule, her expression suggesting resignation rather than arousal. Finally the top popped off.

"There!" I said, triumphantly producing the condom.

She watched with grim curiosity as I began unfurling it over the tip of my erection, which already seemed decidedly more tentative than it had just seconds earlier.

"This is all you wanted," she said. She stated it as a fact, not a question.

"Don't be ridiculous," I muttered. I found it hard enough to put on a condom in the best of circumstances, and almost impossible while conducting a serious conversation.

"I should've known," she said. "This is all it ever comes down to, isn't it?"

The condom was only halfway on, and I could feel the opportunity slipping away. I tried to save it with a speech, telling her that sex between two people who liked and respected each other was a natural and beautiful thing, a cause for celebration, and certainly nothing for anyone to be ashamed of, but by the time I got to that part the whole issue was moot anyway. I watched her blank gaze travel down to the deflated balloon dangling between my legs and then back up to my face.

"There," I told her. "You happy now?"

slices are ready

The phone rang a few minutes after ten. I hesitated, thinking it was probably Cindy, but then picked up anyway. Those were the days just before answering machines really caught on, and if you were curious you didn't really have a choice.

"Get your coat on," Matt barked in my ear. "I'll meet you at Naples in ten minutes."

"What?"

"You heard me."

"I can't."

"Whaddaya mean, you can't?"

"I told you. I've got a date with George Eliot."

"Fuck George Eliot."

"I'll be lucky to get to second base."

"Ha ha."

"Seriously, I'm supposed to read up to page six eighty-seven."

"So?"

"Right now I'm on page two seventy-two."

"See? You're halfway there. Just skim the rest over breakfast."

"Sure," I said. "What the hell. It's either that or the Cheerios box."

Matt sighed to let me know how badly I was disappointing him.

"Listen," he told me. "I don't usually do this, but I'm gonna save you a lot of trouble. You want to know what happens at the end of *Middlemarch*?"

"I'd prefer not to."

"Ha, good one. You know the main character? What's her name?"

"Dorothea?"

"Yeah, her. She throws herself under a train."

"That's Anna Karenina, asshole."

"Oh, right. Sorry. I got confused. There's a big sword fight. Everybody dies."

"Goodbye, Matt."

"You're not gonna do this? You're gonna make me go to bed hungry?"

"Go yourself. You don't need me to hold your hand."

"Yeah, right. I'll really go to Naples by myself at this time of night. First I'll have to make a sign that says, "I'm Pathetic," so I can wear it around my neck."

"That won't be necessary," I assured him.

"Touché," he said, grimly conceding defeat. "Enjoy your reading, weenie boy."

34 **Cindy and I** had ended the summer on bad terms. I came back to school and threw myself into my classes with renewed passion, thanking God every chance I got for releasing me from the bondage of the lunch truck, though my happiness was diluted by the hot flashes of guilt I felt for abandoning my father. Now that I knew what his days were really like, I had to trade in the sustaining illusion of him as a happy and prosperous businessman on wheels for the more accurate and distressing image of him as captain of a sinking ship, an angry, itchy, dyspeptic man tailgating some terrified geezer as he tried to make up for lost time between the perforating company and the lumberyard.

That fall turned out to be a breakthrough semester for me, the first time I ever really felt at home in college. As thrilled as I'd been by the intellectual challenges, my freshman and sophomore years had been emotionally and socially difficult. I felt trapped and resentful a lot of the time, marooned within a small circle of friends and acquaintances, cut off from the wider life of the college, which seemed to be dominated by overlapping prep school cliques I wouldn't have known how to penetrate if I'd wanted to. Junior year, though, the whole place just cracked wide open.

Two changes were responsible for my new sense of excitement and belonging. I got hooked up with *Reality* and went to work in the dining hall. *Reality* was a new undergraduate literary magazine founded by Liz Marin, whom I'd met the previous spring in a class on the epic tradition. Liz was the kind of person I'd never met before coming to Yale. She'd grown up in New York and Paris and had taken a year off after high school to go backpacking through Latin America. She was tall and beautiful and multilingual and fiercely opinionated. One of her opinions held that the rags that passed for literary magazines on campus were so smug and tame and insular that it was hopeless to even try to reform them; they simply needed to be replaced. Her idea was to create a magazine devoted to everything but college, one that focused on exploited workers, violent crime, urban poverty, and moral squalor—the whole wide hardscrabble world spread out like a dirty rug at the foot of our ivory tower—in a word, *Reality*.

"No more sonnets about menstruation!" she proclaimed at our organizational meeting, with what seemed like genuine anguish. "No more wacky stories about summer jobs!"

Our first issue, published that December—the cover photo featured a stray dog with some sort of skin condition straining really hard to take a shit—made a surprisingly big splash on campus. The articles included profiles of a prison guard and a heroin-addicted prostitute, and the poems explored difficult subjects like incest and drug addiction and prison life. There were two short stories—one about a pyromaniac priest, the other about a thirteen-year-old nymphomaniac who poisons her family's dog for reasons the author chose to leave deliberately vague. Liz herself was a talented photographer, and her unflinching portraits of the homeless, the retarded, the weird-looking, and the unlucky were scattered throughout our pages. Despite the grittiness of the content, production values were high; a supposedly anonymous alum—everyone knew he was actually Liz's Uncle George—had donated a substantial sum to insure that we didn't have to cut corners on things like paper stock and high-quality photo reproduction. Just about everyone who mattered agreed that *Reality* was troubling and deeply relevant, a refreshing departure from the usual circle jerk of undergraduate publishing. As deputy assistant literary editor for fiction, I got to bask in some of the reflected glory. Strangers introduced themselves to me at parties; people who'd ignored me for two years suddenly wanted to know me better.

Despite its comparative lack of glamour, though, my job in the dining hall probably had more to do with my improved mood than my association with the magazine. Hot and dirty and hectic as it could be, the work was strangely consuming, sometimes even exhilarating. Three-hour shifts would fly by in a blur of frantic activity and cheerful banter and an unspoken sense of camaraderie I hadn't experienced anywhere else in college.

In my ugly blue shirt and paper hat, I was part of a team, the first one I'd belonged to for a long time. My teammates weren't just fellow students like Matt or Kristin or Sarah, a shy girl I later found out was a world-class oboist as well as a member of the Yale Slavic Chorus, or Eddie Zimmer, who was always trying to recruit people for the Ultimate Frisbee Club, or Djembe, who was supposedly some sort of African prince whose family had fallen on hard times. They were the surly cooks with their unpredictable rages and muttered quips; the black and Puerto Rican women working the serving line, whose private thoughts remained hidden behind masks of polite friendliness; the dishwashers, one of whom weighed three hundred pounds and another who lived in the YMCA and had such a horrible hacking cough I regularly expected to see him start spitting up blood; and Lorelei, this sexy high school girl from New Haven whose job seemed to consist of sitting at the front desk in a pose of provocative languor and pressing a clicker every time someone entered; and Albert, the manager, who enjoyed teaching us restaurant jargon, like "eighty-six" and "sneeze guard." Sometimes I'd get so caught up in the work I'd forget who I was and mutter under my breath about the "fuckin' Yalies," the privileged brats who seemed to think the rest of us had been put on earth to serve their every need and whim.

In late October, at the height of that unexpectedly busy and happy semester, I got a letter from Cindy. It was four pages long, written in red ink on pink stationery in this fat, meticulous, gracefully looping script. "Dear Danny," she wrote:

Guess what? I did it! I broke down and bought a car! A brand new Honda Civic. Silver. It's really cute. You wouldn't believe how good it smells. I woke up in the middle of the night last night and snuck outside of the house in my pajamas just so I could sit in it for a while. Isn't that ridiculous! I'm still learning the stick. I'm all right with everything except starting on a hill. Yesterday I rolled backwards into a cop car at that light by the Hess station! but luckily there was no damage. The cop was nice about it—he just told me to take it easy on the clutch. It was easier once I got myself to calm down a little.

Are you surprised to hear from me?! My heart's pounding like crazy. I don't know why. It's just a letter, right? I'm sure your busy with your friends and all your homework and everything, but I'm curious. Do you think about me sometimes? I'm only asking because I think about you all the time. I mean ALL THE TIME! I've written you like 37 letters I've been too scared to put in the mail, but this one I think I really might send so I'm trying to be EXTRA careful about spelling since I know it is one of your strong points (NOT one of mine!)

You know when I think of you most? Coffee break. When I step outside and see your father's truck waiting in the road. I expect you to be there again, wearing that doofy coin belt (No offense!) or else I remember us kissing in the front seat. Remember that?

I'm really sorry if I disappointed you. It wasn't that I didn't want to be with you the way you wanted to be with me. I guess I was just scared or something. Oh well. You probably have a new girlfriend now. I HOPE not! (Is it all right for me to say that?)

You don't have to write back if you don't want. I mainly just want to tell you about the car, since you spent so much time helping me look. I at least owe you a ride when you get back home for Thanksgiving. Would that be okay?

Wow! I don't think I've written a letter this long in my whole life. I guess I'm like that once I get going I can't seem to get myself to shut up. But I guess I don't have to tell YOU!

Love,
Cynthia

ps—is it all right for me to say love?

Another letter came the next day, and another one the day after that. After her eighth unanswered letter, I finally broke down and wrote her back. I congratulated her on her new car, talked a little about my classes, and told her how much fun I was having working in the dining hall. In passing, I mentioned that I wasn't seeing anyone new, and that I still thought about her from time to time. Three days later, she called and asked if she could drive up for a visit. ("Just for the day," she assured me.) By that time, though, it was November already, and the late semester crunch had set in. I had papers to write, and no time for visitors. We made plans to get together over Thanksgiving break.

My first night home she picked me up in her new car, proud and happy and nervous. She had a new haircut too, shorter and less elaborate and a lot more flattering. We went to the movies, then out for a couple of drinks. We laughed a lot, and took a detour to Echo Lake on the way home. In an empty parking lot by the golf course, she showed me how the front seats of her Honda reclined like dentist chairs. With the heater running and *Greetings from Asbury Park* on the tape player, we kissed till our jaws ached and our tongues were sore, just like the summer had never ended.

At ten thirty the phone rang again. I figured it to be Matt, weighing in with a second round of begging and hectoring, but it turned out to be Polly Wells, the deputy assistant literary editor for poetry at *Reality*.

"Hey," she said, chuckling softly to herself as if remembering a good joke. "What are you doing?"

"Abusing my highlighter. It's an ugly scene."

"Want to go to Naples?"

"Like when?"

"Like now?"

I glanced down at the brick that was *Middlemarch* and weighed my alternatives. Polly had a cloud of reddish blond hair and the mouth of a cherub. We'd kissed each other once, experimentally, at the party celebrating the first issue of *Reality*, and neither one of us had mentioned it since. We were both drunk at the time, but I retained a vivid memory of her whispering, "You're a very strange person," and then kissing me on the mouth, as if to congratulate me on my strangeness. I believe I'd been going on about her name before that, telling her how great I thought it was that there were still people in the world named Polly. (The only thing I remembered after that was vomiting into a storm drain while Sang stood by with some guy I didn't know, waiting patiently for me to finish.)

"Now sounds good," I told her.

Ten minutes later I was sitting across from her in a scarred-up wooden booth near the jukebox, waiting for my glass of foam to revert to its original liquid condition. Polly was one of the few girls I knew who was always up for splitting a pitcher, but she hadn't quite perfected her pouring technique.

"I'm pissed at Peter," she told me, straining to make herself heard over the din of surrounding conversations. Naples at that time on a Tuesday night seemed like the hub of the universe, and one of the few scenes at Yale that actually approximated stereotypical images of "college life"—crowds of more or less rowdy students gathered around dark tables littered with beer glasses and pizza crusts, laughing, arguing, and occasionally bursting into song, though the general aura of medieval revelry was softened by the presence of numerous violin cases stowed under the tables, as well as the healthy population of loners scattered throughout the restaurant, holding folded pizza slices in one hand and open books in the other.

"What did he do now?" I asked, trying to strike a tone that balanced interest and fatigue. I wasn't thrilled with my role as sounding board for her boyfriend troubles, but I didn't want to jeopardize it, either. If her relationship with Peter—I couldn't help thinking of him as Professor Preston—really did go south, I figured the hours I'd put in as sympathetic listener would give me a leg up in the competition to replace him.

"He's got some woman staying in his apartment for the next two weeks, this professor from Vassar doing research at Beinecke Library. He claims she's just 'a friend and colleague,' but maybe it would be better if we didn't see each other while she's around. I bet he's in bed with her right now."

"Not necessarily," I said, secretly rooting for this possibility. "Maybe they really are just friends."

"He's such a hypocrite," she said, shaking her head like a dog to get that beautiful hair out of her pale, almost ashen face. Her eyelids looked pink and irritated. "When we first started going out, he said he didn't care who knew. We used to go to the movies at York Square and hold hands. He'd pick me up in front of Silliman in his car. Now it's all hush-hush, like he's married or something."

Peter Preston was a rising star in the English Department, a thirty-two-year-old assistant professor who'd arrived from Berkeley the year before and made an immediate name for himself with his lecture class on Shakespeare's problem plays, which drew close to three hundred students, myself included. He was boyishly handsome, with a shock of blond hair that kept falling over his left eye no matter how many times he pushed it back on top of his head.

We loved him—most of us, anyway—for his dry wit, his skinny neckties, and his familiarity with our pop culture universe. For the past several months, his relationship with Polly had been an open secret, at least in certain circles. Sexual harassment hadn't quite come into its own as a concept at the time, and most of us were at best mildly scandalized by the idea of a young professor sleeping with an undergraduate who wasn't currently enrolled in one of his classes, though I must say that on a purely personal level, I had found it confusing and painful to make the transition from worshipping him as a teacher to resenting him as a rival.

"What's taking so long with the slices?" Polly cast an impatient glance at the pizza counter, where a crowd had begun to gather. "I'm starving. I haven't eaten all day."

"All day? You're kidding, right?"

She shrugged. "Sometimes I forget."

"That's amazing. I don't think I've forgotten a meal my entire life. It doesn't even seem possible."

"Maybe I should sleep with someone else," she said, unwilling to be sidetracked into a discussion of my fanatically regular eating habits. "Maybe that would wake him up."

"Hmmm," I said, making an effort to look like my interest in the subject were purely theoretical. "That's a pretty drastic step."

"But who?" She exhaled so forcefully I felt the breeze all the way across the table. "Can you think of anyone?"

"Don't ask me," I said, wondering if it would be out-of-line to float my own candidacy. "This is something you'll have to figure out on your own."

"My history TA's pretty cute. But he's got that awful beard."

I rubbed my clean-shaven chin and clucked my tongue.

"Too bad."

"There's got to be someone," she said, squinting into the distance.

From where I sat, I had a clear view of the counter, so I knew what was coming when the pizza guy bent down and put his lips to the silver microphone they kept by the register.

"Slices are ready."

His mumbled announcement crackled through the staticky PA system, silencing the pizzeria like the Voice of God. I jumped up and joined the mad rush for the counter, jockeying for position among the mob of ex–National Merit Scholars and former student council presidents, many of whom were waving plastic plates in the air like extras in a movie about the Depression. I had jostled my way almost to the front of the line when someone shoved me from behind with a force that could only have been deliberate.

"Hey," I said, whirling angrily. "Take it easy."

Matt fixed his paper hat on his head and eyed me with cool disdain.

"*Et tu,* Danny?"

I shrugged an insincere apology, lowering my voice to a conspiratorial level. "I'm with a girl. Good things are happening."

Any of my other male friends would have accepted this excuse without a protest, but Matt's expression didn't change. He raised his hands up to his head like a hold-up victim, and turned slowly, until I was facing his back.

"What are you doing?" I asked.

"Go ahead," he said, glancing mournfully over his shoulder. "Stab me in the liver. Give it a couple of twists while you're at it."

"Yoo-hoo," said the guy behind the counter. "You boys want slices, or you wanna play games?"

So, what about you?" Polly asked, shaking a storm of red pepper flakes onto her slice. "What's going on with you and your secretary?"

I always felt bad when people at school referred to Cindy as my secretary, not only because it was unfair to her, but also because of what it said about my own sad vanity. At some point I'd realized that my association with her struck certain of my college friends as vaguely exotic, and I'd played up the working-class angle for all it was worth.

"Nothing much."

"You going to visit her this weekend?"

"Nope."

"She coming here?"

"Nope."

"I guess spring break's only a couple of weeks away. You must be looking forward to that."

I usually thought of myself as having a quick mind, but I was often slow on the uptake with Polly. For weeks I'd been pretending to her that Cindy and I were still a couple, figuring that this somehow equalized things between us, saving me from looking like what I really was—the second banana, the would-be boyfriend waiting in the wings, the one who kept her company when the other one had better things to do. But all at once it struck me that Polly wasn't just making conversation, that she might actually have a personal interest in my weekend plans, that there might be some hope for me after all.

"It's over," I said.

Her self-possession faltered for a second. She leaned forward, the eagerness in her voice betraying the careful blankness of her face.

"What?"

"It's over with me and Cindy. It's been over since Christmas."

She sat back and contemplated me for a couple of seconds. She couldn't seem to decide if she was angry or amused or simply puzzled.

"Why didn't you tell me?"

"I don't know."

She looked away, momentarily distracted by a commotion across the room. One nerdy guy in a Yale sweatshirt was leaning across a table, beating another nerdy guy in a Yale sweatshirt over the head with a Yale baseball cap. The guy being hit wasn't trying to defend himself. He just sat there with this feeble smile on his face, as if he wanted onlookers like us to think it was all in fun.

"I wish you would've told me," she said.

"Why?" I said, relishing the power that had come from surprising her. "What's the difference?"

"What's the difference?" She seemed offended by the question.

"Yeah. What would be different if you'd known?"

Before she could answer, a hard ball of paper hit me in the forehead. I looked up and saw Matt standing at the edge of our table, holding open his winter coat to reveal a rectangle of pizza box cardboard taped to his shirt. The words "I'm Pathetic" were printed on it in bold capital letters. He smiled at Polly and held out his hand.

"Hi," he said. "I'm Pathetic. You must be George Eliot."

Polly smiled politely. "Excuse me?"

Matt drew back, apparently perplexed. His head was bare, and I realized that the crumpled projectile now resting in my pizza plate was his dining-hall hat. He glanced at me, then back at Polly.

"I'm sorry," he said. "I talked to Danny earlier in the evening, and he told me he had a date with George Eliot. So I merely assumed—" He held up both hands as if in apology. "I hope I haven't embarrassed anyone."

"Just yourself," I assured him.

"That's okay," he said, once again displaying his sign. "I have no shame."

"It's a good thing, too," Polly told him.

"Touché," said Matt. It was one of his highest compliments.

"Good night," I said. "See you Thursday."

Matt put both hands together as if in prayer and bowed to Polly— "Good night, Mr. Eliot"—and then to me—"Good night, Brutus." Then he zipped up his coat and strode off without looking back. He didn't even turn around when I beaned him with his hat from a distance of about ten feet.

"Friend of yours?" asked Polly.

"We work together in the dining hall."

"Isn't his father some kind of big shot?"

"Who, Matt?"

"Yeah. That was what Ingrid told me."

"I don't think so. His father's a car salesman."

"Are you sure?" she asked. "I thought she said it was the guy who went around in the paper hat."

"Positive." Matt had told me lots of hilarious stories about his hapless, overweight father, who was always moving from one dealership to another, never quite meeting his sales quotas. In the one I liked best, Matt had snuck into a lot his father had recently been fired from and soaped lots of crazy things on the windows of the used cars, phrases like *Complete Piece of Shit, A Real Lemon,* and *They Tampered with My Odometer!*

"You must be confusing him with someone else."

"Whatever," she said. "Doesn't matter."

We drank a second pitcher, something we had never done before, and stayed until closing time. Polly talked about her family's summer place in Vermont. She said there was a spring-fed pond there, and a pasture they rented out to a dairy farmer down the road. She said it was possible to really get to know the cows, not only to distinguish one from the other, but to get a pretty good sense of how they were feeling on any given day.

"How do you do that?"

"You talk to them. And look at their faces. Cows have very expressive faces."

I knew her well enough at that point not to be surprised by this. The first few months we'd worked together, I'd found her distant and intimidating, not just because she was Professor Preston's girlfriend, but also because she'd cultivated a very adult reserve that made her seem years older than the rest of us. She was all business at our editorial-board meetings, holding herself conspicuously aloof from the atmosphere of manic jocularity that dominated the proceedings. The more time we spent together, though, the more I'd come to realize that her reserve was rooted as much in shyness as in confidence, and that her quiet sophistication masked a powerful streak of girlish sincerity.

"You should come visit me," she said. "We could go for a mid-night swim."

"Just you and me? Or are the cows included, too?"

"The more the merrier, I guess. What are you doing this summer anyway?"

"Probably helping my dad."

Just thinking about the lunch truck made my head hurt. I had a pretty strong beer buzz at that point, and for a second or two, the physical reality of the summer washed back over me, almost like a hallucination. I felt the weight of the coin belt around my waist, the dent in my forehead from a too-tight baseball cap, the numbness in my hand from fishing around in the ice bed, trying to locate the last can of orange soda. Spring break was only two weeks away and instead of traveling to someplace warm like the Whiffenpoofs, I was going to spend it behind the wheel of the Roach Coach, filling in while my father recuperated from a long-delayed hemorrhoid operation.

"That must be nice," she said. "Getting to spend time with your dad like that. I was always jealous of my father's life at the office. He spent so much time there and I could never be part of it."

"It's not nice," I told her. "It's boring as hell. I'd love to do something else. But he needs the help."

I smiled as though resigned to making the best of a bad situation, thinking, for some reason, of my parents at Camp Leisure-Tyme, playing solitaire at opposite ends of the picnic table. I couldn't help resenting Polly just then for her spring-fed swimming hole and her expressive cows—the whole Vermont summertime idyll—resenting her despite the fact that she'd been kind enough to offer to share it with me. Her foot touched my ankle under the table, as if she understood my bad thoughts and wanted to forgive me anyway.

"I think I'm going to take painting lessons," she said. "I want to learn to look at things. So I can see what's really there instead of what's just supposed to be."

The busboy came to clear away our mess. He couldn't speak English and had to communicate by pointing. Polly said something in Spanish that made him smile, and he began gathering our plates and glasses. Trying to be helpful, I flicked a dirty napkin in his direction, and suddenly felt like a jerk. To him I must have looked like a prince of privilege, drinking beer at midnight with a pretty girl, attending a school that cost more a semester than he probably made in a year. He muttered, "*Gracias,*" and dropped the napkin into the empty pitcher.

"You know the real reason I want to paint this summer?" Polly's foot touched mine under the table again. This time she kept it there.

"What?"

She smiled. "I want to look like an artist. I love those paint-splattered jeans they wear. It makes them look so serious."

"Don't do it," I said.

"Don't do what?"

"The paint-splattered jeans."

"Why not?"

"It wouldn't be fair." My foot felt huge against hers, like someone had inflated it with a pump. "You're too cool already."

Both of us needed to use the bathroom before we left. The women's room was upstairs, not far from the pizza counter, but men had to descend a steep stairway and follow a narrow hallway to a cramped, doorless stall lit by a naked bulb. I unzipped and cursed myself for not wearing a decent pair of underpants or packing one of my lambskins just in case, but these recriminations were beside the point. The night had veered wildly off course, heading toward a destination that hadn't even been on the map when I'd gotten dressed after my shower. I briefly considered ditching my shabby briefs in the garbage can, presenting myself to Polly as more of a devil-may-care sort of guy than I really was, but quickly realized that removing my underwear in the present circumstances was out of the question. If we really did end up in a pants-off situation, she was just going to have to accept me for the slob I was.

This was the thought foremost in my mind when I stepped out of the bathroom and into her arms. I hadn't expected her to be there, and let out an involuntary cry of alarm that she stifled with a kiss. It was an abrupt, determined kiss, almost like someone had dared her to do it, and it was over before I really had a chance to process what was happening. She stepped away from me in the murky hallway, tilting her head to study me from a different angle.

"Walk me home?" she asked. There was an anxious tremor in her voice, as if she'd somehow gotten the idea that there was the slightest chance in hell I might say no.

She lived right around the corner, so we didn't have far to go. It was too bad, in a way, because everything seemed perfect just then. The night was clear and cool, the moon bright; Polly's hand was warm. I would've been happy to walk with her for hours down the quiet streets, traversing the entire campus, past the darkened libraries and lit-up residential colleges, the closed stores and the blank fronts of secret societies, past stone walls and ivy-covered moats and iron gates, never out of earshot of tapping typewriters or the sound of laughter seeping through a closed window.

As it was, the walk lasted maybe a minute. Even so, I remember feeling like Wordsworth on the verge of a sublime experience, one of his "spots of time." I was alert and deeply connected to my surroundings, the familiar world seemed to vibrate with unexpected significance. The revelation it brought me wasn't grand or romantic, though—it was just a simple sense of belonging. *I'm here,* I thought. *I'm happy.*

"Oh, shit," said Polly. Her hand slipped out of mine.

Peter Preston was waiting out in front of the Silliman gate in a leather bomber jacket, leaning against the hood of his Volkswagen Rabbit. Polly looked at him. He looked at me. I looked at her, then back at him, feeling instantly diminished by his presence—shorter, younger, more badly dressed than I'd been a second ago. He made me think of all the books I hadn't read, and all the ones I'd read but hadn't fully understood.

"Hi, Danny," he said, as if it were a chance meeting in the street, involving just the two of us. He knew me from class the previous year—my final paper on *Measure for Measure* had been nominated for one of the sophomore English prizes—and had taken me to lunch to congratulate me on a job well done.

"Hi, Professor Preston."

He gave a weird laugh.

"Might as well call me Peter."

"Okay."

He combed his fingers through his hair and gave a big sigh. He seemed stricken, like he'd just received terrible news but for some reason felt obligated to smile about it. Out of the blue, I remembered this girl in my section remarking on his uncanny resemblance to Andy Gibb.

"Mind if I talk to Polly?" he asked.

I checked with her, already knowing the answer. She bit her lip, dismissing me with a nod.

"I'll call you tomorrow, okay?"

My face felt hot, like I was standing too close to a fireplace. I gave a shrug of what was supposed to be mature resignation and headed off down College Street as though it were all the same to me, as though I'd expected the night to end like this all along. It seemed important not to look back or give too much thought to what they might be doing or saying, so I tried to distract myself by whispering the word "fuck" over and over again, in unison with my footsteps, and thinking about how cool I would be in the leather bomber jacket I was sure I would someday own.

kimchi virgins

By the time I got within striking distance of J. E.—Jonathan Edwards, my residential college—I had cheered up considerably. My initial sense of defeat had subsided, and I was beginning to see the night as a major step forward. Polly had kissed me; I had told her the truth about Cindy. I was off the sidelines and into the game, and the score wasn't nearly as lopsided in Peter Preston's favor as I'd imagined.

Fumbling for my keys by the main gate, I grew uneasy, as though I were being watched. Casting a furtive glance down Library Walk, the elegant bluestone path that separated J. E. from Branford College, I spotted a shadowy figure on the grass between the walkway and the Branford moat, maybe thirty yards away. He had his back to me and was partially obscured by a tree, but something—his distinctive slouch, or maybe just the drape of his coat—told me right away that it was Nick. I was amazed to see him still hanging around campus at this hour.

I wasn't sure if he'd seen me, and could just as easily have slipped through the gate and left him to his business, but I didn't. Part of my hesitation came from a fear of looking like I was snubbing him—grouchy and foul-mouthed as he was, Nick could be surprisingly touchy—but mainly I was just curious. Nick had gotten under my skin over the past couple of months. I'd met a lot of guys like him back home, factory workers and manual laborers who seemed too smart for the jobs they'd ended up with and only knew how to fight back with muttered curses and bitter jokes, guys who played the lottery every week just to remind themselves that you couldn't win. Like them, Nick made me wonder if I was a fool for thinking I had some kind of God-given right to satisfying work and personal happiness, for believing that what separated me from him was anything more than a few points on a standardized test and a little bit of luck that was bound to run out long before I reached the finish line.

I didn't walk any more softly than usual, but for some reason he didn't hear me approach. He just stood there, lost in thought, gazing into a lighted window on the ground floor of Branford, on the far side of the moat. Kristin Willard was framed in the window, her profile angelic in the pale glow of her reading lamp. She seemed to be concentrating hard, as if something in the book didn't make sense to her. Another girl appeared in the doorway behind her, but Kristin read on, oblivious to the intrusion. Our conversation in the dining hall came back to me, Nick and Matt joking about inviting her to our orgy, but it seemed wrong now, creepy instead of funny.

I cleared my throat.

Nick couldn't have reacted more violently to a gunshot. He spun on his heels, emitting a strangled yelp of distress, and flung his arms into an awkward karate stance that couldn't conceal the flinch of pure terror on his face. I jumped backward, raising my own hands in a reflexive gesture of self-defense. We froze in these half-assed Bruce Lee poses for a few seconds, until Nick finally realized who I was.

"You got a good dentist?" he asked me.

"What?"

"If you ever do that to me again," he whispered, "you're gonna be missing a whole bunch of fucking teeth."

He brushed off the front of his coat as if he'd gotten crumbs on it, and walked off without another word. When I checked on Kristin again, she was gone. All I could see through the window was the lamplight falling on her empty desk.

———

My heart still pounding, I opened the door to my suite and stepped into a pungent cloud of pot smoke spiced with the industrial-strength odor of fermented pickled cabbage. *Pretzel Logic* was playing on the stereo and the common room was crowded with visitors from the second floor, including the elusive Vernon Davis, the only black guy on our entryway. I had barely registered my surprise at his presence when Ted lifted the red plastic tube off the coffee table and held it out to me. Sang did the same with a glass jar the size of a human head.

"Bong hit?" asked one.

"Kimchi?" inquired the other.

Over the past couple of months, these two items had become the centerpieces of a popular late-night ritual in our suite. Sang had returned from Christmas break in California with three huge containers of his grandfather's homemade kimchi—it was supposedly aged in the traditional manner, buried in a hole in the backyard—and he invited a couple of his Asian friends over to try some on the night before classes began. Shortly before they arrived, Ted broke open a gigantic Thai stick his prep school lacrosse coach had given him as a Christmas present. Those who partook of these two delicacies in the proper order—I wasn't one of them—pronounced the combination nothing short of miraculous, and word had gotten around.

"No thanks," I said.

"No bong hit?" Ted squinted at me in broken-hearted disbelief. It wounded him when people didn't want to share in his pleasures.

"Sorry," I said, my willpower already starting to erode. "I've got five hundred pages of *Middlemarch* to go before I sleep."

"So?" Ted glanced around the room for support. "What's that got to do with anything?"

"You ever try to read George Eliot stoned?" I felt somewhat sheepish advancing this line of argument after splitting two pitchers with Polly, but it was important to my self-image that I at least try to resist. "You can't get past the epigraphs."

"Eat some kimchi," said Donald Park, a Korean-American straight-arrow who only tolerated our dope smoking out of a deep, almost primal craving for his ancestral staple. "It's scientifically proven to clear the mind and freshen the breath."

"Danny's a kimchi virgin," Sang explained, as though this shameful fact hadn't already attained the status of common knowledge. He passed the jar across the table to Donald, who unwrapped a pair of restaurant chopsticks he'd removed from his shirt pocket and used them to fish out a radioactive-looking wedge of cabbage, its pale surface speckled with chili powder. He munched it slowly, regarding me with undisguised pity.

"I'm working up to it," I assured him. "I'm gonna get there any day now."

Among my friends—especially my more or less omnivorous Asian friends—I was widely celebrated for my strange eating habits. I had grown up in a house where spices were frowned upon, and where eating out inevitably meant pizza or McDonald's. Before college, the only Chinese food I had ever consumed was a mouthful of canned, uncooked La Choy water chestnuts whose unusual texture had left me deeply traumatized. But it wasn't just the cuisine of other lands that gave me trouble; I had also cultivated a profound, unshakable revulsion for a number of common American foods, including eggs, raw tomatoes, mayonnaise, mushrooms, sea creatures, and every vegetable known to humankind with the exception of iceberg lettuce, canned corn, and overcooked green beans. On the other hand, the few things I did like—hot dogs, BLTs (minus the T), French dip sandwiches, chocolate pudding, pancakes, saltines with peanut butter—I consumed in amounts that had made me a minor legend in the dining hall. I justified myself by saying that I more than made up in volume what I lacked in variety, but the truth was that I was often embarrassed by my cowardice, the way I forced my friends to bend over backward for me when choosing a restaurant or even ordering pizza. I had a number of self-improvement projects in the works in those days, and one of the main ones involved forcing myself to become a more adventurous eater.

"Tonight's the night," sang Hank Yamashita, in a credible imitation of Rod Stewart. Hank was a six-foot-tall Japanese-American from the Upper East Side who read *GQ* and had taken it upon himself to act as my informal fashion advisor. It was at Hank's urging that I had replaced my cherished blue suede winter coat with a less eye-catching parka, and had relegated my new Thom McAn cowboy boots to a dusty corner of my closet. (It wasn't that Hank had anything against cowboy boots per se—he owned several pairs himself—but he did object to the peculiar orange glow mine seemed to give off, especially at twilight or in cloudy weather.) "Vernon's gonna take the plunge," he added.

"Tonight?" I asked.

Vernon responded with a skeptical nod, and it wasn't until then that I noticed the chopstick in his right hand. On the tip, impaled like a check on a spindle, was a tiny scrap of kimchi.

"That's the plan," he said, holding the chopstick in front of his face like a sparkler. "How hard could it be?"

Vernon was a short, powerful-looking guy with no neck and the suave baritone voice of a late-night deejay. He lived with Hank and Donald, but generally kept himself apart from the social life of the entryway. If you asked his roommates where he was, they'd just give a vague shrug, as if to suggest that it was a big world out there, and your guess was as good as theirs. Ever since I'd met Vernon freshman year and learned that he'd attended the same Jersey City high school as my mother, I'd been hoping we could become friends, but lately I'd begun to suspect that it wasn't in the cards. I couldn't seem to find a way of talking to him that didn't transform even the simplest conversation into some sort of debate about race in America. He'd been steering clear of me since our last meal in the dining hall, when I'd pressed a little too hard to enlist him on my side of an argument about Richard Wright's portrayal of Bigger in *Native Son*.

"You know what?" I turned to Donald, seized by a sudden jolt of inspiration. "I think I'll try some, too."

"You're kidding," said Sang.

I shook my head. "Why not? I'm as ready as I'll ever be."

"All right!" Sang congratulated me with an upraised fist. I was touched by how pleased he seemed. "I knew you could do it."

Donald plunged a chopstick into the jar and speared a bite-sized morsel of cabbage. I took it from him and smiled at Vernon.

"Safety in numbers," I said.

Vernon gave a barely perceptible nod. Then he brought the kimchi to his nose and gave it a little sniff.

"Here goes nothing," he said, looking me straight in the eye as he closed his mouth over the tip of the chopstick. I followed his lead. He withdrew the chopstick and chewed slowly, his expression shifting from grave suspicion to cautious approval.

As soon as I bit down, my mouth flooded with powerful sensations. The kimchi was cold, briny, crunchy, and spicy, though not nearly as fiery as I'd expected. It was okay.

"Well?" said Sang. "What's the verdict?"

Hank, Donald, and Ted leaned forward in their seats, as if something important were about to happen. Vernon and I traded glances, each waiting for the other to take the lead.

"Not bad," we finally blurted out, almost in unison.

Something about our answer struck the other guys as funny. Sang slapped his leg. Hank and Donald traded high fives in our honor. Ted shook his head, an expression of solemn wonderment taking hold of his face. He held out both his meaty arms as wide as they would go, as if he were thinking about embracing all five of us at once.

"This," he said, pausing to make eye contact with each of us in turn. "This is why I came to Yale."

An hour or so later, I slipped away from the party. It was almost two in the morning, but my breakthrough with the kimchi had given me a second wind. Even after a couple of celebratory bong hits, I felt strangely alert, eager to resume my plodding trek through *Middlemarch*. My mood was such that it didn't even bother me to open the door and find Max sprawled out on my bed, his bare, not-exactly-spotless feet propped up on my pillow.

"Hey," I said, "what's a nice girl like you doing in a dump like this?"

Unaware of the emotional progress I'd made since our last encounter, he scrambled into sitting position, shielding his face with a fat hardcover.

"Sorry." He peeked out from behind the book. "I would've stayed in my room, but Nancy wanted to go to bed early."

"No problem." I dismissed his concerns with a magnanimous flick of the wrist. "Whatcha readin'?"

"Something about Leon Czolgosz. The anarchist who shot McKinley."

"Nice guy?"

Max didn't seem to notice that I was goofing on him.

"I wouldn't call him nice, exactly. But I'll tell you what—that McKinley was a first-class dirtbag in his own right. You want to know what's wrong with America, study up a little on the McKinley Administration."

"Got what he deserved, huh?"

"That's not for me to say. I'm just saying there are different ways to be a killer."

"I hear you," I said, thinking suddenly of my parents, and the way my life sometimes seemed to embody their worst suspicions about college. Was this what they'd scrimped and sacrificed for all those years? So their son could spend his Tuesday nights drinking beer, smoking dope, eating weird food, and learning to see the assassin's side of the story?

Max rose slowly from the bed, a distracted expression on his face. He closed his eyes and squeezed the bridge of his nose with two fingers, as if he had a headache.

"Guess what?" I told him. "I just ate some kimchi. Me and Vernon."

He let go of his nose and turned his attention to his navel area, which he scratched with more than run-of-the-mill thoroughness. The skin down there looked pink and a bit rashy, like he had poison ivy or something. When he was done, he paused for a few seconds to examine his fingernails.

"Cindy called again. She sounded pretty upset."

"I'll call her tomorrow."

He nodded and slipped past me on his way out, stopping short just as he reached the doorway. He glanced over his shoulder, forcing a quick smile.

"Hey," he said. "That's great about the kimchi."

I'd only gotten through a couple of paragraphs when my eyes strayed to the pink envelope resting under the chipped hockey puck I used as a paperweight. The envelope contained Cindy's most recent letter, the only one I'd received from her since we'd parted on bad terms over Christmas vacation.

I put down the book and picked up the letter, though the actual document was something of a formality, since I had it pretty much memorized. Even now, a good three weeks after I'd fished it out of my mailbox at Yale Station, I still felt the urge to reread it once or twice a day.

Dear Danny,

I've been thinking a lot about Bruce lately, I'm not sure why. I think the song the River is about the saddest thing I ever heard my whole life. I love Hungry Heart though. That's sad too if you think about it. the guy just gets in his car and ditches his wife and kid. He doesn't think twice. It's just who he is. Maybe the guy in the River should do that too. He seems so depressed as it is . . .

I always had this idea that if Bruce got to know me—to REALLY know me! then we would fall in love and be together. (I know this sounds kind of stupid, believe me!!! I never told anyone but you) Yeah, I know he's this big rock star he can have any girl he wants. I'm not Cheryl Tiegs or anything but it's like he says on Thunder Road, she's not a beauty but that's all right with him. Hey—he's the one who said it NOT me!

This wasn't some crazy fantasy. It was what I believed. I believe there's one person in the world your meant for no matter what, and that he was the one for me (You know that song For You? I LOVE that song) I've felt this way for a long time, even before Born to Run. But then this afternoon I realized it was all just a big stupid joke. Joke on me. Even if he met me he'd just think so what? What's so special about her?

I cried a little and then I was okay.

Sincerely,
Cynthia

On New Year's Eve, Cindy and I had slept together for the first and only time. Her mother was out of town visiting relatives, and she invited me over for a quiet evening of champagne and Dick Clark. Around eleven thirty, we started making out on the couch. It was her idea to relocate to the bedroom, and the suggestion caught me totally off guard. By that point I'd pretty much given up on the prospect of ever actually having sex with her, a mental adjustment that had made our time together a lot less stressful for both of us. I hadn't even packed a lambskin.

"It's okay," she said. "I have something else."

Already naked, she broke open a package she'd produced from one of her dresser drawers and turned away from me, squatting in a froglike stance. I heard an odd noise, something like the sound of shaving cream foaming out of the can. When it stopped, she turned around and approached the bed, wiping her hands across her thighs.

"What was that?" I asked.

"Birth control."

I wanted to ask her what kind, but she'd already climbed into bed with me. There was no sign of the nervousness she'd exhibited at my house; she was in charge of the situation, utterly at peace with her decision. She looked up at me, and her face was pure invitation.

"Happy New Year," she said, pulling me on top of her.

Her eyes widened as I slipped inside her, and she gasped, as if something profound and transforming had just happened, as though this were more pleasure than she deserved or could bear. I was startled by the urgency with which she met me, the frantic rhythm of our coupling. The noises that came out of her were heartfelt and unpredictable. Sitting at my desk two months later, I could still feel the tension of her legs around my waist as I came, the groan of desolation she gave when we slipped apart.

What I wanted to forget—for her sake as well as mine—was the feeling of wild emptiness that had come upon me the moment I entered her, the awful physical knowledge that she'd been right all along: this really was all I'd wanted, and now that I had it, I knew I'd never want it again. Her passion was embarrassing, not because of what it said about her, but because of what it revealed about me, the person who'd been willing to humor her and string her along for half a year just so I could fuck her and not feel a thing, except maybe that I deserved it for putting up with all those visits to the car lots, all the annoying chitchat, all those letters on pink stationery.

She must have realized it too, because as soon as we were finished she burst into tears and told me to please get out of her house. Five weeks later she mailed me the letter I was now slipping back into its envelope. Why such a shameful memory gave me an erection every time I replayed it, I had no idea, but that was how it always happened. I already had my pants open and the zipper down when my eyes strayed to the face-down copy of *Middlemarch*, the words "George Eliot" thundering off the cover like an accusation. Three hundred ninety-two pages to go.

Fuck it, I thought. *I'll just have to skim the rest over breakfast.*

part two

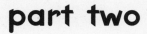

The Return of the Repressed

roadkill manicotti

Between 4:30 and 4:59 the long table by the salad bar was colonized by dining-hall workers—students and full-timers alike—wolfing down last-minute dinners before the early birds started banging on the doors at 5:00 on the dot. I breezed in at twenty of, grabbed a tray and some silverware off the serving cart, and wandered over to the deserted beverage station. One of the perks of dining hall employment was that you didn't get stuck in traffic so often at the height of the dinner rush, trying to appear unruffled as you waited for some weirdo to finish filling a dozen glasses with a precisely calibrated mixture of pink and orange bug juice, or for a chin-scratching professor emeritus of comparative religion to finally take the plunge and choose between the day-old tuna lasagna and tonight's meat loaf with brown gravy.

I had just topped off my third glass of Coke when Matt emerged from the kitchen, already punched in and hard at work. A gigantic sheet cake balanced in his arms, he whistled the theme song from *The Andy Griffith Show*, with a chipper virtuosity he had successfully concealed from the world—or at least from me—until that very minute. He stopped as soon as he spotted me, but it was too late. We both knew he'd been caught in a moment of extreme uncoolness.

"Damn," I said. "That's some mighty fancy whistling. Did you pick that up in Mayberry?"

Matt set the cake down on the stainless-steel countertop and tried to look unruffled.

"And how are you today, Brutus?"

"Seriously," I said, "where does a fellow like you learn to whistle like that?"

He stalled for time, bending to retrieve a trowel-like serving implement from the shelf below the counter.

"Prison," he finally replied, straightening up and gazing at some point above my head with a vaguely troubled expression. "Gotta do something to fill those long hours in the hole."

"I'm sure the other inmates found it very attractive."

"Some of us juggled," he said with a shrug, "and some of us whistled. Some of us fashioned deadly weapons out of small pieces of rusty metal." He shook his head wistfully. "I miss those guys."

He turned his attention to the cake, slashing it up and down with a series of what I assumed were meant to be perpendicular lines. I grabbed my plate and looped around to the other side of the steam table, hesitating between one uninspiring entree and another.

"Go with the bourguignon," he advised.

"You think?"

"No contest. The manicotti's a little gamey."

I plopped a pasty tangle of egg noodles onto my plate, then
smothered them with a ladle's worth of beef and gravy. After a moment's reflection, I added half a spoonful of succotash to the mix, plus a single tube of the questionable manicotti. I was always hungry, and appreciated the mix-and-match, all-you-can-eat spirit of the dining hall.

Matt lifted a small slab of cake out of the grid and deposited it on a dessert plate. Pivoting gracefully, he slid the plate onto the second shelf of the display rack, which was already half-filled with parfait glasses containing butterscotch and chocolate pudding. The top shelf was reserved for desserts provided by the Green Jell-O Fund, a substantial endowment dedicated to the purchase, in perpetuity, of this once-popular foodstuff. As usual, many servings of Green Jell-O had gone uneaten for several days running, and had been poignantly adorned with a last-chance dollop of whipped cream.

"Sorry about the other night," I told him. "Polly called me out of the blue."

"I'm over it."

"You sure?"

He gave me a look.

"I called the crisis hot line. They talked me down from the ledge."

Upon further reflection, I speared another unit of manicotti. My plate was starting to get a little crowded.

"I warned you about that crap," Matt reminded me.

"But I like it gamey," I insisted.

Albert, the dining-hall manager, chose that very moment to burst into the serving area. Ninety percent of the time, Albert was a mellow, easygoing guy who liked to kid around with his employees. The rest of the time he looked like a man being chased by a team of trained assassins.

"Gamey?" He fixed me with a look of wild panic. "What's gamey?"

"The manicotti," said Matt. "Did you fill it with possum or squirrel?"

Albert glanced quickly over his shoulder.

"Don't even joke like that. That's how rumors get started."

"You're right," said Matt. "Our customers can be picky about their roadkill."

Albert let out a deep breath and reached up to massage his tired eyes. He couldn't have been much older than thirty, but the strain of running the dining hall was starting to take a toll on him. Sometimes he reminded me of my father.

"You guys seen Lorelei?" he asked.

Matt and I shook our heads, but that didn't stop him from peering over the top of the steam table, as if he expected to see Lorelei crouched on the floor by the short-order grill, dreamily filing her nails.

"Excuse me," he said, his focus shifting suddenly to Matt. "What the hell is that?"

"What the hell is what?" Matt inquired.

"That thing you just cut. Give it here."

Matt handed the dessert plate to me, and I passed it along to Albert, who squinted for a few seconds at the peculiar wedge of cake resting on top of it.

"I'm curious," he said. "What would you call this?"

"Angel food?" Matt guessed.

"No, shapewise." Albert tilted the plate so we could get a better look. The cake stuck there as if it had been glued on. "Is there a name for this shape?"

"It's almost like a rhombus," I ventured. "Except for that curved part."

"Why does everything have to have a label?" Matt asked. "Why do you think that's so important to you?"

Albert looked like he was about to say something nasty, but then thought better of it. He banged the plate down on top of the steam table and turned to Matt with a plaintive expression.

"Just cut it straight, okay? Is that too much to ask?"

Nick didn't normally work Thursday nights, so I was surprised to see him sitting at the worker's table with Kristin, Sarah, Djembe, and Brad Foxworthy, the weekend dishwasher, who was subbing again for Dallas Little. Dallas weighed three hundred pounds and was supposedly having trouble with his feet, though Milton, the usual Thursday-night chef, viewed this complaint with a certain amount of skepticism. "Oh, yes," he'd mutter, whenever the subject of Dallas's podiatric ailments surfaced, "the man's feet hurt. You bet your feet hurt, you spend all day on the corner with a can of malt liquor in your hand. Bet your head hurt too."

I took the first available seat, next to Brad and across from Nick, who acknowledged my arrival with his customary curt nod. His face was utterly blank, a practiced mask of boredom and reserve. With Kristin just a few seats away, I knew better than to refer, even elliptically, to our strange encounter outside her window on Tuesday night.

"Milton sick?" I asked.

Nick shook his head. "Bowling. His team switched to a Thursday-night league."

"I didn't know Milton was a bowler."

Nick took a moment to dab at his perspiration mustache with a paper napkin. When he took the napkin away, the mustache was still there, but his expression, without changing much at all, suddenly seemed unfriendly.

"What's it to you what Milton does in his spare time? You keepin' tabs on the man?"

"Come on." I chuckled defensively. "I was just making small talk."

"Hey, Brad," Nick said, "Better watch yourself around this one. He's got us under surveillance."

Brad was usually too preoccupied by his meal to bother with conversation. He hunkered down over his plate with the single-minded concentration of a man who didn't always get enough to eat, and had to stock up when the opportunity presented itself. That night, though, he made an exception.

"You a Bonesman?" he asked, his eyes widening with curiosity behind his thick glasses, one earpiece of which was held in place by a cocoonlike mass of electrical tape. Brad had dropped out of Yale Law School a couple of years earlier, and had since developed some sort of paranoid obsession with Skull and Bones, the notorious secret society whose tomblike headquarters was located right next to our dining hall.

"I can't believe this." My face flashed hot with guilt, as though Nick's accusation were somehow true. "All I said was that I didn't know Milton was a bowler."

"And a damn good one," Nick added. "One-eighty-seven average."

"That is good," I said, my indignation already fading into uncertainty. Maybe I'd misread Nick's expression; maybe he'd just been kidding around. "I'm lucky if I break one-fifty."

"The CIA runs this whole place," Brad continued cheerfully. "'Light and Truth,' my ass. 'Darkness and Skulduggery' is more like it."

A moment of silence overtook the table. The only one who didn't notice it was Kristin, who was caught up in an urgent-sounding conversation with Djembe.

"Suck my cock!" she commanded, in a guttural impersonation of a male speaker. "Kneel down and lick it, you prep school bitch!"

Even before she finished, Kristin realized that her audience had expanded beyond Djembe. Blushing sweetly, she reached up to adjust the paper cap she kept pinned to her hair at a charmingly impossible angle.

"My obscene caller," she explained. "I changed my number twice but he still keeps tracking me down."

"Gross," said Sarah. "My roommate gets those all the time."

"Outrageous," Djembe declared in his elegant Nigerian accent. "This should not be tolerated."

Nick gave a soft, derisive chuckle, just loud enough for Brad and me to hear. Djembe had long gotten on Nick's nerves, originally for his regal bearing and exotic good looks, but more recently for his close and sexually charged friendship with Kristin.

"Hey, Jimbo," Nick called out. "You know why they don't have any obscene phone callers in Africa?"

Djembe turned wearily toward our end of the table. He had long ago given up correcting Nick's deliberate mispronunciation of his name.

"Please explain," he said.

"I'll tell you why." A slow grin of triumph spread across Nick's face. "'Cause they don't have any fucking phones."

For some reason, he addressed this punch line to me instead of Djembe. Even after the joke met with a deafening lack of response from the rest of the table, he kept his eyes glued to mine, as if daring me to laugh, to join him in an alliance against the humorless stiffs and African princes of the world. The best I could manage for him was a tight little smile, a cowardly smirk of approval.

The dish line had its own eccentric rhythm, out of synch with the rest of the operation. It was quiet when the dining hall was packed and noisy, and increasingly hectic as the place began clearing out. You got to lounge when your co-workers were hustling, and then had to pick up the pace just as everyone else began slacking off.

At its best, the dirty end of the line was simply unsavory. At its worst, the work was filthy and relentless. Tray after tray—some of them stacked into precarious double- and triple-deckers—came streaming down the conveyor belt at a pace that seemed reasonable enough right up to the moment when it suddenly became demonic. In the space of a couple seconds, you had to grab the silverware, rinse the plates, and empty the glasses, sorting each item into separate racks. When a rack got full, you had to shove it into the dishwasher, which resembled an automatic car wash, and then grab a fresh rack from underneath the conveyor belt, all without missing a beat on the next tray. It was just possible to accomplish these tasks without shutting down the line if the diners did as they were told before bussing their trays—i.e., dispose of their paper trash and uneaten food, and place their silverware on the right—but not everyone found it in their hearts to cooperate. You would get coffee cups half-filled with peanut butter, a mound of mashed potatoes studded with cigarette butts, someone's eyeglasses tucked inside a taco shell. You'd grab for a plate, only to discover that it had been painstakingly coated with mayonnaise, or find yourself staring in confused revulsion at a bowl full of melted chocolate ice cream and green peas. All over the dining hall, it seemed, people were ripping their napkins into confetti, and dropping the confetti piece by piece into nearly empty glasses of water, just to give us the pleasure of reaching in with our bare hands and scooping out clots of saturated paper. By the end of the shift, you were soaking wet and smelled exactly like the webbed rubber floor mat you had to hose down before calling it quits—ripe and meaty and hazardous to the public health.

Eddie Zimmer was late that night, but I didn't mind covering for him. Eddie and I had handled the Thursday-night dish line all year, and had developed a model working relationship. Outside of the dining hall we barely exchanged two words, but inside we looked out for one another. When things got hairy on my end, he was more than happy to pitch in. I didn't have to ask, either; he'd just appear at my side and start grabbing for dirty dishes. If one of his Ultimate Frisbee games ran a little late, I'd discreetly punch him in at five and take care of both ends until he made his entrance. It was no big deal—for the first half hour of the shift, the dish line was basically a one-person job anyway.

It was the Thursday before spring break, and an irrational euphoria had taken hold of me, as though I were heading down to Daytona to judge the wet T-shirt contests instead of facing a two-week stint behind the wheel of the Roach Coach. Part of my good mood was relief—I had dodged a bullet in my George Eliot seminar and would finally have time to catch up on my reading over break—and part of it was anticipation. *Reality* was throwing a big party on Friday, and Polly had called a few hours earlier to find out if I was sticking around for it. It was our first contact since the awk-

ward parting on Tuesday night.

When she hadn't called me on Wednesday, I'd pretty much decided to skip the party, despite my semi-prominent position in the magazine's hierarchy. I figured she and Professor Preston had patched things up and wanted to spare myself a potentially depressing encounter with her—or worse, with them—on the eve of the long vacation. Max's parents were coming to town and had invited our whole suite out to dinner, an obligation that could easily consume the whole night if I let it. But something in her tone alerted me to a new spectrum of possibilities.

"You going with anyone?" I inquired.

"Just Ingrid."

"So what's up with you and Peter?"

She let go of a big breath, a not-quite-sigh of fatigue and exasperation.

"We had a long talk."

"And?"

"I'm not sure. I guess we're taking a break from each other or something."

"A break?" I found it difficult to modulate my voice, as though I were going through puberty all over again. "Does that mean it's over?"

"This is boring, Danny. Will I see you there or not?"

"Are you kidding? Back home they call me Party Guy."

"Great. Save me a dance, Party Guy."

The clean end of the dish line was located in the furthest reaches of the kitchen, near the entrance to a storeroom for dry supplies— bricks of paper napkins, towers of Styrofoam cups, box upon box upon box of Green Jell-O mix, gleaming five-gallon cannisters of pudding that looked like something we might have dropped on peasants in Vietnam. A stairway at the back of the storeroom led down to the basement, a labyrinth of narrow corridors, cubbyhole offices, walk-in freezers and refrigerators, and, most ominously, the prep room, a vast, morguelike space housing six stainless-steel tables big enough to accommodate the average-sized corpse, plus an impressive array of slicing, dicing, peeling, and chopping implements.

I happened to be sorting silverware on the clean end when Eddie and Lorelei appeared at the top of the stairs. She looked nervous; he seemed stunned. Even if their faces had been totally blank, though, I'm pretty sure I would've known what they'd been up to. Three years of college had brought me into frequent contact with couples who had just engaged in some form of sexual activity—not to mention highly infrequent but generally quite memorable contact with couples actually in the process of engaging in some form of sexual activity—and I'd gotten so I could recognize them at a glance. It wasn't that they all looked the same—some were mussed and seemingly drugged, some were fresh from the shower, some were furtive, others smug—but what they shared was an aura of privacy and collusion that sealed them off from the rest of the world, marking them as temporary foreigners in our midst, people you'd need to address in an unnaturally loud voice if you wanted them to understand what you were saying, or even that they were being spoken to in the first place.

Lorelei came out first, stepping tentatively into the heat and chaos of the kitchen. On a normal night no one would have given her a second glance, but that night—maybe because Albert had been looking for her, or maybe because she was blushing (you got the feeling it would take a lot to make Lorelei blush), or maybe just because she was walking so slowly—she might as well have been naked. Her entrance stopped everything.

I gave a quick nod as she passed, trying not to betray anything with my expression. Up to his elbows in soapy water, Brad Foxworthy opened his mouth as if to ask a question, then closed it without making a sound. Sarah, who worked as cook's helper on Thursday night, stood frozen over a tray of manicotti, pinching a sprig of garnish in her raised hand as though it were a dart. Nick was the only one of us who didn't seem to think that silence was an appropriate response to Lorelei's dreamy march down the aisle.

"Well, well," he called out. "Look what crawled out of the basement."

Lorelei stopped short, wincing at the sound of his voice. She raised a finger to her lips, but Nick wasn't about to be shushed. He crossed his arms over his chest, mimicking the tone and posture of a disapproving parent.

"Young lady? Where in God's name have you been?"

Though still in high school—she was employed through some sort of work/study arrangement—Lorelei usually had the self-possession of someone much older, at least when it came to putting men in their place. On any other night, she would have just ignored him and gone about her business. For some reason, though, Nick's question flustered her; she seemed to feel herself under an obligation to answer it.

"Outside," she lied, in a voice bereft of all conviction. "Smoking a cigarette. I lost track of time."

Nick grinned unpleasantly. I had always thought of him and Lorelei as allies, but now I wondered if I'd been paying close enough attention.

"I bet that's not all you lost," he told her.

"Fuck you," she said. "You're not my father."

Lorelei cast a quick, nervous glance in the direction of the store-room, apparently waiting for Eddie to step out and defend her honor. At the same moment, a sudden hush descended upon the dining hall, an absence of sound far more conspicuous than the dull background roar it replaced.

"Maybe not," Nick admitted, grinning unpleasantly, "but I'm sure your brothers would be interested to know what you're up to."

"Leave my brothers out of it," Lorelei shot back, her voice wavering between a plea and a command.

Before Nick could reply, the singing started up, the har-monies startling in their purity and sweetness. Still clutching her parsley, Sarah pivoted in the direction of the music. Brad Fox-worthy extricated his arms from the soapy water and began peeling off his yellow rubber gloves. Matt poked his head into the kitchen.

"C'mon everybody," he called out, beckoning us with his icing-covered trowel. "It's the Whiffs."

It was a tradition for the staff to interrupt work whenever a singing group performed in the dining hall. Like rats summoned by the Pied Piper, we emerged from the kitchen in single file and lined up along the wall near the mouth of the conveyor belt, all of us in our blue shirts and paper caps except Nick, who was decked out in the stained white clothes and absurd hat of the professional chef. Resplendent in their formal wear, the Whiffenpoofs stood in a semi-circle in front of the nonfunctional fireplace, crooning "Surfer Girl" for their captive audience. One of them was black, one Asian, one short, one both short and prematurely bald; the rest looked like close relatives of Vice President Bush. If not for the salad bar separating us from them, we might have looked like two rival street gangs from a highly peculiar metropolis, faced off and ready to rumble.

I had spent enough time at Yale to know that one member of the Whiffenpoofs was known as "the Pitch," and I assumed it was the Pitch—he happened to be the short, bald guy—who stepped forward after "Surfer Girl" to inform us that the group had just learned a whole slew of Beach Boys' tunes in preparation for their upcoming trip to Southern California and Hawaii.

"None of us are surfers," he admitted, absent-mindedly fiddling with the waistband of his tuxedo pants, "but we've been told we look pretty good in our bathing suits."

On cue, the whole group let their pants fall to their ankles, revealing gaudy tropical-print swim trunks, and then struck muscleman poses for the whooping crowd. When the cheers and catcalls had subsided, they launched into a lumbering version of "Help Me, Rhonda" that made the Beach Boys look like a bunch of swinging anarchists by comparison. Spotting her chance, Lorelei slipped out of line and looped around the salad bar to the front desk, where Albert was unhappily holding the fort, reduced to checking IDs and meal cards in her absence. She knew him well enough to know that he wouldn't dream of making a scene while the Whiffenpoofs were singing "Help Me, Rhonda." The worst he inflicted on her was a stern frown, which she countered with an apologetic shrug before taking her customary seat.

The singers had just managed to pull up their pants and wipe the smiles off their faces before the Pitch issued the ritual invitation for any former Whiffenpoofs in the audience to join them for the singing of "The Whiffenpoof Song." A second or two had passed with no takers when Brad Foxworthy, who was standing right next to me, stepped out of line and began retracing Lorelei's path around the salad bar. I figured that he wanted a word with Albert, but instead of veering right toward the front desk, he veered left, defecting to the enemy. Despite his sopping blue shirt and taped-together glasses, the Whiffenpoofs seemed to recognize him as one of their own. They broke ranks to make a space, gathering him like a missing link into their chain. Bug-eyed and happy-looking, he stood between Nelson and Tripp, their arms around his shoulders, his around theirs, as the chorus line of poor little lambs began to baa and sway.

Halfway through "The Whiffenpoof Song," Eddie slipped into line beside me, filling the space Brad had so recently vacated. I turned to him, arching my eyebrows significantly.

"Where the hell were you?" I whispered.

Eddie didn't answer right away. He reminded me of one of those movie gangsters who doesn't realize he's been shot until he looks down and sees the flowery bloodstain spreading across his shirt.

"The compactor room," he said finally, squinting at the Whiffenpoofs as though they were giving off a painful radiance. "It was the strangest thing."

On our way out of the dining hall, I asked Matt if I could buy him a beer to celebrate the official start of spring break and make amends for blowing him off on Tuesday night. I was under no illusions about getting any work done for the next couple of days and didn't figure he was, either.

"Wish I could," he said. "I've got to pull an all-nighter on that Shakespeare paper."

"An all-nighter? Can't you just hand it in after break?"

"Jessica's coming tomorrow. I want to get it out of the way before she gets here."

He held the door open for me like an old-fashioned gentleman, then followed me outside. A light drizzle had fallen during dinner, and now the world smelled fresh and fertile, less like New Haven than it had before. We both noticed it at once, pausing at the top of the steps to sniff at the damp breeze, which wasn't quite strong enough to make me forget about the rank odors wafting up from my shirt.

"Got a topic?" I asked.

"Not even close." He grinned with apparent pride. "Haven't even read the damn play."

The main gate swung open ahead of us, and an attractive senior in a lacrosse uniform—her name was Blinky or Tick, something not quite right that kept slipping my mind—came limping up the path with a cast around one ankle, the rubber tips of her crutches sucking at the wet slate.

"Broken," she announced ruefully, in response to a question no one had asked.

Matt and I nodded sympathetically, then turned to watch her negotiate the sharp turn into the courtyard, the short pleated skirt riding high on her well-muscled thighs.

"I'd sign *her* cast," Matt mumbled under his breath.

"That Women's Studies seminar did wonders for you," I observed.

She was barely out of sight when Nick and Brad burst through the doors behind us, engaged in a heated conversation. Nick was smoking a cigarette and wearing the leather jacket that made him look like a small-time mafia guy. Brad wore an old tweed sportcoat over a flannel shirt; his hair was wet and newly combed, as though he were heading out for the night. I wondered what it had felt like for him, singing with the Whiffenpoofs, then returning to the kitchen to plunge his arms back into that sink full of greasy pots and pans.

"Well, well," Nick grumbled as they brushed past. "If it isn't the two dipsticks."

"Have a good break," Matt called after them.

Despite his hurry, Nick pulled up short, whirling so abruptly you might have thought Matt had insulted his mother. With a fierce squint, he took a last long drag off his cigarette, then flicked it over the fence, into the garden of the master's house.

"Have a good what?"

"Break," Matt repeated.

Nick looked at Brad, then back at us.

"Is this your native fucking planet?"

"Are you referring to Earth?" said Matt.

"Only Yalies get spring break," Nick explained helpfully. "The rest of us get up in the morning and go to our shitty jobs."

"We're on painting crew," Brad informed us.

"But thanks for thinking of us," Nick added. "We'll be sure to wear lots of sunscreen."

"*Excuuuse me,*" Matt said à la Steve Martin, raising his hands as if to fend off blows. "Forget I even mentioned it."

Neither one of us moved or spoke until they'd slipped through the gate and out of sight. Then we looked at each other, shrugged, and drifted down the steps to the path, where our ways parted. Matt took a sidelong step in the direction of the gate, then thought better of it.

"Hey Danny," he said. "You wouldn't have that paper you wrote for Preston last year, would you? The one on *Measure for Measure*?"

"Sorry. It's back home in my closet."

"Too bad," he said. "I think it might help me out to take a look at it."

"Maybe you should just read the play," I suggested.

"I've tried about six times. It would help if the guy could write in plain English."

Visiting on Parents' Weekend the previous October, my mother noticed that many students kept erasable message boards on their doors. In an effort to be helpful, she sent me one a couple of weeks later that featured a large picture of Garfield, along with the ridiculous exhortation, "Hey cool cat, leave me a message!" (For a couple of years, for reasons only she could explain, my mother had been buying me all sorts of Garfield paraphernalia, which I had no choice but to immediately consign to the nearest trash receptacle.) My suitemates were delighted by my embarrassment—so delighted, in fact, that they insisted on rescuing the message board from the garbage when I wasn't around and nailing it so firmly to the door that I doubt I could have removed it with a crowbar.

When I got upstairs that night, two messages were scrawled on the board, both of them directed at me. The first was from Sang, telling me to meet him, Ted, and Nancy at the Anchor at nine o'clock. The second was from Max, telling me that Cindy had called again.

"WOULD YOU JUST PLEASE CALL HER?" he'd scrawled across the whole bottom half of the board in big pleading letters.

Inside, *Gaucho* was spinning on the turntable even though no one was home. I thought about calling Cindy, then decided that it could wait for a couple more days. I was going to be home on Saturday, after all, and would be driving the Roach Coach to her workplace every weekday morning and afternoon for the next two weeks. We'd have more than enough time to talk. Right now what I needed was to get out of my smelly clothes and into a long, scalding shower.

fourteen thousand dollars for this

Parental visits were unsettling for the entire suite. We had to tidy up the common room, stash the bong and whatever liquor bottles had been left out in the open, and suppress any evidence of Nancy's status as fifth roommate that happened to be lying around—the odd tampon, those little white socks with fuzzy pompoms, the elastic bands with two attached marbles that she used to tie back her hair, the dog-eared copy of *Gyn/Ecology* she always seemed to be puzzling over that semester. These purges were her idea, not ours. Although she'd been living with Ted for half a year, her family back in Pennsylvania was laboring under the impression that she was a virgin without a boyfriend, and she didn't want any information to the contrary leaking back to them through some complicated chain of parental gossip.

The presence of responsible adults altered our behavior in both subtle and obvious ways. We became less sarcastic than usual, more affectionate, more serious about our studies. On Parents' Weekend in particular, we transformed ourselves into a suiteful of Eddie Haskells, flattering each others' mothers with a shamelessness that seemed to please them enormously. Only Sang's mom refused to play along. She was a high-powered research biologist who stared at us like we were a bunch of idiots when we tried to comment on her new hairdo or handbag. We'd quickly learned to divert our attention to his father, a garrulous anesthesiologist who had memorized a number of Robert Frost poems shortly after immigrating to the U.S. in the late 1950s and was happy to recite some or all of them on request.

Though taxing for everyone, these encounters were most stressful for the person whose parents had come to visit. How could it have been otherwise? There was something so nakedly revealing about being seen in the presence of the people who had made and raised you. It was the Return of the Repressed, the pasts we had tried to conceal upon arrival at college suddenly taking human form and walking through the door with care packages in their arms and faces a lot like our own. Ted's father wearing those green pants. His mother enunciating as though her teeth had been clamped together with Krazy Glue. One Dr. Lee talking incessantly, the other seeming to have taken a vow of silence. My own father looking around and shaking his head. "Fourteen thousand dollars for this?" he'd mutter over and over again, as if Yale were the biggest scam ever perpetrated in the history of humankind. My mother just wanting to clean the bathroom and do everyone's laundry.

Max's torment in this regard, as in all things, was of a different order entirely. His parents didn't just embarrass him, they infuriated him. Their politics appalled him; their friends made his skin crawl. His mother was a Denver socialite, part owner of a store that—according to Max, anyway—sold hideous and outrageously overpriced clothing, and a highly ranked competitor in the Colorado forty-and-over amateur tennis circuit. His father was a lawyer turned real-estate developer/venture capitalist whose money made money every time he tied his shoes or wiped his ass. They drove matching BMWs and had recently purchased a monstrous vacation home in Vail, two facts that Max frequently cited as evidence of their profound moral and spiritual corruption.

At the same time, Max was closer to his parents than the rest of us, though this closeness took a peculiar form. He was their only child, and if Mr. and Mrs. Friedlin weren't traveling, they called him every evening, the conversations sometimes lasting for hours. They began cordially enough, with small talk about classes and current events, then grew increasingly testy, ending more often than not with Max slamming down the phone and barging out of the suite without stopping to grab a coat. He would return an hour or so later, calmer but still wired, grinding his teeth at the latest outrage: his father was pressuring him to take Econ; his mother was trying to fix him up with a sophomore in Davenport, the niece of one of her tennis buddies. In recent weeks, both of them had encouraged him to stop thinking so much about Arthur Bremer and John Hinckley and get in touch with a therapist.

"They don't think I'm normal," he reported one night, sounding somewhat offended by this verdict.

"Do you?" I asked.

"I reject the category," he replied haughtily. "Especially when it's invoked by people who had electric buttwarmers installed in their cars."

"Buttwarmers?"

"The seats heat up," he explained. "There's some kind of coil hidden under the leather."

"Must feel pretty good on a cold day."

"Actually," he said, "if you leave it on long enough, it feels like you shit in your pants."

The Friedlins were on their way to Paris for the month of April and had arranged their itinerary so they could stop in New Haven on Friday night and take our whole suite out to dinner at Robert Henry's, the fanciest restaurant on Chapel Street. That afternoon, a few hours before they were due to arrive, Max poked his head into my room.

"Just packing a little. I want to catch an early train tomorrow."

He took that as permission to step inside, though he didn't go so far as to sit down in his usual spot at the foot of my unmade bed. Instead he hovered just inside the doorway, dressed, as he often was at that time of day, in baggy fatigue pants and his favorite too-small pajama top that had recently developed a plunging neckline after all but the two bottom-most buttons had popped off. He had a paper airplane in his hand and a grim expression on his face.

"What's up?" I asked, ramming more dirty clothes into my already tumescent duffel bag.

"Not much. Boning up on Oswald."

"Guess you'll have a lot of reading time in the next few weeks."

"I hope so. I'm usually pretty bad about getting work done during vacations."

Max was one of only a handful of students in Jonathan Edwards who had received permission to stay on campus for the duration of the two-week break. The others were foreign students marooned in New Haven for financial reasons; Max was just staying to be perverse. His parents would gladly have taken him to Paris if he'd wanted to join them, and they certainly would have paid for him to fly home to Colorado. I'd invited him to my house as well, but he'd declined after I'd explained that I'd be driving the lunch truck full-time while my father recuperated from his "procedure." I couldn't say I blamed him. The idea of him and my convalescent dad sharing a house for several days sounded like a scenario for a sitcom that was too weird even for Max.

He closed one eye and launched his paper airplane, clearly aiming for my head. The aircraft performed a single loop-de-loop, then promptly crashed on the floor near my laundry basket, its flimsy nose crumpling like an accordion.

"Did you call her?" he asked.

The question caught me off guard. The only "her" on my mind at that point was Polly, and I understood from the careful neutrality in his voice that he wasn't referring to her. In the split second it took me to get up to speed, I'd already spoken.

"Call who?"

His face changed, the spacy blankness giving way to a kind of amazement.

"Wow," he said. "I can't believe you're being such an asshole about this."

"Gimme a break," I said lamely.

"Why don't you give her a break? You had sex with the girl. The least you could do is return her phone calls."

His logic was airtight, but I felt betrayed anyway. The unwritten rule said you gave your roommates the benefit of the doubt. I'd certainly given it to him a few times.

"You know what?" I told him. "It's really none of your business."

"Yeah, right. She calls in tears every night, and I'm the one who has to comfort her, and it's none of my business."

"You don't have to comfort her, Max. All you have to do is take a message, okay?"

He looked away, as if it were beneath him to contemplate my face at that moment. I took a deep breath and tried to strike a less defensive tone.

"Look. It's over between me and Cindy. Talking about it isn't going to help. She's just going to have to get used to it."

"I just don't think she deserves this."

"Nobody deserves it," I informed him. "But it happens anyway. I've been on the receiving end once or twice myself."

"So that makes it all right?"

"It doesn't make it anything. It's just the way it goes."

He ran his hand partway through his tangled hair and left it there.

"I guess I expected better of you."

"Then you overestimated me."

He shrugged and left the room, his hand still resting on top of his head. It wasn't until he'd gone that I realized I'd been clutching a pair of dirty underwear throughout the entire conversation, the same dingy briefs I'd been wearing the night I almost slept with Polly. I shoved them into the duffel bag, then bent to retrieve Max's wreck of a paper airplane from the floor.

I was about to drop it into the official NFL wastebasket I'd brought from home as a souvenir of my misspent youth when I noticed the drawings. With a blue ballpoint pen, Max had inked four porthole windows on the fuselage. Each window contained a crude but easily recognizable caricature of one of our suitemates, Nancy not included. The plane was apparently headed for a crash, because Sang, Ted, and I all had looks of pure terror on our faces. Cartoon bubbles floating overhead detailed our reactions to the impending disaster.

"Rats," thought Ted. "Guess I'm not getting laid tonight."

"Darn," reflected Sang. "Looks like I won't make Phi Beta Kappa after all."

"Hmmm," wondered Danny. "Maybe I should have called her back."

Only Max seemed unperturbed. He held one hand on top of his head, just as he had moments before, and gazed out the window with an expression of philosophical calm, maybe even the ghost of a smile.

"Oh, well," he considered. "At least I won't have to suffer through this fucking dinner tonight."

I laughed in spite of myself, then wandered out to the common room to compliment him on the likenesses, already forgiving him for taking his anxieties about his parents out on me. He wasn't around to receive my absolution, though. The common room was empty, and so were the other two bedrooms. I called his name a couple of times just to make sure, but I already knew he was gone. He'd slipped away so quietly, I hadn't even heard him close the door.

At six thirty that evening he still hadn't returned. This was awkward, because Gail and Howard Friedlin had been sitting in our common room for close to an hour at that point, making small talk and trying not to appear too concerned while we humored them by making phone calls to anyone who might have an idea about their son's whereabouts.

"It's just like Max," his mother said, manufacturing a tense little smile. "Punctuality's never been one of his strong points."

The Friedlins hadn't visited for a long time—Parents' Weekend that year had overlapped with their Australian walkabout—and I was still getting over the mild shock of seeing them in person again. Living as I did with Max's demonized image of his parents, it was easy to forget what attractive people they were—tanned, youthful, athletic-looking—so unlike their son that Max frequently had to insist to people who had just met Gail and Howard that he was not, in fact, adopted. The Friedlins were probably only a couple of years younger than my parents, but they seemed to belong to a different generation. You got the feeling that they would rather be caught dead than listening to Henry Mancini or the Hundred and One Strings on the car stereo, and that, under the right circumstances, they could probably tell you some pretty interesting stories involving hot tubs and controlled substances.

"Just like Max," his father echoed in a less affectionate voice, stroking his salt-and-pepper beard and impatiently flipping through a week-old *Yale Daily* he'd found on the coffee table. He was sporting a stylishly cut silvery blue suit that looked like it might have been pilfered from the set of *Miami Vice*. Like Don Johnson, Mr. Friedlin wore the suit over an expensive-looking black T-shirt, a casual touch I found quite appealing.

Ted, Sang, and I nodded in unison, each of us muttering something to the effect that it was indeed just like Max. All three of us had dressed for dinner, Sang and Ted in khakis, blue blazers, and striped ties, with Sang opting to spice up the uniform with a pair of red Converse high-tops. I myself was outfitted in a daringly eclectic ensemble—skinny black leather New Wave tie courtesy of Hank Yamashita, tan corduroy sport coat, blue Dickey work pants, and my radioactive cowboy boots—that I was beginning to suspect added up to less than the sum of its parts. We were sitting next to each other on the couch, one to a cushion in descending order of size—Ted, Sang, me—like brothers posing for a portrait.

"He better get here soon," Howard Friedlin muttered. "The reservations are for seven o'clock."

"We don't have to get there exactly at seven," his wife reminded him. "It's not like we're going to lose the table."

"That's not the point." Mr. Friedlin had tossed aside the *Daily* and turned his attention to a copy of *Aurora* that Nancy must have picked up from the freebie table outside the dining hall. *Aurora* was a feminist journal specializing in impassioned critiques of the patriarchy and celebratory, sometimes astonishingly explicit poems about lesbian sex, not to mention the occasional frank portrait of sullen, short-haired women with no shirts and hairy armpits. I read it avidly, if furtively, with confused feelings of shame and arousal, but Mr. Friedlin seemed unruffled by what he found there. "The point is, we've got a roomful of hungry males to feed. Right, guys?"

Sang and I made noncommittal gestures meant to suggest that we could wait, but Ted nodded in emphatic agreement.

"I'm starving," he said, rubbing his stomach tenderly, as though it were the head of a sick dog. "I had to work right through lunch to finish my lab report."

"See?" said Mr. Friedlin.

His wife pretended not to hear. Seconds earlier, the Harkness carillon had clanged into action, the gigantic bells ringing out a slow motion, barely recognizable version of Bob Seger's "Night Moves." As if summoned by the music, Mrs. Friedlin stood up and drifted over to the window overlooking the courtyard. She was wearing tailored black pants and an aquamarine silk blouse that interacted with the light in all sorts of strange and shimmery ways. Her body was lithe and girlish from all that tennis; from my angle, at least, you would not have pegged her as the mother of a college-aged son. With exasperation and a certain degree of scorn, Max had once described to me some of her elaborate beauty regimens—the manicures and pedicures, the leg and lip and bikini waxes, the clay masks and diet pills, the massages and hundred-dollar haircuts, the long hours she put in scouring fashion magazines, her brow knitted as though she were working her way through Hegel in the original—but I couldn't help feeling then that all her hard work had paid off.

"I envy you," she said, turning back to the room with a melancholy smile. "Women weren't allowed here in my day."

"Sure they were," her husband quipped, aiming a sly wink in our direction. "Just not on weekdays."

Instead of chuckling, Mrs. Friedlin glanced at her watch. Something went out of her just then; you could see it happen. All at once her face seemed sad and tired in the murky light of the common room, a decade older than her body.

"Do you think he's okay?" There was a meekness in her voice that hadn't been present a moment before. "Should we call the police?"

Sang, Ted, and I traded quick looks, like liars hoping to keep our stories straight.

"I'm sure he's fine," Sang told her.

"Is something bothering him?" she asked. "Does he seem depressed?"

"Not really," said Ted. "He's pretty much the same as always."

An uncomfortable silence ensued, an interlude that allowed the unthinkable to enter my mind. Every year since I'd come to college, there'd been at least one suicide or serious attempt by an undergraduate, including a particularly grisly wrist-slashing episode that took place in a library bathroom just days after we'd arrived freshman year. I'd worried about our old roommate Seth in this regard—his lethargies had been so deep and prolonged, his anger so sudden and explosive—but never about Max. Max had his moods, but he inhabited them with a fierce dignity, as if he'd made a conscious decision to be unhappy as a protest against a ridiculous and unjust world. If he was depressed—and it would have been pretty hard to deny it—his depression seemed to have an ethical rather than chemical origin. It was chosen, I believed, and therefore worthy of respect, if not admiration. But now I wasn't so sure. I thought of the paper airplane on my desk, the eerie calm on Max's cartoon face as we hurtled earthward, and a queasy lump of foreboding took up residence in my stomach.

"Ten more minutes," Mr. Friedlin said, slapping the *Aurora* back down on the coffee table. "Ten more minutes or he's out of luck."

For reasons that were unclear to me, we had decided to place our telephone at the summit of a precarious stack of overdue library books piled on top of a rickety end table that Sang had rescued from a dumpster. Ted was sitting right next to this dubious arrangement when the phone rang, but he didn't have a chance. Mrs. Friedlin whipped past him in a silky blur, snatching up the receiver before the first ring had completed its cycle. She didn't even try to disguise the contest between hope and panic in her voice.

"Hello?"

Her eyes narrowed as she listened; her shoulders sagged with defeat.

"Yes," she said wearily. "He's right here."

She pointed the receiver in my direction, looking as though she might burst into tears at any moment. I shrugged an apology as I took it from her hand.

"Jeez," said Polly. "What was that about?"

I turned my back to the room, thrilled as always by the sound of her voice, stretching the cord as far as it would go.

"I'll tell you later," I whispered. "Things are a little crazy around here."

"I won't keep you," she said. "I just wanted to tell you something. So we can avoid confusion later on."

"Okay."

There was a brief, nervous pause.

"I think I want to sleep with you."

For a second, I wasn't sure if I'd heard her right.

"You do or you don't?" I inquired warily.

"Do," she said. "A lot."

Oddly, ecstasy was not my first reaction. Some deep, permanently frightened part of me could only interpret her offer as some sort of cruel practical joke, something that would be taped and played back for my humiliation at an unspecified later date. Ecstasy was my second reaction. When it hit I found myself transformed into a spacewalker, suddenly liberated from gravity.

"Okay," I told her, with a jauntiness I hadn't known I possessed. "I'll pencil you in for bedtime."

"Great," she laughed. "I'll see you at the party."

"See you then."

When I turned around, my roommates had perked up considerably. For a couple of seconds there, I'd forgotten all about them.

"Pencil you in for bedtime?" Sang repeated incredulously.

"Your girlfriend?" Gail Friedlin asked. I couldn't tell if she was really interested, or was just trying to be polite.

"I hope so."

"And he does mean pencil," Ted chimed in with a smirk.

Only Howard Friedlin seemed oblivious to the now-public drama of my love life. He was too busy glowering at the copy of *Reality* he'd unearthed from the bottom of the coffee-table pile.

"What about Max?" Mrs. Friedlin asked. "Does he have a girl-friend too?"

Before I could answer, Mr. Friedlin raised the magazine like a kindergartner at show-and-tell. He tapped his index finger against the cover photo of the mangy constipated dog, hunched and gri-macing.

"What the hell is this?" he demanded.

"A literary magazine," Sang replied cheerfully. "Danny here is one of the editors."

Mr. Friedlin gave me a look of incomprehension worthy of my own father.

"Did you intend it as some kind of *statement*?" He pronounced this last word with genuine distaste, as if we all knew about state-ments.

"It is what it is," I informed him, grinning like an idiot. I felt positively giddy. Polly wanted to sleep with me. She'd said so over the phone. "It's just reality."

"Why don't you just photograph some dog shit?" he asked. "That's part of reality, too."

"They're saving that for the spring issue," Ted explained help-fully.

a feeling comes over me

Seven o'clock came and went. Mrs. Friedlin refused to leave until she heard from Max, while Mr. Friedlin insisted on forging ahead without him, partly on principle, but mainly as a courtesy to Ted, Sang, and me. He scoffed at our assurances that we'd be just as happy ordering a couple of pizzas.

"Forget pizza," he said. "You can have pizza anytime you want. Tonight we're going to eat some real food."

"Maybe we should wait a few more minutes," Sang suggested, glancing at Mrs. Friedlin for support.

"Go ahead," she told us, breaking the stalemate with a wan smile of encouragement. I got the feeling she'd be just as happy to do her worrying in private. "There's no sense ruining everyone's night. When Max gets back, we'll catch up with you at the restaurant."

It was a little weird to just leave her there and head out into the night, but it was also a relief to finally get moving. Mr. Friedlin must have felt it too. As soon as we stepped outside, he closed his eyes and inhaled the New Haven damp like a man who had just been released from prison.

I had to tap him on the shoulder to get him to make way for Trip, who was transporting a half keg of beer up the slate path on a hand truck and grinning with badly concealed smugness, the way people often did when in possession of large quantities of alcohol. Ted held open the door for him.

"Party tonight," Trip announced, executing a smooth half turn and easing the wheels of the hand truck over the rise and into the entryway. The keg was scuffed and dented, almost like someone had gone after it with a hammer. "After the jamboree."

"Where's the jamboree?" Mr. Friedlin inquired.

Trip didn't even glance behind him as he began his nimble backwards ascent, jolting the hand truck over each successive step with an efficiency that verged on grace. If not for the tuxedo, you might have mistaken him for a professional deliveryman.

"Stiles," he said, pausing on the landing to adjust his grip. "It's the Spring Jailbreak. Us, the B.D.'s, and the S.O.B.'s." He shook his head, paying silent tribute to the firepower of the groups in question. A distant, almost wistful look passed across his good-natured mannequin face, and I couldn't quite suppress a stitch of jealousy, a resentful suspicion that, for all of his shortcomings, Trip was a lucky guy, one of those people who'd found his place in the world. As if to confirm this hypothesis, he smiled with peculiar intensity, like a kid who'd eaten too much cake.

"It's gonna be so great," he told us.

92 **After a cursory** glance at the leather-bound list, Mr. Friedlin tossed off the name of a forty-dollar bottle of red wine the way my own father might have ordered a Big Mac, without hesitation, embarrassment, or the slightest trace of self-importance. Our waitress accepted his order with a nod of approval that was somehow both respectful and flirtatious at the same time. She was around the same age as Sang, Ted, and me, and probably a student herself— maybe a part-timer at a state school or community college—but she barely deigned to acknowledge our presence at the table. The way she acted, Howard Friedlin might have been sitting there all by himself, with three empty chairs for company. I didn't bother to resent her for this because I saw exactly what she did—Mr. Friedlin's quiet authority, the top-dog aura that seemed to emanate from the fabric of his expensive suit. I wasn't sure which had come first, his money or his confidence, but I took note of how impressive the combination could be in a setting like this, the solemn, high-ceilinged dining room with its starchy tablecloths and tasteful chandeliers, the soft buzz of conversation hovering in the background like the hum of insects on a summer night. I couldn't help thinking of my own parents, who insisted on taking me to a Roy Rogers on Whalley Avenue whenever they visited New Haven, their discomfort at being surrounded by black people temporarily offset by their horror at the prices charged by restaurants closer to campus. I wasn't embarrassed by their preferences—I knew how tight money was for us, what a ridiculous luxury it was for me to be attending a school like Yale, even with the generous financial aid available in those days—but it saddened me to think that they could sip the same wine I was sipping just then and not taste anything but a half day's work down the drain.

Mr. Friedlin kept our glasses full and asked a lot of questions. An unforeseeable mellowness had taken hold of him as soon as we entered the restaurant, and I thought I understood why he'd been so adamant about coming here, despite the peculiar circumstances. This was his element. Inside it, his hard edges softened; he seemed to genuinely want to know us better, not because we were his son's roommates, but simply because we were there, sharing his meal, and meals in restaurants like that meant something to him.

93

I'm not sure what it was—the wine, the atmosphere, the fact that Mrs. Friedlin wasn't there—but we answered as though he were one of us, not a parent but a visitor from another school, someone's brother or cousin or hometown friend. With no apparent effort, he got Sang talking about Eve, his girlfriend from sophomore year, a topic he generally preferred to avoid. After their unexpected break-up, Sang had spent the whole fall semester in a state of reckless bewilderment and was only now beginning to regain his mental equilibrium.

"You should have seen the letters she sent me last summer." He shook his head, a fresh note of grievance entering his voice. He had referred to their correspondence a few times in my presence, but had never gone too far in the way of details. "I mean, we had a perfectly normal sex life together. Maybe calmer than normal, I don't know. But something happened to her over vacation. She was working as a counselor at this camp for disturbed kids way out in the woods, and I guess she got lonely. At first there'd just be this

quick p.s., you know, one line saying that she missed me or whatever, maybe mentioning something we'd done before, the kind of
stuff everybody does. And then it started getting more elaborate,
even a little kinky. I mean, it wasn't porno or anything. It was just
Eve talking. She was kind of shy about it, almost apologetic."

Like the waitress, Sang kept his eyes locked on Mr. Friedlin as he
talked, almost as if Ted and I weren't there, but it was uncomfortable
nonetheless. Eve was a friend of mine, one of the smartest, sweetest
people I knew. I had introduced her to Sang and still had lunch with
her every once in a while. She had lovely red hair and big breasts that
she was really self-conscious about and tried to hide under layers of
baggy clothing. I didn't want to find myself across from her in the
dining hall, trying to hold up my end of a conversation about Henry
James or the Russian anarchists while secretly wondering what she
looked like in nothing but galoshes and a firehat.

"So there I am," he continued, "working in my mother's lab at
UC Irvine, and I can barely function. All these phrases of hers just
keep floating through my head. I want to do this to you. I want you
to do that to me. I want so-and-so to join us. You can imagine the
state I was in when I got back here in September. And then she goes
and breaks up with me before I've even unpacked my suitcase."

Ted had spent the past few minutes fiddling morosely with the
date setting on his wristwatch, but now he snapped out of his funk.

"Who'd she want to join you?" he asked, making a transparent
effort not to seem too interested. "Just tell me if it was a guy or a
girl."

Sang ignored him. "The thing that killed me was that she
wouldn't give a reason. I kept demanding an explanation, and she
kept insisting that she didn't have to give one. That became the
whole focus of the break-up. Whether she had to give me a reason
or not. I still don't know why she dumped me."

"Was it someone we know?" Ted had abandoned his previous
pose of casual curiosity and was trying his luck with a more
wheedling tone. "You can't just leave us hanging like that."

"It's none of your business," Sang told him.

"Please? Just give me the initials."

"Forget it."

Ted leaned forward, hands clasped together as if in prayer.

"Pretty please?"

Sang stared at him for a few seconds. Then he nodded wearily, as if Ted had worn him down and he saw no choice but to cooperate.

"Okay," he sighed. "Y. M."

"Y. M.?" Ted's mouth dropped open and his brow furrowed with concentration. He looked like the poster boy for perplexity. "I don't know any Y. M."

"Sure you do," said Sang.

"I do?" Ted checked in with me. "Help me out here, Danny."

"Sorry," I told him. "I'm stumped too."

Ted turned back to Sang, shrugging in defeat. The mystery seemed to be taking a toll on him.

"Come on," he groaned. "Have a heart."

"Y. M.," Sang repeated, as if the solution were obvious to anyone with a brain. He spoke slowly, as if Ted's powers of comprehension were impaired. "Your . . . Mother."

Ted accepted the punch line without protest, almost as if he'd been expecting it, squinting doubtfully in an effort to visualize the proposed encounter. I understood the difficulty. His mother was an erstwhile field hockey star at Smith, a large, no-nonsense woman who dressed exclusively in the kind of clothes you saw advertised in the L.L. Bean catalog and couldn't believe that anyone would actually wear—ankle-length tartan skirts, knee socks, tassled moccasins, sweaters with busy snowflake patterns or reindeer motifs, white turtlenecks that covered every millimeter of her neck with lots of fabric to spare. She was the kind of woman you could imagine walking through the streets of revolutionary Iran in her usual attire and not upsetting the ayatollahs.

"You could try," Ted speculated. "But you'd have to get her pretty drunk."

Everyone laughed at that, even Mr. Friedlin, who expressed his amusement by closing his eyes, tilting back his head, and opening his mouth as far as it could go, like a baby bird waiting for a worm. For some reason the sight of his face contorted like that made me flash suddenly on his wife, alone in our common room. Was she crying? Reading a book? Had she taken her shoes off? If I were her son, I thought, I wouldn't have disappeared on her the way Max had. If I were her husband, I wouldn't have ditched her in favor of dinner with a bunch of college kids. When his spasm of mirth had passed, Mr. Friedlin shifted his attention to Ted.

"What about you?" he asked. "How's your girlfriend treating you?"

Even Ted surprised me that night. Until then, I'd never heard him discuss his relationship with Nancy in anything but the most contented terms.

"Girlfriend?" he huffed. "Wife's more like it."

"Is that good or bad?" Mr. Friedlin inquired.

"It used to be good. But now it feels like the bed's too small."

Mr. Friedlin scratched his chin like a therapist.

"So why don't you get a bigger bed?"

"I meant it metaphorically," Ted explained.

"Perhaps a smaller girl, then?" Mr. Friedlin suggested.

Ted acknowledged the quip with a sad smile.

"We even use the same toothbrush," he confessed.

"Now *that's* disgusting." Sang gave a quick shudder, as if this practice were too distressing even to contemplate.

When Mr. Friedlin turned to me, I was ready. I wanted to tell him about Polly, how just then—that very night, in fact—I felt poised, for the first time in my life, to have a real relationship: not just sex but friendship, too, maybe even love. I'd had some flings over the past few years, but now I saw that they had all just been practice, something to pass the time until someone like Polly came along, a girl I could share all of myself with, not just carefully selected fragments. I was going to tell him how surprised I was to suddenly find myself standing in the doorway of what felt like adulthood with no qualms whatsoever about finally stepping in, but he had something else on his mind.

"Wait," he said, rapping his knuckles against the side of his head, as if trying to dislodge a stubborn fact. "Didn't Max tell me you drove an ice-cream truck last summer?"

"A lunch truck," I told him. "It's my father's."

Mr. Friedlin had maintained a playful expression for most of the conversation, but now it changed. His face grew serious, quietly respectful.

"A small businessman," he said, nodding as if this were a wonderful thing indeed.

"I guess you could call him that."

"The independent entrepreneur is the engine of capitalism," he informed us, as if reciting a line of poetry.

The engine of capitalism. Something about the phrase sounded funny to me, at least in relation to my father. I was debating whether to make a comment about the engine's itchy rectum, but our waitress reappeared just then and asked if she could take our orders.

All my life I'd been an enthusiastic carnivore. In the dining hall, I'd once consumed nine French dip sandwiches in a single sitting, supposedly on a dare from Sang, but mostly just because I thought they tasted so great. Until that night, though, I'd never eaten filet mignon. It wasn't nearly as exotic or elaborately prepared as the name seemed to promise, but that was okay with me. It was just this thick lozenge of beef, maybe the size of a squashed baseball, so tender that employing my teeth in its consumption seemed almost unfair, a form of overkill. I sat there in a daze of primal ecstasy, gazing into its pink bull's-eye center, feeling like one of Plato's cave dwellers who'd suddenly been offered a rare—or should I say medium rare—glimpse of the Real Thing in place of the pale, trembling shadows I'd been settling for up till then: the greasy, paper thin Steak-Ums with their crimped and shriveled edges, the too-round industrial hamburger patties studded with pearls of cartilage, the disagreeably veiny or suspiciously squishy mystery cubes of "meat" floating in bowls of stew or lurking in furtive disgrace beneath blankets of brown gravy. How, I wondered, would I ever face them again?

"So," said Mr. Friedlin, releasing a soft preliminary sigh of resignation. "I don't suppose you guys are big Reagan fans."

The three of us traded a quick round of glances.

"We kind of hate him," said Sang.

"Why's that?" Mr. Friedlin didn't seem upset, just curious. We all knew that he had given a lot of money to Reagan's campaign, and that photographs of Gail and Howard with Ron and Nancy were prominently displayed in the Friedlins' den, to Max's undying shame and outrage.

"He supports all those dictators," I said.

"He acts like the rich are oppressed by the poor," Sang complained. "Like it's the people on welfare who are getting away with murder."

"Plus," said Ted, "isn't he kind of stupid? Didn't he say that trees cause pollution or something like that?"

"And that we could retrieve nuclear missiles after they'd been launched," I added. The litany was lengthy and familiar.

"And what about those idiots he surrounds himself with?" Sang wondered. "Ed Meese and James Watt and those other guys."

Mr. Friedlin laughed. "You're right about that," he conceded. "It's not exactly the Institute for Advanced Studies over there on Pennsylvania Avenue."

I wished I could say that we'd scored a point, but I could tell that we hadn't. He was laughing, but the laughter was affectionate, the way it usually was when people who liked the president contemplated his intellectual deficiencies. It was like they were proud of him, like it was a point in America's favor that a man of such dim wattage could get himself elected to the highest office in the land.

The whole Reagan phenomenon eluded me. I had arrived in

college in 1979 with an open mind and very little political baggage. Freshman year I was too focused on my own life—to be specific, on not flunking out of Yale, which I secretly believed had made an enormous error in admitting me—to pay much attention to the world beyond New Haven. In fact, I had so much reading to do first semester that I didn't learn that Americans were being held against their will in Iran until something like Day 17 of the crisis, when my history TA made an offhand comment about Ted Koppel's hairdo.

My political education hadn't really begun until 1980, when I belatedly began to accept the fact that millions of American citizens not only took Ronald Reagan seriously—a mental leap that struck me as preposterous enough in itself—but were actually prepared to place their lives in his hands. I remember watching the debate between Reagan and Carter and feeling a huge abyss open up at my feet when the commentators began declaring Reagan the winner, even though he'd seemed to me to have performed a fairly plausible imitation of a twinkly-eyed village idiot. I wondered if it was Yale that had made me such a stranger to my own country or having smoked too much pot as a teenager. In any case, it was unnerving to find myself dwelling in a separate reality from the majority of my fellow citizens, my parents included. I was enough of a believer in democracy—or maybe just safety in numbers—to not be able to derive much comfort from the stubborn conviction that they were wrong and I was right.

A couple of years into the Reagan presidency, I'd pretty much come to take this abyss for granted, but Mr. Friedlin made me contemplate it again as if for the first time. I'd already figured out why my parents liked Reagan. He appealed to an idea of America they cherished—i.e., that we were innocent and fair-minded and better than any other people who had ever lived on earth. But what about an educated man like Mr. Friedlin? He hardly seemed the type who thought that the fifties were better days, or that General Pinochet was by definition better than Nelson Mandela, or that welfare queens picked up their checks in pink Cadillacs. I must have been staring, because he looked right at me, as if answering my unspoken questions.

"You guys are missing the point," he said, in a patient and friendly voice. "All that stuff's just window dressing. Foreign policy, who's smarter than who, who's got the better statistic. The bottom line is that Ronald Reagan's been a great president for people like us."

Whoa, I thought. *Stop right there.* "People like who?" I wanted to ask. But before I could open my mouth, Mr. Friedlin reached across the table and topped off my wineglass, filling it so completely that the ruby liquid began to dribble a little over the rim. To avoid spillage, I bent forward like a dog and took a big sucking sip to remove the excess. When I looked up, my lips still pressed to the glass, Mr. Friedlin was smiling at me, and I couldn't stop myself from smiling back, nodding my silent thanks. He stretched his arms overhead like a man who'd just awakened from a refreshing nap.

"So?" he said. "Who wants to check out the Whiffenpoofs?"

100

I had to stop back at J. E. to change my clothes for the party. I'd expected my companions to come inside with me to check on Max and Gail, but they only accompanied me as far as the front gate.

"We're twenty minutes late as it is," Mr. Friedlin said, consulting his watch with an expression of grave concern. "Just tell them to meet us at Stiles."

I looked at Sang, but he just shrugged. He was about as enthusiastic about singing groups as I was, and on any other night I would have been surprised by his decision to go to the jamboree. But we were having a good time with Mr. Friedlin, and I couldn't blame him for not wanting it to come to an end. If not for my date with Polly, I probably would have gone too. Ted delivered a brotherly punch to my shoulder.

"You better go," he said, unsuccessfully fighting a smirk. "Better sharpen up that pencil."

Sang cast a suspicious glance at my crotch. "Hey," he said, "is that the stub of an Eberhard-Faber in your pocket, or are you just happy to see me?"

"All right," Mr. Friedlin said, draping an arm around each of their shoulders and gently steering them away from me. "Enough of this nonsense. Let's get moving."

I'd felt oddly sober throughout dinner, but the sight of them heading down Library Walk without me, their arms snaking around each others' shoulders as if they were Whiffenpoofs themselves, or soldiers helping a wounded comrade to safety, made me feel suddenly tipsy. Reaching into my pocket for my keys, I found myself dreading the prospect of making small talk with Mrs. Friedlin if Max hadn't returned. There was no way around it, though; I was not about to jeopardize my standing with Polly by showing up at a big party in a borrowed leather tie, a sport coat from Sears, and factory-reject cowboy boots.

When my companions had finally drifted around the corner onto York Street and out of sight, I selected the key marked SWOG from the sneaker-shaped key ring my father had given out at Christmas as a promotional gimmick—*Dante's Roach Coach,* it said, *Good Food in a Hurry*—and fitted it into the lock. At almost the same moment, the strangest feeling came over me, a burning, overpowering rush of shame, though what it was for I couldn't say. The intensity of it literally buckled my knees, and I spent a few seconds squatting on the ground by the emergency phone, clutching my head in my hands and moaning in a soft singsong. Then I forced myself to stand up.

"I didn't do anything wrong," I said in a soft, shaky voice, as if answering a question posed by someone other than myself. Then I turned the key in the lock and leaned my shoulder against the heavy wrought-iron gate. It resisted for a moment before giving way, issuing the familiar creak of protest that always accompanied my entrance.

Mrs. Friedlin had, in fact, taken her shoes off. She was resting on the couch with a damp washcloth clamped to her forehead, listening to a Joni Mitchell record that had mysteriously attached itself to our collection, probably via Nancy. At the sound of my arrival, she lifted the washcloth and inclined her head in the direction of the door.

"Oh," she said, not bothering to conceal her disappointment. "It's you."

"I'll only be a minute," I assured her, as if she were the resident and I the visitor. "I just have to change for this party."

Giving in to a delayed reflex of politeness, Mrs. Friedlin forced herself to sit up. Her shirt seemed to have faded to a duller shade of green over the past couple of hours and part of it had come untucked. She looked rumpled and bleary, and I knew better than to ask if she'd heard anything from Max.

"Where's Howard?" she asked, addressing this question to the pink washcloth draped across her palm like a slice of ham.

"They went to see the Whiffenpoofs. He said you should join them if you feel like it."

"The Whiffenpoofs?" She pronounced the name as though it meant nothing to her.

"They're a singing group."

She looked up. The damp part of her forehead was shinier than the rest of her face.

"I know what they are, thank you."

"The concert's at Ezra Stiles. I can give you directions."

She responded with a look of sullen contempt, clapping the washcloth back onto her forehead with unnecessary vehemence. I nodded sagely, jerking my thumb over my shoulder with what I hoped was boyish charm.

"Okay," I mumbled. "Righty-O."

My party uniform that semester consisted of jeans, a green pocket T-shirt, and a tattered tweed jacket with suede elbow patches that I'd recently bought at a secondhand clothing store on State Street. Vacillating for a moment on the subject of footwear, I stepped into, then out of, my new penny loafers before settling on the safer bet of Adidas running shoes. The overall effect was surprisingly good, I thought, taking a moment to admire myself in the full-length mirror a previous tenant had mounted on the inside of the door. The outfit had a way of harmonizing the competing aspects of my personality that caused so much friction rubbing up against each other as I went about my business in the world. A powerful sense of wholeness and well-being descended upon me as I pondered my reflection, as if life were an endless costume party, and I'd finally figured out a way to come as myself.

This feeling lasted about three seconds, until I stepped out of my room and back into Mrs. Friedlin's field of vision. It was clear that she'd been waiting for me and had taken advantage of my absence to pull herself together. Her shoes were back on, her hair brushed, her shirt tucked in and shimmering. The washcloth was nowhere in sight. Something about the way she was staring made me suddenly self-conscious, like a kid playing dress-up, a person no one in their right mind had any business taking seriously. I won- dered if it was my jacket. The sleeves were too long, and I had to fold back the cuffs so they wouldn't swallow up my hands.

"Tell me the truth," she said, and I could hear the effort it was costing her to keep her voice calm and even. "How worried should I be?"

"I don't know," I told her. And I really didn't. My gut feeling was that Max was okay and simply avoiding his parents, but I also had no idea where he could have disappeared to for the past six hours.

"Well, tell me this then," she said. "Would you ever do something like this to your parents?"

I shook my head.

"What's he so upset about?" she asked, almost pleading.

"I don't know."

Mrs. Friedlin shifted her gaze to our fireplace. There was a charred log resting on the andirons, left over from an unsuccessful blaze on Halloween night. She stared at it for a long time, as though it were actually burning. I pushed my jacket sleeve up past my elbow, then tugged it back down again. Nothing ever fit me right. Mrs. Friedlin looked up.

"Oh," she said. "I almost forgot. Someone named Cindy called for you. She sounded pretty upset."

"She's from home," I said, feeling a vague obligation to explain. "It's kind of a mess."

She looked me over for a few seconds, as if something didn't quite add up. I wondered if the jacket would look better if I cuffed the sleeves under instead of rolling them back. That way, at least, people wouldn't be able to see how ridiculously long they were.

"You're quite the little ladies' man, aren't you?" she asked.

I was about to deny the charge when I registered the grudging note of respect in her voice.

"Believe me," I told her. "I'm as surprised about it as you are."

She smiled, as if we'd reached some sort of understanding.

"Have fun at your party."

"Thanks."

I took a couple of steps toward the door, then stopped.

"Mrs. Friedlin," I said. "Can I ask you something?"

She nodded. I moved back to where I was before.

"Is this jacket okay?"

She thought it over.

"I think so."

"What about the sleeves?"

"What about them?"

"Do they look stupid?"

"You look nice," she told me, in a firm, motherly voice. "Very collegiate."

woo!

The party was being held at Manuscript, which was basically the cool people's version of a secret society—i.e., it was coed, and its members were not required to masturbate in a coffin, join the CIA, or leave the room when the name of the organization was mentioned in public. I'd heard numerous reports about their great house and excellent parties—Liz Marin was a member that year—and was thrilled to finally have been invited to one. But the excitement of having achieved temporary insider status was utterly eclipsed by the simple fact that Polly was waiting for me.

Generally speaking, the headquarters of secret societies were hard to miss. They were forbidding windowless structures, reminiscent of bunkers and mausoleums, the kinds of buildings you noticed even when you weren't looking for them. Manuscript was different, though. When I got to the spot where it was reputed to be, a short distance beyond Fitzwilly's restaurant, all I saw was a white brick wall that looked like the backside of a garage or small machine shop. Figuring I'd been given bad directions, I walked a couple of blocks further down Elm Street, until I'd clearly left the campus neighborhood and entered the scarier precincts of greater New Haven. None of the buildings I passed seemed even remotely capable of being mistaken for the opulent headquarters of an exclusive and well-endowed not-so-secret society.

Baffled, I returned to my starting point and stared some more at the brick wall. A mild disorientation took hold of me as I pondered the unremarkable surface. It was a familiar feeling, a muted version of the panic that had regularly seized me during my first few days at Yale, when I'd had a series of urgent bureaucratic errands to run in ninety-five-degree heat and couldn't seem to make sense of the campus map in my blue book. The low point in this frustrating odyssey came when I, along with an honor guard of three other losers, spent a half hour in the pitiless spotlight of the noonday sun, waiting for someone to unlock the door of the language lab so we could take our German placement exam. Fifteen minutes after the scheduled starting time, a passerby helpfully informed us that there were, in fact, two language labs on campus. The other one—the right one, needless to say—happened to be right across the street. We'd spent the past thirty minutes staring right at it, sweating profusely and cracking nervous jokes in bad German while watching one student after another stride purposefully through the open front door. How had they known the right language lab from the wrong one? Why, in the whole freshman class, were there only four of us with bad information? It was no disaster, of course—the graduate students administering the test barely noticed that we were late—but the feeling of bewildered exclusion that had been baked into me that afternoon had returned again and again in the years that followed. What was so great about *Harold and Maude*? What was the story with the blue blazers? Did I really have to say "Boola Boola"?

And where the hell was Manuscript anyway? I wandered half-heartedly down to the end of the block, on the off chance that I'd overlooked an enormous mansion on the first pass, then returned to my skeptical vigil in front of the wall. I'm not sure how long I would have remained paralyzed there, letting my big chance with Polly drain away, second by agonizing second, if I hadn't been jumped from behind. The sudden impact staggered me, and I cried out in alarm as two arms wrapped themselves around my neck. I might have been even more terrified if my assailant hadn't also wrapped his legs around my waist and begun shouting, "Giddyap! Giddyap, horsey!" in a lame cowpoke accent, while a pretty girl in a red baseball jacket stood by, laughing a sweetly musical laugh that just then struck me as one more piece in the puzzle of this particular bad dream.

Once I'd convinced him to dismount, Matt was more than happy to inform me that the wall I'd been communing with was indeed part of Manuscript.

"What are you, stoned?" he demanded. He was wearing a beat-up fishing hat, every square inch of which was plastered over with metal lures, fuzzy flies, and campaign buttons touting candidates I'd never heard of. It had the odd effect of making you appreciate the sober dignity of his usual headgear by comparison.

"Unfortunately not."

"Then you must be a moron."

"I prefer to think of myself as an imbecile."

The girl laughed again, but Matt maintained a straight face, directing my attention to the dark alley between the wall and the tall wooden fence bordering the property next door.

"Didn't you see the path?"

"That's a path?"

"Duh? What did you think it was?"

"It looks like a place you go to be mugged and left for dead."

"Danny, Danny, Danny." Matt shook his head with affectionate tolerance, like he made a habit of rescuing me from jams like this. "You theoretical physicists are all alike. You can unlock the secrets of the universe, but you can't remember where you left your own keys."

"Speaking as a theoretical physicist," I said, "did I mention that I like your hat?"

"We went to a thrift store," the girl said excitedly. "We got tons of great stuff."

"Jess, Danny." Matt performed elaborate curlicues with his hands to facilitate the introduction. "Danny, Jess."

I reached out to shake her hand, but ended up grabbing the limp sleeve of her jacket, which was too long by about six inches. It hit me with the force of a minor revelation that it was okay to wear oversized clothes, just as long as you made people think it was a statement rather than an error in judgment, though it also occurred to me that girls who looked like Jessica might be granted a little more slack in these matters than the rest of us.

"It's a little big," she admitted, flapping her sleeves like wings, "but I couldn't resist."

She pivoted to show me the back of the jacket, the hem of which hung down almost to the level of her knees. It featured a sewn-on decal of a sneering, eyepatch-wearing pirate, along with peeling felt letters spelling out the words, "St. Mary's Buccaneers."

"Isn't that great?" she said, turning back around. "St. Mary's Buccaneers? I mean, who do they play? The Mother Seton Maulers?"

"The St. Francis Sharks?" Matt suggested.

"The Holy Cross Gamecocks?" I laughed, happy to play along. My outlook had brightened considerably now that I knew I was in striking distance of the party.

"*The Holy Cross Gamecocks?*" Matt repeated scornfully. "Why

is that funny?"

"Sleep on it," I told him. "It'll all make sense in the morning."

Jess held up one foot so I could admire her new shoes. They were the kind of clownish bowling shoes you could only rent at the alley, red and green with the size scrawled over the toe in Magic Marker. Matt did a little soft shoe so I could see that he had acquired a pair as well.

"Matching rentals," I said. "How romantic."

"Aren't they cool?" Jess asked proudly. She had Cleopatra hair, flawless features, and skin that was luminous even at night. Although Matt had frequently boasted of her beauty, I hadn't really expected her to live up to—let alone exceed—his extravagant description. That was one of the confusing things about being friends with him. Just when you got used to factoring a certain amount of exaggeration and wishful thinking into whatever he said, it turned out he was telling nothing but the truth.

———

Architecturally speaking, Manuscript was an anomaly at Yale. It had no pretensions to medieval grandeur or even garden-variety academic charm—no ivy climbing, weathered stone walls, no moat, turret, or slate roof. It was a low-slung, unapologetically suburban structure—just a ranch house, really—with a restaurant-quality kitchen, off-white wall-to-wall carpeting, and sliding glass doors that communicated onto a small patio. My first thought upon entering was that I'd returned to high school, to one of those blowout keg parties kids used to throw when their parents were away on vacation.

Matt and Jess plunged into the mob swarming around the beverage table in the main dining room, but I hung back, setting off on a solo search mission for Polly. Nodding and weaving my way down a cramped corridor, I poked my head into a small, atrium-style room where a stereo was blasting "Roxanne." The flagstone dance floor was empty except for two girls I didn't know and a guy I recognized from my Japanese Society class. They were getting down with the grim determination of pioneers, trying to get the ball rolling for the rest of us. I waved politely and ducked out of the room when they beckoned me to join them.

109

My original sense of high school déjà vu began to dissipate as I explored the remote corners of the building. No one I'd grown up with had lived in a house like this, a rambling, sparsely furnished pleasure palace made up almost entirely of denlike communal spaces. Down in the cozy finished basement, four bisexual painters—three tall slender guys and a striking but extremely short Eurasian girl—had installed themselves in front of the humongous TV, which was tuned to an episode of *The Incredible Hulk*. Their faces were somber and transfixed, as if Bill Bixby's imminent transformation into Lou Ferrigno was a spectacle worthy of the gravest consideration.

At the top of the stairs I was accosted by a stocky guy in a black velvet cape whom I didn't immediately recognize as Eric Storm. If

I had, I might have taken more strenuous evasive action when he planted himself directly in my path, thrusting out his chest like some kind of pasty collegiate superhero.

"What's wrong with Socialist Realism?" he inquired in a loud voice, as if issuing a challenge. He didn't seem angry, exactly, just a bit agitated. Besides the cape, he wore a tight black turtleneck, heavy woolen pinstripe trousers, and those rubber boots from L.L. Bean. The last time I saw him he'd been deep in some kind of mountainman phase, complete with bushy beard and loud poncho.

"Excuse me," I said, throwing a head fake to the right as a precursor to my unsuccessful attempt to squeeze past him on the left. "I'm looking for Polly."

"What's wrong with Socialist Realism?" he asked again, this time more plaintively.

"Is this a riddle? Do I have to answer correctly to pass?"

"I'm just curious," he said, calming a little now that he knew he had me cornered. "Everyone acts like it was such a horrible thing."

I knew better than to get sucked into this sort of discussion with him. The one and only time Eric and I had had lunch together—it was back in December, shortly after *Reality* had published his story, "A Match Made in Heaven"—we got into an unrewarding two-hour argument about whether Less really was More. He kept calling me for days afterward, trying to start it up again.

"You look different without your beard," I told him.

He rubbed both hands over his baby-smooth face, compressing his cheeks with a tenderness I found vaguely unsettling.

"You think so?"

"Yeah. It's a younger look. More approachable."

He seemed pleased.

"That's what I was hoping for. The beard was kind of imposing. No one would talk to me."

"The cape's a nice touch too," I added, peering around him to see if I could spot Polly in the hallway. Completely by accident, I made eye contact with Jodie Foster instead. She was standing outside the bathroom, dressed in a pair of baggy overalls and a gray T-shirt, nodding emphatically at something someone was telling her. She looked in my direction the same moment I looked in hers; our eyes met for a split second before she turned back to her conversation.

To my knowledge, it was the first time Jodie and I had ever been present at the same social occasion. The thrill I felt simply upon seeing her doubled when I realized that she was talking to Liz Marin. I could just walk right over and join them! Liz was a friend of mine; I wouldn't have seemed like just another creep hounding Jodie because she was famous. I imagined breaking the ice with a suave comment about Bill Bixby, an actor she'd worked with on *The Courtship of Eddie's Father*. Not everyone remembered that about her. But instead I was trapped here at the top of the stairs, watching Eric pet his cape as though it were a living thing.

"It was a Christmas present," he explained. "This is the first opportunity I've had to wear it in public."

"A Christmas present?" I couldn't help laughing. "Who from?"

"My mom."

I peered around him again to see if I could renew eye contact with Jodie, but she'd disappeared. I relaxed a little, forcing myself to pay closer attention to Eric. He wasn't such a terrible guy, if you could get past the bluster and the affectations.

"Your mom got you a cape?"

"I mean, I asked for it," he said, a bit sheepishly.

"Wow." I shook my head. "I don't think my mom would even know where to look."

Distracted as I was by an image of my mother wandering around Bamberger's Basement, trying to locate the velvet-cape section, I didn't see it coming when Eric jammed his index finger into my sternum. It wasn't a pleasant feeling.

"You didn't answer my question," he said.

"You had a question?"

"Yes. Wouldn't you say that all literature is ultimately in the service of some social or political system? What's wrong with making that explicit?"

"Nothing, I guess." I felt the quicksand sucking at my ankles. There was nothing to do but sink. "The problem comes when you use that as an excuse to lock people up or kill them."

"Stop right there," he said, thrusting out one hand like a traffic cop. "I'm just talking theory here. I'm not trying to defend the practice."

I remembered this tactic from our previous argument. Eric was like a kid at the playground, making up the rules as he went along, always after the fact and to his own advantage.

"All right," I said. "Have it your way. The problem with Socialist Realism as a concept is that it erases the distinction between literature and propaganda."

"Aha." He smiled like I'd played right into his hands. "But literature is propaganda. Any fool can see that."

"Not this fool."

"No?" He drew back a little, as though he feared my ignorance might be contagious. "You like Tolstoy, as I recall. So let's just take *Anna Karenina*, for example. Isn't that propaganda in favor of adultery and divorce?"

"Maybe. But adultery and divorce were frowned upon when Tolstoy wrote the book. He was working against the grain of his own society. That's exactly what you're not allowed to do under Socialist Realism."

Eric frowned. His way of responding to countervailing arguments was simply to repeat his original point in different language.

"I'd say governments have the right to determine what sort of propaganda gets disseminated in their countries, don't you?"

Somebody turned up the music. I had to raise my voice so he could hear me over "Rock Lobster."

"Eric," I said. "You wrote a story about a priest who burns down an altar boy's house on Christmas Eve. What government would be in favor of that?"

"Are you kidding?" He reached behind him and flipped back his cape. It was a reflexive gesture, like a girl pushing hair out of her face. "Priests are class enemies. Stalin would have loved my story."

I took a deep breath and glanced down the hallway, trying to fend off a sudden wave of anxiety. If Polly were here, surely she would have found me by now.

"Listen, Eric. It's not the writer's job to kiss the asses of the people in power. It's the writer's job to go against the grain."

"Like who, for instance?"

"What do you mean, like who?"

"Name me a writer who went against the grain. Besides Tolstoy. Not Shakespeare. Certainly not your precious Hemingway."

There were lots of writers I might have named, writers who'd been murdered, jailed, exiled, or censored—Babel, Solzhenitsyn, Kundera, Joyce, Nabokov, Allen Ginsberg. But for some reason, my mind at that moment was a vast empty space with only a single name rattling around in it.

"George Eliot," I said.

"George Eliot?" He laughed. "Is that the best you can do? Chickenshit George Eliot?"

"Chickenshit?" I said in disbelief. "George Eliot?"

"If I'm not mistaken," he observed, "Mr. Eliot's real name was Maryann Evans."

"So? She had to change her name to publish her books. Women weren't allowed to be serious writers back then."

"Changing your name isn't bucking the system. It's going along to get along. She should have stood up for her rights instead of hiding behind a pseudonym."

"Hiding? George Eliot wasn't hiding from anyone. It's not fair of you to impose twentieth-century values on a nineteenth-century writer."

He waved me away as though I were some kind of intellectual mosquito.

"George Eliot doesn't cut it, Danny. Give me a better example."

I wanted to walk away, but I was already in too deep, just like last time. The guy was a black hole. I felt him absorbing me molecule by molecule. If Polly hadn't grabbed my arm just then I might have vanished from the face of the earth.

"There you are," she said. There was the slightest hint of accusation in her voice. "I've been looking all over."

Not hard enough, I wanted to tell her, but I held my tongue at the last second. She looked rattled, not quite herself. Even Eric noticed. He took one look at her tense, unhappy expression and realized his time was up.

"We'll finish this later," he muttered darkly, pushing me aside and making his way downstairs to inflict himself on the painters.

Polly squinted after him. Her hair was wild and she was wearing a coat I'd never seen before, an ugly orange ski parka zipped, Sang-style, all the way up to her chin. A wrinkled lift ticket dangled from the zipper pull.

"Who was that caped crusader?" she asked.

"Argument Man," I told her. "He had me cornered. I thought you'd never show up."

Instead of smiling, she considered me for a long time.

"Listen," she said, "you're lucky I'm here at all."

Polly maneuvered me away from the stairs to a less-congested sector of the hallway. Maybe because we didn't know each other very well and had such an ill-defined relationship, she had this quality of moving in and out of focus for me. There were times when I was sure I was in love with her and found her beauty obvious and riveting. And then there were times like this—usually when days or weeks had gone by since I'd last seen her—when I was obscurely disappointed by her and couldn't quite remember what all the fuss was about.

"Peter called," she informed me in an unconvincingly matter-of-fact voice. "We had a big argument."

Maybe it's the coat, I thought. She was wearing gray tights and sexy ankle-high lace-up shoes; her skinny legs protruded like sticks from the bulky parka. The contrast gave her a jarring, almost composite appearance, as if the upper and lower portions of her belonged to different people. Normally she wore a secondhand suede coat with frayed cuffs, a missing button, and a prominent coffee stain on one lapel. Its absence disturbed me enough that I couldn't help wondering for a moment if it was Polly I had the crush on or that funky coat of hers.

"I thought you two were taking a break from each other."

"I thought so too. But he kind of lost it when I told him I was seeing you tonight."

"Jesus." It was disturbing enough to imagine Professor Preston "losing it" under any circumstances, let alone circumstances that involved me personally. It seemed somehow beneath his dignity. "Did you have to tell him?"

"Why should I lie? He didn't lie to me about his *colleague* from Vassar." She pronounced the word "colleague" as if it had a different definition from the one that appeared in the dictionary. "If he's not really my boyfriend, then I guess I can do what I want."

She took hold of the lift ticket and unzipped her parka in distracted slow motion. It parted to reveal an apple green cotton dress, the fabric of which was printed with a design that alternated pink clocks and gray lollipops. She laughed as if surprised at herself.

"He's probably standing by the Silliman gate right now, wondering where I am."

"I thought you told him you were going out with me."

Her cheeks ballooned, then collapsed.

"He sort of talked me out of it."

"Sort of?"

"He kept me on the phone for like two hours," she explained, her voice vehement and pleading at the same time. "Peter's a really hard person to argue with. He just wears you down until you can't even think straight."

"So why are you here?"

"It's not fair," she continued, addressing a spot on the wall somewhere above my head. "He thinks he can just bend me to his will. I hung up the phone and thought, *No way, tonight I'm doing*

115

what I want. I didn't even call him back. I just borrowed this coat from a guy across the hall and headed over here."

"What's the coat got to do with it?"

"I didn't want him to notice me if he passed in his car." She pulled a gray rag watch cap out of a pocket. "I wore this too. I bet my hair's a mess, right?"

"You went incognito?" I would have laughed if she hadn't looked so serious. The guy was a Shakespeare scholar, not someone you needed to hide from in an ugly coat.

"He has this way of finding me," she said, casting a nervous glance down the length of the hallway. "And if he finds me I just end up doing what he wants."

She covered her face with both hands and began shaking her head back and forth, moaning like someone who realizes she's making a big mistake, but is going to go through with it anyway. I remembered my own mysterious fit of moaning outside the J.E. gate and wondered if the night was taking me into deeper water than I could handle. But when she pulled her hands away from her face, she smiled like nothing was wrong.

"Come on," she said, grabbing hold of my wrist. "Let's dance."

Despite my cavalier promises to the contrary, I had arrived at Manuscript that night with no intention of dancing. If pressed, I expected to do to Polly what I'd done to other girls at other parties. I'd take her aside, put on a thoughtful, sadly resolute expression, and make her understand that I simply didn't do it, that it wasn't just a preference, like not smoking or not going to church, but an essential and immutable part of my identity.

Why don't you go ahead without me, I might have begun. *I'll just stand here in the doorway and watch . . .*

I'd keep talking for as long as it took—it didn't usually take that long—to convince her that I was serious, accepting her momentary irritation and baffled shrug as the price I had to pay for keeping faith with my high school self, the sixteen-year-old who believed that Disco Sucked and that dancing (for guys, anyway) was a violation of the unwritten code of rock 'n' roll—maybe not Richie Cunningham sock hop rock 'n' roll, which was nearly as pathetic as disco anyway, but the Real Thing, leather-pants guitar-hero sex-with-groupies rock 'n' roll—though the code did permit you to bob your head in time with the music and punch your fist in the air. You just weren't allowed to move your feet unless you were an actual member of the band. It was hard to put all this into words, so I had to smile regretfully and say things I didn't really mean, like *Maybe if I drink a little more*, or *I'm a little self-conscious*, which almost always did the trick. The girls I hung around with at college were very respectful of my feelings of self-consciousness.

That night, though, the flow of events caught me off guard. Before I could launch into my speech or even compose my expression, Polly had led me into the atrium, tossed her parka on the floor, and begun dancing without the slightest hesitation or transition, as though it were a perfectly natural form of behavior. The room was sweaty and crowded now, the loud, pulsating heart of the party. Eyes half-closed, smiling faintly, she held out her hand like a lifeline as she began drifting away from me, insinuating herself into the throng of moving bodies behind her. I pressed back against the wall, shaking my head no, *No, I couldn't possibly*.

I felt so stupid just then, I could hardly bear it. "Rock the Casbah" was playing, a totally respectable song, and no one was paying any attention to me, no one except a ghost floating above the dancers, a long-haired kid with aviator glasses and a Jethro Tull T-shirt. He was watching me warily, his eyes full of quiet pleading. *Remember me?* he seemed to say. *Remember all the good times we had?* I looked at Polly for a few seconds—her eyes were all the way closed now, slender arms aloft, her body in fluid motion—then back at the kid. I would have apologized, but he was already gone, spared the sight of me wading away from the wall and into the crowd of dancers, smiling the way you do down the shore, when the sun is hot but the ocean's colder than you expected.

It was strange and awful in the beginning, a bad dream made flesh. I was the Dork-in-Chief, the Anti-Dancer, the Fred Astaire of Spaz. My arms moved and my legs moved, but these movements had little to do with the music, and even less to do with fun. They were abrupt and jerky, the flailings of a defective marionette. I needed oil. The beat was a distant rumor. If I'd been in water I would have drowned. To make matters worse, everyone else on the dance floor suddenly seemed improbably fluid and limber, full of tricky spins and Soul Train swivels. I mean, they were Yalies. Molecular Biology and Biochemistry majors. People who petitioned to take seven courses in one semester so they wouldn't have to choose between Introductory Sanskrit, Medieval Architecture, and that senior seminar on *Finnegans Wake.* Where had they learned to dance like this? Groton? Choate? Some special summer camp my parents hadn't heard about?

The only thing that amazed me more than their collective grace was their collective lack of interest in the spectacle I was making of myself. I half-expected them to gather in a circle to point and snicker, but whether out of politeness or self-absorption, they moved past me as if I didn't exist. Polly opened her eyes for a second, smiled at me, then closed them again. I couldn't believe I was getting away with it. I felt relieved and bewildered at the same time, like a stoned hippie in a tie-dyed shirt breezing through customs with ten pounds of pot hidden in his guitar case.

Joe Strummer made way for David Bowie. "Young Americans" was a longer song than I'd realized; it just kept going on and on, the sheer tedium of it offering a kind of release. I stopped trying to dance, surrendering my body to auto pilot and reflecting instead on my argument with Eric, the way he managed to get me to take the bait. *Chickenshit George Eliot,* I thought, and the unlikeliness of the phrase made me laugh out loud. Polly looked up. She was waiting out the saxophone solo, shuffling in place, letting her head loll lazily from side to side. Her face was damp, flushed with exhilaration. She stuck her tongue out and panted like a dog.

"God," she said. "We should do this more often."

i broke a sweat on "Pump It Up" and began to unclench a little. I had been dancing for maybe fifteen minutes at that point, and my anxiety had ebbed to a manageable level. I'm invisible, I kept reminding myself, *No one knows I'm here.* I wasn't having fun exactly, but I did register the first rumblings of self-congratulation, the secret pride that comes when you face up to fears that other people don't even know you possess.

"Super Freak" was my breakthrough. As soon as I heard those familiar bass notes, I began to move differently. My legs felt bouncy and strong, like I'd just removed a pair of ankle weights. The beat was obvious and I let it take me where it wanted. *When I get to her room, she's got incense, wine, and can-dles . . .* Polly swung her hair back and forth as she sang along; there was a startled look of illicit pleasure on her face, as if she'd achieved a state of mystical union with Rick James. *It's such a freaky scene . . . Yow*!

In fact, the whole room seemed to have undergone some sort of transformation, like water come to a boil. People collided and spun, careening through the crowd, changing partners and moving on in some kind of manic, free-form square dance. A sweaty football player banged into me, almost knocking me down. When my balance returned I found myself moving at a higher frequency, my arms and legs churning effortlessly, as though my body were a machine powered by the song.

"Woo!" I shouted, punching the air like John Travolta.

Once, back in high school, I'd gotten stoned and watched a Popeye cartoon. In this particular episode, at the low point of the pre-spinach narrative, Popeye had been turned into a punching bag, his feet rooted to the ground, his arms pressed uselessly to his sides. Bluto pummelled him without mercy, his fists a blurry windmill of

119

punishment. Popeye's clothes fell off first, followed by a host of strange objects they'd apparently been concealing—a lantern, a spy glass, a ship's wheel, a life preserver, an anchor—the tools and debris of a lifetime spent at sea. I wondered if something similar wasn't happening to me as I danced, if burdens I hadn't even known I was carrying were falling away from my body. High school dropped away. The 1970s. New Jersey. The years I'd spent sitting on the bench, waiting for my shot at gridiron glory. The guitars I'd never quite learned to play. The girls who wouldn't look at me. The friends I'd lost. The people I'd hurt. My crummy summer jobs. The whole accumulated weight of the past. I felt lighter and lighter, pumped full of fresh air, and though my feet remained rooted to the ground, I experienced an odd sensation of rising, a slow inexorable ascent, as though I were moving upward on an invisible escalator, dancing my way into a brighter and easier future.

"Woo!" I shouted again, just in case anyone hadn't heard me the first time.

fornicators

"Oh man." **Matt** shook his head, resting a compassionate hand on my shoulder. "Man oh man."

"Yes?" I was standing next to him at the beverage table, sipping flat club soda with no ice while Polly waited on line for a turn in the bathroom. A struggle for control of the stereo had resulted in a string of REO Speedwagon and Journey tunes that had cleared the dance floor as effectively as an attack of poison gas. We were biding time, charging our batteries for the inevitable counterstrike.

"Sweet Lordy," he replied, administering a gentle squeeze to my trapezius muscle. "Are you the worst dancer in the world or what?"

"Fuck you," I said, twisting out of his grasp.

"I didn't mean it as an insult," he assured me. "It was more of an observation."

"Oh well in that case, fuck you."

"Just ignore him," Jessica told me. "You did fine."

"You know what?" I said. "No one was even watching me."

"I was," Matt volunteered. "Wanna know what you looked like?"

He set his plastic beer cup down on the table, twisted his face into a moronic grimace, and lurched into motion, shifting his weight from one leg to the other like a clumsy giant while simultaneously jabbing at the air in every possible direction, as though trying to punch out a swarm of flies.

"Come on everybody," he called out, the lures on his fishing cap flapping up and down as he stomped. "Let's do the Danny."

Under normal circumstances, I would have felt exposed and mortified by this sort of personalized public mockery, but that night I had attained a lofty state of detachment. This was about Matt, I realized, not about me. The longer he kept up the joke, the sorrier I felt for him.

"Help me, Jesus!" he cried out. "I'm a dancing fool!"

He tucked his chin down into his chest, hunching his shoulders like Frankenstein as he began to run in place, pumping his knees and elbows with jerky exaggeration. There was a startled, almost desperate look on his face.

"I can't stop!" he shouted, loud enough that people around us began to take notice. "I've got dance fever!"

I was distracted for a moment by the sight of a girl in equestrian clothes—the weird beige pants, the shiny knee boots, even the little black jockey's cap—squeezing between Matt and Jess on her way to the table, like a lawn ornament come to life. All she needed was the little lantern. Without the slightest hesitation or change of expression, she plunged her hand into the punch bowl and pulled out a Rolex watch.

"I've been looking all over for this," she informed me in a sweet Southern accent. "My Daddy would've killed me if I'd lost it."

Though privately I thought she might have at least used the ladle, I shrugged to indicate my lack of jurisdiction in the matter and turned back to Matt. By this time, his imitation of me seemed to have evolved into some sort of one-man impersonation of the Three Stooges. He'd begun slapping himself in the head with distressing enthusiasm, emitting little whoops of joy in response to each self-inflicted blow. I watched in pained fascination, oddly unsurprised by the spectacle, as if something latent in his everyday behavior had finally found its way to the surface.

"Take that!" he growled, striking himself in the forehead with the palm of his right hand while his left fist spun threateningly in the air above his head. "Why I oughta—"

Before he could make good on this threat to clobber himself, Jessica grabbed a cup of beer off the table and flung it in his face. The splash stopped him cold. His shoulders sagged; he dropped his arms to his sides and stood there helplessly, breathing hard and looking vaguely bewildered as the yellow liquid ran down his face and dribbled off the brim of his crooked hat. He glanced at me, then shifted his attention to the floor.

"Sorry," he muttered, sticking out his tongue to catch a stray droplet about to detach itself from the tip of his nose.

"It's okay," I told him. "Forget about it."

"It's not okay," Jess said sharply. "Can't we go to a party just once without you doing something stupid?"

"I was trying," he insisted, his voice contrite and defiant at the same time. He wiped his sleeve across his mouth. "I thought you'd like it."

"Oh yeah," she said. "I love it when my boyfriend makes an ass of himself in public."

The polo player—or whatever she was—stood nearby, licking the punch off her Rolex as she eavesdropped on this discussion. She kept this up for longer than could have been necessary, almost as if she'd come to think of the watch as a lollipop. I got so engrossed in watching her that I failed to notice right away that Polly had returned from the bathroom. Her presence didn't really register on me until she'd dug her fingers into my wrist and yanked so hard on my arm that both of us almost ended up on the floor.

"Come on," she said, addressing me in a no-nonsense voice I hadn't heard from her before. In her borrowed coat and hat, she seemed no more familiar to me than the jockey. "We're outta here."

123

Polly wasn't running exactly, but she was walking so fast that it was hard to keep up with her, let alone carry on a conversation. We had already turned the corner onto Park Street and were rushing past the sub shop before she managed to explain that we were fleeing from Peter Preston, who had apparently crashed the party a few minutes earlier.

"You didn't see him?" she asked breathlessly.

I shook my head. "There was all this weird stuff going on by the punch bowl. Did you have a scene?"

"No, thank God." She glanced quickly over her shoulder. "I was in the bathroom when he went by. Ingrid saw him go downstairs. She said he looked furious."

"Maybe he ran into Eric," I speculated. "That should give us a couple hours' head start."

I thought that might get a chuckle out of her, but the next thing I knew she had dropped to her knees right there on the sidewalk, gesturing feverishly for me to do the same. We waited like that, crouching in the shadow of a parked car, until three sets of head-lights had passed, then jumped up and hustled across the street, darting into the labyrinth of footpaths behind the drama school. Once we were safely hidden from the street, Polly leaned back against a skinny tree and pulled off her watch cap. I felt a huge surge of relief as her hair spilled out, softening the angles of her face, making her look like herself again.

"God," she said, wiping one hand across her brow and sighing like an actress. "That was close."

The pause that followed was so awkward and romantic, I had no choice but to kiss her. Her lips parted and her arms tightened around my back, and I understood right away that her plans for us to sleep together remained unshaken. This was a relief to me, of course, but not as much as it should have been. For reasons I couldn't quite identify, I felt disturbingly insulated from the moment and from Polly herself. I'd spent months waiting to kiss her like this, and now that it was happening all I could think about was the party we'd just left—the thrill of dancing, the sound the beer made slapping into Matt's face, the blank expression on the face of the girl licking her wristwatch—and what a good teacher Professor Preston had been, how much he'd taught me about Shakespeare.

"Is something wrong?" she asked.

"No," I said, my voice trailing off. "I just . . ."

She looked at me for a few seconds, her lips thoughtfully puck-ered, then reached up to unzip her jacket. She did it slowly, like a stripper, watching me the whole time.

"Try it this way," she said, wriggling out of the sleeves and letting the coat drop to the ground. "I'll be more like kissing a girl."

We crossed York Street and slipped like thieves into Jonathan Edwards. We needed to be somewhere with a bed, and her room had been declared off-limits, due to the fact that Professor Preston supposedly had a key and no compunction about using it.

"I just hope my roommates are out," I said, giving her hand a little squeeze. "It'll be hard for us to fornicate with them right in the next room."

"Not for me," she laughed. "I'll copulate right in the common room if I have to."

These words weren't our own; they'd been given to us by the strangers who'd stumbled upon us only moments before. Polly's decision to remove the coat had done wonders for my concentration, and by that point we were dry humping on the grass, using the borrowed parka as a kind of makeshift blanket. As a rule, dry humping was not a favorite activity of mine, but Polly's dress had crept up around her hips and I could see the white of her panties glowing dimly through the stretchy opaque fabric of her tights as she pushed herself against me, and I felt as gratified and excited by this sight as an astronomer who discovers a new galaxy after a lifetime of pondering the emptiness of space. I was so transported, in fact, that my reaction to the sound of approaching footsteps was simply to ignore them, in the hope that the people attached to the feet would just mind their own business and go away.

"Mark it, uncle," a cheerful male voice called out. "Behold the beast with two backs."

"Oh stop it," a woman said, giggling nervously. "Leave them alone."

"Are they fornicators?" a second male voice inquired. It was deep and booming, but tinged with uncertainty. "Has the knave found his way to the forfended place?"

With a groan, I rolled off Polly and squinted in the direction of our audience. Maybe twenty feet away, clearly visible on the well-lit path, three people stood watching us—two men in Elizabethan regalia, plus a woman in jeans and a long sweater. The shorter man, who happened to be carrying a pizza box, was decked out in patch-work tights and a jester's cap; the other was tall and stooped over, with an unconvincing white beard glued to his young and handsome face. He had a crooked walking stick in one hand, a six of beer in the other. Polly sat up too, tugging the dress down over her thighs.

"Is that Lear?" she wondered out loud.

The white-bearded actor thumped his stick on the sidewalk. "I am the king himself."

"Sorry to bother you," the woman said, tugging none-too-gently on King Lear's arm. "They're just jealous is all."

"Carry on," the fool told us, balancing the pizza box in one hand and throwing us a quick salute as he scurried to catch up with his companions.

I watched the three of them disappear around a bend, then turned to Polly, worried that the encounter had embarrassed or troubled her. But she couldn't have looked more delighted.

"I guess that's what we get for making the beast with two backs behind the drama school," she reflected.

"I'm just glad it wasn't Titus Andronicus," I told her.

She rose to her feet, extending a hand to help me up. In the distance, we heard King Lear shouting into the night: "Let copulation thrive, for Gloucester's bastard son was kinder to his father than my daughters got 'tween lawful sheets!"

"Speaking of sheets," she said. "Have you washed yours recently?"

"Don't worry," I assured her. "Once a semester, whether they need it or not."

I was hoping we could slip into my bedroom unobserved, making a clean transition back to the good place we'd been before King

Lear had so rudely interrupted, but I'd forgotten about the Whiff-enpoof party across the hall. It looked like the whole jamboree had transported itself to Entryway C; a mob of well-dressed people were swarming around the brightly lit doorway, talking and laughing in unnaturally loud voices, trying to compete with "Racing in the Street," which was blasting from an open window on the second floor, the speakers turned out to face the courtyard.

"I love this song," Polly told me. "It's so utterly desolate."

"It's okay," I said. "Not one of my favorites."

I wasn't a huge Springsteen fan, but I always felt a bit proprietary about his music when I heard it at Yale. It didn't sound right in this context, played for the enjoyment of people who were going to end up being the bosses of the people the Boss was singing about. Nobody in Entryway C was born to run; no one in the whole college—none of the students anyway—came home from work and washed up, and went racing the streets. I didn't either, but I did take a certain pride in actually knowing a few people who did, or at least could have if they'd wanted to.

The stairwells were packed wall-to-wall with revelers holding enormous plastic cups and shouting in each others' ears. Polly and I had to push and squeeze and thread and hello our way through the festive masses; it was a little like moving through a tilted subway car at the height of rush hour. Already I could imagine the stale beer reek we'd wake to in the morning, the way the gummy stairs would grab at our shoes as we tiptoed down to breakfast.

It must have taken us five minutes to climb three flights, ample time for me to consider the various scenarios that might confront us when we finally made it inside. The best one involved an empty suite, Polly's dress on the floor, her bra draped over the back of my chair. The worst case had Mrs. Friedlin prostrate on the couch, still stubbornly waiting for Max, but it was after midnight and hard to imagine that the situation hadn't resolved itself by now. In between those two extremes was a host of likelier possibilities, most of which would require us to make a few minutes of small talk with some combination of my suitemates before making a transparent excuse to escape to the bedroom. ("We're *tired*," Ted and Nancy always lied, holding hands and smirking cheerfully just in case anyone was unclear about the true nature of their mission. "Gotta catch some shut-eye.") If you lived in a dorm, it was pretty much a given that your sex life unfolded in the public domain. You either moved off-campus, took a vow of celibacy, or learned to put up with it like everyone else.

"Well." I smiled nervously at Polly as I selected my room key from the Roach Coach key chain and slipped it into the lock. "Here goes nothing."

I blinked and staggered slightly as we entered the common room, almost as if several flashbulbs had exploded at once. My immediate impression was of a large group of people, all of them staring expectantly at me, waiting for a signal to leap up and shout *Surprise!*

Letting go of Polly's hand, I blinked a few more times and tried to get a handle on the situation. It quickly became clear to me that the room was not as crowded as I'd thought. Sang and Ted were there, looking about as uncomfortable as it's possible to look when you're trying to pretend that everything's cool. Nancy wasn't present, nor was Max, though for a second I assumed that he was, since his parents were sitting on the couch, one on either side of a person it took me a surprisingly long time to recognize as Cindy. Part of it was that the bottom of her face was concealed by a Kleenex she was weeping into, but mainly it was just that it made no sense to see her flanked by the Friedlins, both of whom were patting and stroking her as though she were their adopted child. It felt unreal, like I'd stepped into one of those dreams where you find your dead grandmother working the drive-thru window at McDonald's.

"Well, well." Gail Friedlin glared at me, her red-rimmed eyes brimming with accusation. "Looks who's back from the big party."

"You have a visitor," Howard Friedlin said, his voice containing both a taunt and a warning.

"Is something wrong?" Polly asked.

I brushed the question aside with an unconvincing shake of my head and turned back to Cindy. She balled the Kleenex inside her fist and sat up straighter, sniffling to pull herself together. My initial shock had faded by now, displaced by a raw surge of annoyance. It was bad enough that she called me all the time, I thought, disrupting my schoolwork. But to ambush me like this on the Friday before vacation was just plain rude.

"You know," I said, forcing myself to sound casual and friendly, "I'm not sure this is the best time."

"I've been calling you for weeks," she said, her voice trembling like she might start crying again at any second. "You never called me back."

It was strange: Cindy wasn't wearing anything that lots of girls at Yale wouldn't have worn—jeans, sneakers, denim jacket—but on her the effect was entirely different; one glance and you would have known that she didn't belong. Her jeans were designer, sausage-skin Sergio Valentis that she'd once told me took several minutes to wriggle into. Her jacket was two-tone, the collar, cuffs, and chest pocket a distinctly lighter blue than the rest of the garment, and her sneakers were just too damn white. As usual, she'd taken great pains with her hair and makeup, and I couldn't help but wonder what she made of Polly's wild tangle of curls, her five-dollar vintage dress.

"Look, Cindy, I've been really busy. You have no idea what midterms are like."

"Cindy?" Polly said, finally catching on. "Your secretary?"

She clapped a hand over her mouth as soon as she said it, but it was too late. Cindy didn't say anything in response; she just stared at Polly for a few seconds, letting the word hang in the air. Her voice was stronger when she finally spoke, as if the insult had given her courage.

"I came to tell you something."

"Couldn't it have waited a day?" I asked, surprised to hear myself pleading with her. "I'm going home tomorrow."

"No," she said. "I think you need to hear this."

"Okay," I told her. "But it better be good."

Up to that point, I hadn't been able to give much thought to the purpose of her visit. But all at once, in the brief space between my comment and her reply, I knew exactly why she was here and what I'd been hiding from these past several weeks.

"Oh my God," I said, before she'd even uttered a word.

part three

The Roach Coach

tito the snack king

With exquisite deliberation, my father lowered himself into the kitchen chair. It was early evening, just after the ritual viewing of *60 Minutes*, which had long ago replaced church as my family's Sunday obligation of choice. All three of us watched with righteous pleasure as Mike Wallace showed hidden camera footage of dangerous and unsanitary conditions at a poultry-processing plant to a stammering, heavily perspiring executive who moments before had insisted that his company adhered to "the highest possible standards of safety and cleanliness."

"The highest possible standards?" Mike Wallace repeated incredulously. "Those are your words, sir, not mine. Would you say that workers trampling on a chicken carcass and then putting it back on the assembly line represents the highest possible standards of cleanliness for an industry that feeds millions of Americans? Would you say that inspectors who regularly ignore high levels of salmonella and fecal bacteria—*fecal bacteria*, sir—represent the highest possible levels of safety?"

"Ha!" my father called out. These were the moments that he loved, when the mighty were humbled. "What do you say to that, you pompous bastard?"

"I don't . . . we can't—" The executive held one hand in front of his face, shielding himself from the camera like a criminal on the TV news. "I must insist that we terminate this interview."

After Andy Rooney's closing sermon, my mother remained in the living room to clip and alphabetize coupons from the Sunday paper while my father and I retired to the kitchen to talk business. He opened a spiral-bound notebook and cleared his throat, but instead of speaking he tilted his upper body to the right at a severe angle. In this awkward position, with the distracted expression of someone who'd just lost a filling, he mapped out the route and timetable I'd be following for the next two weeks.

"There've been a few changes," he explained.

In fact, the new route was significantly different from the one I'd gotten used to over the previous summer. He'd picked up a couple of new stops— the Department of Public Works in Darwin and a big construction site in Springville—but had lost half a dozen. He exhaled slowly, raising himself into a position halfway between sitting and standing up, and spoke through gritted teeth.

"We don't go to Union Village anymore."

"You okay?"

"Yeah." He worked his mouth into an unconvincing simulation of a smile. "Never better."

"Can't you put on some ointment or something?"

"They only go up to Preparation H. For the thing I got, you'd need Preparation Z."

"Oh well," I said, ever philosophical about other people's distress. "Tomorrow morning it'll all be a distant memory."

"I don't know if I can last that long." He lowered himself back onto the chair as if onto a bed of nails. "I'm tempted to grab one of those steak knives and do the job myself."

I followed his gaze to the phalanx of gleaming Sliceco knives arranged in ascending order of size along a magnetic strip above the stove. I'd been a Sliceco sales representative for a couple of months my senior year in high school, but hadn't been able to close on any customers except my parents. The knives turned out to be too sharp to use and now served a purely decorative function in our kitchen.

"Be my guest," I told him. "Just don't ask me to assist."

"On second thought," he muttered, "maybe a pair of pliers would do the trick."

"What's that you were saying about Union Village?" I asked, pulling him back from the abyss of do-it-yourself surgery.

"It's history."

"What? Even Via Commercial?"

"Gonesville." He mimed the act of crumpling a piece of paper and tossing it over his shoulder. "It makes it a lot easier to get to the rest of the stops on time."

Via Commercial, the industrial park off Vauxhall Road, had been one of the linchpins of my father's route. He'd serviced three of six plants laid out along the sinuous cul-de-sac, including Re-Flex Industries, where Cindy worked, and where I'd been expecting to meet my fate in the morning.

"What happened?" I asked, torn between relief on my own behalf and concern on my father's. To lose three prime stops in a single blow was a bitter setback for the Roach Coach.

"The Lunch Monsters." He spoke the name in a grim, matter-of-fact voice, as if there were nothing even remotely humorous about it.

"The who?"

He shrugged. "That's what they call themselves. They're a bunch of bodybuilders who've outfitted their trucks with those ridiculous monster tires. They've pretty much taken over the entire town."

"How? I mean, they just can't just drive up and steal your stops, can they?"

"These guys don't mess around, Danny." My father lowered his voice. "Their boss is an Italian from Staten Island."

"So? What's that supposed to mean? You're an Italian from New Jersey."

"You're not listening." He looked away from me, taking a few seconds to peruse the simulated wood grain of the tabletop. "If these guys want your stop, you give them your stop."

I couldn't believe what I was hearing. My father wasn't a tough guy, but he knew the rules as well as anyone. Lunch-truck drivers didn't just hand over their stops without a fight. It didn't matter how old or small or sick or peace-loving you were; if someone tried to take what was yours, you had to go after them. If you didn't you were dead meat.

"They took over the whole town?"

He nodded. "You know Tito? Big red truck?"

"Tito the Snack King? The guy who drives around with the Chihuahua?"

"Drove," he said pointedly. "They went after him first. He pulled into a stop—this warehouse he's been going to for years—and these assholes were already there, doors open and everything. Tito's been around the block, right? He doesn't say a word, just walks over to the driver's side of their truck, rips the keys out of the ignition, and throws them on the roof of the warehouse. It's one of those flat roofs, you know, so the keys don't slide down or anything. They just sit there. The muscleman driver comes after him, but Tito shows the guy his tire iron, and that's the end of that. The driver slinks off and Tito goes on about his business. He said that when he pulled out, the asshole was up on the roof on his hands and knees, sniffing around for his keys."

"Good for Tito."

"Wait. That's not the end of the story. Same night, Tito takes his dog for a walk. He lives in Elizabeth, but not a bad area. Nice quiet street. Except that night two big white guys jump out of some bushes and work him and the dog over with baseball bats. They don't take his money or anything. But when it's over, they fish his keys out of his pocket and drop them down a storm drain."

"Did they hurt him bad?"

"Bad enough. Broke one of his arms. Knocked out a couple teeth. Killed the dog, though. And you know how much Tito loved that ugly little mutt."

"Jesus."

My father tilted himself to the left for a few seconds, then back to the right. Neither adjustment seemed to do him much good.

"Listen," he said. "They've got their eye on this construction site I just picked up. It's right on the border between Union Village and Springville. These are bad people, Danny. If they come after you, just walk away. I don't want you getting into a fight with them, understand?"

"They killed the Chihuahua?"

My father jumped up like his chair was on fire and began moving his butt around with both hands in a way that would have seemed obscene, or at least funny, under other circumstances.

"I'm telling you, Danny, these are not nice people."

There was a phone in my room, but I only gave it a fleeting glance before flopping down on my bed and reaching for the copy of *On the Road* on my night table. I'd bought the book a couple of summers before, but for some reason hadn't gotten past the first few pages. The previous night, though, I'd cracked it open again in a fit of restless anxiety, only to find myself startled by its raw hypnotic power. I stayed up until close to three in the morning, my mind racing along with the run-on sentences, the descriptions of driving that just went on and on like the highway itself, as if life were nothing but a perpetual cross-country road trip fueled by diner coffee, crazy talk, and whatever dope and liquor happened to be on hand. It made me want to pick up the phone and wake Matt in the middle of the night—he was staying with Jess in her apartment near Columbia—to find out if he'd ever read it, and how, if he had, he'd ever managed to stand living a normal life afterward, going to classes, eating three square meals a day, only studying the books some stuffy old professor with tuna fish in his beard insisted were the classics. *Man*, I wanted to tell him, *let's just get in the car and drive*, realizing even as I fantasized about this conversation that neither one of us had a car.

The manic buzz of Kerouac had stayed in my blood all day, making the thought of calling Cindy even more impossible than it already was. I mean, what was I supposed to tell her? I wished she wasn't pregnant; I hoped she wouldn't have the baby. The idea of fatherhood seemed like a kind of insanity to me, a nightmare on the level of paralysis or imprisonment. I actually knew one guy at Yale—Stew Johnson from Burlington, Vermont—who'd had a kid freshman year with his high school girlfriend. His parents had money, and were paying to support the kid and his mother while Stew finished college. Every now and then the kid came to visit, and whenever I saw Stew pushing the carriage around campus in his untucked paisley shirt and state trooper sunglasses, smirking like the whole thing was some absurd prank played on him by the gods, I smiled politely and averted my eyes from the spectacle of his misfortune.

But as difficult as it was to imagine turning into a hard-luck version of Stew—after all, my parents didn't have money and weren't going to be supporting anyone while I finished college—it was no easier to imagine going the route of Larry Messina, this guy who'd graduated Harding High a year ahead of me. Larry was the long-time boyfriend of Monica Brady, one of the smartest girls in my class. Monica had received a full scholarship to study engineering at Bucknell, but her plans changed when she got pregnant the night of her senior prom, supposedly the first time the two of them had done the deed. Her father was a bigwig in the Knights of Columbus, and he refused to even consider the possibility of allowing his daughter to get an abortion. Instead a quickie wedding was arranged for late that summer, on what turned out to be a beautiful breezy Sunday afternoon, though the auspicious weather couldn't quite compensate for the inauspicious absence of the groom, who had allegedly gone to a Grateful Dead concert the night before and disappeared into a two-tone VW van with Oregon plates. Nearly three years later, Larry was still at large in the Deadhead underworld and still spoken about in hushed tones by the people who'd known him, as though he were a draft dodger or fugitive from justice, someone who'd brought nearly unspeakable shame on himself and his family. Meanwhile, Monica had taken a part-time job at Stop & Shop, and whenever I shopped there I tried to avoid getting on line for her register, to spare us both the awkward conversations we always seemed to have about what a great time I must be having in college.

If someone had put a loaded gun to my head, I thought I'd

probably choose Stew's route over Larry's, though I wasn't sure if this was a sign of decency or cowardice on my part. I couldn't imagine embarrassing my parents the way Larry had, and I couldn't stand the idea of people I'd grown up with thinking badly about me, especially since a flattering consensus seemed to have developed around town that my life was shaping up pretty well. I'd rather have them feeling sorry for me, like I'd given up the world to pay for one stupid mistake, which was the way everybody felt when they saw Monica Brady biting her lip, trying to remember the price code for eggplant. On the other hand, the last thing I wanted was for Cindy to know that I felt this way, for fear that it would encourage her to actually put me in a position where this hypothetical dilemma would become horrifyingly real, and God only knew what I'd have to do to save myself.

Oddly enough, Cindy and I hadn't really managed to discuss the situation on Friday night, despite the fact that she'd driven all the way up to New Haven to bring it to my attention. The words were barely out of her mouth when she rose from the couch and walked calmly out of the common room with a dramatic flair I hadn't known she possessed, turning sideways to slip between me and Polly on her way to the door. I stood paralyzed in her wake, everyone's eyes on me in the stunned silence that accompanied her departure.

"Holy shit," I exclaimed, grinning the stupid grin I reserved specially for moments of crisis.

If it had been left up to me, I would have just gone into my room and laid down for a while, but it was clear from the intensely interested gazes of my audience that something a little more dynamic was required of me at the moment. I touched Polly lightly on the wrist.

"Don't go anywhere," I told her. "I'll be right back."

She pulled her hand away as though I were a stranger who'd accosted her in the elevator, rather than the guy she'd just been making a spectacle of herself with on the lawn behind the drama school.

"What a night," she muttered, loud enough for everyone to hear.

It was misery to plunge back into the chattering mob on the stairs, squeezing my way through the press of bodies like a salmon struggling in the wrong direction, away from where I wanted to stay toward a destination I didn't want to reach. When I finally managed to force my way to the ground floor and fresh air, I walked straight into Max, who was standing outside the entryway in his bare feet and skintight pajama top, squinting skeptically at our third-floor windows.

"Aha," he said. "Just the man I wanted to see."

"Jesus, Max. Where the hell have you been?"

"Around." He gestured vaguely at the wider world. "Killing time."

"Your mother's pretty upset."

"They still up there?"

"Yeah," I said, wondering where you could go to hide out for nine hours looking like an escaped mental patient, even at Yale. "They'll probably still be there in the morning."

He shook his head. "Bastards can't take a hint."

"They came all the way from Colorado. The least you could do is say hello."

"No," he observed, improvising a little dance to protect his naked feet from the cold slate. "The least I could do is a lot less than that. Where you off to anyway?"

"Tell you later."

I patted his shoulder and looped around him on my way to the York Street entrance, where I found Cindy standing like a prisoner with her face and hands pressed against the bars of the locked gate. I jingled my keys to let her know the cavalry had arrived.

"Need some help?"

She turned slowly. From the look on her face, you might have thought she knew dozens of people at Yale, any one of whom would have been preferable to me at that particular moment.

"What's it look like to you?"

She let me walk her to her car, which was parked right in front of WaWa's. Three homeless guys hit us up for money in the half-block it took for us to get there.

"It's not as pretty as I expected around here," she observed. "You made it sound like heaven or something."

"It's better in the daytime."

"Princeton's a lot nicer," she said, snapping open her purse and fishing around for her car keys. "I thought this was going to look more like that."

"Princeton?" I scoffed. "Princeton's a country club."

"Well, this looks like downtown Elizabeth."

"I like being in the city. It's not so much like being locked in an ivory tower."

She'd gotten too engrossed in her search to answer. She kept pulling things out of her purse—a travel packet of Kleenex, a silver whistle, a squeeze tube of Vaseline—and shoving them back in with small sighs of exasperation.

141

"Damn," she said. "I hope I didn't leave them in your room."

She pried the purse open as far as it would go and pressed her face into the aperture, like an animal trainer peering into a lion's mouth. I struck a pose of pensive waiting, rubbing my chin and pondering the night sky. It felt like we were on public display, lit up like movie stars in the fluorescent glow spilling out from the plateglass windows of the convenience store, which just then seemed to be the dazzling hub of all New Haven. Behind her I could see a pack of local kids gathered in front of Demery's, shouting at passing cars, and farther down, a big silver tour bus parked in front of Toad's. Branford was having a Motown party that night, and you could hear the muffled voices of the Jackson Five rising above the hum of Elm Street traffic.

"I give up," she said finally, turning the bag upside down and dumping the contents onto the hood of her car.

Her purse was normal size, but it disgorged a bewildering tor-

rent of stuff, including about forty sticks of Juicyfruit gum, a bat-
tered issue of *TV Guide* with Peter Falk on the cover, an unopened
deck of cards, maybe half a dozen film cannisters, a few stray
jujubes, the obligatory container of Tic Tacs, and the two letters I'd
written her the previous fall. It was odd to see the envelopes tum-
ble out with the rest of the junk, my familiar scrawl staring back at
me like an old friend. I had to suppress an urge to reach down and
claim them as my own.

"I'm such an idiot," she said, straightening up and laughing. She
reached into a slash pocket on the side of her jacket and produced
the keys with a bashful flourish. "I can't believe I'm so stupid."

She handed them to me for safe-keeping—like my own, they
were dangling from one of my father's souvenir sneakers—and
began jamming the mess back into her purse, muttering all the
while about what an unbelievable ditz she was. I was taking a
moment to admire the contours of her ass in the snug jeans, drawing encouragement from the fact that she didn't look the slightest
142 bit pregnant, when a car pulled up alongside hers and honked
twice. The sound itself was high-pitched, almost toylike, but there
was something urgent and imperious in the delivery, and I
snapped to attention as if my name had been called. The driver's
side window descended in jerks, revealing Peter Preston's agitated
face.

"Where is she?" he demanded.

My instinct was to play dumb, until I realized I didn't have to.

"How should I know?"

He scrutinized Cindy for a few seconds, apparently trying to
determine if she was Polly in disguise, then resumed glaring at me.
His voice was more tentative now, though still aggrieved.

"They said she was with you."

"I guess they were wrong."

He closed his eyes and nodded slowly, trying to get hold of himself. It struck me then with surprising force—saddened me,
almost—that Cindy's Civic was a lot nicer than the professor's dirty
yellow Rabbit. I wondered if he was making some sort of statement

about materialism, or if he simply couldn't afford a better car. The least he could have done was wash the one he had.

"Okay," he said, more to himself than to me. "All right, then."

By the time he drove off, Cindy had finished repacking her purse. She unwrapped a stick of gum and carefully folded it in half before tucking it in her mouth.

"Who was that?"

"Polly's old boyfriend."

"Is Polly—?"

"Yeah."

"She's pretty," Cindy said, with the tone of melancholy objectivity girls often struck when pronouncing verdicts on their rivals.

I nodded without enthusiasm. Cindy risked a smile.

"Sorry to mess up your night."

"That's okay. I guess I deserve it."

She extended her hand to me, open palm up. There was a shy, expectant look on her face, almost as if she were asking me to dance.

"It's really nice to see you again," she told me. "I've been missing you a lot."

I opened my mouth to say something similar but couldn't bring myself to mouth even the blandest pleasantry. *You were a mistake,* I wanted to tell her. *Is that so hard to understand?* In my embarrassment I looked away, pretending to be distracted by the bright interior of WaWa's, full of Yalies loading up on bags of Doritos and pints of Häagen-Dazs. Completely by chance, I found myself locked in goofy eye contact with my dishwashing partner, Eddie Zimmer, who was standing on line with three rolls of toilet paper balanced on top of his head like a smokestack. Lorelei was standing next to him, shaking her head in mock disapproval of his wacky antics. I took a deep breath and turned back to Cindy.

"Your car looks nice," I told her, dropping the keys into her palm. "Do you still wash it every week?"

She hesitated, as if she hadn't heard me correctly.

"I worked hard for this car." There was an edge to her voice, as if she were trying to suggest that I'd been handed things on a silver platter. "It'll be a long time before I can afford another one."

"I'm so far from being able to afford a new car, you wouldn't believe it."

"Yeah," she said, "but when you do it'll be a lot nicer than this."

"I'll keep you posted."

"You do that," she snapped, whirling away from me with startling abruptness, as if she'd just realized she was late for an appointment. She had trouble with the lock, jabbing the key at the target three or four times before hitting the bull's-eye. The button popped with a solid thunk.

"Yo, Danny," a voice called from the doorway. "Heads up."

I turned just in time to see a wobbly missile spinning toward my face. Acting with admirable autonomy, my hands flew up and snagged what turned out to be a roll of toilet paper.

"Nice grab," said Eddie, who was busy shoving the two remaining rolls up and under his Penn sweatshirt in what my George Eliot professor would have called "an act of gender transgression." Lorelei seemed to interpret this gesture as some sort of challenge, and promptly pulled open her army jacket like a flasher to exhibit her own breasts straining against the fabric of a too-small Mötley Crüe T-shirt.

"Mine are still bigger," she said, giggling with drunken pride. She smiled at me, and I felt a sudden jolt of electricity, as if our bodies were tuned to the same frequency. "Don't you think?"

"We'll have to make a more thorough comparison back at my place," Eddie told her, thereby earning himself an affectionate punch in the arm. "Hey, you guys wanna party? We still got half a bottle of tequila left."

I glanced at Cindy, who was staring at Lorelei as if she knew her from somewhere. For a second, in spite of everything, I felt like saying yes. Maybe that's what we need, I thought, a night with Eddie and Lorelei, a lesson on how two totally different people can hang out together and simply enjoy one another's company, free from expectations or recriminations. But then I admitted to myself that what I really wanted was to trade places, to slip off and get drunk with Lorelei while Eddie figured out what to do about Cindy.

"Maybe some other time," I told him.

"No problem. We'll be over at the Taft if you guys change your mind. Apartment seven-B." Eddie glanced at Lorelei. "If her brothers don't kill me first."

Lorelei nodded to confirm this possibility. "They want to kick Eddie's ass."

"Really?" I said. "How come?"

"They're greasers," she said, as if this were a term that people still used everyday. "They think it's funny."

"Nick ratted me out." Eddie shook his head. He was a shaggy-haired Applied Math major who looked like a wiseass even when he was trying to be sincere. "Now Ronny and Tony want to beat the living shit out of me. It's just so *primitive*."

"So what are you gonna do?" I asked.

"I dunno," Eddie admitted, cupping his hands beneath his toilet-paper breasts. "Guess I'm gonna get my ass kicked."

Lorelei snickered. "My hero."

They headed off down the block, laughing as if the whole thing were a big joke. By the time I turned back to Cindy, she had climbed into her car and shut the door. She cranked the window down a couple of inches, looking up at me with a familiar scrunched-up expression.

"You okay?" I asked. "You sure you're all right to drive?"

"I'm fine."

She started the engine and released the brake, staring at me the whole time, waiting for me to say something else. All at once the tears just started dropping out of her eyes and sliding down her face like a special effect, one perfectly formed droplet after the other.

"I'm sorry," I finally managed to stammer, but by that point she'd already pulled away, leaving me alone at the curb with a roll of toilet paper in my hand.

———

I was still deep in a Kerouac trance when my father knocked on my bedroom door a couple hours later. Dean and Sal were zooming through Nebraska in a borrowed Cadillac limousine, going "a hundred-and-ten miles an hour straight through, an arrow road, sleeping towns, no traffic." He shuffled into my room in flannel pajamas and an old plaid bathrobe he only wore when he was feeling sick or downhearted.

"You still up? It's after eleven."

"Reading." I set the book down next to the legal pad I'd been using to copy out my favorite sentences.

"Schoolwork?"

"Pleasure."

He gave me a look I was beginning to recognize, the one that often took up residence on his face when the conversation shifted to matters that could broadly be termed intellectual. His eyes narrowed and he leaned forward a little, concentrating harder than usual, as if he hadn't paid proper attention to me in the previous two decades of our acquaintanceship and now had to play catch-up.

"You even take notes on your pleasure reading?"

"Not usually. This is a pretty amazing book, though."

"Oh yeah? What is it?"

"*On the Road.* By Jack Kerouac."

"*On the Road*?" He studied the ceiling while gently ministering to his ass with his left hand. "Doesn't ring a bell."

"You sure? It's a pretty famous book. Published back in the fifties. This is the Twenty-fifth Anniversary Edition."

"Hmm," he said, moderately impressed. "What's it about?"

I picked up the book and read from the back cover. "'*On the Road* is a saga of youth adrift in America, traveling the highways, exploring the midnight streets of the cities, learning the vast expanse of the land, passionately searching for their country and themselves.'" I left out the part about the book being . . . *an explosion of consciousness—a mind-expanding trip into emotion and sensation, drugs and liquor and sex* . . . and jumped right to the end. " 'It is, quite simply, one of the great novels and major milestones of our time.' "

"I wasn't much of a reader back then." He shook his head, as if saddened by all the major milestones he'd missed out on. "Maybe things would be different now if I was."

"You should check it out sometime," I said, an invitation I would never have extended if I'd thought there was the slightest chance he'd take me up on it. I couldn't quite imagine him reading sentences like the ones I'd scribbled in my pad—*The madness of Dean had bloomed into a weird flower*, say, or *To Slim Gaillard, the whole world was just one big orooni*—and feeling like he was making productive use of his time.

"Maybe I will," he replied, smiling to let me know he was only kidding. "By the way, did you remember to turn on the coffee stoves?"

"Damn," I said. "I'll go do it now."

"Don't forget." His face turned serious. "Maybe you should get some sleep when you come back in. Believe me, four o'clock'll be here before you know it."

Prosaic and dependable by day, the Roach Coach took on a more alien aspect at night, the silver storage cube haloed in moonglow, as if lit from some internal source. Sometimes it seemed as startling to me as a lunar module parked in one of our neighbors' driveways might have been. I tiptoed across the dewy lawn in my flimsy corduroy slippers, unlocked the back door of the cube, and pushed it up on its groaning hydraulic arms to expose the familiar flat faces of the coffee urns and sandwich oven.

Making coffee for a lunch truck isn't anything like making it at home. You can't just flip a switch and expect piping hot coffee to come pouring out a couple of minutes later. The Roach Coach was outfitted with two twenty-two-gallon double-spigot tallboy urns, each divided into two chambers—left side for coffee, right for hot water. The last thing you did at the end of the day was fill the two right-hand tanks almost to the top with water from the garden hose (it's important to use a black hose; water from the green ones tastes like plastic). Then, ideally around ten at night, you lit the propane stoves under the urns to heat the water overnight. While you slept, the ten gallons of water heated to the optimum temperature of two hundred degrees; eight gallons would be poured through a flannel coffee bag containing two pounds of GoldPak restaurant-quality coffee first thing in the morning. The remaining two gallons of water would be held in reserve for the occasional tea drinkers and Cup-a-Soup fans among our clientele.

Aside from failing to extinguish the pilot lights before filling the propane tank—an oversight that could be potentially fatal or at least hazardous to the eyebrows—probably the single stupidest mistake a lunch truck operator could make was forgetting to turn on the stoves before going to bed. Every driver had a cautionary anecdote on the subject—never autobiographical—about some bozo in Bergen or Hudson County, or maybe someone his cousin

had heard about in western Pennsylvania, a fuck-up too stupid or hungover to realize that his urns were dispensing cold water coffee to the biggest, meanest, most unforgiving construction workers around (ironworkers, usually, though some guys substituted pipe-fitters, apparently for variety), who retaliated for this outrage, depending upon who was telling the story, by 1. dumping cup after cup of the undrinkable stuff on the head of the hapless driver until he was thoroughly marinated in the juice of his own error, or 2. teaming up to push the truck on its side, or, most simply, 3. beating the living shit out of the guy, who absolutely deserved it, because people need hot coffee in the morning, and lunch-truck drivers have undertaken a sacred trust to provide it to them wherever they might be.

So I lit the stove and averted these potential humiliations, at least for the time being. My task complete, I lowered and locked the door and headed back across the lawn and up the steps, fully intending to take my father's advice and try to get some sleep. At the last minute, though, I let go of the doorknob and turned around to look again at the truck. It seemed to be shining a little more brightly than before.

A voice spoke in my head.

This is it, it said.

I waited for clarification, but the voice didn't return. I gave a short, uncomfortable laugh and closed my eyes, thinking I must have been more tired than I'd realized. But when I opened them, a strange feeling of lightness filled my body.

I can do this, I thought. I didn't have to be Joe College or Jack Kerouac. I could just be myself, my father's son, living out my life in the town where I was born, growing old among people who'd known me as a kid. I could accept the world I'd unknowingly volunteered for the night I started a new life in Cindy, learn to love her the way my father had learned to love my mother, learn to be content with the things other people learned to be content with. What was in front of me right now—the anonymous suburban street, the silent trees, the truck glowing with its hidden fires—all that could be enough.

"I can do this," I said out loud, and admitting it was such a mighty relief that I might have sunk to my knees there and then if our next-door neighbor, Mrs. deFillipo, hadn't stepped out onto her own porch at exactly the same moment and begun chanting, "Muffin, oh Muf-fin," into the night in such a plaintive, melodic voice that it seemed like prayer enough for both of us.

a shitload of salad

I was back outside a few minutes after four the following morning, feeling distinctly less upbeat. The previous night's epiphany hadn't vanished, exactly, but it had already begun to slip out of reach, like a good dream interrupted by the alarm clock. Part of me wanted to close my eyes and summon it back to life, but the lunch-truck driver in me knew better than to try. If I closed my eyes for even a couple of seconds, I would have passed out in the driveway like the beleaguered heroine of a Victorian novel. The paperboy would have found me three hours later, curled up and snoring on the blacktop in blue sweatpants that spelled out Y-A-L-E in enormous white letters marching all the way down the length of one leg.

I raised the back door again and stared dumbly at the steam leaking out of the coffee urns before remembering that all I had to do was turn on the stove to heat the sandwich oven, which just then contained no sandwiches, only single serving cans of pork and beans, Chef Boy-R-Dee ravioli, and Campbell's soups. Unlike the urns, the sandwich oven wasn't outfitted with a thermostat; if you accidentally left it on over the weekend, it would just get hotter and hotter until the cans exploded. You'd open it up on Monday morning and find the oven dripping with goop, like the walls of a gory crime scene.

Concentrating hard, I twisted the knob and listened for the whoosh of ignition. Then I shut the door and rested my forehead against the cool metal for a couple of minutes before stumbling back inside for a shower, several cups of double-strength Folger's crystals dissolved in hot tap water, and a Snickers bar, the first of many I'd consume in the course of a long day on the Roach Coach.

Most people have never seen a coffee bag. It's a reusable flannel filter that looks like a diaphragm custom-made for a woman who just happens to be a hundred feet tall. You fit it into the basket on top of the urn, dump in a couple pounds of ground coffee, and then pour hot water over it, one gallon at a time, from a stainless-steel pitcher. It's not that easy to do; a gallon weighs a lot, especially when you're balancing on the back bumper of a truck and your hands are shaky from lack of sleep. Aside from not spilling too much, the main thing you need to worry about is keeping track of how many pitchers you've poured. It's easy to space out around five or six, and end up skipping or repeating a number. You wouldn't think an extra gallon one way or the other would make that much difference, but our regular customers were surprisingly discerning in this respect. They could tell from a single sip if we'd screwed up and would be happy to remind us of our failure for months to come.

Once the coffee was taken care of, I made a quick trip to the basement fridge to grab the box of sandwiches my father had been storing there since Friday afternoon, the usual mix of Turkey, Liverwurst, Roast Beef, Ham & Cheese, Taylor Ham & Cheese, Sausage & Cheese, Steak & Cheese, Pastrami & Cheese, Beef Patty on Roll, Monte Cristo, et cetera, all of them wrapped in filmy plastic at the warehouse, their names and prices neatly handwritten on circular white labels. The cold sandwiches went on the bottom shelf of the display side of the truck, right above the ice bed, and the hot sandwiches went into the oven. You wouldn't expect sandwiches to taste that good nearly three days after they'd been assembled, but picky as our customers were about the coffee, none of them ever complained that Monday's sandwiches tasted any less fresh than the sandwiches we served any other day of the week.

It was five thirty by the time I closed the doors, climbed into the cab, and started the engine. I changed the radio station from

WPAT to WNEW, then ran down a mental checklist—made the coffee, got the sandwiches, loaded my change gun—before releasing the parking brake and shifting into reverse. Then I backed out of the driveway and into the world, already singing along with the Boomtown Rats' "(Tell Me Why) I Don't Like Mondays," which the deejay was playing especially for me and all the other poor stiffs just like me, a whole legion of us up before the crack of dawn, driving with our headlights on into the long dark tunnel of another work week.

The warehouse—Central Jersey Lunch & Canteen in Roselle—was hopping at quarter to six, more than a dozen trucks crammed into the narrow spaces, parked so close that their raised doors formed a broken silver roof stretching the length of the lot. I waited in the street until one of the drivers finished loading—it was the surly Lithuanian everyone called Pete the Polack—and then nosed the Roach Coach into the space he'd vacated, threading the needle between Chuckie's Chuck Wagon and a truck I'd never seen before, the door of which sported the words *"Lunch" by Anthony*, painted in flowery cursive and framed by a wreath of laurels.

"Well, well," said Chuckie when I hopped out of the cab. He was a shaggy-haired, foul-mouthed fireplug of a guy with a droopy mustache, wearing his usual cool weather outfit of an orange down vest over a green hooded sweatshirt. We'd gotten fairly close over the previous summer, had even gone out for beers a couple of times at the end of the workday. "Look who's back from the groves of academe."

"*The groves of academe*? Where'd you get that?"

Chuckie looked hurt. He claimed to have taught seventh-grade social studies for a couple of years—at which institution I couldn't imagine—before quitting to take over his father's route, and I'd forgotten how prickly he could be when he thought I was pulling rank on him.

"It's a common fucking idiom," he informed me.

153

"Not as common as you think."

Chuckie grinned to let me know he was giving me a free ride on this one.

"Well," he said, "I'm a special fucking guy."

"Special's a nice way of putting it."

"Whadja take a class in smart-ass remarks this semester?"

"Howdja guess? Don Rickles was a visiting professor in the groves of academe."

"Eat me," he said, giving his genitals a hard upward yank.

"Lovely," I told him, popping up my storage door at the same moment he pulled his display door down. "I miss you when I'm away."

Chuckie breathed into his cupped hands and then rubbed his palms together. His face grew thoughtful and concerned.

"By the way," he said. "How's your dipshit father?"

154   **You entered the** warehouse through a curtain of heavy strips like the ones that slap your car at the car wash, and found yourself in a no-frills supermarket specializing in snack cakes, soft drinks, and paper goods, all of which you loaded onto a flat-bottom cart big enough to sleep on. When you had what you needed, the owner's daughter, a hot number named Sheila who dressed like every day was Saturday night, tallied up your order and sent you on your way with a sweet smile and a few words of encouragement. No money changed hands in the mornings; the whole point was to grab what you needed, throw it on the truck, and get the hell out of there. There would be time enough to settle up at the end of the day, when everybody had cash in their wallets and a little more room to breathe. Besides, Sheila's father didn't have to worry too much about getting paid. If you wanted to drive a lunch truck in central Jersey, you had better stay on Pat Swenson's good side. Either that or make your sandwiches by hand and buy your Tastykakes at the A & P.

The truck was pretty much cleaned out on Monday mornings,

so I loaded up on baked goods, box after box of icing-striped danishes sweating inside their crinkly cellophane, tiny packs of Rich Frosted Mini Donuts, individually wrapped buttered rolls, Mell-O fruit pies, peanut butter crackers, and sandwich creme cookies, not to mention the all-important milk for the coffee—whole, skim, and half-and-half—plus some SnakPak cereals, a big jar of nondairy creamer, a three-week supply of plastic stirrers, two cartons of cigarettes—one Marlboro, one Kool—and a dozen copies of *The Daily News*. Sheila barely glanced at my haul; instead she looked me up and down, smiling like I'd just offered her a surprise gift. She was wearing a black polka-dot miniskirt and sheer black stockings, an outfit my mother would have said she didn't have the legs for, but even so, she was a welcome vision inside that drab warehouse full of wooden pallets and metal racks and cardboard boxes. The only other women in the place were the sandwich makers, four sweet-tempered middle-aged ladies who seemed completely at peace with the fact that they had to wear plastic bags on their heads for eight hours at a stretch.

155

"Oh my," Sheila said, scribbling mechanically on the pad attached to her clipboard. "You get better-looking every time I see you."

"Thanks." I might have been more flattered if I hadn't heard her say the exact same thing a minute earlier to Ted McGee, the three-hundred-pound operator of Fat Teddy's Belly-Bustin' Chow Barge. "You're looking pretty good yourself."

Her expression grew momentarily uncertain, and I wondered if my compliment had broken through her thick shell of boredom to the actual person inside.

"You know what?" she told me. "You're half a dozen short on the buttered rolls."

Chuckie's space was empty by the time I rolled my cart back out to the Roach Coach, but a muscular man with a shaved head and an honest-to-goodness waxed handlebar mustache—I assumed he was the Anthony of *"Lunch" by Anthony*—was busily rearranging the storage compartment of the truck to my right. Like most drivers, my father treated his storage area like a big car trunk, tossing in anything that didn't fit anywhere else, crucial supplies mingling freely with mysterious junk, gold foil coffee packets nesting inside an old sweater, threadbare road maps scattered among stray napkins and winter gloves with cut-off fingertips, a broken change gun resting on top of a case of eight-ounce cans of Bluebird orange and grapefruit juice. One of our shelves was broken, and the other had been permanently bowed into the shape of a smile. Anthony's storage compartment, on the other hand, was more neatly organized than our own display side, everything lined up and readily identifiable, not a candy wrapper or soda can in sight, the metal buffed and gleaming.

"Maybe you can whip mine into shape when you're done with yours," I told him, raising the lid on the sorry jumble of sandwiches and candy and chips that was the business end of the Roach Coach. Everything had shifted during the ride; boxes were out-of-kilter and a couple of roast beef subs had tumbled into the ice bed, which luckily had no ice in it just then. Even the stainless-steel shelving looked dull, as if all the shine had been sucked out of it somewhere down the line.

"I'd need about a week for a monstrosity like that." Anthony's he-man build and novelty mustache made him look a little like a circus strongman in a Fellini movie, but his voice was as pixieish as Truman Capote's. He was wearing jeans, black combat boots, and an unzipped hooded sweatshirt over a white T-shirt, but on him there was nothing casual about this outfit. Everything was crisp, snug, considered. He reminded me of men I'd seen in Greenwich Village, fierce-looking guys who sometimes wore leather chaps over their Levis and checked each other out with startling candor, almost like they were spoiling for a fight.

"I'm Danny," I told him, holding out my hand. "I'll be filling in for my dad for the next couple of weeks."

"Anthony," he said. "Delighted."

"Did you just start this route?" I asked, loading the danishes on the second shelf from the top. "I didn't see you here in January."

"I've been catering for three years," he explained. "The lunch business is an experiment. In fact, it's not really lunch as we know it. That's why I put the word in quotation marks. It's an entirely new vision of lunch."

"How so?" I asked, clearing space for a box of fruit pies at the end of the sandwich shelf.

"I only serve salads and healthy foods. No lunch meats full of nitrites, none of those horrible fattening danishes wrapped in plastic, none of those carcinogen-filled cherry pies." He shuddered at the litany, then steeled himself to continue. "And no Twinkies! My God, are you aware of the crap that goes into Twinkies? If there was a nuclear war tomorrow, people would come back a thousand years from now, open a package of Twinkies, and basically taste exactly what you or I would taste if we opened that same package this very minute. Isn't that frightening?"

"I guess," I said, though I actually felt a certain grudging admiration for a snack cake that could withstand Armageddon. "But who wants to eat salad for lunch?"

Anthony smiled like a man holding a winning hand.

"Come here. I want to show you something."

I followed him around to the display side of his truck, which looked nothing like any other lunch truck I'd seen. Where standard trucks were outfitted with four shelves, Anthony had customized his truck to accommodate six. The shelves contained nothing but plastic containers full of salads, three deep and two high the entire length and width of the box, packed as tight as books in a library.

"That's a shitload of salad," I observed.

"I make them myself."

"You're kidding."

"What? You think they're going to make them here?" Anthony pulled one of the containers out and held it in front of my nose. It was nothing fancy, just iceberg lettuce topped with a couple of cherry tomatoes and a tuft of alfalfa sprouts. "Dollar fifty a pop," he said proudly. "You know how many I sell on an average day?"

"How many?"

"Two hundred."

"*Two hundred?*"

"Two hundred," he repeated, replacing the container on the shelf.

"Where?"

"Hospitals. Big office buildings. Anywhere you got nurses or secretaries. Half the phone company eats salad for lunch."

Anthony pulled his display door shut, then did the same for his back and storage doors.

"I'm telling you," he said, climbing into his cab, "it's the wave of the future."

"Two hundred salads," I said, my incredulous voice drowned out by the sudden roar of his engine.

Anthony waved to me as he backed out of his space, then tooted the horn for good measure as he pulled into the street and headed off to wherever it was you went to sell salad at six in the morning. I waited until he was decently out of sight before pulling a pack of Twinkies off the shelf and tearing open the wrapper. The sweaty yellow missile slid easily off its cardboard base, and I sunk my teeth into it in the spirit of scientific inquiry, tasting the spongy sweetness as if for the first time and chewing thoughtfully, like an archaeologist savoring the glories of a lost civilization.

There was a long line at the ice house, so I left the engine running and hopped out of the cab to resume my conversation with Chuckie, who was standing outside the Chuck Wagon a couple of trucks ahead of me. A cigarette in one hand and a cup of coffee in the other, he surveyed the activity with a calm, almost proprietary air, as if he were the owner of this bustling warehouse instead of an anxious customer cooling his heels while precious minutes ticked away.

"Hey," he said. "Whose dick were you sucking?"

"Pardon?"

"You got white shit on your face."

"Oh that." I wiped at my lips. "It's just Twinkie filling."

"Twinkies? At six in the morning? What are you, eleven fucking years old? You gonna have Ding Dongs for lunch?"

"I was just talking to Anthony back there. He said something that got me thinking about Twinkies, and once you start thinking about Twinkies you might as well eat one. Otherwise you'll spend your whole day thinking about them."

"Kind of like jerking off," Chuckie pointed out.

"Kind of," I agreed, understanding him more readily than I would have liked to admit. "Anyway, Anthony was ragging on Twinkies, how they could survive a nuclear war or something, and I hadn't really eaten breakfast or anything—"

Chuckie cut me off. "You sure you weren't sucking his dick?"

I swirled my tongue around the inside of my mouth.

"Pretty sure. I mean, it's hard to be a hundred percent certain about anything, right?"

Chuckie's expression was stern.

"He's a faggot, you know."

"Yeah, I kind of got that impression. He's got a pretty good thing going with the salads, though."

"Yeah, right," Chuckie scoffed.

"He said he sells two hundred a day."

"That's this week," Chuckie said, shaking his head with sad amusement. "I got one word for your pal Anthony. One fucking word."

"What's that?" I asked, bracing myself for the word in question.

"Crepes," he said. It wasn't the word I'd expected.

"What?"

"Crepes," he said again, nodding like a man in the know. "It's just like crepes a couple of years ago. The next big thing and all that bullshit. Everybody loves crepes, right? America's going apeshit over crepes. Cover of *Time* magazine and everything. You start seeing these crepe places opening up at the malls, people are buying special pans so they can make crepes for supper, you can't wipe your ass without hearing about crepes. This one buddy of mine fell for it. He got his whole truck re-outfitted for crepes. Monsieur Crepe, that was the name of his business. Well, you wanna know where Monsieur Crepe is today?"

"Where?"

"Vocational school." Chuckie laughed to himself, as if this were a particularly pathetic place for a guy who called himself Monsieur Crepe to end up. "Majoring in lawn-mower repair."

"Crepes were a novelty," I said. "Salads are pretty much here to stay."

Chuckie had made his point and wasn't about to get enmeshed in a broader discussion. His eyes had narrowed, and he was gazing into the distance, like a philosopher lost in thought.

"I wonder how they do it," he mused.

"Who?"

"Fags. What would possess them to put another guy's cock in their mouth."

"I guess it's a matter of taste."

"I guess," he conceded. He seemed to be making a genuine effort to take the imaginative leap. "I could see maybe taking it up the ass. Maybe. But sucking another guy's cock? What's the point of that?"

"You don't have to do it if you don't want to," I reminded him. "Unless you go to prison or something."

"I don't even understand how women do it," he confessed.

The conversation trailed off. I could see Chuckie still had some hard questions to work through.

"By the way," I said. "What's the story with the Lunch Monsters?"

That snapped him out of his reverie. He turned to me like I'd slapped him in the face.

"What's the story?" he repeated. "I'll tell you the fucking story."

He yanked open the storage door of the Chuck Wagon and

fished around in the pile of trash he had painstakingly accumulated over the years. It looked like the hopper of a garbage truck in there.

"This is the fucking story with the Lunch Monsters," he said, unwrapping a plaid dish towel to reveal a small, snub-nosed revolver, the kind police officers carried. "I don't care if their boss is Don Corleone himself. They better not fuck with my stops."

I filled the ice bed and propane tank and then I was off, roaring down North Avenue toward Springville Boulevard. It was a pleasure to be driving so early in the morning, before the congestion turned everything sluggish and ugly, before school buses began stopping at railroad crossings and funeral processions began their somber crawls through major intersections, before gigantic trailers had to be backed into narrow loading docks by drivers who would have enough of a challenge navigating a shopping cart into an airplane hangar.

The radio was on, but I wasn't really paying attention to anything but the voice of Jack Kerouac chattering in my head, narrating the morning as if the man himself were sitting beside me in the damp-smelling cab, playing Dean to my Sal, giving the drab landscape back to me in the breathy cadences of beat rapture: *The gas stations sleeping in the heartbroken light of the wild New Jersey daybreak . . . The babbling American madness of the billboards . . . The lost parking meters crying Violation! to the empty spaces on Main Street . . .*

My first stop was Franklin Typographics, a huge print shop that ran three shifts. I set up near the main entrance and caught the people coming and going, the fresh-faced newcomers—*the dreamy typesetters of the Garden State, smelling of sleepy love and the first cigarette of the mad romantic morning*—buying coffee and danishes to take inside, the bleary-eyed nightcrawlers—*zombies of the third shift, heads swimming with commas and despair*—blinking in pained amazement at the light of day, grabbing hot sandwiches and candy bars to fuel their dazed journeys home.

It was all self-service; my job was to calculate prices, make small talk and change, and watch that nobody was ripping anything off. These early stops were just warm-ups, with none of the frantic hurry of factory coffee breaks, where sometimes you had to clear thirty customers in three minutes, a few of them wanting to break big bills, others paying off debts from last week, still others needing credit till payday. Every now and then so many people descended on the Roach Coach at once that the truck actually started rocking on its wheels, and it seemed for a few seconds that it was in the process of getting stripped to the bones, that there'd be nothing left of it when they got finished but four tires, a steering wheel, and a gas tank.

One nice thing about driving a lunch truck: people are almost always happy to see you. You're deliverance, sustenance, a break in the monotony. With me that morning the effect was multiplied by my long absence and the fact that my father was in the hospital. It was old home week, customers I hadn't seen since January slapping me on the back, calling out "Hey kid" and "Where the fuck you been?", making polite inquiries about the state of my old man's bunghole before demanding to know whether I'd finally stopped jerking off and begun applying myself to the serious business of getting into Jodie Foster's pants, as if she and I were the only two people at Yale and destined to get together sooner or later. (Of course, as far as most of them knew, we *were* the only two people at Yale.) Even the guys at the Department of Public Works, whom I'd never met before, were eager to get an update on my progress with Jodie.

"I'm working on it," I assured them. "She can't hold out much longer."

It was like climbing onto a bike for the first time after a long winter. After a few false starts and fumbles the rhythms came back to me, the names and faces, the quirks and the banter. This guy's Walter, that one's Pete. Jerry eats split-pea soup for breakfast. The metal painters wear white protective suits and respirators that look like they were designed to withstand an attack of poison gas. Factory workers owe money; construction workers pay cash. Wooden skids are everywhere, and rusty metal drums. Dexter at the car wash is a dead ringer for B. B. King and buys three cherry pies every morning, one for each of his remaining teeth. "Hoo Wee," he says. "Got to be cherry. Yes sir, got to be cherry." They let you use the bathroom at the carpenter's school; don't forget to wash your hands. The salesmen at Everett Chevrolet are always pissed off; the secretaries from Pearl Industries giggle among themselves. By eleven o'clock I was working the change gun like it was part of my body, adding numbers in my head while taking money from the guy on my right and trading insults with the guy on my left, pausing to scribble a sum on my IOU sheet while shouting out the price of a Milky Way to a regular who knew exactly what it cost, but was hoping I might slip up and maybe charge him a nickel less than my father did. Keeping track of so many little things at once was engrossing and even oddly exhilarating, if only in a private way, like I was putting on a circus act for my own enjoyment, juggling small talk and numbers instead of bowling pins and flaming batons.

163

Without the Union Village stops to slow me down, I made all my coffee breaks with time to spare, and was unusually relaxed for the late morning downtime, which I filled by stopping for gas and making a quick trip to the bank to break a few tens and reload my depleted change gun. Lunch flew by in the same way; by one thirty I was back at the warehouse to pay my bill for the morning and loading up sandwiches for Tuesday. By two thirty I was back home in the driveway, filling the coffee urns with water from the hose. By three o'clock I was back in my room, pulling the covers down and belly flopping into bed, the workday already behind me.

If not for a single strange encounter, I would have counted the day a complete and unqualified success. It happened in the early afternoon, after I had completed my final lunch stop. I was waiting at a red light down the road from this big construction site my father had warned me about—they were building a state-of-the-art twenty-four-hour supermarket and mini-mall on the border between Springville and Union Village—when another lunch truck pulled up even with me on my left. This was a fairly common occurrence, since we all fished in the same greasy waters. Noticing it out of the corner of my eye, I turned to give it the obligatory wave when I was struck by an odd shrinking sensation, as if the Roach Coach and I were suddenly growing smaller.

The truck beside me was all wrong. It was too big, too shiny, out of proportion with the rest of the world. I had to tilt my head to make eye contact with the goon in the passenger seat—my first impression was of a neck with sunglasses—who smiled down at me like we were old pals, his veiny, implausibly muscled arm protruding from the open window at an uncomfortable-looking angle, as if he were signalling for some sort of complicated traffic maneuver the rest of us hadn't been taught in driver's ed. I barely had time to take in the preposterous tires and the amateurish Frankenstein head painted on the box before he spoke.

"Hey chief," he said, laboriously jerking his thumb in the direction of the construction site. "You don't need to go there tomorrow. We'll take care of it, okay?"

His voice was amiable, like he was offering to do me a favor, and I almost nodded my assent before catching myself.

"Excuse me?" I said.

"That stop's ours." With another herculean effort, he pushed the sunglasses on top of his head and squinted down at me. His voice was flatter now, more matter-of-fact. "You don't go there anymore."

I felt a brief flicker of fear, but it vanished as quickly as it came, leaving an unexpected sense of calm in its wake. Now that his whole face was visible, I couldn't help noticing the acne on his cheeks and the almost alarming smallness of his head in comparison with his neck and torso. The overall effect of the mismatch was freakish and comic at the same time, as if a twelve-year-old dork had somehow succeeded in grafting his head onto the body of Mr.

Universe. It must have been to the twelve-year-old that I addressed my next question.

"You got a dentist?"

The non sequitur seemed to annoy him.

"Whuh?" he demanded, sticking his head a little further out the window.

"Make an appointment," I advised, a split second before the light changed and we parted ways. "Tell him you're gonna be missing a whole bunch of fucking teeth."

The whole thing happened so fast it was almost like it hadn't happened at all. And yet this brief exchange dominated my thoughts for hours afterward, filling me with a strange and giddy pride that nothing could dispel, not even the creeping suspicion that I'd just made a really big and really stupid mistake.

the squidman and me

My parents made it home from the hospital around six. They were both in the kitchen by the time I dragged myself out of bed and marched groggily downstairs, my mother crumbling a brick of ground beef into the frying pan, my father standing by the refrigerator, clutching what appeared to be an infant-sized life preserver and looking around uncertainly, as if he'd wandered into a stranger's house by mistake.

"Hey," I said. "How'd it go? Was the exorcism a success?"

"It went fine," he said, in a tone that suggested that even a "fine" hemorrhoidectomy didn't quite qualify as a life-enriching experience. "How'd it go for you?"

"Okay. A little rusty at first. But tell me about the operation."

"Nothing much to tell," he muttered, subjecting me to the kind of scrutiny my mother used to inflict on me when she suspected me of coming home drunk or stoned from a high school party. "You sure you're okay?"

"A little tired," I conceded. "Why?"

"Just curious. I was worried about you today."

I shifted my gaze to my mother. "So everything went okay? No complications or anything?"

My mother looked up from the sizzling meat, arching her eyebrows with playful significance. She seemed oddly merry for someone who'd spent most of her day in a hospital waiting room.

"Let's just say that your father was not exactly a model patient."

He didn't deny it. He just stood there, frowning slightly and shifting his weight from one foot to the other, holding the little tube in front of his chest and squeezing it as though it were an accordion.

"What happened?"

"He was a little—" My mother paused, searching for a word I had a feeling she'd already found. "I guess *uncooperative* is a good way of putting it."

"Uncooperative?"

"Recalcitrant?" suggested my mother. "Bordering on belligerent?"

My father didn't protest any of these characterizations. Instead he just kept staring at me, as if I were the one who'd behaved badly during a minor operation.

"Next time," he said, "I don't care how simple the procedure, I'm going for the general. It's not natural to be awake when they start passing out the scalpels."

"What about those guys in the Civil War?" I reminded him. "Some of them were wide awake when they got their legs amputated. At most they got a shot of whisky or something to calm them down, maybe a bullet to bite on. And the surgeons back then were just using these rusty old hacksaws."

I moved my arm back and forth, grimacing from the effort of forcing my rusty old hacksaw blade through a stubborn mass of muscle and bone. My father raised one hand in a subdued plea for mercy.

"Spare me, okay?"

"By the way," I said. "What's with the inner tube?"

"It's a donut. I'm supposed to sit on it to keep the weight off my stitches."

"Speaking of sitting," my mother said, steering him gently out of the room on her way to the refrigerator, "why don't the two of you go somewhere else and let me cook in peace?"

i followed my father into the living room, saddened to see him walking with such obvious discomfort, tiptoeing almost, his legs wide apart, shoulders hunched and arms dangling, looking like something on the far left side of one of those Ascent-of-Man charts. He stopped in the middle of the room, as if confused about what to do next.

"Want the couch?" I asked.

"Nah." He dismissed the suggestion with an almost haughty air, as if he had not been in the habit of sitting down for many years now and didn't expect to return to it anytime soon. "I'm fine right here."

I plopped down on the couch and smiled up at him. He returned the grin without enthusiasm, slipping his right hand into his pocket and striking as casual a pose as you could strike while holding a rubber donut.

"So tell me," he said, lowering his voice and glancing quickly over his shoulder before speaking. "Did those guys give you any trouble? The ones I was telling you about?"

"You mean the Lunch Monsters?"

He nodded, casting another swift glance in the direction of the kitchen.

"Did something happen today?"

I hesitated for a second or two, long enough to register how pale and tired he looked.

"No," I lied. "No hassles at all."

"Good." It wasn't until I heard the relief with which he uttered the word that I realized how upset he'd been. "I was worried sick. I was sure something had happened."

"Why?"

"One of their trucks was parked across the street."

"Across the street from what?"

"From our house," he said. "Right in front of the Wetzels'."

"When?"

"Just now. A few minutes ago. They drove off as soon as your mother and I turned into the driveway."

"Wow." I tried to look puzzled instead of frightened. "That's pretty weird."

"That's the kind of crap these people pull." He took his hand out of his pocket and crossed his arms on his chest, shaking his head in disbelief. "Can you imagine? Trying to intimidate people in their own homes?"

I looked down at the rug, my mind flashing suddenly on the image of a baseball bat making contact with a Chihuahua. When I looked up, my father had uncrossed his arms and was leaning forward with both hands clasped behind his back. It made me nervous to have him looming over me like that.

"You sure you don't want to sit down?" I asked him.

I was restless after supper. My afternoon nap had revived me, but not to the point where I felt clear-headed enough to start working on my George Eliot paper or even to tackle the last thirty pages of *On the Road*. What I needed was distraction, diversion, a cold beer, and someone to talk to. But I couldn't think of anyone in the immediate vicinity I wanted to call, anyplace I wanted to go.

Yale's spring break was out of synch with those of other colleges—the big weeklong parties in Florida had already come and gone by the time our vacation began—so most of my high school friends were already back to the grind at Rutgers or Kean or Stockton State. Even if they'd been home, though, the sad fact of the matter was that we'd drifted apart in the past year or so in a way that had begun to seem irrevocable.

Zeke, Woody, the Squidman, and Steve—the litany was popular among my friends at Yale—these were the guys I'd hung out with in high school, guys I'd smoked pot and drunk beer and gone to countless concerts with. We called ourselves the Teenage Diplomats, after a phrase from "Blinded by the Light," and made drunken pledges on graduation night not to let college and adulthood get in the way of our friendships. Less than three years later, though, any one of them would have been shocked to get a call from me out of the blue on a Monday night. None of us would have liked to admit it, but I had become for them—as each of them had become for me—a voice out of the past, a guy they used to know.

Woody and Steve were at Rutgers, pledged to the same frat whose name I could never remember—Alpha Kappa Gamma, Gamma Kappa Alpha, Gabba Gabba Hey, it was all the same to me—and excelling at their respective majors (accounting for Steve, food science for Woody) while getting shit-faced three or four times a week and scoring with the occasional freshman girl too drunk to judge them on their merits. Zeke and the Squidman were living at home, Zeke half-heartedly attending Kean while spending the bulk of his time pumping iron at the gym where his on-and-off fiancée, Suzy, taught aerobics. Meanwhile, the Squidman had fallen into a dispiriting rut, loading trucks part-time for Jersey Express, delivering pizzas in the evenings, and spending his nights at the bar in Darwin Lanes, in the company of hard-core alkies and sad old guys in bowling shirts.

True to our pledge, the Diplomats had managed to stay pretty close through our freshman year of college and reached what in retrospect appeared to be the pinnacle of our togetherness the summer after that, when all five of us played softball for the Stay-A-While Tigers, a team affiliated with a bar the Squidman had become a regular at while flunking out of his first semester at Union County College. Most of the teams in our league decked themselves out in double-knit uniforms closely modeled on the colors worn by their professional namesakes—the Chem-Lawn Mets, for example, and Frank's Wholesale Seafood Cardinals—but we just wore sweatpants and T-shirts bearing the two-part motto of our sponsor, *Stay-A-While* . . . *THEN GET THE HELL OUT!*, the first part set in tasteful cursive on the front, the second part printed in huge block letters on the back. Despite our humble attire, we made it all the way to the league finals, where we got our butts whupped by the Lemon Tree Transport Padres, a team of trash-talking school-bus drivers who slid into second with their sharpened cleats aimed at your shins.

During the spring of our sophomore year, the Squidman fell into a bitter argument with the owner of the Stay-A-While, a wide-ranging dispute that began with a disagreement over whether he had, in fact, ordered a bag of peanuts and ended with "you and your asshole friends" being barred from the Tigers the following summer. Even without that particular setback, though, a kind of entropy seemed to have taken hold of the group. Steve and Woody rented a place in Manasquan with some of their frat buddies. Zeke and Suzy announced their second re-engagement, insisting that this time they were serious. That left the Squidman and me to carry on the tradition, or let it expire quietly.

Despite the fact that we only lived a few minutes apart, the Squid-man and I managed to go a full month after I returned from college without even running into each other. When we finally did—I was in the driveway one Saturday morning, hosing down the Roach Coach; he was passing by in his rustbomb Dodge Dart—we greeted each other effusively, trading solemn promises to get together as soon as possible, promises we knew were lies even as we uttered them.

"Call me," he said. "I'm around."

"Sure. Or you call me."

"Whichever," agreed the Squidman. "Doesn't matter."

Our wariness wasn't all that surprising. The Squidman and I were an unlikely pair, and the most tenuously connected members of the entire group. Where the other four of us had grown up together in Darwin and knew each other from kindergarten, Cub Scouts, and Little League, the Squidman—his real name was Paul Skidarsky, his original nickname of "Skid" somehow evolving into "Squid" and finally into "the Squidman"—had only moved into town in eighth grade, and didn't attach himself to our group until midway through our junior year in high school, when he and Zeke took Auto Shop class together and discovered that they both had a lot more fun messing around with engines when they were stoned.

Given all the time we'd spent in each other's company since

then, I still didn't know him very well. For reasons that were unclear to me, he'd been raised by his grandmother and didn't talk much about his parents. He liked AC/DC and Molly Hatchet, bands the rest of us despised, but never complained when we dragged him to concerts by Yes and Genesis, or even Renaissance. (Our moment of greatest intimacy had come during a Richie Blackmore's Rainbow show at the Capitol Theater, when he barfed on my sneakers and promptly fell asleep with his head on my shoulder, where it remained through three raucous encores.) He thought it was okay to call black people "niggers" and seemed annoyed when Steve and I tried to convince him that it wasn't, though he finally agreed not to use the word in our presence. He never talked much, especially if the rest of us were discussing books—we were big fans of *The Lord of the Rings* and anything by Kurt Vonnegut—or current events, and his silences had grown longer as the rest of us got more and more absorbed in our college lives. Still, you never got the feeling that he felt excluded. He just seemed happy to have us all back in one place again.

173

In the end, we spent a grand total of one night together that whole summer, and even that was an accident. Woody and Steve had invited us down the shore for a weekend in late July—there were rumors of wild parties, sorority sisters in microscopic bikinis—but when I climbed into the Squidman's car that Friday night, he confessed that he'd lost the paper with the phone number and directions to the beach house. We tried calling Woody and Steve's parents, but no one was at home in either place. After toying with the idea of driving down anyway and trying to locate them through trial and error—the Squidman was pretty sure they lived on a street with a name like Lighthouse or Seagull or something like that—we finally gave up and decided to stay in town until Saturday morning.

"At least we can fire up a doober," he said by way of consolation, producing a fat joint from behind his ear with a magicianlike flourish.

It wasn't good pot; the buzz I got from it was heavy and vaguely alarming, with an edge of paranoia aggravated by the Judas Priest tape we were shouting over. We smoked the joint down to nothing, driving up and down the familiar empty streets, then stopped at the bowling alley for a couple of beers, making awkward stabs at conversation over the background thunder of exploding pins.

"How's it going with the lunch truck?" he asked, stroking the half-assed mustache he'd been cultivating for the past year or so. Other than that, his appearance hadn't changed much since high school. He still had the same limp hair parted in the middle, still wore the same flannel shirts with the sleeves cut off and the untied work boots that had been his uniform at Harding. I usually got pissed off when my friends mocked me for going preppy on them, but sitting next to the Squidman in my jeans and Hawaiian shirt and penny loafers, I understood why they might think so.

"Not bad. Kinda sucks getting up at four in the morning, though."

"There's a truck that comes by the loading dock," he said. "Coffee tastes like shit."

"Our coffee's not so bad until about ten o'clock. After that it's a little iffy."

A panicky feeling came over me just then, like I'd forgotten to do something important but couldn't remember what it was.

"Fuck," he said. "I wish I hadn't lost those directions. I can't remember the last time I went to a party."

I closed my eyes for a few seconds, trying to get everything to slow down so I could think a little.

"Did you get a weird buzz off that pot?" I asked.

The Squidman ignored my question. He looked me over for a few seconds, like he was trying to figure out if he could trust me.

"You wanna go to Cousin Butchie's?" he asked. "I bet Jenny's dancing tonight."

Cousin Butchie's looked like a regular neighborhood bar, except for the fact its only neighbors were a few rundown houses on one side and the Bayway Refinery on the other, a sprawling, mysterious facility fenced in and lit up like a maximum-security prison. Every time I saw the storage tanks, dozens of them laid out in neat rows like a suburban development, I couldn't help remembering the massive explosion that had ripped through the refinery when I was a kid. Even eight miles away in Darwin, the sky had turned a bright blazing orange, and people came spilling out of their houses in pajamas and robes, pointing heavenward and wondering out loud if the Russians had started World War III.

Despite the universally glowing reports I'd gotten from my friends, it struck me as soon as I coughed up the three-dollar cover and stepped inside that Cousin Butchie's wasn't a place you came to have fun. There was a charge in the air, an aura of bottled-up tension and impending violence; with each step I took I felt myself becoming younger and younger, a little boy wandering into a circle of embarrassed and angry men. They were working men, mostly, guys in dusty jeans and steel-toed boots who probably bought their coffee off a truck, clutching beer bottles and staring at a sullen Puerto Rican girl in moccasin-style go-go boots and a feathered headdress who was gyrating to that song about how "they took the whole Cherokee nation, and put us on this reservation."

The Squidman and I claimed a pair of stools and ordered expensive beers. The bar was circular, and I found myself struggling not to make eye contact with the man directly across from me. He was about my father's age and I had him pegged for a salesman of some sort, a chubby, exhausted-looking guy in a rumpled gray suit with an overstuffed three-ring binder resting on the bar next to his bottle of Bud. The stools on either side of him were empty, and I couldn't help wondering what would drive somebody like him to a place like this at ten o'clock on a Friday night. His studiously blank expression only changed once the entire time we were there, after a black dancer wearing a leopard-print G-string squatted right in front of him and shook her ass in his face for a long time. When she finally stopped, he looked like a different man, his eyes bulging and his mouth hanging open, his whole face shining with a look of awestruck gratitude. He took a bill out of his wallet and waved it back and forth over his head until the dancer took pity on him and did it again.

There were five girls trading off in a round robin, dancing for a song or two, then making way for the next. Each one had her own meager costume and matching style of music. Besides the Puerto Rican Cherokee and the black woman, who had a kind of Sheena thing going (her signature tune was Jethro Tull's "Bungle in the Jungle"), there was a voluptuous California girl ("Surfin' USA"), and a petite Asian woman in a waitress uniform ("Brass in Pockets," followed, for some reason, by Aretha Franklin's "Respect"), and finally Jenny, who came bounding out to "Sugar, Sugar" by the Archies in an honest-to-goodness Harding High cheerleader outfit, complete with saddle shoes and green-and-gold pom-poms.

It was a surreal moment, made even stranger by the fact that I didn't recognize her right away. Part of it was that she'd dyed her hair black since I'd last seen her and was wearing it in pigtails, but

mostly it was just the sheer incongruity of the costume. If they'd given out an award for the girl least likely to be mistaken for a cheerleader at Harding, Jenny would have been a shoe-in. She'd always been perversely proud of her identity as the school slut and was probably as scornful of the perky and cliquish cheerleaders as they would have been of her.

Even if you hadn't been her classmate, though, it wouldn't have taken you long to figure out that Jenny hadn't logged a lot of hours at pep rallies, or in drama class, for that matter. Her impression of a cheerleader was fairly minimal. It basically consisted of shoving the pom-poms in one direction and jutting her hips in the other, and then reversing the procedure, all the while making absurdly lewd faces at the audience. When this got old she did a few jumping jacks and then gave up on the pom-poms altogether, tossing them over her shoulder to a wiry bouncer with a slicked-back Sha Na Na haircut whose job it was to collect the discarded items before they fell into the hands of the paying customers.

The next segment of her routine played off the illusion—given the skimpiness of the G-string, it was a fairly convincing one—that she wasn't wearing anything under her short pleated skirt. She skipped a quick circuit around the elevated walkway, flipping up her skirt every couple of steps to give the viewers a good peek at what was underneath. The Squidman, who was normally pretty shy around girls, clutched my arm as she approached and let out a roar of delight when she gave us the obligatory eyeful.

"All right!" he bellowed, pumping both fists in the air. "Woo-hoo!"

Pleased by his enthusiasm, Jenny skipped back in front of us and gave a brief encore performance for our benefit, adding a couple of well-rehearsed bumps and grinds to the mix. The way the walkway was rigged up, my eyes were level with her knees, so I had to tilt my head at an uncomfortable angle to look at her face. I wondered for a second if she might recognize me, but she just kept staring at nothing, her eyes glittery and hollow, as she ran her hands slowly up her thighs and over her breasts.

She stripped before the next circuit, gathering the sweater over her navel and lowering it a couple of times before pulling it off completely. Wriggling out of the skirt with a similar lack of ceremony, she kicked it through the air to the bouncer, and then, for the first time since she'd made her entrance, really started to dance, turning in slow circles so that everyone could appreciate her small upturned breasts, bare except for the nipple-concealing pasties required by state law, and the shapely contours of her ass.

I had been mildly troubled by the other dancers, embarrassed and aroused by the spectacle of their near-nudity at the same time that I was amused by the goofy theater of it, but with Jenny these mixed feelings intensified to a different level of magnitude. I was riveted by the sight of her, but also a little sickened, like I was looking at something I shouldn't have been allowed to see. My face burned as I watched her make her way slowly around the platform, pausing for a few seconds in front of each audience member so he could have a chance if he wished to reach up and tuck some money into her G-string.

"Woo-hoo!" the Squidman was screaming beside me. "Shake those titties!"

She was on the other side of the bar at the time, a few stools down from the salesman, but she turned and did as he'd requested, raising her arms and arching her back to give her breasts more forward thrust. That was when our eyes met. I felt the shock of recognition when it happened, saw the momentary flicker of startled displeasure pass across her face before she turned away from the Squidman and me, and got back down to business.

Her reaction caught me off guard. I'd gotten the impression that lots of our high school classmates had been coming to see her dance—the Squidman claimed to have caught her act a half-dozen times—so it wasn't like she objected in principle to being ogled by people she'd grown up with. And it wasn't like I was a special friend or enemy of hers, either. I'd barely exchanged a word with her in high school—she had dropped out in the middle of junior year, after getting pregnant by one of the Coletti brothers, all three of whom had allegedly taken turns with her in their backyard toolshed—and had hardly given her a passing thought since the day I'd left for college.

The last time Jenny and I had had anything to do with each other was way back in the summer between seventh and eighth grade, when we'd been part of the same big group of kids who hung out at the town-sponsored recreation center at the Little League. Even then she was way beyond me, letting high school boys get her stoned and take her out to the woods, but sometimes during the day, we'd kill time playing nok hockey or ping-pong, Jenny holding a cigarette in one hand and a paddle in the other, a box of Marlboros tucked inside her tube top. She never talked much or bothered to laugh at my jokes, but she didn't seem to mind having me around, either.

The only problem we'd ever had came at a dance near the end of the summer, when a bunch of us—five or six boys and Jenny—

were playing tag in the outfield. At some point, tag changed into something else, with whatever boy was It chasing after Jenny and tagging her on the chest or ass, copping as much of a feel as he could before she squirmed out of his grasp. Everyone was doing it, and Jenny didn't seem to mind; she just let out this weird high-pitched giggle whenever anyone groped her. Then she always ran after another boy and tagged him to keep the game going.

Finally my turn came and I ran after her like everyone else, my heart pounding like crazy. In the parking lot, the band had just started up again after a break, grinding out "Sunshine of Your Love" at a brutal and exhilarating volume, and I could feel the music surging through me as I chased her. The game had pretty much been confined to left field until then, but this time Jenny just kept running, a lot faster than I'd thought she could go, past the scoreboard, almost to the right field line. I was just about to grab her when she stopped in her tracks and turned around.

"Don't," she told me, breathing hard and holding both hands in front of her chest.

"What?"

"It's over," she panted. "I quit."

"What?" I repeated. She was wearing a tight shirt, a dance leotard with glittery planets painted on the front, and I couldn't keep my eyes focused on her face. "You can't just quit. I have to tag you."

"Come on," she said, not quite pleading, but still holding her hands up, as if she thought I might take a swing at her. "Just cut it out, okay?"

"It's not fair. Everyone got to tag you but me."

Jenny bought time, looking off toward the first-base bleachers. A bunch of older kids were sitting with their backs to us, facing the band.

"Can't you just leave me alone?" she asked.

"Please?" I whimpered. "It'll only take a second."

She stared at me for a moment, then dropped her arms in defeat. Saturn was located over her left breast, and that was where I placed my hand. I'd never touched a girl like that before, and it felt great. I cupped her breast from underneath, lifting as gently as I could, testing the weight in my palm, listening to the sound of my own breathing. If she hadn't yanked my hand away, I might have stood like that for hours.

"Okay?" she said, glaring at me with helpless fury. "Are you fucking happy now?"

A long time had passed since that night at the Little League. The Coletti brothers and lots of other guys had done lots of worse things to her in the meantime. She was a professional stripper who'd had her baby taken away by the state and put into foster care. It was hard for me to believe that she'd even remember that stupid incident at the dance, or hold it against me if she did. But when she finally came around to our side of the bar, she rushed past the Squidman and me without even stopping, not giving us the chance to add our carefully folded bills to the impressive bouquet of money that had sprouted between her hips.

"**I don't know** what was wrong with Jenny tonight," the Squidman observed, reaching into the open sack of burgers between us. "She's usually a lot more friendly. Once she even came out and talked to me during her break."

"It was weird seeing her up there." We were perched on the warm hood of his car in the parking lot of the White Castle in Union Village, our customary destination after a night on the town. "I mean, imagine if you had a sister and that was what she did for a living."

The Squidman chuckled lasciviously. "I wish I had a sister who did that for a living."

"Why? What good would it do you if she was your sister?"

"I don't know," he admitted. "Maybe she could introduce you to her friends or something."

"I guess. But would you still want to go out and see your sister and her friends dancing naked in front of a bunch of strangers?"

"If they looked like Jenny I would."

White Castle hamburgers are small and square, not much bigger than a driver's license, and it wasn't unusual for me to consume ten or twelve in a sitting. That night, though, despite a wicked case of the munchies, I found myself feeling a little queasy around burger number six.

"Damn," I groaned. "I can't eat as many of these as I used to."

"You're not quitting, are you?" The Squidman sounded concerned. "We still got a half a bag to go."

"I don't know. My stomach feels like the Love Canal."

He studied me for a couple of seconds, puzzled by the reference, then decided to let it pass.

"I guess we can save the leftovers," he said. "Then we won't have to stop for breakfast tomorrow morning."

"Cold ratburgers for breakfast?" The thought made me shudder. "You're kidding, right?"

"They're not bad," he said, a bit defensively. "I do it all the time."

The Squidman slid another burger out of its little cardboard sleeve and stuffed the whole thing straight into his mouth. He chewed slowly, his eyes narrowing in contemplation, like a connoisseur searching for the precise adjective to describe the miracle taking place in his mouth.

"I wish we'd made it to that party," he said finally. "Those college girls are pretty hot."

"You visit Woody and Steve a lot at the frat house?"

"Not really. Not since Halloween."

"How come?"

He shrugged, shook his head, then shrugged again, as if the whole thing were too complicated to go into. Against my better judgment, I reached into the bag for burger number seven.

"You know what would be cool?" he said. "If you could join a frat without going to college. That would be pretty cool."

———

On the way home, he invited me back to his house to watch a porn movie. He said he had a projector set up in his basement and five or six different movies, all given to him by this retired guy he'd gotten to know at the lanes. The guy apparently had an extensive collection and had started giving the Squidman the stuff he'd gotten sick of.

"One of them's this lesbian fistfucking thing," he said, shaking his head in respectful amazement. "This girl's whole hand disappears."

By then my gastric distress had reached a crisis point. The fumes from the leftover burgers weren't doing me much good, nor was the Squidman's choice of topics.

"Yeesh," I said.

"See for yourself." He made a fist and slowly straightened his arm. "It's only like ten minutes long."

"I don't think so," I said, pointing discreetly at my stomach by way of explanation.

"You sure? It's pretty unbelievable."

"Maybe next time. Right now I kind of need to get to a bathroom."

He nodded, unable to conceal his disappointment, and then fell into a deep silence that lasted all the way to Darwin. I just sat there, trying not to move or think too hard about the pressure in my abdomen. Just saying the word "bathroom" out loud had made everything that much more urgent.

"You ever seen a porno movie?" he asked, as we pulled to a stop at the traffic light by the Hess station.

"Once," I said, staring desperately at the light, hoping to change it from red to green by sheer force of will. "At college."

Even as I said this, I wished I could take it back. Freshman year I'd gone with a couple of roommates to a soft-core midnight feature at the law school, which had been interrupted by a feminist group that had burst into the auditorium and begun chanting, "Shame! Shame!" and "Women are not Meat!" One of the protesters was a girl I worked with at the art and architecture library, someone I'd thought of as a friend, and she refused to talk to me for months afterward. The whole subject remained a touchy one for me, a can of worms I didn't feel like opening with the Squid-man, especially in my present condition.

He didn't press for details, though. He just turned to me with a certain amount of pride and said, "Bet it didn't have any fistfucking, right?"

By the time we pulled up in front of my house, I had broken out in a cold sweat. I said good-bye through gritted teeth and hurried inside as quickly as I could without actually breaking into a run, something I'd learned from experience could be counterproductive at a moment like that. I still wasn't right the following morning, so the Squidman had to go to Manasquan without me. The Friday after that I had my first date with Cindy, which gave me a standing excuse to avoid him for the rest of the summer, an excuse it turned out I didn't need, because he never called me again, either.

the emperor of ice cream

Sang called from California around nine o'clock. It was a huge relief to hear his voice, to remember that I wasn't lost in space or marooned on a desert island.

"Hey," he said, his tone friendly and cautious at the same time. "How's it going?"

My nerves were pretty much shot. For the past hour and a half I'd been bouncing around the room like a caged hamster, traveling a fidgety circuit from my bed to the window, where I checked the street below for signs of the Lunch Monsters, and then over to the bookcase, which I scanned in a halfhearted way for something that might save me from lying back down on my bed and staring some more at the bewildering paragraph in *On the Road* that began, "Remember that the Windsor, once Denver's great Gold Rush hotel, and in many respects a point of interest—in the big saloon downstairs, bullet holes are still in the walls—had once been Dean's home . . ." before giving up and returning to the window.

185

"Not bad," I replied. "How's it going your way?"

"Okay. Except for the blind date my folks set up for me. They think I need to meet some nice Korean girls. Like Yale's not full of them."

I was intimately familiar with Sang's position on Korean girls and the tension it caused between him and his parents. He had nothing against going out with them per se, but, as a committed pluralist and enthusiastic participant in the sexual melting pot, he objected strenuously to the idea that he was *supposed* to go out with them, and even more strenuously to the idea that he was more or less required to marry one at some point down the road. Not to mention the fact that—according to Sang, anyway—most Korean girls still believed that they needed to remain virgins until their wedding day, a tradition he respected from a cultural and intellectual standpoint, but found to be a bit of a drag on a day-to-day basis.

"Know anything about the girl?"

"Not much. Her name's Katie Kim. She's a junior at Wesleyan, and she's out here visiting relatives. Her uncle's my uncle's old school chum or something."

"Where you gonna take her?"

"Nowhere. She's coming over with her aunt and uncle in about an hour."

"Katie Kim," I said. "Katie Kim. You gotta admit, it's kind of a cool name. I've always liked women who alliterate. Greta Garbo. Sally Struthers. Katie Kim. If I were you, I'd keep an open mind."

"I guess." The pause that followed felt purposeful rather than awkward, as if Sang wanted me to know that he wasn't going to let the conversation wander any further afield than it already was. Even though I knew he was home in Pacific Palisades, probably gazing out the sliding glass doors that overlooked the ocean, I pictured him sitting on the beat-up couch in our common room, running one hand over the brushy stiffness of his crew cut, a somber, almost paternal expression on his face. "That was a pretty gnarly scene the other night."

"You're telling me."

He couldn't help laughing. "That was quite a look on your face when you opened the door."

I laughed too, re-imagining the scene from his perspective. "I thought I was about thirty seconds away from getting really lucky."

"That Polly . . ." he said, his voice trailing off in admiration.

A fresh wave of desolation washed over me, along with a sense of injustice I knew better than to put into words. For months I'd been biding my time, waiting for the planets to come into alignment just so I could be alone with Polly. To have come so close and still have had it taken away was almost too much to bear.

"You okay?" he asked.

"Yeah. Tell me something. How long did she stick around?"

"Who, Polly?"

"Yeah."

"Not very long. Maybe a minute or two. Why?"

"Just curious."

He must have heard the disappointment in my voice.

"What did you expect? I mean, what was she supposed to do? Sit down and make small talk with the Friedlins till you came back? *If* you came back." Sang's voice grew sober and neutral. "So, what's up with you and Cindy?"

"Nothing."

"What do you mean?"

"We haven't really talked yet."

I could sense his mystified disapproval from three thousand miles away.

"Don't you think you should?"

"I keep meaning to call her. There's just a lot going on around here. My dad had his hemorrhoid operation and we've been having a weird situation with the lunch truck and—"

"Danny, you've really got to call her and talk this over. It's not fair to leave her hanging like this."

"I know."

"If you talked to her a month ago, maybe you wouldn't be in this bind right now."

"I know. I know. Fuck."

"Call her," he instructed me. "Tonight. Right after you hang up with me, okay?"

"Okay."

"Promise?"

"Promise."

"She's cute too," he said, after a brief pause to clear the air. "I can see how you fell for her."

Right then, I almost blew up at him. *Fell for her?* I wanted to scream. *I didn't fucking fall for her. I was just stuck here in this*

hellhole, driving a lunch truck all day and trying to find a little
company so I wouldn't have to spend my nights listening to Judas
Priest and watching fistfucking movies. It was just a stupid little
diversion that got out of hand, that's all it ever was. But I didn't say
any of it. I took a deep breath and got ahold of myself.

"I'm glad you liked her," I said.

"Call her," he repeated.

"Right this minute," I assured him.

I meant to. I think I really meant to. I had the phone off the
hook and everything when it occurred to me that Cindy wasn't
the only person who might have been frustrated by my silence
over the past couple of days. Distracted as I'd been by more
immediate dilemmas not to mention shamed by the memory of
how I'd been forced to abandon her on Friday night—I'd done
my best to shut Polly out of my mind. But now, quite suddenly—
it must have been Sang's assumption that to praise her, it was suf-
ficient simply to utter her name—I found myself overwhelmed
with longing for her, or at least for the sound of her voice,
some sort of long-distance reassurance that she wasn't lost to
me forever.

Polly liked to complain about how her father was never home,
but it was Mr. Wells who finally answered on the seventh ring,
barking out the word "Hello," in such a way as to make it unmistak-
ably clear what an enormous inconvenience and potential waste of
valuable time it was for him simply to have to pick up the phone.
Polly had described him as a thwarted, gentle soul, a brilliant tax
attorney who lived to paint watercolor landscapes on the weekends,
but he sounded to me like the kind of guy it would be best not to
cross.

"Yeah, uh, hi," I mumbled, meek as a seventh grader whispering
into a pay phone outside the 7-11.

"What?" he demanded. "Would you speak up?"

I cleared my throat and forced the words out at an audible volume.

"I'm, uh . . . looking for Polly."

"Who's calling?"

"Uh . . . Danny."

"Danny?" he repeated, as if there were something preposterous about the name.

"I'm a friend of hers from college."

Polly seemed groggy, and I wondered for a second if I'd dragged her away from a nap. But then I remembered that it was nine thirty at night, hardly optimum nap time, even for a college student.

"You okay?" I asked.

"Not really. I've been killing myself over this paper for my Stevens and Frost class. It's just a stupid little close-reading exercise. I should be able to do it with one hand tied behind my back."

"Which poem?"

" 'The Emperor of Ice Cream.' I'm analyzing the sexual imagery."

"So what's the problem?"

"I don't know. I mean, I see all the code words and hidden meanings. I just don't know what to do with them."

"Can't you just say that the poem seems to be about one thing, but really it's about sex?"

"But I don't even know what it seems to be about. Isn't that a little weird, when you can understand the hidden meaning, but not the surface?"

"Maybe you could finesse that and get right to the sex."

"But what's it saying about sex?"

"Beats me," I admitted. Not having read the poem, I was on shaky interpretive ground.

"And who's the emperor of ice cream?" Her voice broke as if she were on the verge of tears. "I've read the thing a million times, and I still don't know what the title means."

"It's a catchy title," I observed, hoping to extricate myself from the nitty-gritty of her analysis.

"You know what the worst part is?" she continued. "I could pick up the phone and call Peter, and he'd just laugh like I was an idiot and say something like, *Can't you see it? Hamlet is the emperor of ice cream.* And as soon as he said it, it would all be completely obvious."

I should have seen that coming. It wasn't possible for us to have a conversation without Peter Preston popping up at the most inopportune moment. *Well, excuse me,* I wanted to say. *Excuse me for not being a Yale professor with a Ph.D. from Berkeley. Excuse me for not being able to identify the emperor of ice cream.*

"Why don't you do a Frost poem instead?" I suggested. "I bet 'The Road Not Taken' is full of hidden sexual imagery too."

"I don't think so," she said. If she detected the sarcasm in my voice, she kept it to herself. "I'm determined to nail this down. How will I survive in grad school if I can't even do a five-page explication?"

"You'll figure it out. Sometimes you just have to keep banging your head against the wall until something comes loose."

"Or you suffer irreversible brain damage." She laughed in spite of herself. "I may have already reached that point."

"So anyway, I was just calling to apologize. For the way things turned out the other night."

A moment of uncertainty followed, as if my reference to "the way things turned out" were as inscrutable to her as a line from a Stevens poem. But then it fell into place.

"So what happened?" she asked. "Is she getting an abortion?"

"I wish."

"She wants to keep it?"

"I haven't talked to her about it. But she doesn't really believe in abortion."

"Wow."

I didn't know what to say after that, and a deep silence opened up between us, almost like the line had gone dead.

"I'm sorry," I said. "I wish this wasn't all so messed up."

"You don't need to apologize," she assured me. "The whole thing was hopeless from the start."

"Hopeless? What do you mean?"

"It should have been obvious, Danny. Peter wasn't going to let it happen."

"Peter? What's Peter got to do with it?"

"He always gets what he wants. I don't know why I even bother to fight it."

"Peter had nothing to do with the mess between me and Cindy," I reminded her.

"I know," she said, but there was something grudging in her concession, as if she didn't really believe that on some level Professor Preston hadn't orchestrated the entire fiasco.

"Jesus, Polly. He's not God."

"You don't know him," she insisted.

"He's not even the emperor of ice cream."

She waited a couple of seconds before responding. The pause lasted just long enough for me to realize my error.

"Speaking of which," she said, "I really need to get back to this paper."

"I really miss you," I blurted out. "I'm going crazy down here."

"I know." There was a kindness in her voice that hadn't been there before and made me wonder if things weren't quite as hopeless as she claimed. "I'll see you in a couple of weeks."

"Maybe we can go dancing or something," I suggested. "I really enjoyed that."

Polly laughed out loud, as if I'd made some sort of joke.

"You were a wild man," she told me. "Where'd you learn to move like that?"

It poured on Tuesday and Wednesday, and I spent a lot of time thinking about how much it sucked to be driving a lunch truck in the rain. Traffic was heavier than usual, but business was light. No matter how careful I was, I somehow managed to get a load of cold water dumped on my head and down my neck every time I raised or lowered the doors. My clothes were soaked, my fingers achy, my customers grumpy. An average of three people per stop felt compelled to ask if it was wet enough for me, and at least one appeared genuinely interested in receiving an answer.

I knew it was useless to curse the weather, but I couldn't help myself. The rain affected me less as a natural phenomenon than as a personal insult, a taunting reminder that I was cut out for finer things than selling soggy sandwiches to grumbling factory workers in a relentless March downpour. When the Lunch Monsters failed to show at the construction site, I saw it more as a sign of good sense than as evidence of a possible surrender.

Sang called again on Wednesday evening to get an update on my negotiations with Cindy. He was usually a mellow guy, an unflappable adherent of the live-and-let-live credo that was California's contribution to the world, but that night he lost his temper.

"I can't believe it," he said. "I can't believe you're being such an asshole."

"Give me a break," I said, realizing even as I uttered it that I'd made the same plea to Max on Friday afternoon.

"You of all people," he continued, in a thoroughly disgusted voice. "The Working-Class Hero. Mister Man-of-the-People. You're as big a snob as Dobb Stoddard."

"Dobb Stoddard?" I said, wounded by the comparison. Dobb was a columnist for the *Yale Daily News,* a tweedy arch-conservative who made William F. Buckley seem like a beer-swilling regular Joe in comparison. In his columns, he expressed frequent and heartfelt nostalgia for the days when Yale was all-male, predominantly WASP, and everyone wore ties to dinner. "That's a low blow."

"Well, you deserve it. You can't just get a girl pregnant and then pretend she doesn't exist."

"It's weird," I explained. "I really do want to call her. But there's this—this mental block or something that keeps holding me back."

"That's not a mental block. You're just a wuss."

I opened my mouth to protest but no words came out. A hard ball of something was rising in my throat, and it took everything I had to force it back down.

"I'm scared," I whispered.

"Of what?"

I squeezed my eyelids shut to trap the welling tears, but they oozed out anyway.

"Of ending up like Seth." I was mortified by the weepy tremor in my voice. "It was like he dropped off the face of the earth. He was one of us, and then he just . . . disappeared. It was like he died or something."

"Seth was depressed. You're just being a selfish jerk."

By that point it was too late to defend myself; all I could do was sob into the phone. It took a minute or two for me to pull myself together.

"Sorry," I sniffled.

"I'm not the person you need to apologize to."

"I'm going to call her," I promised. "I'm going to hang up right now and call her."

"It's your life, dude. Don't call her on my account."

That night, at least, I was as good as my word. I hung up the phone, wiped my sleeve across my eyes, and dialed Cindy's number. The line was busy. It was busy when I tried again five minutes later, and still busy a couple of minutes after that. I would have kept trying, but my father knocked on my door and asked if I wanted to play Monopoly. He'd been cooped up in the house all day and was desperate for some diversion besides the TV. I didn't have the heart to tell him no.

Thursday was a bitch too, a damp miserable slog beneath a seemingly permanent canopy of gloom and drizzle, and a depressing number of my customers had run out of money in advance of payday. When I wasn't entering their debts on the water-swollen legal pad I'd discovered in the storage compartment of the Roach Coach, I tormented myself by drawing up a list of all the great places in the world I'd probably never get to visit—New Orleans, San Francisco, the Mekong delta, the Amazon Basin, Reykjavík, Ketchikan, Baja California—because in all likelihood I'd still be right here five, ten, maybe even fifteen years down the road, a Yale dropout slouching in the misty rain of West Butt-fuck, New Jersey, keeping detailed accounts of the purchases of men who worked their asses off every day and still couldn't afford to pay cash for a liverwurst sandwich and a package of Funny Bones.

In the end, for all my promises to Sang and myself, Cindy was the one who called first. I'd been home for about two hours on Thursday afternoon when my father looked up in the middle of our third game of checkers and broke the news.

"Oh yeah," he said, wiggling a little to position himself more comfortably on the donut. "I almost forgot. Cindy called this morning."

"Who?" I stared at the board with more concentration than the game demanded.

"Cindy from Re-Flex. The one you dated last summer."

"Oh yeah? How'd she sound?" I asked, trying to approximate the tone of someone just making conversation.

He didn't answer right away, and when I looked up he was making a face like I'd just asked him to explain Max Weber's theory of capitalism.

"Whaddaya mean, how'd she sound?"

"I mean, what did she say?"

"She said she wants to cook you dinner."

"Tonight?"

"What am I, your secretary?"

No, I thought. *That would be someone else.*

"Sorry," I said. "Your move."

I picked up the phone after supper with a sense of grim obligation and impending doom, beneath which ran a barely perceptible current of relief. I was finally doing the thing I dreaded, stepping up to learn my fate and take my medicine. At the very least, I'd be spared the agony of further suspense.

"Oh, hi," she said, sounding relaxed and chatty. "You didn't tell me you were driving the truck."

"I didn't?"

"No-o-o. It really threw me for a loop when your dad answered the phone."

"Yeah, well, he had a kind of a . . . minor surgical procedure."

"I heard." Her voice was full of amused sympathy. "I never knew hemorrhoids could get so bad you'd need surgery."

Listening to her, you would have thought everything was fine between us, that we had nothing more to decide than whether to go car shopping or catch a movie. Her tone had me so off-balance I didn't even stop to wonder at the fact that my father had confided the intimate details of his affliction to her. For months he had gone to great lengths to avoid using the word "hemorrhoid" in my presence, instead referring vaguely to "a problem" with his "you know."

"He was in a bad way."

"Poor man. Maybe I should send him flowers or something."

"No need. He's on the road to recovery."

Cindy didn't even pause to signal a change of topic.

"Are you busy Sunday night?"

"Me?"

"Is there anyone else there?"

She was playing with me. I deserved it, but it was the last thing I expected under the circumstances.

"I don't think so."

"You don't think there's anyone in the room, or you don't think you're busy?"

"Both, actually."

"Good. Then come over to my house for dinner. Six thirty okay?"

"You don't have to cook for me, Cindy."

"I'm not cooking for you. I'm just inviting you to dinner. I think it's time we had a talk."

"All right," I said, surrendering to the inevitable. "See you at six thirty."

Even after a morning of uninterrupted sunshine, the supermarket construction site was a swamp of mud when I pulled in at Friday lunchtime. I tapped the horn three times to announce my arrival, and set up shop as close as I could to my usual spot near the storage area for welding generators and bottled gas. A spot check for Lunch Monsters turned up no signs of danger, and in a matter of seconds the Roach Coach was besieged by a horde of smiling, muddy-faced men in hard hats, calling out to one another and jockeying for position on line.

Fridays were different from other days, busier and easier all at once. Lots of guys who'd brown-bagged it all week gave their wives a break and bought lunch off the truck. Sullen, preoccupied men who hadn't looked at me twice in the previous four days suddenly knew my name, wanted to know how I was doing. Half the customers who reached into the ice bed asked if I had any beer in there, and chuckled appreciatively when I informed them that I'd just chugged the last one on my way over. A sweaty kid in a tipped-up welding mask told me he was going camping in Pennsylvania with his girlfriend over the weekend and couldn't wait to get away to the woods, away from all the cars, people, and pollution.

"Away from this fucking thing," he said, jerking his thumb at the skeletal supermarket, the tarp-covered girders rising from the enormous pit, the green-and-white cement mixer hypnotically spinning. "Out of fucking Jersey."

The line had shrunk down to about half its original size when the bronze Continental turned into the site. I spotted it out of the corner of my eye and tracked its progress through the graded but as yet unpaved parking lot without thinking much about it one way or the other. All sorts of people visited a site like this in the course of a day—architects, developers, inspectors, suppliers, salesmen— and some of them drove fancy cars. I didn't really start to pay attention until it pulled to a stop about ten feet from the Roach Coach, and the white-haired guy stepped out.

I was busy tallying orders and making change so I couldn't study him that closely, but my first impression was that he didn't look like an architect or developer or anyone else associated with the supermarket project. Dressed in high-waisted gray trousers and a pale blue windbreaker with epaulettes, he reminded me of someone's prosperous Italian grandfather, a retired guy who spent his winters in Florida and the rest of the year in the old neighborhood, a hunch I based as much on his no-longer-immaculate white shoes as I did on the tan that created an odd affinity between his face and the car. The second thing I realized, after he shut the door and took a few careful steps in my direction, was that he hadn't come for lunch.

One foot propped on the Continental's bumper, he crossed his arms and watched me work. His scrutiny felt benign, but it was unsettling nonetheless. He watched me the way you watch an employee or your own child, someone you have a right to stare at as long and hard as you please, and made it hard for me to concentrate on my work. When I'd finally taken care of the last customer, I turned to face him straight on.

"You want something?"

Instead of answering, he took a few more steps in my direction, resorting to some surprisingly nimble footwork to avoid the puddles. Stopping just outside of handshake range, he rubbed a closed eye with two fingers and spoke without introducing himself.

"You seem like a good kid," he said. "Why you want to make trouble for yourself?"

"I don't want to make trouble."

"That's not what I hear."

"I'm just minding my business," I insisted.

He nodded for a few seconds, as if to imply that my point was taken. Though there was nothing otherwise clownish about him, he had the kind of hairdo I associated with clowns—bald on top, bushy on the sides—and a vaguely melancholy face. There was something about his watery blue eyes that made me think he might listen to reason.

"You really go to Yale?" he asked. I detected a note of skepticism in his tone.

"Yeah. Why?"

"I got a niece goes to Dartmouth." He puckered his lips and made a sucking noise, like there was something caught in his teeth. "She's got a lot on the ball. Pretty, too. Wants to be a doctor." I wondered for a second if he was going to try and fix me up with her, but he tapped himself in the forehead with two fingers instead.

"My son's not like that. He doesn't have a lot going for him upstairs, know what I mean? He's not gonna have all the opportunities a kid like you has." He shook his head, as if saddened by the thought of his son's limited prospects. "Even now, all he wants to do is lift the weights with his buddies. I try to tell him that he's a businessman, that it's not all about muscles anymore, but I can't seem to get through to him. If it was up to him, he'd live in that goddam gym."

"I'm sorry," I told him. "I'm having a little trouble figuring out what any of this has to do with me."

"My guys didn't like the way you talked to them the other day. I think it would be a good idea if you apologized."

"Apologize?" I said. "They started it."

He made the sucking noise again, then reached into his jacket pocket for a cellophane-covered toothpick. He stripped off the wrapper and went to work on one of his top molars, cupping his free hand over his mouth to spare me the gory details.

"For a smart kid, you're acting pretty stupid," he told me when he was finished with the excavation.

"They came after me," I said indignantly. "I was just minding my own business."

He shook his head slowly and sadly, then flicked the toothpick past my ear, in the general direction of the Roach Coach. His voice was soft but firm.

"You don't get it, do ya? It's not your business anymore."

won't that be something

I arrived at Cindy's on Sunday evening with a bottle of rosé and a heavy heart. My misgivings were hardly put to rest by the wonderful aroma of roast chicken that pervaded the house or the casual way she pressed a Molson into my hand before steering me in the direction of the living room, suggesting as she did so that I might keep her mother company while she mashed the potatoes and tossed the salad. This was an unwelcome twist—she hadn't mentioned anything about her mother joining us for dinner—and Cindy noticed my dismay.

"Don't worry about her. If she says anything crazy, just ignore it."

"Does she know—?" Instead of finishing the question with words, I pointed in the general direction of her stomach, struck again by the fact that she looked about as pregnant as I did.

She placed her hand beneath her rib cage and moved it downward, smoothing the fabric of her velour sweater.

"Sort of," she said.

"Sort of?"

She made a face that looked like it might be a prelude to an explanation, but the stove timer erupted before she had a chance to continue. The sound was harsh and mocking, like the buzz that follows a wrong answer on a game show.

"Go on," she said, propelling me out of the kitchen with a gentle, two-handed shove. "You can do it."

The living room didn't look like a chamber of inquisition. Dan Fogelberg was playing at low volume on the stereo and the lights were dimmed as if to set the mood for a romantic encounter. Without rising from the couch, Cindy's mother introduced herself in a soft, halting voice as Nicki. She was a plump woman in plaid pants and a dark turtleneck sweater, her eyes hidden behind gigantic brown-tinted glasses that made her resemble some kind of mutant insect creature in a science fiction movie. A heart-shaped throw pillow was resting in her lap.

"Have we met?" she whispered, mechanically stroking the pillow.

"I don't think so."

I was pretty sure I'd never seen her before in my life—not once, not at the supermarket, not at church, not at any school or municipal function, not even just passing on the sidewalk—a circumstance that seemed pretty close to amazing, considering that I'd lived about a half mile away from her for the past twenty years and was on more or less intimate terms with her daughter.

"I don't get out much," she admitted, speaking in a loud whisper for no apparent reason. "I go to my class and that's about it."

"Your class? What are you studying?"

"This term it's Freud and Literature. I'm trying to finish up my Bachelor's."

"Where?"

"Kean," she said, still whispering as though a baby were sleeping nearby.

"Wow. I can't believe you and Cindy go to the same college. She never mentioned it."

"Our paths don't cross much," Nicki explained. "Cynthia takes all those boring business classes. I prefer the liberal arts."

"Me too," I said, starting to relax a little. Whatever Nicki's agenda was, grilling me about my place in Cindy's life hardly seemed to be at the top of it. On the other hand, it was a bit disconcerting to discover that I might have more in common with the mother than with the daughter I'd gotten pregnant. "So what do you think of the Freud class?"

"The prof's okay," she said, somewhat distractedly. "But I think Freud needs to see a psychiatrist."

I started to laugh, but stopped myself when I realized that she wasn't joking.

"Why's that?" I inquired. I had taken a seminar on "Freud and Philosophy" in the fall, and considered myself something of an expert on the subject.

She leaned forward. I got the feeling she was studying me a little more closely, but those impenetrable glasses made it hard to tell for sure.

"What did you say your name was again?"

"Danny."

"Danny what?"

I told her. Her attention seemed to wander for a few seconds, but then it came back.

"Is your mother Linda?"

I nodded. "Do you know her?"

Nicki ignored the question. "She's big in the PTA, right?"

"No," I said, momentarily thrown by her verb tense. "I mean, she used to be, back when I was in grade school."

Nicki leaned forward even further. She cupped one hand around her mouth, as if to frustrate eavesdroppers.

"They're not fooling anyone," she told me.

"Who's not fooling anyone?"

"The PTA."

I tried to look interested rather than confused.

"What do you mean?"

"Who do they think they're kidding?" she asked, in a tone that mixed pity with contempt for the poor saps who thought they were putting something over on the rest of us. "So high and mighty."

"My mom was an officer for a couple of years," I went on, hoping to get the conversation back on track. "She said the politics got pretty exhausting after a while."

"What do they want from me?" Nicki's voice was louder now; there was a vehemence to it that was hard to connect with the subject at hand.

"Excuse me?" I said, unable to suppress a nervous chuckle.

Just then the light went on in the dining room. I was startled by the sudden flash of brightness, the unaccountably surreal sight of Cindy with a carving knife in one hand and a serving fork in the other.

"I know they're tapping my phone," Nicki stated matter-of-factly. "I can hear the little click when I pick it up."

"Okay, you two," Cindy called out, grinning the way people do when there's nothing to grin about. "Enough chitchat. Time to eat."

204 I looked down at the pale feast on my plate—the moist slices of white meat, the mound of mashed potatoes awash with beige gravy, the golden-brown dinner rolls still smoking from the oven—and wondered how long Cindy had been taking care of her mother. Her parents had divorced when she was in second or third grade, but I couldn't imagine that the judge would have given custody of a small child to a woman who believed her phones were being tapped by the PTA. I wished I understood more about the onset of mental illness, if it built up gradually over the years until a person was irrevocably changed, or if something just snapped one day. My only direct experience was with Seth freshman year, and I'd been too busy trying to keep my own head above water to devote a lot of attention to the sequence of events leading up to his breakdown.

When I looked up, Cindy was smiling at me, as if to ask if something was wrong. I smiled back, feeling like an idiot. She had frequently referred to her mother as "crazy" in my company, but I'd understood the word not as a clinical diagnosis but in its colloquial sense. After all, what person our age didn't think his or her parents were crazy? I used the word to describe my father's habit of eating head cheese every Sunday, and used even stronger terms than that—"sociopathic" was one of my favorites—to characterize my mother's insistence on buying perfumed toilet paper.

"Mom?" said Cindy. "Did I tell you Danny goes to Yale?"

"Yale?" Nicki frowned, as if the name didn't ring a bell.

"It's a college," I added helpfully.

"I know what it is," she informed me. "My brother-in-law's a groundskeeper at Princeton."

"Oh yeah? How's he like it?"

"Fine," said Nicki. "He's only got a year to go before retirement."

"Mom?" Cindy seemed upset. "Uncle Al's dead, remember? We went to his funeral last year." She looked at me. "He had a heart attack on the golf course."

"Did he like to golf?" I asked, thinking that it was at least a blessing to die like that, doing something you enjoyed.

"He wasn't playing," she explained. "He was cutting the grass."

"So what's it like?" Nicki inquired, unfazed by the news about Uncle Al. "Do you like it?"

"It's okay," I said, uncomfortable as usual discussing my college life at home, though I was generally quite happy to talk about Darwin in New Haven. "I'm just about done with my junior year. How close are you to getting your degree?"

"Three more classes to go," Nicki said proudly.

I smiled at Cindy. "Your mom was telling me about her Freud and Literature class."

"Mom." Cindy spoke sternly, like a parent addressing a misbehaving child.

Nicki ignored her, calmly cutting up her chicken.

"That's my class," Cindy told me. "My mother hasn't taken a class in five years."

Cindy washed and I dried. It felt good, this momentary domesticity, even oddly natural, and blessedly free of all the baggage that usually cluttered up the space we shared, making it hard for either of us to actually see the other: tension about our different stations in life, worries about sex or new cars or who had or hadn't read which books, or what my friends at school might think about her feathered hair or the fact that she typed a hundred words a minute. None of the free-floating nervousness that made her babble and me smile stiffly. Just the two of us standing side by side, the sound of running water.

"I really pigged out," she said, squirting what I thought was a shocking amount of dishwashing liquid onto her sponge. "I'm hungry all the time these days."

I was about to say I'd been like that for years when it dawned on me what she was talking about.

"Do you get sick?" I asked. "In the morning?"

"I used to. Everything's a lot better now, knock on wood."

Being the kind of person who took her superstitions literally, Cindy handed me a rinsed plate, set her sponge on the edge of the sink, and turned around to knock three times on the table before returning to her post. I rubbed the plate with my soggy dish towel till it squeaked and shined.

"What's it feel like?" I asked.

We were alone by then; Nicki had begun nodding off midway through dessert, and had excused herself as soon as the table was cleared. Cindy blamed her mother's fatigue on a new medication, and predicted that she would sleep at least until noon. Still, she said, it was better than the alternative. In the old days, Nicki had suffered from some sort of nervous disturbance that left her wide awake in the middle of the night. A couple of times she'd slipped outside for epic nocturnal walks that didn't end until the police found her wandering around at daybreak, exhausted and incoherent, a long way from home.

"What's it feel like?" Cindy touched her stomach and made a

skeptical face, as if this were a question she hadn't considered until this very moment.

"Inside, I mean. Is it any different than usual?"

"Are you kidding?" She laughed out loud. "I feel like there's a factory in there and this baby's working three shifts."

I don't know what it was about this image, but all at once I could see it—the fetus, I mean. Until then, I'd only thought of the pregnancy as a disaster for me, a clot of bad luck gathering like a storm cloud inside Cindy's stomach. But now I could visualize the baby too—my baby. A boy, I thought. A little curly-headed boy nestled inside the cloud, wearing safety glasses and a hard hat, working overtime to get himself born.

I didn't ask permission. I reached out and pressed my palm against her flat stomach. A few seconds later Cindy placed her damp hand over mine, pressing down harder.

"I'm so sorry," I whispered. "I didn't mean for this to happen."

In a firm voice, she told me not to worry about it. She said I'd done her a big favor by treating her so badly, not giving her any excuses to fall under the spell of wishful thinking.

"I do that sometimes." She bit her bottom lip and shook her head, as if ashamed of herself. "It's a bad habit of mine."

"It's not you," I assured her, though she probably knew as well as I did that this wasn't precisely true. "I'm just not ready to be a father. It's not even funny how not ready I am."

She accepted this explanation without protest or visible disappointment, nodding emphatically as though I were articulating her thoughts rather than my own.

"I'm just glad you were honest. The worst thing you can do is pretend to somebody that you're going to be there and then back out. That's what my father did. It's much better to be up front with them to begin with."

"My schoolwork's really demanding," I said, glancing uneasily at the faucet. The water was running full blast while we talked, and it was starting to seem wasteful. "I just can't afford to concentrate on anything else right now."

As if she'd read my mind, Cindy stepped back to the sink and reached for a wineglass on the counter. She swabbed it out with her soapy sponge, then held it under the faucet, letting the clean water overflow the rim for way longer than necessary.

"You're lucky to be going to a school like that. It's too good an opportunity to pass up."

"I know."

"It was interesting to finally see it," she said. "I liked your room-mates."

"They liked you too."

"Really?" She seemed genuinely pleased by this information. "What did they say?"

"I talked to Sang the other night. He thinks you're cute. I got the feeling the Friedlins liked you too."

"They were great. I'm just sorry Max wasn't there."

"He's been having some problems with his parents."

"I know." She gave me a funny look. "He told me all about it.

Five or six times at least."

"He did?"

"We talk a lot on the phone," she said. "You didn't know that?"

I should have known, of course. The evidence had been right there in front of me for weeks. Why else would Max have been so pissed at me? Why else would he have treated my private business as though it were his private business too? Even so, the possibility that he and Cindy might have struck up an independent friendship had never occurred to me. They belonged to different worlds, separated by borders only I was allowed to cross, or so I liked to pretend. Objectively speaking, I understood that it was the height of arrogance to think this way, but it was hard for me to be objective about my own life and harder still not to feel like they'd betrayed me in some way, sneaking around behind my back.

"I know you talked," I lied. "I just didn't know you talked about his parents."

"Are you kidding?" She laughed, scraping a piece of something off a fork with her thumbnail. "That's all he talks about. That and *Taxi Driver*."

"And what an asshole I am."

"That too," she agreed, without smiling to soften the blow.

All that was left to wash was the roasting pan. She transferred it from the counter to the sink and squirted some detergent onto the greasy bottom. When it had filled up with hot sudsy water, she turned off the faucet and wiped her hands on her jeans, leaving sharp imprints on the denim.

"I have such a sweet tooth these days," she said, wandering over to a cabinet by the refrigerator and pulling out a bag of gumdrops. She ripped open the bag and dumped the candies into a bowl. "His parents were a lot nicer than I expected. The way he talks about them, you'd think they were these horrible rich people dripping with diamonds and furs."

"That's what he can't forgive," I explained. "They're not-so-horrible rich people with good taste who love him."

She rolled her eyes, as if to suggest that everyone should have such problems, and popped a yellow gumdrop into her mouth.

"I can't believe they're in Paris." She shook her head in what appeared to be genuine wonderment that anyone could actually be in Paris. "Can you imagine?"

"They travel all the time. Anywhere you can think of, they've probably been there."

"I can't wait to go to Hawaii." She glanced at the clock over the sink as if her flight were departing in a matter of minutes. "I hear it's incredible."

"There's a girl from Hawaii in my entryway," I said, unable to stop myself. I recognized this habit as a bad one, my need to establish a personal connection with any subject under discussion. I hadn't been this way before college, I was almost sure of it. "She says that after you've lived there for a while you don't even notice how beautiful it is. You might as well be in New Jersey."

"Kevin's taking me," she said.

"Kevin?"

"My old boyfriend. We're going there for our honeymoon."

I held up one hand, trying to get her to slow down. The moment of truth had apparently arrived, much sooner than I'd expected, and already I was stumped. I couldn't remember her ever mentioning an old boyfriend named Kevin. In fact, there was only one old boyfriend of hers that I knew of.

"Your boss from Medi-Mart? I thought he was married."

"It's sort of a pre-honeymoon," she admitted. "The divorce won't be final for about a year."

"Doesn't he have kids of his own?"

She looked at me. For the first time all night, I thought I detected signs of hostility in her face. After a few seconds, her gaze traveled slowly downward to the soggy dish towel in my hand, which I'd unconsciously twisted into a tight rope, as if I'd been trying to wring it dry.

210   **The gumdrops were** stale and chewy, with more than enough adhesive power to make you fear for your fillings. Nonetheless, I kept reaching for the next one and the next one and the one after that, matching Cindy drop for drop as she tried her best to fill me in on the strange turn her life had taken.

"I made the decision on the way home from New Haven. The next day I went down to the store and told him I would marry him."

"You told him?"

"Yup."

"And he said yes? Just like that?"

She nodded, clearly gratified by the amazement in my voice.

"He never really got over me. After I broke up with him he kept calling and writing these crazy letters. He said he'd leave his wife, run away with me to California, anything I wanted."

"Did you tell him?"

"Tell him what?"

"You know. That you're pregnant . . . with—"

"With *what*?"

My voice faltered. "Someone else's kid."

"What do you think?" There was something almost playful in her smile, and I could see she enjoyed having the upper hand for once. "He's not stupid, you know."

"And he didn't mind?"

"I don't hear him complaining."

I still felt lost, like I'd wandered into the theater when the movie was halfway over. I needed to backtrack a little, to start somewhere a little closer to the beginning.

"So why did you guys break up in the first place? I don't think you ever told me."

"You never seemed very interested."

"I'm interested now."

She made a face. The mischievous pleasure of a moment ago had faded; she seemed a lot more like herself or at least the version of herself I was familiar with.

"I got pregnant." She glanced up at the clock again. "The fall after we graduated."

"I didn't know that."

"It's not something I advertise."

"So what happened?"

She examined her fingernails. Her voice was soft.

"I went to a clinic."

"Is that what Kevin wanted?"

She seemed impatient with the question, as if I hadn't been listening closely enough.

"He wanted to marry me. That's all he's wanted since the day we met."

"So why didn't you?"

She looked at me like I was an idiot.

"I didn't love him. I thought I deserved to spend the rest of my life with someone I was in love with."

"But you don't think so now?"

I meant the question to sound sincere and apologetic, but it must not have come out that way. Her smile was bitter.

"Right now he seems like a pretty good bargain."

She was watching me closely, and I squirmed under her gaze, grappling with an unexpected sense of loss. I'd never thought of Cindy as a person to be madly in love with, someone you'd ruin your life to run away with. But now that she had revealed herself as precisely this kind of person, I wondered how I'd missed it.

"Anything else you need to know?" she asked me.

I had lots of questions, but it didn't seem like the right time to ask any of them.

"I don't think so."

"Okay," she said. "Then let me ask you something."

"Fire away."

"How do you feel about all this?"

"All this?" I asked.

"Yeah," she said. "This mess we're in."

"That's a hard question."

"Take your time."

I certainly knew how I should have felt. I should have felt awful about putting Cindy in a position where she thought she had no choice but to marry someone she didn't love and even worse about indirectly helping to break up Kevin's family. Most of all, though, I should have felt ashamed of myself for letting another guy take responsibility for a child I'd fathered. This was a direct violation of what I'd been taught all my life was the most basic definition of manhood—a man took care of his kids. You could have the crappiest job in the world, a wife you couldn't stand to be in the same room with, a rustbucket car with bald tires and a cracked windshield, and a house with a leaky roof, but if you took care of your kids, you could hold your head up around anyone. Certainly this was the principle on which my father had based his own life. If it ever slipped my mind, he reminded me every time we saw something on the TV news that mentioned a single mother on welfare. "Where's the father?" he demanded time and time again, his anger undiminished by repetition. "Off making a baby with someone else? Drinking wine out of a paper bag on the street corner? Why don't they ask her where the father is?"

But when I looked inside myself in response to Cindy's question, I could detect only muted traces of guilt and embarrassment, and even then I couldn't help wondering if what I was noticing were not these emotions themselves but the void created by their absence, since what I was mainly feeling just then was a combination of wild gratitude and awestruck relief, as if I'd just been rescued from a riptide or carried out of a burning building. I sat up straight in my chair and let go of a deep breath, like someone who had just completed some serious reflection.

"I feel okay," I said carefully. "This seems like a pretty good solution for everyone involved."

There wasn't much left to be said after that. We exchanged searching looks—mine meant to communicate sorrow, hers stoical determination—and made a few futile stabs at small talk that ended when I looked at the clock and pretended to be surprised at how late it was.

"Jeez," I said. "I better get going. Tomorrow's a work day."

"You sure?" she asked. "Kevin's coming in a few minutes. I thought you might like to meet him. Only if you want to, I mean."

Sometimes people you think you know say things that suddenly make them seem like total strangers. Did she really think I wanted to meet Kevin? Or was she just trying to exact some kind of payback for the humiliation I'd inflicted on her in New Haven? Neither theory seemed to add up—she didn't seem naive enough for the first or calculating enough for the second. Maybe she just thought it was a good idea for Kevin and me to at least know what each other looked like, given the peculiar bond we'd be sharing for the rest of our lives.

"I'd like to," I said, in a tone that clearly indicated otherwise. "But I'm trying to get to bed around nine these days. I can barely open my eyes at four in the morning as it is."

"Whatever," she said. "It was just a suggestion."

Without another word, she got my coat from the hall closet and walked me to the door. She put her hand on the doorknob, but didn't turn it.

"I guess I won't be seeing you for a while," she said.

"I guess not."

She looked up at me, her eyes shining strangely in the dim hall-way.

"You're just going to go back to school and forget all about me."

"No, I won't."

She shook her head, but I didn't know if she was asking me not to talk or apologizing for making a scene at the last minute.

"Cindy," I said.

I put my arms around her, unable to fathom how it had come to this. Her breath was hot and damp against my neck, and I was startled by how good it felt to be holding her again.

"I wish you could have loved me," she said. "It would have been so much better."

I held her tighter, willing myself not to think about the life I wasn't going to have.

"You deserve to be happy," I whispered.

She pulled away with a gasp, looking up at me with an expression that seemed to combine hope and alarm in equal measures.

"We all do," I added, in case she'd misunderstood me. "Everybody deserves it."

I'd long ago formed an image of Kevin as a middle-aged Lothario in a short-sleeved polyester shirt, so it took me longer than it should have to identify the cool-looking guy leaning against his car in front of Cindy's house. He was tall and skinny, with shaggy blond hair hanging past the collar of his denim jacket and a kind of loose-limbed slouch that had probably been perfected during years of smoking in high school bathrooms; he looked like a soft breeze might knock him over. If it hadn't been for his work clothes, the gray trousers and skinny tie, you might have pegged him for a musician, or at least a guy who worked in a record store. He couldn't have been much older than twenty-five.

Cindy didn't flinch when she saw him or make any attempt to conceal the fact that she'd been crying, but she did tighten her grip on my hand as we descended the steps and made our way down the front walk. I lagged a half step behind her to signal my reluctance to everyone involved.

"You didn't have to wait out here," she told him. "You could have rung the bell."

He gave a sullen shrug, sucking long and hard on his cigarette before flicking it onto her front lawn, staring at me the whole time. I made a complicated face in response, trying to convey discomfort, friendliness, and a desire to be elsewhere in a single expression. Probably I just looked like a moron.

"Kevin, Danny," Cindy said, liberating my hand for the ceremonial shake. "Danny, Kevin."

Kevin's grip was as limp and unenthused as my own, and I felt a strange kinship with him when our eyes met. He seemed no more suited for marriage and fatherhood than I did.

"Man," I said, hoping he understood that I meant it as a compliment, "you don't look like the manager of a Medi-Mart."

"Assistant manager in training," he corrected me, smiling sadly. "It just means I have to work nights, weekends, and holidays."

"You'll be a manager soon," Cindy told him.

Kevin didn't dispute this assertion. Reaching into the pocket of his nicely faded jean jacket—I'd never been able to get my jackets to fade like that and would have liked to know his secret—he pulled out a soft pack of Winstons and extracted another cigarette. I tried not to stare as he struck the match and brought the tiny quivering flame to his face, but I couldn't help myself. He blew a cloud of smoke at the sky and watched it dissipate.

"Won't that be something," he said, so softly that it seemed to be addressed more to himself than to me or Cindy.

It was a little after nine when I pulled up in front of my house, late enough that I could light the coffee stoves on the Roach Coach and save myself a trip later on. I'd gotten into the habit of watching my back in the past couple of days, in case the Lunch Monsters decided to pay me the same sort of surprise visit they'd paid to Tito, but that night my mind was elsewhere. The whole way home I'd been thinking about Kevin and Cindy and the baby and myself, wondering if everything hadn't worked out in the best possible way for all of us. Kevin loved Cindy, so he couldn't complain. Instead of being a single mother, Cindy would have a husband and a father for her child, a good-looking young guy with a decent job and not some portly middle-aged lech like I'd imagined. I'd be going back to school, picking up right where I left off. The baby would have a normal childhood, just like the one I'd had, maybe even going to the same schools and learning from some of the same teachers. I felt a small pang of sadness imagining all the milestones I'd miss out on—the first steps, the first words, the birthday parties and school plays and Little League games, the lost teeth and Christmases and trips to the beach and points of historical interest—but the thought that Kevin would be there in my stead seemed right somehow, as if the baby were as much his as my own. I even toyed with a fantasy in which I became rich and famous and returned to Darwin years later as a kind of fairy godfather, showering my wealth not only on the child whose life I hadn't been able to share, but on Cindy and Kevin too, rewarding them for their years of sacrifice, buying them a fancy car and sending them on an all-expenses-paid trip to Paris while Polly and I stayed behind and looked after the kid. I tried not to think about Kevin's broken family or the sadness and fatigue that had come over him when he talked about his job. He'd reminded me of my own father then, and I'd found this association more upsetting than comforting.

I pushed open the back door of the Roach Coach and turned on the burners. Just as the flames ignited, a voice spoke in my head, as loud and clear as if another person were standing next to me. *He died for my sins,* it said. I wasn't religious, so this message caught me completely by surprise. Incongruous as it was, the phrase repeated itself with such urgency that I must have spoken it out loud, even as my attacker came charging across the driveway.

"He died for my sins."

Our driveway was narrow, and I was standing right by the edge, which was a good thing, since I was tackled with such force that my feet left the ground. I landed on my back on the dewy front lawn, the wind knocked out of me by the impact, my arms and legs spread as if I'd been crucified. Stars swam on the inside of my closed eyelids, and a strange calm settled over me as I awaited the first blow. I had already decided not to fight back, but instead to accept the punishment I had so deliberately called down upon my own head.

A few seconds passed, though, and still nothing happened. Cautiously I opened my eyes. Instead of a ferocious goon, I saw Matt crouching over me, looking down with an expression of sarcastic glee.

"What the hell—" I sputtered, too short of breath to complete the question.

"Who died for your sins?" he demanded with a smirk.

I sat up slowly, drawing my knees to my chest and shaking my head to clear away the cobwebs. I saw his paper dining hall cap lying in the driveway, not far from the Roach Coach, and wondered why I felt irritated rather than relieved.

"Kevin," I told him. "Who died for yours?"

vito meatballs

Matt was thrilled by the sight of the Roach Coach in the driveway, as excited as a little kid at the firehouse. "Is this really your truck?" he kept asking me, once I'd picked myself up from the lawn and begun breathing more or less normally. "I can't believe this is really your truck." He begged me to take him for a spin and wouldn't stop until I promised to let him ride shotgun with me in the morning.

His gung-ho spirit faded overnight, however, and he was still fast asleep on my bedroom floor when I tiptoed outside in a chilly dawn drizzle and climbed into the truck. I'd tried waking him at four and then again an hour later, but both times he'd flopped onto his stomach and pulled the sleeping bag over his head. I could have kept shaking and prodding him until he surrendered, but as much as I would have enjoyed his company, I sympathized even more with his desire to remain where he was.

It had been awkward introducing him to my parents so close to bedtime—they were both in their pajamas and less than thrilled to learn that a visitor had arrived, let alone a crazy-eyed stranger in bowling shoes and a paper cap who blithely announced that he'd just been kicked out of his girlfriend's apartment for insulting Emily Dickinson—but once we cleared that hurdle I was surprised at how happy I was to see him. The events of the previous week had left me feeling troubled and isolated, and I was glad to finally be able to talk about them with a friend, a more or less kindred spirit I could count on for unswerving empathy and moral support, if not for good judgment.

On a normal day, my arrival at the warehouse generated about as much fanfare as the appearance of the next garbage truck at the dump. That Monday morning, though, people were waiting for me. I could feel it as soon as I pulled into the lot. The other drivers stopped what they were doing and stared at the Roach Coach as if the Pope himself were perched on top, dispensing his blessings from inside a bulletproof glass bubble. By the time I shut off the engine and climbed down from the cab, a small receiving committee had gathered in my honor in the middle of the lot. Chuckie was there, and Anthony, and Ted McGee, and even Pete the Polack, as well as a couple of guys I wasn't even on nodding terms with.

"Way to go," said Fat Teddy, almost knocking me to the pavement with a friendly swat between the shoulder blades. "Show the bastards what you're made of."

"Kid's got balls," said one of the strangers, a gangly six-footer with a receding hairline and a prominent adam's apple.

"Fock dare modduhs!" exclaimed Pete the Polack, ejecting a gob of spit from the corner of his mouth with startling conviction and velocity. It exploded against the blacktop with a clearly audible splat.

Another stranger, a taciturn guy known as Corduroy on account of the ratty beige sport coat he wore on all but the hottest or coldest days of the year, stepped up and pressed my hand between both of his. His eyes were watery and his breath smelled like last night's beer.

"Your father must be proud," he told me.

"Fock dare sistus!" Pete added for good measure, launching an equally impressive projectile from the other side of his mouth.

"Stand up to the bullies," Anthony added quietly, raising a clenched fist and nodding his approval.

Chuckie placed his right hand gently on my shoulder. His expression was so solemn I thought I was being knighted.

"We're with you," he said. "We're all pulling for you."

"Fock dare dogs!" Pete continued, getting a bit carried away. I thought he was going to spit again to complete the outburst, but this time he just cleared his throat and smiled.

"You goot boy," he told me.

My hero's welcome continued inside the warehouse, where I received numerous pats on the back and muttered words of encouragement that made me feel like the star quarterback must feel in the locker room on the morning of the big game. Even Sheila joined the chorus. She tallied up my order with a few quick scribbles in her pad, then pressed her icy palm against my cheek in an incongruously maternal gesture.

"You be careful now," she told me. "Come back in one piece, you hear?"

i wasn't displeased by all this attention—I wouldn't have objected to being treated like that on a daily basis, in fact—but I couldn't help wondering what I'd done to deserve it. It was true that I'd managed to elude the Lunch Monsters for several days running, but as far as I knew nothing had happened over the weekend to account for the apparent jump in my status between last Friday and today. I loaded up the Roach Coach and headed around back. There was a long line for propane, as usual, but Chuckie was alone at the ice house, so I pulled up behind the Chuck Wagon and jumped out, hoping for some enlightenment.

"Here he is," Chuckie said, announcing my arrival to an invisible audience. "The man himself."

"That's right," I said. "*Ecce homo.*"

I figured the homo thing would get a rise out of him, but he let it pass without comment. He dumped three shovelfuls of ice into his ice bed before pausing to look at me.

"You sure you know what you're doing?"

"It depends," I said. "What am I doing?"

His eyes narrowed; he studied me for a few more seconds, trying to decide if I was pulling his chain.

"You're too much," he said, shaking his head and chuckling

indulgently. Almost immediately, though, his expression darkened. "You want to borrow my piece?"

"Do I need it?"

"I dunno," he shrugged. "Maybe. After what you said to Vito Scalzone . . ."

"Vito Scalzone?" The name rang no bells. "You mean the kid?"

"What kid?" He looked at me like I was being purposely dense. "Vito Meatballs."

"The old guy?"

"Vito Meatballs," he said again, as if this were a household name. "The one and only."

"*Vito Meatballs?*" My heart sank. "Is that really what they call him?"

"Either that or Mr. Scalzone, I guess." Chuckie gave a soft laugh, as if sharing a private joke with himself. "I can't believe you told Vito Meatballs to suck your dick."

"What? Where'd you hear that?"

"Fat Teddy told me."

"Who told him?"

"I don't know. Lots of people are talking about it."

My face got hot. I wasn't an expert on these things, but I had read *The Valachi Papers* in seventh grade and came away from it with a clear understanding that you shouldn't say things like "Suck my dick" to people with names like Vito Meatballs.

"That's bullshit," I said.

"So modest." Chuckie jabbed the shovel into the sparkling pile of ice. "That's one of the things I like about you."

"I didn't," I insisted. "It's just a stupid rumor."

Chuckie must have heard the fear in my voice. He turned around a little too quickly, accidentally tilting the shovel in the process. The ice cubes slid off, raining down on the cracked pavement and scattering like marbles.

"You didn't?"

There was such naked disappointment on his face that I shifted my gaze back to the ground. I wanted to explain that the basic story was right but the details were all wrong, that instead of inviting Mr. Meatballs to perform a sex act, I'd really just advised one of his flunkeys to make a dentist appointment, but the distinction hardly seemed worth making. If the Lunch Monsters felt like making an example of me, setting the record straight to Chuckie wasn't going to change anything. And besides, I was tired of letting people down. It was nice to be the hero for once, if only for a handful of lunch-truck drivers.

"Cock," I explained, crunching an ice cube beneath the heel of my work boot. "Not dick. I told him to suck my cock."

Chuckie hooted with laughter and relief.

"You're too much," he told me. Then he shook his head and patted me on the shoulder. "Watch your back, okay?"

The only other time I'd felt myself in such immediate physical danger was in the spring of my senior year in high school, when I'd gotten myself on the wrong side of a maniacal wrestler named Mark "Psycho Midget" Barnhouse. Though technically not a "little person," Barnhouse was very short, maybe five foot one, with a strikingly handsome face and an impressive weightlifter's torso that began just north of his knees. I'm not sure if he was bitter about this lack of proportionality and as a result felt some compensatory need to prove his manhood through violence, or if he was just a vicious person with unusually stumpy legs, but it was widely accepted at Harding, even by football players who towered over him and outweighed him by fifty or a hundred pounds, that it was a good idea to steer clear of Barnhouse. Don't talk to him, don't look at him, don't even think about him. Stay off his radar screen, because you just don't know what's going to set him off. He beat the crap out of Phil Derry, this totally harmless band nerd, for wearing an ugly sweater. Steve Mullaney, a well-liked jayvee goalie, ended up with a black eye and three stitches in his lip for taking an especially smelly shit in the locker room while Barnhouse happened to be within sniffing distance.

The thing that made Barnhouse so singularly terrifying wasn't his improbable strength, or the obvious pleasure he took in inflicting pain, or his contempt for the widely accepted concept of "fair fighting"—it was his unpredictability. You never knew when or where he might strike. He'd gotten suspended for spitting Tabasco sauce in someone's eyes in the cafeteria during the first week of his freshman year, and after that had made it a point only to go after people off school grounds. Mike Donlevy opened his front door on Halloween night and got socked in the mouth, right in front of his mother, by a suspiciously short trick-or-treater in a Frito Bandito costume. Dave Repetto got his septum deviated in the bathroom of the Park Cinema during a Sunday matinee of *Monty Python and the Holy Grail*. It was like Barnhouse kept a list of people he needed to beat up in his pocket and selected a name off it at random whenever he was in a bad mood. You could offend his sensibilities in September and not find out about it until April, when Psycho Midget materialized out of nowhere and began smashing your head repeatedly against a car door in the parking lot outside Echo Lanes.

Barnhouse was a year older than me, so he wasn't even at Harding anymore when he decided to add my name to the list. The trouble started at the Battle of the Bands, held in the gym/cafeteria of St. Lucy's school in Springville. My friends and I were pushing our way out with the rest of the crowd when I noticed that Zeke had struck up a conversation with Ronnie Barnhouse, Psycho Midget's average-sized younger brother. This might have made me nervous under normal circumstances—Ronnie was only slightly less unpopular and belligerent than Mark—but the Squidman had turned us on to some Thai stick that night, and I was distracted by the realization that everyone around me was wearing Two Shoes, a phrase whose comic potential I had grossly underestimated until that very moment. *I am wearing Two Shoes,* I thought, giggling to myself while Zeke and Ronnie exchanged what appeared to be pleasantries. *And you are wearing Two Shoes too.*

Later, when the altercation was re-enacted, I learned that the conversation was anything but pleasant. Zeke had accidentally stepped on Ronnie's foot during the rush to the exits, and Ronnie had taken offense.

"Hey," he said. "You stepped on my fucking foot."

"Sorry," said Zeke, and because he was as stoned as I was, something about this exchange made him giggle.

Ronnie smiled in return. This was a favorite Barnhouse tactic, to act like your victim's best friend just before you clobbered him, but Ronnie didn't have his brother's discipline, which was one of the reasons people found him merely hateful rather than frightening.

"You better be sorry," he said, the surly tone of his voice cancelling out the lulling effects of the smile.

It was weird, Zeke explained later. Just like that, he wasn't stoned anymore. His head was clear; he saw what was coming from a mile away. He and Ronnie continued walking side by side, out the doors and onto the lawn in front of the school. They had almost reached the sidewalk when Ronnie put his hand on Zeke's shoulder.

"Hey," he said. "No hard feelings."

Even as he said this he was swinging his right fist at Zeke's temple, but it was already too late. Zeke had ducked out of the way and was in the process of delivering what by all accounts was a beautiful uppercut to the tip of Ronnie's jaw. I was looking the other way, at this sweet-faced girl I'd been talking to earlier in the night, the sister of the bass player in Sweet Home Cranwood, a country-rock band that had come in third in the Battle of the Bands, behind Spread Eagle and Total Extinction. Martha was her name, and she smiled and waved to me as she headed across the street with her friends. I was waving back, wondering why I hadn't bothered to ask for her phone number, when I heard the fleshy smack of a landed punch. By the time I turned around Ronnie Barnhouse was flat on the ground at Zeke's feet, looking like he'd been struck by lightning. Zeke was rubbing his hand and smiling down at Ronnie, as though the punch had been offered in the spirit of friendship.

"Fucking Barnhouse," he said, surveying the ring of onlookers that had been called into instantaneous existence by the murmured word "Fight!," repeated by one person after another until it filled the air like the sound of crickets.

What happened next must have happened quickly, but for me it unfolded in the slowest of slow motion, as if everyone around me were moving and speaking through an element more like motor oil than air. The words "Fucking Barnhouse" had barely finished vibrating in my ear when a kind of collective gasp rose from the crowd. The next thing I knew Mark Barnhouse had breached the human ring and was striding toward his brother. He was wearing a green-and-yellow varsity jacket with leather sleeves and a shock of hair had fallen over his forehead, concealing one eye. Ronnie was conscious, but clearly dazed, and I remember being struck by the gentleness with which Mark knelt down and helped his brother into sitting position.

"Ronnie," he said, in the wooden voice of an actor auditioning for a role he'd never get. "Who did this to you?"

To my surprise and dismay, the first person Ronnie looked at was me. I'd felt very much the innocent bystander until then, but all at once fear cleared my head, and I saw that a neutral observer might reasonably assume otherwise. The ring had formed in such a way that the only people inside it were me, Woody, Zeke, and the Barnhouse brothers. I held up both hands in a gesture of surrender and shook my head, but by then Ronnie's glassy eyes had shifted to Zeke.

"Him," he said.

"He started it," Zeke protested, too scared to realize that trying to reason your way out of a fight with Mark Barnhouse was a lot like trying to persuade a dog not to eat a piece of meat on the floor.

"He stepped on my fucking foot," Ronnie Barnhouse complained. His voice was full of grievance, like he might never recover from the indignity of having his fucking foot stepped on.

That was when Mark Barnhouse transformed himself into Psycho Midget. You could see it happen, and the sheer theater of it was weirdly compelling. He stood up, puffed out his chest, and placed his hands on his hips, in a posture borrowed from Mighty

Mouse. It was disturbing to realize how handsome he was, like a movie star or model, from the waist up. He stared at Zeke for a couple of seconds, giving him time to get good and scared, and then took a couple of swaggering steps forward. To his credit, Zeke didn't retreat, even when Barnhouse got within striking distance.

"Go ahead," Barnhouse invited him, extending his right foot rather daintily, until the toe of his work boot was almost touching the rubber tip of Zeke's Converse All-Star. "You wanna step on someone's fucking foot, step on mine."

"I don't wanna step on anyone's fucking foot," Zeke muttered.

"Step on it, you pussy."

Zeke looked at me, silently begging for help. I shook my head, trying to look apologetic. I had already been accepted to college, and the last thing I wanted in the few remaining weeks of my high school career was to find myself on Barnhouse's shit list.

"Come on, big man. Step on my fucking foot."

Zeke turned to Woody this time, and Woody shamed me by responding to the call, shuffling into the danger zone with obvious reluctance and placing his hand on Zeke's elbow.

"Come on," he said. "Let's just get the fuck out of here."

"Yeah," I added, though later none of my friends claimed to have heard it. "Let's just get the fuck out of here."

The only person I'd seen do what Barnhouse did next was Moe of the Three Stooges. Reaching up with astonishing quickness, he grabbed hold of Zeke's head with one hand and Woody's with the other and cracked them together. There was no hollow-coconut sound effect, though, just the sickening thud of solid objects colliding and a moan of disbelief from the crowd as my friends collapsed on the grass, clutching their skulls and writhing around in agony.

Now it was Barnhouse time, two wounded adversaries just begging to be finished off. He kicked Woody in the ribs and then turned to Zeke, who had struggled onto his hands and knees and was looking around in animal bewilderment, a trickle of blood working its way down his forehead. Barnhouse had his back to me, but I could see from the way he was lining himself up—carefully, like a placekicker studying the goalposts—that he was preparing to deliver a savage kick to Zeke's face with his work boot.

There was no way out for me. I could already hear the story as it moved through the halls of Harding, how I'd just stood there and watched it happen. It would be better for me to get my own teeth kicked in than to be forever remembered for that. Releasing a puny war cry of misery and regret, I rushed across the lawn and grabbed Barnhouse from behind, wrapping my arms around him like the sleeves of a straitjacket and locking my hands tight against his abdomen with all the panicky, adrenaline-fueled strength I could muster, apparently knocking the wind out of him in the process.

"What . . . the . . . fuck . . . ?" he gasped, screwing his head around as far as it would go in an attempt to ascertain my identity.

Like Zeke, I found myself in the grip of an uncontrollable desire to reason with him.

"I'm not fighting with you," I explained slowly and carefully, as if speaking to a toddler. "I'm just trying to keep you from hurting my friend."

"Fuck you," he replied, twisting his torso from side to side with furious energy, trying to fling me off his back. My grip began to loosen and I pulled tighter, my fists digging into the cavity below his rib cage. His body went limp again.

"What . . . the . . . fuck . . . ?" he repeated.

I almost laughed out loud when I realized what was happening. Without meaning to, I had given Barnhouse the Heimlich maneuver. As I recalled from tenth-grade Health class, this simple but remarkably effective lifesaving technique worked its magic by abruptly forcing the air out of a choking person's lungs, thereby dislodging stuck food or other obstructions from the windpipe.

Barnhouse caught his breath and resumed struggling; I administered another Heimlich. It was amazing to feel the strength leave his body at my command, to fold him in two with a single jerk of my fists.

228

"You're . . . a . . . fuc . . . king . . . dead . . . man," he informed me.

After a minute or two went by, my exhilarating sense of mastery began to wear off, and I faced up to the difficult reality of the situation. I couldn't hold Barnhouse in this Heimlich embrace forever, but I couldn't let him go either, especially since he seemed to have fallen into the throes of demonic possession. He was bent over in my arms, groaning and cursing and thrashing his head from side to side. I couldn't see his face, but I wouldn't have been surprised to learn that he was foaming at the mouth.

"Let . . . go . . . fuck . . . face . . ."

"I'd like to," I told him. "But I can't."

By that point, Barnhouse was completely doubled over, and was addressing me from the vicinity of my left knee. He slumped even further after the next Heimlich, forcing me into an uncomfortable crouch. I didn't realize that this was a calculated strategy on his part until I noticed a strange tightness and a sudden burning sensation on the meaty part of my calf.

"My leg," I told the crowd, speaking in the calm voice of a golf announcer. "He's biting my leg."

The smart thing would have been to administer another Heimlich, but it's hard to be smart when someone's gnawing on your leg. I unlocked my hands and reached for his face, raking my fingernails across his eye and down as much of his cheek as I could find. He kept biting, though, so I did it again, this time forcing my fingertip against his eye like I was trying to push it through the socket and down into the sinus cavity. The pressure on my leg let up abruptly; Barnhouse was rolling on the ground, holding his face and wailing, "My eye! My fucking eye!"

"You shouldn't have bit me," I told him sternly.

Gingerly, he removed his hand from the wounded eye, blinking like a flashbulb had just gone off. His eye was still there, but his cheek was scored by scratch marks, four parallel gashes traversing his cheek on a diagonal.

"Shit," he said, looking at his hand. "I'm bleeding."

Ronnie Barnhouse picked himself up from the ground and went over to examine his brother's wounds. By then, both Woody and Zeke were back on their feet as well.

"Come on," Woody said, grabbing hold of my arm and pulling me toward the sidewalk. "Let's get out of here."

I turned my head, taking one last look at Barnhouse before slipping through the crowd and away from further trouble. He was kneeling on the grass, holding a pristine white handkerchief to his cheek and glaring at me. I remember being surprised by this; Barnhouse hardly seemed like the kind of guy who carried a handkerchief.

"You're a fucking dead man," he told me again.

I took him at his word. For the next two and a half months, I never left my house without first picking up a smooth gray-and-white striped rock that I kept stashed at the base of a sugar maple in front of our house. In the event of what I saw as an all-but-inevitable revenge attack by Barnhouse, my strategy was simple: I would wait until he got about ten feet away and then I would show him the rock. If he still kept coming, I would throw the rock at his face as hard as I could, and then accept the consequences. I promised myself that I wouldn't chicken out, that I wouldn't let myself run away or beg for mercy or take a beating without fighting back. After all, the only thing Barnhouse had on me was a psychological edge. He was willing—even eager—to hurt me; if I could make myself just as willing to hurt him, the playing field was leveled, and maybe even tilted in my favor, since Barnhouse operated on the assumption that his victims would be paralyzed by fear and were therefore easy prey.

Because deep down I doubted that I was really capable of throwing a rock at someone's head—even Barnhouse's—I spent a lot of time mentally rehearsing my counterattack. Over and over that summer, I lay in bed imagining my enemy's approach, feeling the cool weight of the rock in my hand, forcing myself step-by-step through the sequence of events in which I'd have to let it fly. I could get that far, but I could never quite cross the border of visualizing the impact, of figuring out what would happen—how I'd live with myself—if the rock actually made contact with its target. I understood this failure as a potentially dangerous weakness and tried my best to conquer it. But all this futile mental exertion really accomplished was to make me hate Barnhouse even more than I already did. It wasn't enough for him to terrorize me; he had to poison my mind with fantasies of violence and troubling questions about how far I was willing to go to save myself.

Luckily for me, I never had to find out. A few days before that Fourth of July, the Barnhouse brothers got bored and decided to play hot potato with a lit M-80. Ronnie lost; the tiny bomb exploded in his hand, blowing off two fingers and the thumb, a small piece of which was later reattached by doctors using revolutionary microsurgical techniques.

From what I heard, Mark changed overnight. He walked around pale and chastened and was often seen at church, sobbing as he prayed. Whenever he bumped into people he'd beaten up, he apologized and volunteered to let them take a swing at him, just to even the score. He was so sincere that a couple of people actually took him up on this offer, though later they felt lousy about it.

I didn't see him again until the summer after my freshman year in college, when I bumped into both Barnhouses at the Stay-A-While. Mark waved at me from across the bar and beckoned me over like we were old friends.

"Hey," he said. "Aren't you the guy who gouged my eye?"

"You bit my leg," I reminded him. "I've still got the teethmarks to prove it."

He shook his head. He'd put on a lot of weight and gotten glasses in the year since our fight.

"I'm surprised I didn't give you rabies," he said with a laugh.

Ronnie asked me what I was drinking. He reached into his pocket with his mangled right hand—it looked rudimentary but still functional, a little like a miniature catcher's mitt—and slapped a wad of crumpled bills on the bar.

"This one's on us," he told me.

I was thinking about the Barnhouses that morning as I approached the construction site, my mood swinging wildly between bravado and terror. I was thinking that I was a basically lucky person, that bad situations had a way of working out in my favor, and I was thinking how glad I was that I'd decided to defend myself back then, how much better it was to walk around with a rock in your hand than to cower in your room until it was safe to go back outside. But then the terror kicked in, and I was hearing Barnhouse's voice in my head, telling me I was a dead man, and sounding even more convincing than he had the first time. By that point, though, there wasn't anything I could do about it, because I was already through the gate and inside the site, bouncing over the dirt toward a bunch of guys in hard hats and muddy boots who were busy forming a ragged line in honor of my arrival.

i'm not even here

Whether out of courtesy or calculation, the Lunch Monsters waited until I had closed up shop and was heading out of the site to spring their trap. In an elegantly choreographed example of what military documentaries called "a pincer movement," two of their jacked-up monster trucks—one emblazoned with the crude Frankenstein head I'd seen before, the other with an equally primitive rendition of Count Dracula—converged on the front gate from opposite directions, sealing off my exit. I stopped about twenty yards away and watched as four musclemen spilled out of the cabs and began moving toward me without haste or hesitation across the flat dirt expanse of the parking lot, the emptiness of which was relieved only by the gooseneck light poles that had been cemented into the ground at regular intervals. Given the numerical mismatch, I was relieved to notice that only one member of this contingent, the kid whose dental health I'd threatened, was armed with a baseball bat.

I couldn't say I was caught off-guard. A jittery air of anticipation had hung over the construction site that afternoon as I exchanged money and small talk with my customers, whose number had shrunk considerably since the previous week. A couple of guys insisted on shaking my hand and made cryptic remarks suggesting that they didn't expect to be seeing me again. The young welder I'd gotten friendly with, the one who'd gone camping with his girlfriend over the weekend, seemed particularly concerned for my safety. He was off by himself as usual, perched on the hitch of a spare generator, eating from a single-serving can of ravioli and watching anxiously as I closed up the truck.

"Yo chief," he called out.

I looked up just in time to see a yellow hard hat spinning through the air like a misshapen frisbee. I snagged it with one hand, the brim biting into my palm. Along the back was a piece of duct tape with the word "MURPH" written on it in shaky block letters.

"Who's Murph?" I asked, impressed by the hat's no-nonsense protective heft, the illusion it provided that you could tap dance safely through a downpour of hammers, wrenches, and metal beams.

"He fell off a scaffold," the welder told me. "He won't be needing it anymore."

I pressed Murph's hat more firmly down on my skull, but otherwise made no move as the Lunch Monsters approached the Roach Coach, the kid with the bat leading the procession. He was wearing a gray sweatshirt with the sleeves and collar ripped off, the better to display his meaty biceps and thigh-sized neck. One of the guys behind him was even more pumped than he was, a blond giant with the overcooked, slightly radioactive complexion you could only acquire at a tanning salon. The other two were bodybuilders as well, but they were slipping past their prime, going a bit thick in the middle and thin on top.

I should have been terrified but instead a strange calm came over me, and I found myself thinking, for some reason, of Christmas dinner my freshman year at Yale. My roommates and I had dressed in jackets and ties, as we'd been instructed, and had arrived at Commons to find it transformed by ice sculptures and wreaths made of fresh spruce branches studded with holly berries and pine cones. After being serenaded by a series of singing groups, we were treated to the main spectacle of the evening, a medieval procession in which a whole roast pig—eyes and snout intact, a bright red apple stuffed ignominiously into its mouth—was paraded through the hall like Cleopatra on a wooden bier, held aloft by two grim-looking chefs in puffy hats and preceded by a team of student carolers and bell ringers. I stood at attention along with everyone else, my mouth hanging open in disbelief, feeling like I'd gotten lost a long way from home.

This isn't my life, I remembered thinking. A similar sense of unreality washed over me as the goon with the little head started tapping on the driver's side window of the Roach Coach with the handle of the baseball bat, yelling for me to get the fuck out. *This isn't my life,* I told myself again. *I'm not even here.*

"Get out!" the kid was screaming, his voice muffled by my rolled-up window. "Get the fuck out!"

There must have been something I'd been trying to prove by picking a fight with these guys, but I could no longer remember what it was, or who I was trying to prove it to. I just sat there in the locked cab of the truck with my hands clamped around the steering wheel, smiling stupidly and shaking my head no, as if he were one of those volunteer firemen who sometimes knock on your window at busy intersections on Saturday afternoon, hoping to collect a donation.

"Fucking asshole!" He pressed his face right up against my window, so close his breath left an oval of fog on the glass. My assailant's name, I later discovered, was Junior, but even if I hadn't come across this bit of information, I would have known right away that he was Vito Meatballs' son, the kid without much going for him upstairs. There was something about his face that made you think immediately of his father, even if the impressions they left with you were entirely different. Where Vito Senior seemed avuncular and basically good-hearted, tired in a seen-it-all sort of way, Junior just looked puzzled and mean, like he suspected you were going to put one over on him sooner or later and wanted to wring your neck before you got a chance to do it.

I didn't snap out of my daze until he started whaling on the truck. He seemed to be retreating in frustration at that point, backpedaling away from me in the direction of his buddies, but he stopped suddenly near my front tire, shifting from a right-handed batting stance to a left-handed one, and took a leisurely swing at my headlight, which exploded in a spray of sparkling fragments. Switching back to his right-handed stance, he wandered back to my door, smiling like a genius in the grip of a new idea.

"How you like that?" he yelled, bending his knees and raising the bat like he was posing for a baseball card. The proximity of his massive arm to his chin made his head seem even smaller than it had before. "How you like that, Big Man?"

This time he swung for the fences, the meat of the bat connecting with the metal of my door. It was a savage collision, and several things happened as a result, more or less simultaneously. An alarming thud resounded through the cab, the whump of buckling metal, and I imagined my father at home, doubling over and clutching at his stomach, as though he and the truck were one. I unlocked the door and reached for the handle—I did this on reflex, not really thinking about what I meant to do next—when I realized that my assailant had just screamed and dropped the bat, the way you do when you hit something wrong on a chilly day, the wood shivering your arms and turning your hands to jelly. I followed through with the motion I'd begun—"Hey!" I was yelling. "Not the truck!"—flinging open the door just as Junior bent down to retrieve the bat. The whole sequence couldn't have worked better if we'd rehearsed it: his hands were just inches away from regaining control of his weapon when the bottom of my door caught him square in the forehead, knocking him onto his butt. Before his thugs could make a move to assist him, I was out of the truck, standing over him with the bat in my hands.

I raised the Louisville Slugger like the Sword of Damocles and smiled down upon my enemy sprawled in the dirt. He was ignoring me, looking more pensive than frightened as he massaged the sore spot on his furrowed brow, and for some reason this bothered me.

"This is a really nice bat," I told him, unable to suppress a burst of nervous laughter. "Do you mind if I keep it for a while?"

I should have known better than to taunt him like that, but I couldn't help myself; it was too exhilarating to suddenly have the upper hand, to have won it so unexpectedly in the teeth of such lousy odds. But the feeling only lasted a few seconds, just long enough to mark off the interval between the giddy surprise of knocking him down and the uncomfortable realization that there was no way in hell I was going to hit him or anyone else with a base-ball bat, even after what he'd done to my father's truck—not to mention Tito and the poor Chihuahua—and what he undoubtedly would have done to me if the situation had been reversed.

"Did I mention that I was home-run champ of my Little League?" This wasn't precisely true—I'd always been a better fielder than hitter, as a matter of fact—but it hardly seemed like the moment to be a stickler for the historical record. It was starting to get pretty awkward out there, the two of us frozen like we were posing for a picture, the other three musclemen looking on, pondering their options. "I'm told I have a very natural swing. The trick is knowing that your power comes from your legs and hips, not your arms."

"You fucking hit me you're dead," he muttered, rallying a little. "My boys'll eat you for lunch."

He was right, of course, but only in theory. In practice, his boys were about ten yards away, and I had a feeling that even with a three-to-one advantage, they might be a little reluctant to get much closer.

"You ever drop a pumpkin out a window?" I took a lazy practice swing, the fat end of the bat passing close enough to his face that he must have felt the breeze, but he didn't even flinch. "My friends and I used to do that a lot when we were growing up. It's incredible. The thing just splatters when it hits the ground, just splits right open. All the seeds and pulp and that weird stringy shit come flying out. Kind of like a piñata. You ever go to a party where they had a piñata?"

I swung harder, stepping into an imaginary fastball. The kid was cringing now, holding his hands up in front of his face like a boxer on the ropes. I couldn't help noticing the distinctive gold-and-silver band of a Rolex on his wrist and found myself thinking for some reason of the horsewoman who'd lost hers in the punchbowl. The kid spoke to me through the gap between his forearms. He sounded a bit worried.

"Do you know who my father is?"

"He seems like a nice man." I took another cut, wondering if it could really be true, as Hank Yamashita had once informed me, that Rolexes could cost as much as five thousand dollars. "Some piñatas you hit once, they break right open. Others you got to beat the shit out of to get one lousy piece of candy."

"You shouldn't fuck with my family," he warned me. "I'm telling you this for your own good."

"Thanks." I swung again, and this time he felt it necessary to duck out of the way "I appreciate your looking out for me."

I sensed movement to my right—the goons were closing in slowly—and my concentration faltered. I glanced over my shoulder in the direction of the unfinished supermarket, wondering why none of the construction workers were coming to my assistance. I could see a cluster of them gathered in front of the Port-a-Johns, watching the action from a distance of maybe a hundred yards, which seemed impossibly far away from my perspective. If worse came to worst, I figured I could just drop the bat and run like hell—I doubted any of the weightlifters could catch me—but that would mean leaving the truck behind, something I didn't want to do unless I absolutely had to. Besides, I wasn't sure if it made more sense to run toward the Port-a-Johns and throw myself on the mercy of the spectators or to make a break for the street, which happened to be a lot closer. The Lunch Monsters took note of my confusion.

"Get up, Junior," the blond giant called out, in a calm and confident voice. "He's not gonna hit you."

Junior dropped his guard for a second and looked up at me with a hopeful expression, like a kid asking for permission. I made the mistake of turning away from him and addressing his comrades, who by that point had crept up to within a few feet of the truck.

"Just fucking try me," I said.

The words were barely out of my mouth when I heard a sudden movement and felt Junior's hand on my ankle, the fingers wrapping around the top of my work boot. I tried to hop away—he was lying on his stomach, his arm extended as far as it could go—but precarious as it was, his grip was tenacious. He wriggled forward a bit, raising his left hand to take a swipe at my other leg, his face scrunched and grimacing.

"Yeah!" someone screamed. "Get 'im, Junior!"

You couldn't really say I swung at him. I just sort of let the bat fall in a gentle arc in front of me, a motion not so different from the one you might use if you were cutting grass with a scythe. It was an easy, almost graceful gesture; gravity did all the work. Even so, the impact was more dramatic than I'd expected: the bat bounced off Junior's head like it had just come in contact with a fully inflated tire. At approximately the same instant, he let go of my foot and began screaming and rolling around on the ground like his clothes were on fire. I watched him for a few seconds, trying to gauge the seriousness of his injury, one part of me wanting to get down on my knees and apologize, and another part wanting to hit him again, now that I realized it wasn't as hard to do as I'd thought. In the end, though, I decided to simply act as though I'd proven a point.

"See?" I told his buddies, standing over Junior like a gladiator. "What did I tell you?"

None of them responded. At some point in the past few seconds, they had turned away from the spectacle of Junior's anguish and shifted their attention to the front gate. Their broad backs were blocking my view, so I had to step around Junior—he was calmer now, moaning and cursing at a civilized volume rather than wailing like a wounded animal—to see what was going on. A new lunch truck had just arrived on the scene—it was parked in the middle of the street, its front door flung wide open. I identified it as the Chuck Wagon at almost the same moment I caught my first glimpse of the stocky guy in a green sweatshirt squeezing with some difficulty between the front bumpers of the Frankenstein and Dracula trucks.

Chuckie walked slowly across the dirt lot, his arms hanging loosely at his sides, grinning like he was late for his own party. It was a drab March afternoon, one of those frustrating days when you keep thinking the sun's about to break through, but it never does. The whole world felt flat and dull beneath a low ceiling of clouds. Even the diamond-patterned silver box on the Roach Coach had surrendered its usual luster, mirroring instead the gray monotony of the sky. I think that's why the gun in Chuckie's hand seemed so conspicuous. I could have sworn it was glowing, that his little pistol was the only bright and shiny thing for miles around.

"Is there a problem here?" he inquired.

The Lunch Monsters respectfully assured him that there was not. In fact, one of the older guys reported, they were about to be getting on their way, just as soon as Junior was ready to get up.

"I think he's ready," said Chuckie.

Junior needed a little help getting to his feet, but he actually looked pretty good for someone who'd just gotten beaned by a truck door and a baseball bat in quick succession. At least there was no blood or anything. He rubbed the bump on his forehead and looked around with the slack-jawed bewilderment I often saw on the faces of Yalies who'd nodded off in the library.

"My father's not gonna like this," he told me.

"Mine's not gonna be too crazy about it either," I assured him.

dust in the wind

The first couple of days after his operation, my father had greeted me the minute I walked into the house, peppering me with questions about the day's business. Toward the end of the week, though, his interest had begun to flag, and I'd come home to find him sacked out on the living room couch, exactly the way he was that Monday afternoon—flat on his back, his mouth wide open to the ceiling. He wasn't snoring, exactly, but he was making a weird guttural noise, like a beginning reader sounding out the letter *K*.

"Kuh . . . Kuh . . . Kuh," he rasped, releasing a dreamy, doglike whimper every third or fourth breath. He looked relaxed and innocent, like a man who'd finally found his place in the world.

I left the money and paperwork on the kitchen table and tiptoed upstairs to the bathroom, locking the door behind me and turning on the shower full blast. My parents had recently installed one of those high-tech massaging showerheads. It featured a variety of settings, from a soft spritzer-bottle mist to pulsing bursts of pressurized pellets that might have been shot out of a firehose. I twisted my way through the dial several times that afternoon, soaping in the mist, rinsing in the pellets, soaping in the pellets, rinsing in the mist. If the hot water hadn't given out, I might've stayed there for hours, shrouded by the steam cloud and the pea-green plastic curtain, trying to scrub away the fear with a washcloth.

A towel wrapped around my waist, I pushed open the door of my bedroom and stepped into a maelstrom of scattered books and papers and articles of clothing and sporting goods. It looked as though my closet had become ill and vomited its contents across the bed and floor. For a moment I entertained the possibility that an intruder had ransacked the room, but then I saw Matt sitting at my desk, his back to me and the chaos, calmly reading my Shakespeare essay.

"Well, well," he said. He hardly seemed real to me at that moment, turning slowly in the chair and adjusting his paper cap. "The great sahib returns from the jungles of New Jersey."

"Jesus Christ," I said, letting my eyes rove over the mess, too tired to formulate a fresh metaphor. "It looks like a cyclone hit."

"Hurricane Matt." He smiled proudly. "That's what my mother used to call me."

"Did you find what you were looking for?"

He nodded, flipping the paper to its cover page and pronouncing my title in a stuffy British accent, as though he were the host of *Masterpiece Theater,* his lower lip jutting out like Churchill's.

" 'Bastard Authority: Legitimacy and Subterfuge in Shakespeare's *Measure for Measure.*' " He retracted his lip and shook his head, chuckling like I'd just told him a good joke. His hands bobbled up and down in front of his chest, as though he were juggling invisible oranges. " 'Legitimacy and Subterfuge.' Oh, baby."

"They're actual words," I told him. "You can find them in the dictionary."

His expression grew serious, even a bit skeptical.

"This paper won a prize?"

"Second runner-up. Why? Doesn't it meet your standards?"

I must have sounded annoyed, because he held up his arms in front of his face as if to fend off an expected attack, momentarily re-creating Junior's posture in the parking lot.

"It's good," he conceded. "But your thesis feels a bit contrived. I mean, isn't it unfair to superimpose a modern definition of political legitimacy on a pre-modern text?"

"I can't talk about this now," I told him, trying not to think about the weight of the bat in my hand, the cringing expression on

Junior's upraised face. "I'm totally exhausted. I'm going into my parents' room to take a nap, okay? I'll be out in an hour or two."

When I got downstairs, Matt and my father were immersed in another round of Monopoly. I wandered over to the dining room table and pretended to be interested in who was the thimble and who was the winged shoe, and which of them owned the houses on Baltic and St. James. My father asked Matt to give him a minute.

"Come into the kitchen," he told me. "I need to have a word with you."

His expression was unusually serious, and I wondered if he'd somehow found out not only about the damage to the truck, but about the whole mess I'd gotten myself into over the past few days.

"Not in here," he whispered, when I stopped in the front of the dishwasher. "In there."

Following him into the cramped and chilly laundry room, I couldn't help noticing that he was walking a lot better, almost like a fully evolved specimen of *Homo sapiens*. His face looked better too, unshaven though it was. His eyes were clear and engaged with the world; he seemed ten years younger than he'd been a week ago, as if the doctors had removed a lot more than one angry hemorrhoid.

"Shut the door," he said.

"I'm sorry," I told him, before he could get another word in. I had already made up my mind to throw in the towel. The moment had arrived for me to take full responsibility for the lies and the damage to the truck, to apologize for putting his business and his only child at risk for no good reason. "It's all my fault."

He looked confused.

"It is?"

"It's not?"

"You didn't invite him," he said with a shrug. "He just showed up on our doorstep."

"Who, Matt?"

243

He gave me a disapproving look, as if I wasn't keeping up.

"Don't get me wrong, he's okay in small doses, he really is." He frowned, running his fingers through his matted hair. "Why don't you take him somewhere tonight? Out to a movie, whatever. My treat."

"Sure," I said.

My father smiled with relief. "And maybe bring him with you on the truck tomorrow?"

"No problem. I could use the company."

"Great." He started toward the door, then stopped. He looked happy and relaxed, eager to return to his game. "Oh, by the way, how'd it go today?"

I hesitated only a fraction of a second.

"Fine," I told him. "Business as usual."

"Forget the car," Matt called out, as I headed down the front walk toward my parents' Malibu wagon that evening. He was standing by the dented front door of the Roach Coach with a hopeful, slightly pathetic expression on his face. "Let's take the truck."

I was all set to explain that insurance regulations prohibited me from using the truck except for business purposes—we ignored this prohibition all the time, but Matt didn't need to know that—when it occurred to me that it wouldn't be a terrible idea to get the Roach Coach out of the driveway for a few hours. I still hadn't told my father about the damage and didn't want him to discover it on his own if he or my mother decided they needed to make a quick run to the store while Matt and I were out. He might have overlooked the dent—it wasn't that conspicuous in the dark, just a slight depression in the thorax of our cockroach—but he wouldn't have missed the busted headlight.

"Okay," I said, reversing course with the aid of the decorative lampost at the edge of the lawn. "Might as well get used to it. You're going to be spending a lot of time in there in the next few days."

I should have known Matt would get all excited when he saw the hard hat resting between us on the seat. He picked it up and studied it from a variety of angles, as though it were a relic from a distant and peculiar land.

"Well, lookey here." He brought the helmet to his ear and rapped on it with his knuckle. "Is this real?"

"I guess. As real as anything can be in an age of mechanical reproduction."

"Cool." He jammed it on over his dining-hall cap, then scooted over on the seat to admire himself in the rearview mirror. "I've always wanted one of these."

Against my advice, he was still wearing the hard hat when we entered Scotch-Wood Lanes, his face set in a proud smirk as he acknowledged the grins and double takes his headgear inspired in the league bowlers, men around my father's age sporting team shirts with the names of factories and small businesses sewn on the back: Freez-Dry Incorporated, A-1 Paving, Reliable Auto Body, On-Time Trucking. I picked up the pace a bit, hoping to place some distance between us as we approached the front desk.

Scotch-Wood was cramped and a bit dingy, but I'd chosen it that night as a protest against Echo Lanes, which had recently installed a computerized scoring system. Magic Score was supposed to be the next big thing in bowling technology; it kept track of your score automatically and displayed it on an overhead screen, relieving you of the burden of calculating it on your own with pencil and paper. Aside from insulting the intelligence of bowlers, the real purpose of Magic Score was to prevent you from taking a couple of practice rolls before starting your game, a custom some consultant must have decided was costing the bowling alley thousands of dollars a year in lost revenue and needed to be eliminated.

There was no computerized scoring at Scotch-Wood, just like there was no "pro shop" in the lobby and no foreign beers at the bar and no new coat of varnish on the saggy, dead-sounding lanes and not a lot of chitchat from the surly-looking guy who was reading

The New York Post at the front desk. He waited until he was finished with his article to peer at me over the top of his glasses, which were perched way down over the tip of his nose.

"Yeah?"

"Any lanes free?"

"One or two?"

"Just one."

"Shoes?"

"Eight and a half."

"No halfs."

"Make it eight."

The counterman was a wiry, gray-haired guy with a military-style crew cut. Without looking, he reached into one of the cubbyholes behind him, grabbed a pair of worn-out, three-tone rentals and slapped them on the counter. One glance and I knew exactly how they'd feel: loose and slippery and none-too-sanitary, the soles eroded to the thickness of cardboard. The counterman shifted his glance to Matt, taking in the hard hat with a look of mild, pursed-lip disapproval that passed so quickly I wasn't sure if it had been there at all.

"What about you?"

Matt looked puzzled.

"What about me what?"

"Shoes," I said, acting as his guide and interpreter. "What size?"

"Don't need 'em." He stepped back, lifting one foot to show the guy his footwear. "I'm an owner, not a renter."

Something changed in the counterman's expression. What had been a kind of habitual, impersonal disdain turned into something much more specific and hostile. He laid his glasses down on the folded newspaper and stood up a little straighter, smiling the way people do when they don't like you and don't care if you know it. He wasn't a big man and he wasn't young, but reading glasses aside, there was something in his ramrod posture and quiet self-confidence that made you suspect that he was either an ex-Marine or ex-cop or both. His veiny forearms, I noticed, were decorated with faded, hard-to-decipher tattoos.

"You're a thief is what you are," he said in a quiet conversational tone. "Where'd you steal them?"

"I didn't steal them," Matt protested with more amusement than indignation. "I coughed up four bucks for these babies."

The counterman shook his head.

"A thief and a liar. Nice combination."

"I'm serious," Matt told him. "I got 'em at a secondhand shop on Whalley Avenue."

"In Connecticut," I explained, offering this fact as a kind of indirect apology for Matt's faux pas. "That's where we go to school. He's just visiting for spring break."

The guy looked at me like I was babbling in a foreign language.

"New Haven," Matt added, trying to help me out. "Yale University."

I groaned to myself. It was better to leave Yale out of it.

"Yale University, huh?" The counterman nodded, pretending to be impressed. "That's a good school. Do they teach you anything besides lying and stealing?"

"I didn't steal anything," Matt insisted, placing his hands on his hips and thrusting his chest defiantly forward, as though we were doing improv and he had just figured out how to play his role. "What kind of villain do you take me for?"

"You can't buy these shoes," the counterman informed him. His face was visibly pinker than it had been a moment before. "You can only steal them from people like me. People trying to make an honest dollar. But you wouldn't know much about that, would you?"

"This is slander!" Matt crossed his arms on his chest and emoted in a stentorian voice he may well have considered Shakespearean. "It's knavery, pure and simple."

"Shut up," I muttered under my breath, but he gave no sign of hearing me.

The counterman shook his head.

"I suppose you bought that hard hat too."

"That's mine," I volunteered. "I loaned it to him for the night."

The guy ignored me. "It takes a lot of gall to walk into a bowling alley wearing something you stole from another bowling alley. A lot of gall. Do you have any idea how much a pair of these shoes costs?"

"Four dollars," Matt told him, reverting to his normal voice.

"You got a smart mouth," the counterman told him in that same flat tone. "I'm fifty-eight years old with a bum leg, but I'm about two seconds from jumping over this counter and kicking your ass."

Matt cowered like a mime, his face a mask of exaggerated fear.

"Can you believe this guy?" he asked me. He had that frenetic, out-of-control look in his eyes, the same one he had when he launched into that stupid imitation of my dancing at the party.

Things were drifting in a bad direction. I grabbed him roughly by the wrists and forced him to look at my face.

"Listen," I said. "I have an idea. Why don't we just rent another pair of shoes. We'll pay the money and everyone will be happy. Just tell the man your shoe size."

Amazingly, I seemed to get through to him. He closed his eyes for a second or two, trying to calm himself down. Then he nodded and opened them again.

"Nine and a half," he told the counterman, capping the request with a patently insincere smile.

"No halfs," I broke in, trying to help him out.

Instead of reaching for another pair of shoes, though, the guy picked up the phone next to the cash register and began dialing. When he was finished he looked at us, cupping one hand over the mouthpiece.

"If you leave now maybe you'll be gone by the time the cops get here."

"The cops?" I said. "You're calling the cops?"

He turned away from us, speaking loud enough that we'd be sure to hear him over the background noise.

"Frank? This is Lou. Lou from the bowling alley. I got a couple troublemakers down here. College kids. You wanna send a car? Thanks."

Matt was shaking his head, grinning like this was the best thing that had happened to him in years.

"This calls for civil disobedience," he said, dropping onto his knees and curling into fetal position on the grimy linoleum floor. "Lock arms! Go totally limp! Call the ACLU!"

"Do what you want," I told him, stepping over his body on my way toward the exit. "I'm getting the hell out of here."

Matt wanted to go to Cousin Butchie's after that, but I told him that all the topless joints were closed on Monday night, an excuse that sounded fairly plausible despite the fact that I'd made it up on the spot. After my misadventure with the Squidman I'd had little desire to visit another go-go bar, and I had even less desire to visit one with Matt. God only knew what sort of trouble he'd get us into at an establishment full of all-but-naked women. We settled instead for the calmer alternative of a pitcher at the Stay-A-While and the promise of an early night.

"Here's to New Jersey," he said. "Where you can go to jail for wearing the wrong shoes."

"To New Jersey." I touched my glass to his and took a sip of Budweiser aged to the perfect degree of flatness by the expert staff at the Stay-A-While. "You don't know the half of it."

"Did you see that guy? I thought he was gonna have a stroke or something."

"It was bizarre." Now that we were out of there, I could more fully appreciate the irony of nearly getting arrested as the accomplice to a person wearing an illegal pair of bowling shoes on the same day I'd suffered no consequences whatsoever for hitting someone in the head with a baseball bat. "Those shoes must be a real sore point for him."

Matt puffed out his chest, re-creating his finest moment.

"This is slander!" he bellowed. "It's knavery, pure and simple."

"I thought he really was going to jump over the counter and kick your ass."

"For a principle like this, I'd be willing to get my ass kicked," Matt declared with a grin. "How'd you like it when I hit the deck? I was all set to break into 'We Shall Overcome.' "

His eyes were bright; I could see how much fun he was having reliving the incident, how exciting it was to reflect on a dangerous moment after you'd escaped it unscathed. There had been a similar expression on Chuckie's face as he'd paraded me around the warehouse that afternoon, telling everyone the story of how I'd held off four goons on my own with a baseball bat—"It was like Sergeant Fucking York!" he'd insisted, over and over again—and how lucky those bastards were that he (Chuckie) had broken it up before the whole bunch of them were lying in the dirt with their heads split open like watermelons. All I had to do was stand at his side, nodding modestly like Gary Cooper to confirm the report of my bold deeds. I wasn't relishing the prospect of returning to the warehouse in the morning to another hero's welcome only to inform my admirers that I was throwing in the towel, that there was no way in hell Sergeant York was going back to the battlefield. Just thinking about it made me want to crawl into bed and stay there for a week or two.

"What's wrong?" Matt asked. "You seem a bit distracted."

"Sorry. There's just all this bizarre shit going on."

I waited for him to probe a little deeper, but all he did was nod sympathetically and pour me another beer, filling the glass in tiny increments, like a mad scientist mixing his secret formula.

"Your father's a nice guy," he told me. "You should hear him talk about you."

"What do you mean?"

"He's just so unbelievably proud of you. It's like no one in the world ever went to Yale before."

"Your father must be proud of you too."

Matt shook his head. "He thinks I'm the world's biggest fuck-up."

"You?" I smiled. "A fuck-up?"

"I know." Matt shook his head. "Once these misconceptions get started, they take on a life of their own."

"Still," I said, "he's gotta be a little proud. How many other car salesmen have kids who got into Yale?"

Matt looked puzzled for a second, then waved away the question like it was smoke.

"Nah," he said. "Now he just thinks Bart Giammati's a fuck-up too."

The glasses that came with our pitcher were small, the size of juice glasses at a diner. You could finish them off in a swallow or two, and Matt and I were feeling solicitous toward one another. As soon as my glass was empty, he filled it, and I did the same for him. Before long, the pitcher was history.

"It's too bad," I said. "That beer was starting to taste pretty good."

The bartender must have heard me. He finished rinsing a few more glasses in a tub of brown water topped with a thin layer of soap scum, wiped his hands on the towel tucked into the waistband of his pants, and shuffled over to our end of the bar. He picked up the empty pitcher and moved it in front of our faces like a hypnotist.

"Another one, fellows?"

"I don't know," I said, checking with Matt. "We've got to get up at four in the morning."

Matt glanced at the clock. He rubbed his chin, adopting the demeanor of a person involved in a complex cognitive operation.

"It's still pretty early," he mused. "I don't see that our impending work obligations necessarily preclude further consumption."

I looked at the bartender, shrugging as though the matter were officially out of my hands.

"You heard him," I said, happy to pretend for the moment that four in the morning was a long way off. "Bring it on."

———

There are two kinds of drunk drivers: the ones who know it and the ones who don't. I was the first kind. My mind was racing a little too quickly, so I tried to compensate by driving very slowly, turning and braking with great care, as though maneuvering my way through a blizzard.

"Jesus," I said. I was perched way up on the edge of my seat, squinting through the dirty windshield. "Visibility's not so good."

"Maybe it would help if you turned on the lights," Matt suggested.

"Good idea," I said. Even one light was an improvement.

The Stay-A-While was in Springville, only a few miles from my parents' house. It was an easy drive sober, over before you knew it. That night, though, Springville Boulevard seemed to last forever. It was like some crew of practical jokers had blown through town while we were in the bar, stringing up traffic lights at every possible intersection in a diabolical effort to prolong my misery and confusion.

252

"I'll tell you what's weird about *Measure for Measure*," Matt remarked as we negotiated the tricky stretch of the boulevard that runs past Nomahegan Park. "Can you imagine living in a place where you can get the death penalty for premarital sex? Would that be a drag or what?"

"Don't talk," I instructed him as we puttered past the county college, moving at about the clip of a riding mower. It felt to me like the truck was standing still, the world rushing madly at my windshield. "It's hard enough for me to concentrate as it is."

"You'd be a dead man," he announced, patting me consolingly on the shoulder.

"Me? What about you?"

"In my own mind I'm a virgin."

I tightened my grip on the wheel as I turned off the main road onto the squiggly back streets that cut through Cranwood and into Darwin. Somewhere around here, back when I was in high school, Jill Arnott drove a driver's ed car over somebody's front lawn and into their house, crashing right through the wall of the family room.

No one was hurt, and she said that the people who lived there were cooler about it than you might have expected. Matt leaned over and turned on the radio. After a couple of commercials, the David Bowie song "Changes" came on.

"Mind if I turn on the radio?" he asked, about halfway into the song.

"Be my guest," I said, riding the brakes through the unexpectedly sharp curves of the residential streets.

A feeling of preliminary relief washed over me as we crossed the border into Darwin and "Changes" segued into "Dust in the Wind"; we weren't there yet, but we were getting close. Matt reached over and turned up the volume.

"Oh man," he groaned, drumming on the glove compartment with both hands. "I love this song."

" 'Dust in the Wind'? Are you serious?"

"You don't like it?" He stared back at me, mirroring my incredulity. "It was my high school anthem."

"I don't know," I said. "It's kind of bleak."

"That's the whole point."

"What's the whole point?"

"That we're dust in the wind," he said, nearly shouting to make himself heard over the lugubrious strains of the song. Something about this concept seemed to amuse him, and he laughed out loud. "Dust in the wind, dude."

That didn't seem like much of a point to me, and I was about to say so when I was struck by the realization that, impaired as I was, and despite the fact that I hadn't the heard the song in years, I knew all the lyrics by heart. Matt did too; in fact, he'd rolled down his window and begun shouting them to the sleeping town.

He seemed to be enjoying himself, so I figured what the hell. By the time the chorus arrived I was right there with him, broadcasting the mournful news at the top of my lungs.

Dust in the wind
All we are is dust in the wind

"Oh shit," I said.

" 'Dust in the wind,' " Matt continued, both hands pressed over his heart, his exuberance undiminished by the fact that he was on his own again. I was too busy to sing; it was all I could do to pull the Roach Coach over to the curb without actually driving it up onto the sidewalk in front of Mr. B's Pet Supplies and Grooming, my own heart pounding as the flashing red lights painted their swirly designs on the glass of my sideview mirror.

I had a hard time falling asleep, but it wasn't because the bed was spinning or anything like that. Getting pulled over had gone a long way toward sobering me up, and throwing up afterward had taken me the rest of the way there. A bad taste lingered in my mouth, a sour sediment that four glasses of water and a marathon Listerine session hadn't washed away, but my head was clear, my thoughts racing in the darkness as Matt snored peacefully beside me in his sleeping bag on the floor.

I hadn't gotten arrested for drunk driving. I hadn't even gotten a ticket for the broken headlight, which was the reason I'd been pulled over in the first place. The cop who came swaggering up to my window, shining a flashlight in my face and barking at me to hand over my license and registration, suddenly burst into a big grin when he realized who I was.

"Danny?"

"Yeah?" I said, cringing at the light, struggling to locate a face in the blinding glare. "Who's that?"

The cop snapped off the flashlight and took a couple steps back from my window so I could get a better look.

"Do I know you?" I asked, pronouncing the words with great care so I wouldn't sound drunk.

The question didn't seem to surprise him.

"Larry," he said, pulling off his hat to reveal the closely cropped hair underneath. "Larry Barlow."

"Jeez," I said. "You're a cop?"

"Just got hired. Hard to believe, huh?"

"Not really," I lied.

Larry was the older brother of Mike Barlow, the biggest stoner in my class. Mike wasn't a close friend of mine, but we'd known each other since kindergarten. When we were sophomores at Harding, Larry used to drive Mike to school, and sometimes in bad weather they'd pull up to the bus stop and offer me a ride, their car a rolling cloud of reefer smoke. Back then, both Barlows had long blond hair that fell way past their shoulders.

"Aren't you at Harvard or something?" he asked.

"Yale. It's our spring break."

"Yale, Harvard." Larry pronounced these names as a pair, the way people often did in Darwin, as if it were somehow beside the point to distinguish between the two. "Same bullshit, right?"

"No kidding," I said. "How's Mike?"

"Okay." Larry shook his head like he wasn't too keen on elaborating.

"Tell him I said 'hi.' "

"Hey," he said. A sly smile spread across his face. "Know who I saw from your class?"

"Who?"

"That girl Jenny. The one who did the Coletti brothers. She dances at Cousin Butchie's."

"I know. I saw her there last summer."

"Fuckin' amazing." The walkie-talkie crackled on Larry's belt. He brought it up to his mouth and mumbled some numbers into it. Then he shoved it back into its holster and pointed at my front end. "You got a broken headlight."

"I know. My dad's taking it to the shop tomorrow."

"Take care, man."

"You too."

I watched in the sideview mirror as Larry climbed back into his patrol car, turned off his overhead lights, and swung what would have been an illegal U turn if anyone else had done it. We were free to go, but I just sat there in the driver's seat, waiting for the turbulence in my stomach to subside.

"That was weird," said Matt.

"Excuse me," I told him.

Cheeks bulging, one hand cupped over my mouth, I stuck my head and shoulders through the open window into the cool night air, wriggling forward as far as I could go to protect my father's truck. At the crucial moment, I uncovered my mouth and spread my arms wide, as if preparing to take flight.

Things could be worse, I reminded myself. I wasn't in jail, I wasn't in the hospital, and I wasn't married. My life was pretty much on track, unchanged by the obstacle course of potential disasters I'd been running for the past several days. A week from now I'd be back at school, picking up where I'd left off, re-dedicating myself to my studies, hanging with my friends, hopefully straightening things out with Polly. Things could definitely have been worse.

In general, I had a fairly high opinion of myself at that stage in my life. I considered myself an intelligent person, trusted my instincts and judgment, and didn't spend a lot of time brooding about mistakes I'd made in the past. I believed that my success in the world, such as it was, was my own doing and no one else's, a well-deserved reward for years of hard work, perseverance, and good-humored self-denial. I believed that I was a decent person and expected the future to be good to me.

But that wasn't how I felt just then. Lying in bed long after midnight, the darkness streaming into my wide open eyes, I saw my life as a car with no brakes careening down a dangerous mountain road. Get in my way and I'll run you down, or at least leave you in the dust. Not because I want to, but simply because I have to. There's Cindy. Whoops. Oh hi, Kevin. Sorry. Zeke, Woody, Steve, the Squidman, my old roommate Seth. Later, dudes. Even Junior. Who else would I have to bowl over or whack with a Louisville

Slugger on my way to wherever the hell it was I was going? My parents and teachers, the women I'd love and the one I'd eventually marry, my unborn children, my current and future best friends? Might as well bring them on, get it over with, because I'm on my way, there's no stopping now, no way, not even if I wanted to.

i must have fallen asleep, because the phone woke me at eight minutes after three in the morning. Maybe I was dreaming of Polly, because I remember thinking it was her—it had to be!—as I threw off the covers and launched myself out of bed, forgetting as I did so that Matt's recumbent body was positioned midway between me and my desk. I stepped on his arm and stumbled over his torso, eliciting only a feeble groan of protest from the deepest recesses of the sleeping bag, while at the same time managing to maintain my balance well enough to snatch up the receiver before the completion of the third ring.

"Polly?" I gasped.

A confused moment of silence followed.

"Danny?"

The voice was unfamiliar, but definitely not Polly's, and I found myself retroactively gripped by the fear that usually accompanies a 3 A.M. phone call.

"Who's this?" I asked.

"Alice," she said. "From next door. DeFillipo."

"Oh hi," I said, sounding cheerfully idiotic even to myself. "How's it going?"

"Your truck's on fire."

It wasn't until that very moment that I became aware of the unusual brightness in the room, a warm orangey glow filtering in through the window shade.

"My truck?" I said.

"Your father's," she said, a certain edge of impatience creeping into her voice. "The truck in your driveway."

"It's on fire?"

"I called 911. They should be there any minute."

"Thanks," I told her. "That was nice of you."

It seemed like a long time before the fire department arrived. I stood beside my father on the front stoop and watched the Roach Coach burning in our driveway. It wasn't a big deal, really, nothing too spectacular. It was the cab that was on fire, the toxic-looking flames licking out of the empty spaces where the windows and windshield used to be, a cloud of acrid gray smoke gathering over the remains of my father's big dream like a cartoon illustration of bad luck.

"I don't think you two should be out here," my mother said, sticking her worried face out the front door. "What if it blows up?"

My father didn't answer. He seemed riveted by the tiny inferno, as though he were making an effort to memorize it down to the smallest detail: the strange chocolatey undertone beneath the stench of burning plastic, the abrupt way the truck sank—like an elephant kneeling in the grass—when one of the front tires blew, the disappearance of the paint on the front door—like an eraser moving from the bottom up—our trademark bug turning to vapor before our eyes, followed in turn by my father's own name. All the while the storage cube kept gleaming brighter and brighter, as though it were being polished and purified by the flames. I remember wondering if maybe it was fireproof, if, when it was all over, we could just pop open the display door and treat ourselves and the neighbors, many of whom had gathered on their own front stoops to bear witness to our misfortune, to a miraculous breakfast feast of warm but intact fruit pies and Ring Dings and Funny Bones.

"Come on," my mother said. "Both of you."

Neither one of us moved.

When the firemen came, they sprayed our Roach Coach with chemical foam. They kept spraying long after the flames had been snuffed out, until the husk of the cab was barely visible beneath the frothy meringue and the whole truck seemed to be made of soap suds rather than steel and rubber.

I wanted to say something to my father, to tell him how sorry I was, how it was all my fault, how much I knew the truck meant to him and how I'd figure out some way to make it up to him, but I was scared just then, scared not only to look at his face but to have him look at mine. I thought he might be able to see beyond my shame and sorrow to the secret feeling underneath, the purely self-ish sensation of having been saved yet again—saved from the Lunch Monsters, from the expectations of Chuckie and the rest of the guys at the warehouse, from having to get up at four in the morning for the rest of my vacation.

My father must have mistaken my silence for sadness, because he laid his hand on my shoulder and left it there for what began to seem like a long time. We didn't touch each other much, and when we did it didn't usually last much longer than a handshake or a pat on the back.

"It's okay," he told me.

Finally I turned to him, expecting to see any number of things on his face—anger, grief, panic, maybe even tears—anything but what was actually there, the mild expression of acceptance, maybe even the ghost of a smile hovering underneath.

"It's okay," he said again, nodding at the piece of smoking, foam-drenched wreckage in the driveway. "That goddam thing was killing me."

part four

Townies

ted?

From a distance, it makes perfect sense that the people and the things you think will save you are the very ones that have the power to disappoint you most bitterly, but up close it can hit you as a bewildering surprise.

At least that's how it was for me, returning to school after spring break. In my mind Yale was the garden from which I'd nearly been expelled, a haven of learning and friendship, the one place in the world where I could really be myself. My roommates would be waiting to welcome me back into the fold, and so, eventually, would Polly. All we really needed was some time together, a few long talks to burn away the shadows Cindy and Peter Preston had cast on our budding relationship. The weather would warm and we'd spend our days reading under flowering trees and our nights pressed together on my single bed, giggling under the covers.

I passed the two-hour drive to New Haven fine-tuning this fantasy, while Matt perplexed my parents with a barrage of devil's advocate–style questions meant to provoke serious discussion of controversial issues, not my family's preferred method for killing the time on long car rides. Didn't they think everyone should spend at least one night in jail, just to know what it was like? Didn't the Iranian militants have a point about the U.S. being the Great Satan, at least from their perspective? And really, what was the difference between a religion and a cult? Looked at from a certain angle, wasn't the Pope every bit as preposterous as L. Ron Hubbard or the Reverend Sun Myung Moon? And what was the story with deodorants? Did we really need them, or were we just being duped into using them by the big corporations? On this last subject, at least, my parents had strong opinions.

"Believe me," my mother said. "No one was ever sorry they put on deodorant."

"But do we really smell bad?" Matt wondered. "Or have we just been trained to think of normal human odors as somehow being repulsive?"

"Stop using it and see how many dates you get," my father suggested.

"You should get a whiff of some of the guys I work with." My mother waved her hand in front of her nose as though the offenders had joined us in the car. "Between the B.O. and the bad breath . . ."

"The Europeans don't believe in deodorant," Matt remarked.

"Some of them aren't too big on bathing either," my mother pointed out. She thought it over a moment, then added, "I guess if everybody smells bad, they don't notice it so much."

"The ladies don't even shave their underarms." My father glanced in the rearview, checking Matt's reaction to this little tidbit.

"I don't mind," Matt told him. "I had a girlfriend once who didn't shave her pits, and I kind of liked it." Neither of my parents had any response to this, so he forged ahead. "It's completely natural."

My father chuckled. "That's one way of putting it."

"I'm sorry," my mother said. "It's not very attractive."

"But who's to say what beauty is?" Matt inquired. "Doesn't it differ from culture to culture?"

On another day I might have intervened to spare my parents the interrogation, but I was happy just then to let Matt give them something to think about besides what my father was going to do on Monday morning, his first official day as a lunch-truck driver without a lunch truck. They'd have more than enough time on the ride home to be alone with each other and their worries, and they seemed as grateful for the diversion as I was.

"Beauty is in the eye of the beholder," my father declared.

"That's original," my mother told him.

"You can quote me," he said, winking at the mirror.

My parents came up to my room to help me "get settled," but they barely stayed long enough to marvel at what a pigsty it was, though I must say that it looked fairly clean to me. None of my roommates were around, and they were eager to get a jump on the long ride home. I offered to walk them back to the car, but they told me not to bother.

"Stay put," my mother said. "I'm sure you've got a lot to do."

Ushering them to the door, I was gripped by a feeling of wild desolation. *Please,* I wanted to tell them. *Please don't leave me here.* I hadn't felt anything like this since the first day of freshman year, when I waved good-bye and burst into tears on College Street.

"You all right?" my father asked.

I nodded, reluctant to open my mouth for fear of what might come out.

"You sure?"

"Honey?" my mother said. "Is something wrong?"

I was mystified by their blindness. They didn't seem to understand the first thing about what had happened. My father had been furious when he heard the highly sanitized account I'd given the police about my trouble with the Lunch Monsters—and even then he'd been more upset by my silence than my actual behavior—but aside from that one brief outburst, he'd absorbed the whole calamity with bizarre composure. My mother had been more openly shaken by it, but in all her dark mutterings, there hadn't been a single word of blame directed at me.

"I'm sorry," I said, my voice quivering like a child's. "It was all my fault."

"What was?" my father asked.

"The truck."

"That wasn't your fault."

"Yes, it was."

"You have nothing to be sorry about," my mother told me. Her face was kind, and she spoke with such gentleness and certainty that I almost believed her. "You didn't do a single thing wrong."

"Don't worry about us," my father added, giving me a supportive pat on the elbow. "You just worry about yourself."

I had just begun unpacking when the phone rang. It was Albert, the dining-hall manager.

"Jesus," he said. "Where the hell have you been?"

"What do you mean?"

"I've been calling all afternoon. I need you to work the dish line."

"The dish line? Isn't it Eddie's night?"

"Didn't you hear? He's in the hospital."

"He is?"

"He got mugged last night. Beat up pretty bad."

"My God. Is he—"

"No, no. He's okay. Can you take his shift?"

I looked at the clock. It was four thirty, and I was totally unprepared. I'd barely have time to change my shirt and grab a bite before being besieged by an armada of dirty dishes. The only thing worse was the thought of sitting alone in my room, doing absolutely nothing.

"Okay." I sighed wearily, as if submitting to his relentless pressure. "I'll be right there."

In the dining hall I received the kind of warm welcome I'd been fantasizing about in the car. Albert shook my hand and thanked me profusely for bailing him out. Kristin and Djembe applauded when I sat down at the worker's table, and Sarah inked the words "Our Hero" on my paper hat with a fountain pen and yellow highlighter. Even Nick seemed happy to see me.

"Hey Pencil Dick, have a good time in Florida?"

"Yeah." I offered up a pasty arm for his perusal. "Like my golden tan?"

Lorelei arrived a couple of minutes before five and glided past our table without a word of greeting, her face its usual mask of self-containment and private amusement. Looking at her, you wouldn't have had any idea that her boyfriend had just been hospitalized after a brutal attack. I searched more closely for signs of distress when I bumped into her by the time clock, but there was only that faint mocking smile that was her basic response to the world.

"How's Eddie?" I asked.

"Okay," she said. "Much better since they took out his spleen."

"They took out his spleen?"

"They had to," she said, removing her time card from its metal sleeve. "It was ruptured."

"Jesus. Do you know what happened?"

She shoved her card into the slot; the machine bit down.

"He got jumped. In the lobby of his building." She squinted at the card as if something was wrong with it, then slipped it back into the sleeve. "I wasn't there."

"Was it your brothers?"

She looked me square in the face for the first time, examining my face as closely as I was examining hers. Her voice was calm, matter-of-fact.

"Probably."

"What do they have against Eddie?"

"They're just assholes. They think it's funny." She shook her head in disgust, like it wasn't worth going into it. "What's that on your hat?"

"It says 'Our Hero.'" I turned my head to give her a better look. "Sarah did it."

"How come?" Lorelei seemed annoyed, like this was one of those stupid college pranks we were always pulling.

"Beats me."

"Hey." She smiled like she'd just remembered something. "Who was that girl you were with the other night? Outside of WaWa's?"

"Her name's Cindy."

"She's not a Yalie, is she?"

I shook my head. Lorelei narrowed her eyes and studied me with a newfound interest. Her voice was playful, laced with a tiny dose of sarcasm.

"I didn't know you dated townies."

Like "weenie," "townie" was one of those words I'd never heard until I got to Yale, and it still had the power to make me wince. I was about to object on the grounds that Cindy wasn't from New Haven when I realized that it didn't matter. By Lorelei's standards—and my own too, now that I thought about it—Cindy was a townie.

"I date all sorts of girls," I said with a shrug.

"I'll keep that in mind," she said, brushing past me on her way to the front desk.

I punched myself in and headed over to the dish line. As the workers' trays floated lazily in my direction, I replayed Lorelei's last statement in my mind, amazed that she could sink so low as to flirt with me while her boyfriend was in the hospital, and even more amazed that I could sink so low as to like it.

Max was sitting in the common room when I got back, reading *The Wretched of the Earth* while Ted and Nancy fucked in the double. I knew they were fucking because Nancy kept saying *Fuck-meohfuckmepleasefuckme* while Ted kept answering with these weird little grunts, like he was trying to lift something that was bolted to the floor.

"Hey," I said. "How's it going?"

Max looked at me for a second or two before responding. The look wasn't friendly.

"Fine," he said.

I sat down on the armchair and tried to ignore the noise.

"How was your vacation?"

Max stared at his book and pretended not to hear me. Before I could repeat my question the action in the double kicked into high gear, a shift signalled first by a rhythmic pounding on the wall and followed almost immediately by a pronounced change in Nancy's monologue.

"Ted," she began chanting. "Ted, Ted, Ted . . ."

She didn't say it exactly the same way every time. Sometimes it was *Ted?* and sometimes it was *Ted!* Every once in a while it even sounded like *TEEEDDD!!!* And then *tedtedtedtedted.* She said his name like she was talking to him across the room and like she was calling him from down the street. She said it like he'd done something cute, and also like he'd done something stupid. She said his name like she hadn't seen him for years and then again like he was getting on her nerves. She sang and muttered and chortled it. Once she even yodeled it. She said *Ted* like it was the only word she knew, like it had to do the work of the whole damn dictionary. And then finally she screamed it so loud, with such ecstatic finality, that even Max had to look up.

"My vacation sucked," he told me. "How was yours?"

I thought about calling Polly, but decided to pay her a surprise visit instead. I had the feeling that what was required of me was some sort of grand spontaneous gesture, something that would throw her off-balance and give me at least a small amount of leverage over the situation, and just showing up at her door was the only tactic I could think of. And besides, I had important news for her, news I wanted to deliver in person and as soon as possible.

I moved across the campus in a blur of anticipation, a sudden and unaccountable surge of optimism inspired by Ted and Nancy. After all, Ted was nothing special, just an all-around regular guy, slightly out-of-shape and a little on the boring side when you got right down to it. And yet, there was Nancy, this intelligent and attractive and charming woman, crying out his name as if he were the God of Love lowered down from the clouds to give her a taste of heaven on that rickety old bunk bed. If Ted and Nancy were a plausible couple, why not Polly and I? If they could make each other happy, why couldn't we?

Yale was security conscious, and I would normally have had to get through a locked gate and locked entryway door before reaching my destination. That night, though, people were still moving back in, and everything was wide open. I passed through everyday obstacles as though on an errand in my dreams, barely registering my good luck. On top of everything, Polly's room door was cracked open too. I could hear her inside, laughing with her roommate.

"I can't believe he did that."

"Well, he did."

"Oh, Ingrid, that is *so* gross." Polly's giggly voice was almost unrecognizable to me. "That is so unbelievably disgusting."

It was there that I hesitated and almost lost heart, partly because I was reluctant to intrude on a private conversation, but mainly just because of how happy she sounded. I couldn't remember Polly ever laughing like that with me, like she was a goofy high school girl and not some earnest would-be intellectual clutching her head about Peter Preston or Wallace Stevens. She seemed so far away just then, like I barely even knew her, like there was a lot more separating us than one partially open door. What right did I have to think that I knew the first thing about her or had the first clue about how to make her happy? I took a step backward, uncertain whether to knock or retreat. Before I had time to choose, the door flew open and I was face-to-face with Ingrid.

"I gotta pee so bad I can taste it," she said, talking to Polly but looking straight at me. She stopped short, her face turning an instant crimson. "Oh, hi."

"I was just about to knock," I told her.

"Ingrid?" Polly called. "Is someone there?"

Ingrid poked her head back into the room.

"You know what?" she said. "I'm just gonna run upstairs and see if Chitra's back."

My plan worked in the sense that I clearly caught Polly off-guard. She was sitting on her couch in a pair of baggy sweatpants and a pink thermal undershirt, one arm buried to the elbow in an econo-sized bag of nacho-flavored Doritos, and staring at me in naked confusion, as if she'd misplaced the word for hello.

My plan failed in the sense that I was just as tongue-tied as she was. I'd never visited her in her room before—had never seen her in sweatpants or a thermal shirt, for that matter—and was over-whelmed by the unexpected intimacy of the situation, the simple, enormous fact of Polly in person again, after a separation that felt like months instead of weeks.

"It's me," I told her, just in case she was wondering.

She withdrew her hand from the bag and licked her fingers clean like a cat, watching me the whole time.

"I wasn't expecting visitors."

"I should have called."

"That's okay."

I understood that it was my turn to talk, but the effort of con-versation seemed utterly beyond me. I just wanted to sit down next to her and hold her hand.

"I like your shirt," I said finally.

She looked down at herself, checking to make sure we were talking about the same piece of clothing.

"Really?"

"Not every girl looks good in thermals."

She smiled, but it was a headachey sort of smile, the kind you get from someone who's trying to be nice.

"Are you all right?" she asked.

"I think so."

She lowered her voice, as if there were a third party in the room. "Is she getting the abortion?"

271

I shook my head, wishing I could just skip over the whole mess, pretend that none of it had ever happened.

"She's marrying an old boyfriend. This guy named Kevin. He's an assistant manager at Medi-Mart."

"Huh." She made a face. "That's weird."

"Tell me about it." Seeing it through Polly's eyes made it seem even weirder than it had before. "He really loves her, though."

"Does she love him?"

"Not really. But at least she won't be alone. The baby will have a father."

Polly took a few seconds to absorb this. She looked like she was about to protest, but then thought better of it. When she looked up again, her expression had brightened. There was a finality in her voice that made me nervous.

"So it worked out for you."

"Kind of. It was a strange vacation. These bodybuilders torched my father's truck."

"Bodybuilders?"

"From Staten Island. They call themselves the Lunch Monsters."

"They burned his truck?"

"Right in our driveway," I said. "It's a long story."

She didn't invite me to elaborate. "That's quite a town you live in."

All I could do was shrug.

"What about you?" I asked. "How's it going with that Stevens paper?"

She looked at me a long time before answering, long enough for me to identify the emotion she was beaming at me as compassion. It was coming off her like a radio signal.

"Peter came up for a visit," she said. "He really helped me out."

"Peter?"

It wasn't until I said his name that I noticed the bouquet of tulips on her coffee table, and the sight of them struck me with shame. Some guys show up with flowers, I thought; other guys just show up.

"We had a really good talk," she explained. "I was imagining all sorts of bad stuff that just wasn't true."

"So you're back together."

I'd meant it as a question, but it came out as a statement. Polly couldn't have looked at me with more kindness if I'd just lost a leg.

"I'm sorry, Danny."

I would have preferred to make a clean getaway, but she insisted on hugging me good-bye at the door, a gesture that I guess was meant to make me feel better, but only made me that much more aware of what I was losing. I'd done the exact same thing to Cindy only a week before, a painful memory I tried to erase by grabbing two handfuls of Polly's shirt and pressing my face into the springy tangle of her hair, murmuring her name over and over again with such mournful intensity that she finally had no choice but to pry herself loose and send me on my way.

mercy

Mostly what I was that spring was lonely. Just when I needed my friends the most, they suddenly went AWOL on me. Much to his own amazement, Sang had fallen madly in love with Katie Kim, and when he wasn't visiting her in Middletown, he was hiding out in Machine City, making feverish declarations into a pay phone. Max, who wasn't feeling particularly well-disposed toward me in any case, had decided to ditch the Hinckley project and make up for a semester's worth of slacking off with a few weeks of heroic cramming. Ted and Nancy had gotten hold of the library's dog-eared copy of *The Joy of Sex*, and were holing up in the double every night, practicing exotic positions and bursting into frequent, irritating fits of laughter. When the phone rang for me it was either Matt, trying to apologize, or Eric Storm, hoping to continue our recent and highly rewarding discussion of Socialist Realism.

Even my father seemed to be having a better time than me. Only a week after the Roach Coach had gone up in flames, he'd taken a job as manager of the Deli Department at Stop & Shop. My mother said he was in his glory, supervising a staff of hardworking middle-aged women, garrulous semi-retired men, and a couple of cranky part-timers. He loved the hours—banker's hours, he called them—and didn't mind spending a good part of the day on his feet behind the meat case. He also enjoyed walking back and forth to work and listening to the morning weather report on WPAT with the bland curiosity of someone whose day could no longer be ruined by it. The insurance company had paid off on the truck, and he had sold a good portion of his route to Chuckie at what he said was a more-than-fair price, so my parents actually had some money in the bank for the first time in recent memory. He said he had half a mind to send a thank-you note to Vito Meatballs.

The trouble with Matt started on a Friday afternoon about two weeks after we'd returned to New Haven. Friday was laundry day for me, and I was alone in my room, sorting through my vast collection of white tube socks, when Peter Preston called. He said he needed to see me immediately.

"Right now? I'm kind of busy."

"I strongly suggest you get yourself over to my office as soon as possible."

I was more put off than alarmed by his brusque tone. He wasn't my teacher anymore and had no right to order me around, especially now that he and Polly were a couple again. I'd passed them the day before on High Street, in the midst of a sudden downpour. They were sharing an umbrella, leaning into one another and laughing. They either didn't recognize me or pretended not to as I rushed past them, soaked to the skin, vainly trying to shield my head with a waterlogged paperback of *Daniel Deronda*.

"Is this about Polly?"

It was an obvious question, but for some reason it threw him off-balance. He didn't hesitate for long, but when he spoke again he sounded a lot more courteous.

"Listen, Danny. You know I wouldn't be bothering you if it wasn't important."

I frowned at the jumble inside my cracked laundry basket. Some of my socks had two stripes, some had three, some had stripes of two different colors. Once you started a job like that, it was a drag to leave it unfinished.

"Okay," I said. "Give me fifteen minutes."

Preston's office hadn't changed much in the year since I'd taken his class. It still seemed more like the work space of an undergraduate than a member of the faculty, the desk strewn with papers and anchored at all four corners with slapdash towers of books and academic quarterlies, the walls plastered with unframed, crookedly hung posters of rock stars and movie idols, many of them curling at the edges.

What had changed was Preston himself. He looked tired and beleaguered and his hair seemed thinner on top than it had the day before. You got the feeling that the clock had just run out a few seconds ago on the Boy Wonder phase of his life, an impression thrown into sharper relief by the presence of the fresh-faced graduate student in his office, a hipster TA with engineer boots and rockabilly sideburns.

"Do you know Lyman Cooper?" Preston demanded, before I'd even had a chance to sit down.

"Lyman? I don't know anyone named Lyman."

"Matt," the TA broke in. "He goes by Matt."

"Matt's name is Lyman?"

"Lyman Cooper III," the TA explained with the slightest hint of a smirk. He was leaning back in his chair, his head resting just below the ecstatic poster of Hendrix at Woodstock. "I'd go by Matt too."

"So," Preston inquired, "is Mr. Cooper a friend of yours?"

"I guess you could say that. We work together in the dining hall. He stayed at my house a few days over break. Why?"

Preston watched me carefully.

"I figured you'd have to be pretty close friends," he said.

Despite the presence of the TA, I still couldn't quite separate myself from the idea that this was all somehow connected to Polly. I tried to remember if I'd told Matt anything about Preston that I wouldn't want repeated.

"Did he say something?"

Preston and the TA traded glances. Sheepishly, the TA let the front legs of his chair drop back to the floor.

"You mean, did he implicate you?" Preston asked.

"Implicate me? What's that supposed to mean?"

"You tell me," Preston suggested, pulling open one of his desk drawers and peering inside.

"I'm stumped. You're going to have to help me out."

With a Perry Mason flourish, Preston removed a graded student essay from the drawer and waved it half-heartedly in the air.

"How do you explain this?" he inquired, sliding the paper to me across the desktop.

One look at the cover explained everything. "Legitimacy and Subterfuge. Bastard Authority in William Shakespeare's *Measure for Measure*, by Lyman Cooper III." Across the bottom, in red block letters, someone had scrawled, "MATT—WE NEED TO TALK—MARCO." A hot blush spread across my face, as though I were a criminal instead of a victim. Just to be sure, I flipped the page and began reading:

> Shakespeare's comedies frequently end with the celebration of one or more marriages, and *Measure for Measure* is no exception. So why, then, does the final scene of this so-called "problem play" ring so hollowly in comparison to a more "conventional" comedy, such as *A Midsummer Night's Dream*? Has the "Bard of Avon" simply failed to write a satisfying ending, or has he succeeded in doing something far more subversive and interesting—namely, calling into question the very genre of comedy itself?

My first reaction to this familiar opening wasn't anger, but embarrassment. It seemed so lumbering and obvious, not nearly as good as I remembered.

"Son of a bitch," I said, louder than I meant to.

"It was an incredibly stupid move," Preston informed me. "We used your paper as part of a grading exercise in one of our staff meetings. All the section leaders read it."

The TA laughed. "He barely bothered to change the title."

"Were you in on it?" Preston asked.

"Are you serious?"

"Did you give him your permission?"

The question seemed so absurd I couldn't help laughing.

"How dumb do I look?"

There was a knock on the door before anyone could answer. Matt poked his head into the room—he was smiling jauntily, wearing the yellow hard hat that had become his new trademark on campus—and took in the scene with a look of slowly dawning comprehension.

"Oh shit," he said.

"Just give us a minute," Preston instructed him. "We're almost finished."

Matt nodded, looking shaken as he withdrew to the hallway. Preston turned to the TA.

"Why don't you keep him company, Marco. I'd like a word with Danny in private."

Marco left, but Preston gave no sign of actually wanting a word with me. He seemed much more interested in the paper clip he'd found on his desk and had begun twisting into some sort of abstract sculpture. I cleared my throat to make sure he hadn't forgotten me.

"I guess you need this back," I said, tossing the essay onto the small clearing in the middle of his desk.

He glanced down at it with an expression of distaste.

"Some friend, huh?"

He sounded sympathetic, so I figured I'd just get it over with.

"Am I in trouble?"

He looked at me in an almost pleading way, as if I'd hurt his feelings just by having to ask. Until that moment, I'd been operating under the assumption that he still thought of me mainly as a guy who'd tried to steal his girlfriend—someone he might enjoy having in his power—but now I saw that it wasn't that way at all.

"I hate this disciplinary crap." He shook his head and let out an exasperated sigh. "This isn't why I got into academia."

I sat silently while he fiddled with the clip, feeling oddly flattered by the lack of attention. In the past he'd been all business when I met him in his office. Now it was as if I'd stopped being his student and had become his peer, someone he could just hang out with while he wrapped a piece of wire around his index finger. I wondered if Polly had had a similar revelation, if one day she looked up and realized that he'd forgotten he was her teacher.

"I'm sorry this is so awkward," he told me.

"That's okay," I said, not quite sure what he was apologizing for.

Preston's expression turned somber as he unwrapped the wire from his swollen-looking finger.

"I didn't mean for this to happen. I'm sorry you got caught up in it."

"Don't worry about it. Things never would've worked out between Polly and me. We're just really different people."

Preston's face tightened with thought. He was listening carefully, chin cradled in his hand, as though I were telling him about a problem I was having with a paper.

280   "These past few weeks haven't been easy for her. She feels pretty bad about the way she treated you."

"Coulda fooled me."

He nodded like a friend offering sympathy, like my bitterness was more than justified.

"You have every right to hate me," he said.

"I don't hate you."

"I'm serious," he insisted. "You have every right."

I didn't say anything, and he seemed to interpret my silence as assent. All I was thinking, though, was that it was no fun to hate people who invited you to hate them.

"I was a late bloomer," he explained, with an odd mixture of pride and embarrassment in his voice. "When I was in college, girls like Polly wouldn't even look at me."

Preston was watching me closely, as if my reaction to this meant a great deal to him. We stared at each other until the silence grew uncomfortable.

"Okay, then." He smiled sadly, as if we'd reached some sort of understanding. "I guess it's Mr. Cooper's turn."

i could feel Matt trying to make eye contact with me in the hall-way, but I brushed past him like a stranger, my eyes locked straight ahead. I ignored his numerous phone calls over the weekend and didn't see him again until the dinner shift on Tuesday night. He was manning the dessert station, wearing his hard hat and whistling "Midnight at the Oasis" as he carved a tray of brownies into his sig-nature amorphous chunks. My anger had cooled a little by that point and, aside from simple social discomfort, the main thing I felt upon seeing him was confusion, since he seemed so oddly cheerful for someone who should have been facing the academic equivalent of the death penalty. He stopped whistling when he saw me and tried to look serious.

"I think something's wrong with your phone," he told me.

"Yeah?"

"I keep getting disconnected."

"That's not the phone," I explained. "That's me telling you to fuck off, Lyman."

"Ouch." He nodded to acknowledge the blow. "I guess I deserve that."

"You deserve way more than that."

He tugged on his earlobe for an extended period, as though it were a secret signal.

"Have you considered the possibility that you're over-reacting?"

"Over-reacting? You mean to the fact that a person I thought was my friend came to my house and took advantage of my family's hospitality to steal something I'd put my heart and soul into, and then tried to pass it off as his own? Over-reacting to the fact that you could have gotten me kicked out of school? Is that what I'm over-reacting to?"

"Huh." He looked troubled. "When you put it that way . . ."

"Is there another way to put it?"

"Preston said it was a cry for help." Matt shrugged, apparently reluctant to endorse this view. "He thinks I need counseling. He made me call Psych Services right there in his office. My first appointment's tomorrow."

"That's it? That's your whole punishment?"

"He gave me an F for the paper. If I write a new one by the end of the week, he says he'll average the two grades together. If I'm lucky I can still get out of the class with a C."

"He didn't report you?"

Matt lowered his voice. He seemed a little perplexed by what he was telling me.

"He gave me this big lecture about *Measure for Measure*, how it was ultimately a play about mercy, and maybe we all need to show each other a little more mercy, to have a little more understanding of the fact that we're all human, we all make mistakes, et cetera, et cetera. He was really very nice about it."

Just then Nick wandered into the serving area with a big grin on his face. He scooped some ice into his glass and filled it with a fizzy blast of Coke before turning in our direction. If I wasn't mistaken, he seemed at least moderately pleased to see us.

"Well, well, if it isn't the Scrotum Twins."

Matt responded with an elaborately servile bow, the kind that Ed McMahon bestowed on Johnny Carson.

"At your service, Herr Chef."

"Here's one," Nick told us, rubbing his hands together in anticipation. "What does Joan Collins put behind her ears to attract men?"

He barely managed to wait for the two of us to exchange blank looks.

"Her ankles!" he cried, pressing both forearms against his head in a misguided attempt to illustrate his punch line. "Get it?"

"I guess that'll do it," Matt agreed.

Nick turned and headed back out to the worker's table, still chuckling to himself.

"Oh yeah," Matt told me. "There's one more thing. I'm supposed to write you a letter of apology."

"I haven't received that yet."

"I'm working on it," he assured me, reaching for his trowel.

"Matt?" I said.

"Yeah?"

"Your father's not really a car salesman, is he?"

He hesitated for a second before answering. It was the first time I'd ever seen him blush.

"Only in the broadest sense," he conceded, addressing his answer to the wall behind my head. "He's a big executive at GM. The number two or three guy, depending on how you look at it."

I'm not sure why this upset me so much. The plagiarism I'd written off as an act of desperation, but this seemed more personal somehow, more like an insult. I remembered all the stories he'd told me about his dad, a chubby guy in a plaid coat who'd tell any kind of lie imaginable to make a sale, and how we'd laughed at poor Mr. Cooper's incompetence and sweaty desperation. Before I was even conscious of my intention, my hand had curled into a fist. I drew back my arm and smacked him in the jaw, a sucker punch of Barnhouse proportions.

He was still flat on his back when Lorelei stepped into the serving area from the kitchen, her mouth opening for a question she couldn't seem to ask. Her expression wavered between uncertainty and delight as she watched Matt struggle into sitting position, the hard hat still miraculously attached to his head.

"I didn't mean anything by it," he explained, blinking his eyes and wiggling his chin around to make sure nothing was broken. "I just wanted you to like me."

283

something you said

Matt had scheduled his end-of-the-year bash for the Friday before reading period, the busiest party night of the semester, and all my suitemates had other plans. Ted and Nancy were going to the Pierson formal, the social highlight of their year. They buzzed around the common room like high school kids on prom night, practicing their dance steps, pinning flowers on one another, posing for pictures in front of the fireplace. Sang was looking sharp as well. Katie Kim was coming down from Middletown for the first time, and he'd made reservations at the only decent Korean restaurant in town, to be followed by dancing at the New Wave Study Break/Sock Hop at the Asian-American Students' Association. Even Max seemed to be preparing for a special occasion of some sort, though, as usual, he wasn't too forthcoming about the nature of the occasion.

Ted and Nancy left around eight, and Katie Kim showed up a few minutes later, looking sweetly self-conscious in her black cocktail dress and high heels. Sang had said she was beautiful, but I didn't agree with this assessment, at least not at first. She was more accurately described as cute, I thought, or even sisterly. Still, their faces lit up the moment they saw each other, and you had no choice but to envy them. They were in love; Max and I were just bystanders.

Katie was easily amused. She had a pretty smile and an explosive, slightly horsey laugh that she tried to apologize for by placing her hand over her mouth and looking mortified. It was a charming gesture—for some reason it came off as ironic rather than self-effacing—and it wasn't her only one. She just had that thing that some people have, that mysterious quality that makes you not want them to leave the room or turn their attention to someone else. Sang had tried several times to explain the giddy sensation that had come over him about an hour after meeting her, and after only ten minutes in her company I understood the feeling all too well, though in my case it was more dispiriting than giddy, because she was already heading out the door, leaving me alone with Max in the suddenly desolate common room.

"Damn," I said, nodding sadly at the empty space she'd left in the air.

Max was lounging in the legless armchair, looking suspiciously presentable in one of Ted's oxford shirts and Hank Yamashita's skinny leather tie, which by now had attained the status of community property. An hour or so earlier, I'd stepped out of the shower and found him standing shirtless in front of the mirror, shaking a dangerous quantity of Old Spice into his palm and massaging it into his chest and stomach as though it were suntan lotion, and now I was catching powerful whiffs of manly fragrance whenever he shifted position.

"You think?" He gave an I-could-take-her-or-leave-her shrug. "Not my type, I guess."

I wanted to ask him to define his type for me—I was curious to know more about the intended beneficiary of the aftershave and thought this might be a good way to broach the subject—but I couldn't bring myself to do it. Max and I had had a bitter argument about Cindy a few days after I got back from vacation, and our friendship still hadn't fully recovered. He'd kept in close touch with her over the break and knew all about her "engagement" with Kevin, which he considered a disaster and blamed on me. He'd launched into a complicated indictment of my behavior, claiming it was tantamount to a violation of Cindy's human rights, as if she were Steven Biko and I were the apartheid government of South Africa. Things had improved a little in the weeks since then, but there was still a palpable tension in the air whenever we were alone together.

He grew more visibly agitated as it approached nine o'clock, glancing at his watch every few seconds and working through the whole repertoire of body language meant to convey impatience, but I still couldn't bring myself to get off the couch. My party spirit, never too strong to begin with, was fading by the minute.

"Shouldn't you be going?" he asked.

"I'm having a little trouble getting motivated."

Max normally regarded the ringing phone with a pronounced lack of enthusiasm, but that night a different set of assumptions was clearly in effect. He sprang out of the chair, snatching up the phone and pressing it to his ear with a look of dread that quickly turned to relief.

"It's for you," he told me.

I rose wearily and accepted the receiver, which smelled like it had just been dipped in a vat of Old Spice.

"Hello?"

"Do you know what time it is?" Matt demanded, shouting to make himself heard over the loud music in the background.

"What time is it?" I obediently replied.

"It's party time!" he bellowed. "Everybody's waiting for you!"

"Who's everybody?"

"Don't waste my time with questions. Just get your ass over here. And bring your damn roommates."

He hung up before I could fill him in on the roommate issue, leaving me with an earful of dial tone. Conscious of Max's scrutiny, I listened to it for a few seconds before setting the phone back in the cradle. I knew he wanted to get rid of me, knew he would have made himself scarce if I were the one wearing the leather tie and too much aftershave. Now that I was up off the couch, walking a few blocks to Matt's house no longer seemed like such a craven act of surrender. As hard as I'd tried in the past few weeks, I found myself unable to stay mad at him. It was as if I'd discharged all my anger with that punch in the dining hall, and had nothing left to do but forgive him. And besides, it was just a party. Everyone was waiting for me.

"All right," I said. "I guess I'll be heading out."

"Have a good time," he told me. "Stay out as late as you want."

Cindy was on my mind a lot those days, way more than she'd been when we were actually going out together. By my calculation, she was about five months pregnant at that point, far enough along to be showing, and I had fabricated an image of her as a lovely and energetic mother-to-be, her face shining with contentment, her body unchanged except for the huge but still graceful swelling of her belly, which I sometimes pictured as being so large that she needed to support it from below with both hands, as though she were lugging a watermelon home from the supermarket. On some level I understood that this was not a realistic vision—I had taken to watching pregnant women on the streets of New Haven and realized pretty quickly that they were just as likely to be cranky and out-of-breath as they were to be radiant and full of vitality—but that didn't make the image any less necessary or appealing to me.

Perhaps because the imaginary Cindy was so familiar to me, I almost charged right past the real one on the steps of Entryway C, offering her no more than the obligatory nod I would have given to any passing stranger. But something—some muffled explosion in some remote region of my brain—made me pull up short and look again.

"Cindy?"

She stopped on the landing between the first and second floor. Her confusion seemed to mirror my own.

"Danny?" she said. "What are you doing here?"

"I live here."

"I know that." She rolled her eyes. "I thought you were supposed to be at a party."

The strangeness of the moment fell on me all at once, and all I could do was stare at her.

"What?" she said, looking worried in spite of her smile. She was wearing the tight blue dress I remembered fondly from the previous summer. "What's wrong?"

So many things were wrong just then it took me another few seconds to break the wrongness into its component parts. She had cut and lightened her hair and was going a lot easier on the makeup. She looked good, better than ever.

"You aren't—" I began, then stopped myself. "Where's the baby?"

Her smile disappeared. I hadn't meant it to come out like that, more like an accusation than a question. She looked down, placing one hand on the flat of her stomach, as if she needed to double-check.

"It's not . . . I couldn't—" Her voice broke and she started over. "I couldn't go through with it."

"Did something happen with Kevin?"

"It was me," she said, shaking her head. "I just couldn't—"

I looked down, hoping to conceal the surprisingly sharp sense of disappointment that had taken hold of me, a feeling I had no right to and couldn't fully account for.

"I'm sorry," I mumbled. "I'm sorry you—"

"It's done," she said. "I'm trying not to think about it."

I was about to thank her for taking the trouble to come all the way to New Haven to let me know, when my brain finally started functioning at full power.

"You're here to see Max, aren't you?"

"I thought I should at least meet him face-to-face," she said. "I mean, we are going to be sharing a house this summer."

"You're what?"

"He didn't tell you?"

"We haven't been talking too much."

"His mother offered me a job," she said, unable to keep herself from smiling. "They need someone to manage the store."

"The store?"

"Cara Mia. The boutique."

It took me a second to call up the fact that Mrs. Friedlin was part owner, along with a couple of friends, of a small clothing store in a fashionable neighborhood in downtown Denver. Max had explained it to me as an expensive hobby, a way for over-educated and under-employed women to convince themselves that they had a purpose in life beyond shopping and tennis and travel.

"You're moving to Denver?"

"That's the plan," she said, looking like she couldn't quite believe it herself. "The Friedlins said I could live in their house until I found a place of my own. They're going to be in Ireland all summer anyway."

"When are you leaving?"

"I already did. My car's all packed and everything. I just figured I'd make a quick stop up here and say hi to Max before getting on the highway. Can you believe it? I'm gonna drive all the way to Colorado."

"What about your mother?" I said. "What's going to happen to her?"

Her face wasn't happy, but it wasn't apologetic, either.

"She's just gonna have to manage."

"You think she can?"

"She'll have to," she said. There was a hardness in her voice I wasn't familiar with. "I've taken care of her since I was a little girl. Now it's someone else's turn." Almost as an afterthought, she added, "Her sister's only an hour away."

"What about Kevin? How's he feel about all this?"

"What do you want from me?" she demanded. "How many chances like this you think I'm gonna get?"

She wasn't that far away, but for some reason I couldn't bring myself to climb the three steps that separated us, joining her on the landing so I could hug her and tell her that it would be okay, that she was making the right choice, that her mother would be fine and everything would turn out right in Colorado, which is what I wanted to do. Instead I looked up at her and said, "Was it Max? Was this his idea?"

An odd little smile came onto her face.

"It was you," she said.

"Me?"

"Something you said."

"What did I say?"

She watched me closely, like she was trying to catch me in a lie.

"That I deserve to be happy. Didn't you tell me that?"

"Maybe," I said. "Probably. I just wonder if you've thought this through."

She didn't answer right away, and it struck me, pretty much out of nowhere, how empty the entryway seemed that night, as if the two of us were the only people in the building, and how different it had been during her last visit, this same stairwell packed tight with partying students, everything reeking of beer and echoing with laughter. She seemed a lot more at home this time around, no more out of place than I was.

"I couldn't make up my mind at first," she told me. "Then I asked myself what you would do."

dark side of the moon

Matt answered the door in his hard hat and a Boy Scout shirt, a pair of expensive binoculars hanging from a cord around his neck.

"Come on in," he said, leading me up a creaky wooden stairway to his second-floor apartment. "Things are a little slow getting started."

Technically speaking, he hadn't been lying when he said that everybody was waiting for me; he'd just neglected to explain that aside from himself, "everybody" meant Nick and Matt's landlord, Lance, a skinny, wolfish guy I often saw prowling around the library, chatting up lonely undergraduate girls. They were sitting on lawn chairs in a room full of outdoor furniture, not to mention a potted palm and a nonfunctioning barbecue grill, regarding me with a certain amount of disappointment.

"Step inside the Conceptual Patio," Matt told me, drawing my attention to the keg in one corner of the room and the garbage can in another. "There's the Michelob and there's the Apollo Love Juice."

"Apollo Love Juice?"

He handed me a rinsed-out mayonnaise jar filled with a nasty-looking orange concoction. "Grain alcohol and Tang. One glass and you're in orbit."

"Two glasses and you're on the dark side of the moon," Lance added, popping a pretzel into his mouth. He had stringy, gray-streaked hair that fell well below his collar, and the haughty demeanor of a flamenco dancer.

"Three and you're on the edge of the known universe," Matt continued with a giggle.

"All right." Nick held up his hand, silencing Lance before he could describe the effects of glass number four. "I'm gettin' a little tired of this."

I pulled up a chair to form a circle of sorts with Matt and Lance, who were sipping their Love Juice and bobbing their heads in time with "Cold as Ice," looking like they were about two seconds away from jumping up and dancing. Nick was sitting off to one side, glancing nervously in our direction.

"There are going to be females at this party, aren't there?" he asked.

Matt and Lance exchanged amused glances.

"What do you think, Karnak?" Matt asked his landlord. "Will there be females at this party?"

Lance closed his eyes, pressed two fingers to each of his temples, and gave the question his full psychic consideration, struggling unsuccessfully to maintain a straight face.

"Yes," he said finally, sputtering with suppressed laughter as he carved an hourglass figure into the air. "I foresee a large number of females."

"Just checking," Nick told him. "I don't want to get in over my head here."

The mood on the Conceptual Patio darkened as time passed and our number remained steady at four.

"I don't know what's wrong," Matt was standing by the window, training his binoculars on the street below. "I figured more people would be here by now."

"It's early," Lance reminded him. "The real party animals haven't even climbed out of their coffins yet."

"You sure you invited girls?" Nick asked again, this time more anxiously.

Lance sat up straight in response to this question, crossed his arms on his chest, and treated Nick to an imperious, heavy-lidded stare. I half expected him to leap up from his lawn chair, snap his fingers, and shout, *"Olé!"*

"Do I look like a fool?" he inquired darkly. "I invited only girls."

"Thirty-seven of them," Matt added. "We made a list."

"Fifteen were possible no-shows," said Lance. "Twelve were likelies, and the rest were probables."

"What about the band?" Nick asked. "Didn't you say there was going to be a band?"

"They backed out," Matt informed him. "There was some confusion about the date."

"No girls, no band," Nick grumbled.

"Don't worry, though," Matt continued, trying to cheer us up. "I've got some live entertainment lined up that's even better."

Nick wasn't reassured.

"You call this an orgy?" he asked, glaring at me like the party was my idea.

"I never said it was an orgy. It's just—" I paused, searching for the right description. "It's just a little get-together."

"Don't pull this get-together shit on me," he warned. "You called it a fucking orgy."

By ten thirty, Lance and Matt had each consumed enough Apollo Love Juice to have pushed beyond the boundaries of the known universe, though neither one of them seemed particularly drunk to me. Nick was halfway through his second cup, and he had become a lot more cheerful since making the switch. I was the laggard, not even in orbit yet, content to sit on my lawn chair and sink deeper into the melancholy that had taken hold of me since my talk with Cindy. I wondered if she and Max were still in the common room, making awkward stabs at small talk, or if they had migrated to a fancy restaurant, where they were laughing over a bottle of wine, planning their big summer in Colorado. I was jealous, of course, but not in the obvious way—it seemed to me that Cindy was the interloper, not Max, that she was the one horning in on something that was rightfully mine, though it was hard for me to identify what that something was.

"Oh, I could have continued with my graduate work," Lance declared, drilling Nick with the unnerving gaze he used to plumb the souls of the girls he befriended at the library. "I could have finished my thesis, taken a professorship, and committed slow intellectual suicide. But I chose the road less traveled."

"Took some guts," Nick commented. "Professors got a pretty good deal."

"I respect the life of the mind too much to reduce it to a job," Lance replied, pausing to shovel a handful of peanuts into his mouth. "I prefer the Greek ideal of leisurely contemplation."

"That's Greek?" Nick seemed puzzled. "The Greeks I know work their asses off. A lot of them are in the restaurant business."

"I'm not talking about modern-day Greeks." Lance's expression soured, as if the mere thought of non-ancient Greeks left a taste in his mouth. "I'm working from a classical model."

Nick swirled the Love Juice in his plastic cup as though it were expensive brandy. "So what do you do for a living?"

"I *live*," Lance told him, delivering this pronouncement with melodramatic conviction.

"I mean for money," Nick explained patiently.

"Ah, money." Lance's face relaxed. "It always comes down to that, doesn't it?"

"The almighty dollar," said Nick.

Lance smiled in rueful agreement. "The monthly pound of flesh."

"What can you do? Gotta pay the man his money."

"Render unto Caesar and so forth."

"Amen," replied Nick. "You mind passing those peanuts?"

Matt excused himself to make some phone calls and returned with a somber expression. He shook his head in response to whatever question it was Lance hadn't yet asked him.

"Really?" Lance looked baffled. "Not even Caroline?"

"No answer," Matt told him.

"Maybe she's on her way," Lance speculated. "What about Sarah and Mary Beth?"

"Sarah thinks she's got food poisoning. Mary Beth's line was busy."

"At least Amy and Michiko will come," Lance insisted. "That much I'm certain of."

"I'm sorry," Matt told me. "I didn't expect it to turn out like this."

"Don't worry about it," I said. "It's a perfectly good party."

"Don't forget Allison," Lance called out. "She said she'd probably be a little late."

Just then the doorbell rang, the harsh cry of the buzzer slicing through the accumulated gloom. Matt cocked his head at a drastic angle, like a dog hearing a distant whistle. When it rang again, he stumbled backwards, clutching at his chest.

"Oh my God. It's gonna happen. I can feel it."

"See?" Lance held out both hands with an air of personal vindication. "What did I tell you?"

Matt took a couple of steps toward the door, then turned back around. He stared at us for a couple of seconds, shaking his head as if we didn't quite measure up.

"Come on, you guys. At least try to look like you're having fun."

In spite of this injunction, we fell into an immediate and embarrassed silence the moment he left the room. Nick whipped a comb out of his back pocket and went to work while Lance sprayed a few blasts of Binaca into his mouth, then made some last-second adjustments to his eyebrows. I untucked my shirt and began polishing my glasses. By the time Matt stepped back into the apartment with the new arrival in tow, all three of us were staring right at the door, unable to conceal first our curiosity, and then our disappointment. Matt's crestfallen expression mirrored our own.

"Guy's," he said. "This is Eric. Eric, this is the guys."

Eric was a bold statement in his orange flight suit and black velvet cape, his eyes glittering with intellectual challenge. To my amazement, he only considered me for a fleeting second before turning the full force of his attention on Lance, who had suddenly become very interested in what may or may not have been a spot on his pants.

"You," Eric said, as if picking the landlord out of a lineup. "I've been looking for you."

Lance looked up and nodded sadly, a condemned man accepting his fate.

"Hello, Eric," he said. "It's nice to see you again."

Eric pounced on the empty chair next to Lance and immediately launched into a diatribe against Carl Jung.

"Don't tell me you fell for that archetype bullshit," he said, as if he couldn't believe that such a terrible thing could happen to such a nice person.

"I think there's some validity to it," Lance countered. "I think all of us are born with a certain set of images and beliefs buried deep in our unconscious minds."

"That's garbage," Eric shot back. "If there really was a collective unconscious, we wouldn't all feel so alone."

I glanced at Nick, curious to see what he was making of this face-off, which looked like it might go on for a while. After a few seconds, he turned to meet my gaze, then got up and walked across the room. He sat down in the chair to my right, scooting it closer so he could whisper in my ear.

"Am I confused, or is that guy wearing a cape?"

"Either that or a really big handkerchief."

I thought it was a pretty good line, but Nick didn't crack a smile. He just grunted quietly, as if in confirmation of his own thoughts.

"Live and learn," he said. "Live and learn."

By midnight it was a whole different scene, not a blowout but at least a halfway respectable party. Kristin, Djembe, and Sarah had arrived around eleven, along with half a dozen of Sarah's friends from the Slavic Chorus. They were followed a short time later by a contingent of dining-hall workers that included Lorelei, Brad Foxworthy, Milton, and Dallas Little, the three-hundred-pound dishwasher, and now Matt's apartment was humming with activity. Lance had escaped from Eric's clutches and had installed himself by the garbage can, where he was ladling out the Love Juice and happily explaining its supernatural powers to anyone who cared to listen. In the meantime, Eric had glommed onto Djembe, who was nodding without enthusiasm and glancing around anxiously for assistance as he bobbed and weaved to avoid Argument Man's jabbing index finger. Kristin couldn't rescue him, though; she was too busy dancing with Brad and Lorelei and Dallas in the big empty room that separated the Conceptual Patio from the actual kitchen. I was watching all this from my lawn chair, while carrying on a conversation with Nick and a member of the Slavic Chorus who'd introduced herself as Katrinka, though I'd known her freshman year as Michele.

"Have either of you been to Russia?" she asked, fixing us with her urgent green eyes. Her thick eyebrows formed a single emphatic bar across her forehead.

"Russia?" Nick snorted. "Why would I want to go to Russia?"

"Me neither," I said, leaning forward to get a better look at Lorelei, whom I'd never seen dance before. Her jeans were tight and her eyes were closed. Her leotard top looked like it was made for a much smaller girl, and all the sexual energy in the house seemed to have gathered around her like a halo. "I've never even been on an airplane."

"You're kidding," said Katrinka. "I'm going to Moscow this summer."

"Why would you want to go there?" Nick asked.

"I'm in love with Russia." She said this with real emotion in her voice, as if Russia were a person. "The music, the language, the history."

Nick looked offended. "What are you, some kind of Communist?"

"Not at all," Katrinka explained. "I'm a Russophile."

I had to lean forward at an extreme angle to see around Dallas, whose enormous body was blocking my view of Lorelei. He barely moved at all when he danced, yet he had a way of standing not quite still that was oddly graceful, as if he were completely at one with the music, as if dancing were less an activity than an attitude toward the world.

Nick tugged on my shirt. "Yo, Pencil Dick, where's the bathroom?"

"Through the kitchen," I told him. "There's no light switch, though. If you need to see what you're doing, there's a flashlight in the sink."

Nick smiled uncertainly. "You're shittin' me, right?"

"See for yourself."

"Unbelievable." He smiled at Katrinka as if she, at least, would understand. "A flashlight in the sink."

Nick headed out the room and across the dance floor. Lorelei caught me looking and waved for me to join her. I waved back, pretending not to understand.

"Who is that guy?" Katrinka asked.

"Who, Nick? He's a cook in the dining hall."

"You hang out with a cook? That is so cool."

"Yeah," I said. "Just like Russia."

Her smile faded. "What's that supposed to mean?"

Luckily, Matt sat down in Nick's chair before I had a chance to answer. He shoved a fat white envelope in my face like he was serving me with a summons.

"This is for you," he said.

"What is it?"

"The letter."

"Oh, right." I accepted the envelope. On the front, in elegant calligraphy, Matt had inscribed the words, *Mea Culpa*. "You really didn't have to."

He watched with a peculiar half-smile as I tucked it into the back pocket of my jeans.

"Aren't you gonna read it?"

"Now?"

"What is that?" Katrinka asked.

"A letter of apology," he told her.

She seemed pleased by the concept. "What are you apologizing for?"

"I was bad." Matt grinned. "I committed a heinous act of solipsism."

Lorelei had slipped back into view on the dance floor and was beckoning me with her index finger, a sweetly pouty expression on her face. She seemed oblivious to the fact that Brad Foxworthy was lying at her feet, waving his arms and legs in the air like an insect. I held up one finger, trying to buy some time. Beside her, Kristin was staring down at Brad with a gaze that mingled pity and disgust in equal measures.

"Give her the letter," Matt told me.

"What?"

"Give Katrinka the letter."

On the way back from the bathroom, Nick walked past Brad without a glance. I pulled the letter out of my pocket and surrendered it to Katrinka.

"You sure it's okay?" she asked, glancing nervously at Matt.

Matt didn't answer, though. He was staring with dismay at Lance, who had leaned over the rim of the garbage can and lowered his head into the Apollo Love Juice as though bobbing for apples.

"Oh shit," said Matt, rising suddenly from the chair.

As if the move had been choreographed, Nick reclaimed his seat the instant Matt vacated it.

"First time I ever pissed with a flashlight," he announced with a smile. "It's a little confusing."

Katrinka smiled at him, still clutching my letter.

"Are you really a cook?" she asked him.

All hell was breaking loose. Matt had his arms around Lance's waist as though he were trying to yank him out of the garbage can. Djembe was clutching his ears, shouting at Eric to leave him alone, to go find someone else to torment. Dallas Little was standing over Brad, attempting to pour a beer into his open mouth, though much of the liquid was missing its mark. Kristin looked on, utterly appalled by this display. Lorelei seemed to have disappeared.

"Are you really a pinko?" Nick shot back.

"Excuse me," I said, though by that point neither of them seemed to know I was even there. "I'll be right back."

She was waiting in Matt's room, sitting on the edge of the bed in total darkness. I shut the door behind me and sat down next to her. After the chaos of the party, it was a relief to be someplace calm and private.

"Took you long enough," she said. Her voice was playful, but there was a hint of irritation in it as well.

"What do you mean? You couldn't have been here for more than a couple of minutes."

"I don't mean tonight. I've been trying to get your attention for weeks."

My eyes were just beginning to adjust to the darkness, and I could have sworn Lorelei was glowing a little around the edges, this nearly invisible corona of sex lighting up the air around her head and shoulders.

"Well, you've got it now," I told her.

She put her hand on my knee, a gesture more comradely than seductive. I felt light-headed and wondered if the grain alcohol was finally kicking in. Maybe Matt and Lance were right; maybe two glasses of the Love Juice really did put you on the dark side of the moon.

"So how's your townie girlfriend?" she asked. There was a taunting note in the question, but I decided to ignore it.

"It's over. She's not my girlfriend anymore."

"Too bad."

"What about you? What's up with you and Eddie?"

"Nothing. He won't even talk to me."

"He got beat up pretty bad," I pointed out.

I'd only seen Eddie once since he'd gotten out of the hospital, and he looked awful. He was using a cane to get around, and one side of his head had been shaved for reasons that were unclear to me. He said he was having trouble concentrating and was thinking of taking a medical leave.

"He was kind of a pussy about it," she said. Maybe it was the moonlight leaking in around the edges of the shade or something, but she seemed to be burning a little brighter than before. Her eyes had an odd catlike gleam. "He didn't even try to defend himself."

By that point, I couldn't help myself. I reached up and began stroking her hair, surprised to discover that it wasn't giving off heat. She leaned into the caress, pressing her head into my palm. She closed her eyes and let out a low moan of pleasure.

"That's nice," she said. "Don't stop."

I brought my face down to hers. Like her hair, her lips felt unexpectedly cool against mine. Her tongue explored my mouth with strange thoroughness, as if she wanted to make contact with every nook and cranny in there, every taste bud and ridge, the whole topography of teeth and gums and skin. I pulled away from her, trying to get my bearings.

"Why am I doing this?" I asked. "I don't even know you."

"You don't have to *know* me," she laughed.

I kissed her again. She reached down and tugged my shirt free from my pants. Her hand slid over my belly and onto my chest. She pressed her lips against my ear.

"Aren't you worried about my brothers?"

I touched her breast. There were only two weeks left in the semester. Her brothers had never laid eyes on me. They didn't even know my name.

"I love how tight your clothes are," I told her.

"This is nothing. I've got stuff way tighter than this."

"I want to see you in it."

"You like the way us townies dress, don't you?"

"You know I do."

She pulled off her shirt and lay down on the bed. Her breasts were perfect.

"You're an easy one," she told me, reaching down to unbuckle her jeans. "I'm gonna make you so happy."

We might have been in there for twenty minutes or two hours. All I knew was that I was lying on top of her, dazed and naked, when the door creaked open and the light came on. I rolled over in a panic, blinking through the glare, and saw Matt standing in the doorway, scrutinizing us with drunken interest.

"Here you are," he said. "I've been looking all over."

"Go away," I yelped, snatching up a pillow for a fig leaf. "Leave us alone."

"Get your clothes on," he told us. "Everyone's waiting for you."

"Leave us alone."

"Hurry up," he said. "I don't want to start the entertainment without you."

"The entertainment?"

"Come on. Just get your clothes on."

Lorelei was sitting up, arms crossed over her breasts, the lower half of her body concealed by a sheet, her expression hovering somewhere between anger and embarrassment. When I glanced back at the doorway, Lance was peering in over Matt's shoulder, scrutinizing us as though we were a museum exhibit. There was a towel wrapped around his head like a turban.

"Shut the door!" I snapped. "We'll be right out."

We dressed as quickly as we could, pausing occasionally to trade shy smiles of disbelief. Lorelei's face was red; her hair was a mess.

She had already wriggled into her jeans by the time I located her panties inside one of my sneakers.

"You can keep them," she told me.

I shoved them into my pocket and followed her out the door.

It seemed like a different party than the one we'd left. Order had been restored. The dancing had stopped and everyone was packed into the Conceptual Patio, staring at us as we entered, as if we were the entertainment.

There's nothing you can do at a moment like that except pretend that everything's normal. Holding hands, Lorelei and I walked past our friends and co-workers and acquaintances as if we'd just returned from a quick trip to WaWa's. Although a number of people were standing, one empty seat remained, a bronze folding chair with the number twenty-two stenciled on it in faded black paint. I sat down in it, and she made herself comfortable on my lap.

"Excuse me," Dallas Little called out. He was holding Lorelei's pink panties in his enormous hand, dangling them in front of his face like a handkerchief. "I think you dropped something."

The whole room burst into laughter as Dallas handed me the panties. I was mortified, but all I could do was smile and act like I was in on the joke.

"I always carry an extra pair," I mumbled. "Just to be on the safe side."

My quip was drowned out by a noise that sounded something like a herd of cattle being driven up a flight of wooden stairs, or a football team charging out of a locker room. When the door opened, though, what it disgorged was not cows or football players, but a dozen or so clean-cut college boys in tuxedos. The Whiffenpoofs surged into the apartment, then drifted over toward the edge of the Conceptual Patio, their faces collapsing into assorted degrees of confusion as they took the measure of our unlikely gathering. I made momentary eye contact with Trip, who shot me with an imaginary gun, his hand encased in an immaculate white glove. Through a gap between two tuxes, I saw Matt hugging the Pitch, the two of them clapping each other on the back like old buddies.

Relieved to no longer be the focus of attention, I let my eyes stray around the room as the Whiffs began to assemble themselves into their usual formation, in the shadow of the potted palm. Nick and Katrinka were right where I'd left them, though I saw that they'd removed my letter from the envelope and appeared to be reading it with great interest and amusement. Sensing my gaze, Nick looked up and wagged his finger at me, as if scolding me for being a naughty boy.

Standing behind Nick and Katrinka, also peering in my direction, were two guys I hadn't seen before. They were scrawny and criminal-looking, definitely not Yalies. One of them wore a leather biker vest over a black T-shirt with a skull and crossbones on the front. His hair was long and greasy, and when he smiled at me I saw that one of his front teeth had turned brown. The other guy had a denim jacket and the ducktail hairdo of a 1950s juvenile delinquent. He gave me a little wave that didn't make me want to wave back. Something about their faces seemed oddly familiar.

"Lorelei?" I said. "Do you see those guys?"

She looked where I was looking.

"Oh shit." She stiffened in my lap. "What are they doing here?"

At that same moment, the Pitch tooted on his little pipe. The Whiffenpoofs looked at each other. A hush settled over the room, but it wasn't an ordinary hush. It was an almost miraculous absence of sound, the kind of quiet that seems to begin in your body and spread outward, a silence trembling with possibilities, the kind you only ever notice the instant before something terrible happens, or a large group of singers burst into song.

306

READING GROUP GUIDE

JOE COLLEGE
TOM PERROTTA

1. In their final encounter, Cindy suggests that Danny has taught her an important lesson. What is this lesson? Is it helpful or harmful to Cindy?

2. When he returns home for Spring Break, Danny has an epiphany of sorts, courtesy of a voice in his head: "I could just be myself, my father's son, living out my life in the town where I was born .... I could learn to love [Cindy] the way my father had learned to love my mother .... all that could be enough." Is this true? Or is Danny kidding himself?

3. Who grows and changes more over the course of the novel, Danny or Cindy?

4. Some readers feel that Danny gets off too easily in JOE COLLEGE, that he's never really held accountable for his actions. How does Danny himself feel about this issue? What about the characters around him?

5. What does Danny's journey in JOE COLLEGE tell us about social mobility and social class in America?

6. Is Danny simply living out the American Dream, an updated version of the Horatio Alger myth? Or is he the beneficiary of a flawed system that gives special privileges and opportunities to a chosen few?

7. The Lunch Monsters are a particular Perrotta creation. How do the thugs represent the author's attempt to flesh out Danny's guilt? Danny says, "There must have been something I was trying to prove by picking a fight with these guys," but it's not clear what Danny is trying to prove, or to whom. What do you feel he's trying to prove? Could it be an attempt to assuage his guilt over Cindy?

8. At several points in the story, the author uses a pause and an absence of sound to indicate that a significant event has just occurred. How do these pauses provide a framework for the momentum of the story?

For more reading group suggestions visit www.stmartins.com

St. Martin's Griffin